MERDE
IN EUROPE

Stephen Clarke lives in Paris, where he divides his time between writing and not writing. His five *Merde* novels, *A Year in the Merde*, *Merde Actually*, *Merde Happens*, *Dial M for Merde* and *The Merde Factor* have been bestsellers all over the world – including France. Stephen also writes non-fiction books, which include *Talk to the Snail*, an insider's guide to understanding the French, *How the French Won Waterloo or Think they Did*, an amused look at France's continuing obsession with Napoleon, *Dirty Bertie*, the story of King Edward VII's youthful follies in France, and *1000 Years of Annoying the French*, which was a number one bestseller in Britain. Research for Stephen's novels has taken him all over Europe and America. For *Merde in Europe*, he ventured deep into the cloistered corridors of Brussels. He has now returned to Paris, and is doing his best to live the Entente Cordiale.

D0715901

9 40332143

Also by Stephen Clarke

Fiction
A Brief History of the Future
A Year in the Merde
Merde Actually
Merde Happens
Dial M for Merde
The Merde Factor

Non-fiction
Talk to the Snail: Ten Commandments for
Understanding the French
Paris Revealed
1000 Years of Annoying the French
Dirty Bertie: An English King Made in France
How the French Won Waterloo (or Think They Did)

EBook Short
Annoying the French Encore!

For more information on Stephen Clarke and his books,
see his website at www.stephenclarkewriter.com

Read Stephen's tweets at @sclarkewriter

Stephen Clarke

MERDE
IN EUROPE

arrow books

1 3 5 7 9 10 8 6 4 2

Arrow Books
20 Vauxhall Bridge Road
London SW1V 2SA

Arrow Books is part of the Penguin Random House group of companies
whose addresses can be found at global.penguinrandomhouse.com

Copyright © Stephen Clarke 2016

Stephen Clarke has asserted his right to be identified as the author of this
Work in accordance with the Copyright, Designs and Patents Act 1988.

First published by Century in 2016
First published in paperback by Arrow in 2016

www.penguin.co.uk

A CIP catalogue record for this book is available from the British Library.

ISBN 9781784755577

Typeset in India by Thomson Digital Pvt Ltd, Noida, Delhi

Printed and bound in Great Britain by Clays Ltd, St Ives plc

MIX
Paper from
responsible sources
FSC® C018179
www.fsc.org

Penguin Random House is committed to a
sustainable future for our business, our readers
and our planet. This book is made from Forest
Stewardship Council® certified paper.

All the characters and events in this novel are completely fictitious, even those that might seem alarmingly real.

The author would like to thank everyone who showed him around, or talked him through, the darkest corners of the European Union's institutions. For obvious reasons, it is impossible to name them, or even give both their initials.

So thanks, *merci* and *dank uwel* most of all to E, P, N, G, J, I and S.

And also, in no particular order, to J, A, J, R, W, T, O, D, K, S, V, B, C, L, S, F, H and M.

Thanks as always to N and to the UEA crowd for their support, and to SLA for getting things moving.

'Insanity: doing the same thing over and over again, and expecting different results.'

Albert Einstein

1

'Euro banknotes can make men impotent.'

Report in the British press, 2002

'VIOLENT THINGS, oysters,' the Englishman said. I didn't know why he was telling me this. We were just two drinkers sitting side-by-side at a bar in Brussels.

'Violent?' I asked.

'Brutal,' he said. 'Vicious.'

'Really?' My own encounters with oysters had all been pretty one-sided, usually ending in a twelve–nil victory in my favour. 'You mean the way they can shred your fingertips if you try and open them yourself?' I asked.

'No, they're evil little bastards. They sneak up on you. Didn't you know?'

'No.'

I turned my attention back to my nearly empty glass. I didn't feel like listening to some drunkard's paranoid rant about being followed everywhere by molluscs.

But he nudged me, threatening to empty my glass completely.

'People don't realise that it's not always a bad oyster that makes you ill,' he said. 'It can be a good one that you haven't killed cleanly.'

'Killed cleanly?'

I tried to work out how you'd do this. A karate blow to the neck? Assuming oysters have necks. Or with a shotgun, perhaps? Might be a bit messy.

'Yes, you have to chew the whole thing up into a mush, so it's well and truly dead before you swallow it. If you don't, it'll slide down into your guts alive, and pump out antibodies until it finally dies.'

He burped. Apparently his digestive system wanted to join in the conversation.

'So what you're saying is that oysters are intestinal terrorists sent on suicide missions to destroy humanity?' I asked.

'You may take the piss,' he said, perceptively, 'but if you're not careful, a perfectly fresh oyster will redecorate your insides with its antibodies, and you'll be sick as a dog for twenty-four hours. You can stay allergic for ever, too. You eat another oyster and you'll be vomiting through the bathroom wall.'

'Delightful.'

'Sorry, but that's just the way they are. Evil, vindictive, slimy bastards.'

Luckily I hadn't been feeling like dinner anyway. We were in a raucous pub in the centre of Brussels, and after several glasses of a thick, dark-brown liquid brewed by sadistic Belgian monks, I didn't even fancy a plate of perfectly non-aggressive lettuce. Nourishing stuff, that beer.

'You've had a bad experience yourself, I take it?' I asked him.

'Yes, but that's not why I want to ban them.'

'Ban them?'

'Make outlaws of the little slimeballs. A new European law making them illegal.'

'That's a bit extreme, isn't it?' I said. 'If Europe went around banning anything that makes us chunder, schnapps would be outlawed in twenty-eight countries by now. And late-night kebabs would be a thing of the past.'

'Well, maybe not ban them outright, but make them damn near impossible to sell. We might introduce a law whereby oysters have to be humanely killed before being served. You know, oblige restaurants to stun each one electronically before opening it. Or apply the old straight-cucumber principle, so oysters can only be sold if they have perfectly oval shells. That'll have those Frogs weeping into their seaweed, won't it?'

'And you can do all that, can you?'

'I work for an MEP who's into food practices. So I can try. '

'Wow.'

Even I knew enough about Brussels to realise that Members of the European Parliament were people who had the power to turn their personal crusades into law.

So my new friend was right about making Frenchmen weep. An embargo on oysters would scuttle the economy of a large slice of the French coast, as well as sabotaging the menus of some very chic *brasseries* in Paris.

And not only Paris.

'I've seen lots of people eating oysters in London, too,' I said.

'Yeah, a few posh posers who don't vote in European elections. We don't care about them.'

'Are you planning to do the same thing to mussels?' I asked him.

'What, outlaw the Belgians' national dish? No, couldn't do that to our generous hosts, could we?' He gargled a laugh through a deep swallow of Flemish ale. 'Anyway, mum's the word on all this. You're English, right?'

'Yes, but the MEP I'm working for is French.'

'French?' Suddenly he was sitting bolt upright, and looking as if a dozen oysters were pumping antibodies straight into his bulging eyes. '*French?* You're joking?'

'No joke. I usually live in Paris, but I've come to Brussels to do some work on protecting endangered local languages in France. You know, Breton, Basque, Corsican and all that.'

'You're not actually French, though? You haven't given up your passport?'

'No. But the woman I'm working for would be very interested in your scheme to ban the oyster. She's the MEP for Brittany West.'

'Oh, shit,' he groaned.

'I think you mean merde,' I corrected him. 'Unless you were trying to speak Breton, in which case it's kaoc'h.'

I must admit that I wasn't being entirely truthful with my loose-tongued English friend. I wasn't really working for a French MEP. Not yet, anyway.

In fact, I'd only arrived in Brussels that same day. I'd come at the invitation of my friend Elodie, the daughter of my former boss in Paris, Jean-Marie. Well, I say invitation, but it was more like a summons: 'Reserved a room for you at the Hotel Empereur Napoléon Bonaparte in Bruxelles. Call me and I'll tell you more.'

I'd asked for details, of course, but all she'd been willing to say was that she wanted to offer me a ridiculously well-paid job working on endangered languages. When I asked whether this would mean trekking through Amazonian rainforests, she'd laughed and said, 'No, more like Breton pigshit.' But she'd sent me a first-class train ticket, and so here I was in Brussels, intrigued but wondering whether it might not be a very bad idea indeed.

I tried to convince myself that any doubts I had were symptoms of gross ingratitude. After all, Elodie had promised me a generous slice of Europe's budget to come and work for her on a short-term contract. What was I worried about? She'd even paid me a sizeable chunk up front. Whatever happened, it was going to be a profitable few weeks.

The trouble was that I had been screwed by Elodie before, both literally and metaphorically.

We'd been (very briefly) lovers, but only because she wanted to shock her *papa*, who was my boss. Then a few months later she'd tried to sabotage a new job I had, promoting the UK as a tourist destination in America. That little rivalry ended in a vicious fruit-fight in Los Angeles that had left her dad smothered from head to foot in fresh strawberries. But since then we'd made up, and I'd even done the catering for her wedding to a filthy-rich Parisian banker. So I hoped I could trust her now.

My instinct was that her trustworthiness depended on whether her father, Jean-Marie, was involved in whatever scheme she had bubbling in her cauldron. Too often the pair of them were side-by-side in the family kitchen, cooking up mischief.

Jean-Marie was the *député* (Member of the French Parliament) for a country town in Mayenne, just south of Normandy, an election he'd won by promising the local farmers that they would be able to give up the tiresome business of growing things, and live for ever on the subsidies that he was going to obtain for them from Brussels. Although, come to think of it, that's what most French politicians promise their farmers, so maybe Jean-Marie wasn't so bad after all.

It seemed only logical that Elodie should follow her dad into politics and get herself elected as an MEP. What better way for him to obtain those subsidies for his farmers?

Even so, there were two things that confused me about her move to Brussels.

One: how did she get herself elected in the far west of Brittany where, to the best of my knowledge, she'd never been in her whole life?

And two: she'd studied at France's most expensive business school and recently married into a Parisian private bank, so why give up sky-high earnings in the world of wealth management to go to Belgium and spend half her life listening to debates about the minimum size of haddock and whether to reclassify British chocolate as 'sugary brown fat'?

It seemed almost certain that her dad was involved somehow.

Early next morning I was due to find out. So it was time to say 'au revoir' to the Brussels pub and its talkative English barfly, get back to my hotel and have a bit of shut-eye.

The only problem with that idea, I realised when I finally located the pub exit and emerged into a cobbled side street, was that Belgian beer seems to coagulate somewhere behind the knees, making the act of walking unusually difficult.

Worse, thanks to some quirk in the Brussels climate, the evening had suddenly become rather blurred. I found that I couldn't recognise the street I was in, or see clearly enough to call up a map on my phone. I couldn't even aim my fingers at the phone to unlock it.

It occurred to me that maybe the beer was slightly stronger than I thought.

I still had a vague idea of the name of my hotel, so I just needed to ask someone for directions. And there was a friendly-looking woman standing a few metres away on the street corner. She seemed to be smiling at me, as if she wanted to help.

'You English?' she called out. 'Français? Deutsch? Italiano?'

'Oh, one hundred per cent English. Not French at all,' I replied, and laughed for some reason.

She seemed pleased to hear this, to judge by the way she thrust out her ample chest, which was, I now noticed, only half-covered by a tight, low-cut T-shirt. She began to totter towards me on perilously high heels, and I was afraid that she would topple over on the cobblestones and scuff her knees, which were totally unprotected by her tiny shorts.

'Can you do something for me?' I asked her. 'Something very kind?'

'Anything you want,' she said, which was highly thoughtful of her, considering that we'd only just met.

2

'Brussels to force farmers to give toys to pigs.'

Report in the British press, 2003

NEXT MORNING there was one reason to feel grateful, but only one. On waking up (or oozing back into the swamp of consciousness), I found a message from Elodie saying that she'd had to go to Paris, and would be arriving back in Brussels about eight hours late for our meeting. This was a huge relief, because my body was quivering at the idea of getting anywhere near vertical, never mind having to walk, think or speak.

As hangovers go, it was an astonishing 3D experience. A non-stop barrage of beer bottles was being thrown at my head by a stone-cold-sober Belgian monk. Those brothers certainly know how to make you feel guilty about over-indulging the flesh. I've never prayed so hard for forgiveness.

And through the shroud of physical pain, I got a vague sense that I'd sinned in more ways than one. I'd drunk far too much, that was certain, but hadn't I also committed some other awful misdemeanour?

Fortunately, my memory seemed to have shut down.

I devoted the whole day to foetal moaning, until about five o'clock when I dragged myself to the bathroom for a frost-bite-inducing shower. After that, it only took a quadruple espresso to give me enough strength to crawl into a taxi and beg to be taken as smoothly as possible to Bruxelles-Midi station. A strange name, I thought, 'Midday Station' – was it just for lunchtime trains? Did they also have a 'Bruxelles-Soir' or a 'Bruxelles-Petit Déjeuner'? I decided to ask Elodie, if I could still remember the question when she got there. Her train was due in from Paris at six fifteen.

As the taxi rattled through the busy streets, I closed my eyes and tried to force my brain to focus on the task ahead – namely, to appear sober, sane and employable. Despite all the dangers of associating with Elodie and her dad, I needed the money. The tea room I part-owned in Paris was doing well, but virtu-ally all the profits were being re-invested in the business. We were also hoping to open up a second branch. Consequently, filling my empty pockets with cash was top of my to-do list.

I must have dozed slightly, because I opened my eyes to see the driver mouthing something at me.

'Monsieur, la gare, we are arrived,' I heard him say.

I gave him some euros, asked him to wait and did my best to walk straight as I entered the station.

The new section, where Elodie was due to arrive, put Paris's Gare du Nord to shame. The concourse running below the tracks was a bit gloomy, but this was a relief for someone with a blinding migraine. And there was nothing shabby about it. The shops were posh, wafting out fresh baking smells and chocolaty aromas that would have been highly attractive if I hadn't had a force-nine hangover. There was a fresh-juice bar and even a flower shop. It was all a pleasant change from the Gare du Nord's wind-blown, pigeon-pooped coffee cabins and its gangs of beggars on the hunt for open bags and loose pockets. It always seemed to me that the French had spent so many years whingeing because London's original choice as its Eurostar terminal was Waterloo that they forgot to doll up their own station.

Bruxelles-Midi wasn't bad at all, I decided. I even found a bench with no one living on it, so that I could relax while I waited for Elodie.

Her sudden appearance at the foot of the platform steps cut short my brief rest period. She looked as if she'd been drinking, too, though in her case it had been cocaine cocktails. She came charging at me, her black raincoat billowing behind her like a parachute. Oh no, I thought, this was exactly what I didn't need in my fragile state – Elodie in supercharged business mode.

She was looking good, I had to admit – long-legged and lithe, her dark skirt hugging her hips affectionately. Her blonde hair was tied back classily to reveal a face that had matured in the year or so since I'd seen her. Her red lips looked determined rather than pouty, and her eyebrows were plucked and lasered into perfect symmetry.

'Allez, Paul, wake up, we're late!'

One thing hadn't changed, then. She was as rude a bitch as ever.

'Bonsoir, Elodie,' I replied pointedly.

'Oh, we'll have time for all that "hello, kiss-kiss, how are you?" stuff in the taxi. You *did* get a taxi?'

'Of course.'

'Well, let's get in it. Europe is paying for the meter to go round.'

I trotted along beside her, walking twice as fast as my body really wanted to, and ushered her towards the chic black Audi with a yellow chequered stripe that was waiting outside the station.

We wasted a few seconds while she stood by a car door waiting until someone (*moi*) opened it for her, and then the taxi set off along a narrow, semi-pedestrian street.

'Does he know where we're going?' Elodie snapped at me.

'No. Because I don't.'

'Well, why has he started driving, then?'

'I think it's one-way.'

'Oh.' She leant forward. 'Au parlement européen, s'il vous plaît,' she told him, almost politely. 'Le plus vite possible,' she added, with a note of girlish pleading that she turns on whenever necessary.

'OK, madame,' he said, and explained that there were lots of traffic jams, so he would have to take a route that would feel as though it wasn't very direct.

'Très bien, très bien,' Elodie huffed, instantly reverting to her true impatient-diva personality.

The driver swung us deep into a criss-cross of narrow roads. Occasionally there came the shock of cobblestones that turned my aching skull into a cocktail shaker, so I tried to focus on the thrill of discovering a new city. It all looked like France, and yet it didn't.

It seemed that Brussels architects had been told to design French styles in red London brick, but with all the Parisian curves knocked off. The bricks were often laid in horizontal lines, like hoops on a T-shirt, to make the slim, one-room-wide buildings look fatter. They were low-rise and individual in style, not like nineteenth-century Paris streets, where all the buildings come from the same mould. Here in Brussels there were balconies and bay windows all over the place, pointed Gothic next to flat-topped modernism.

It was all very cute and provincial for an international capital. Only the chicness of some of the shops gave away the fact that the euro is domiciled here. I guessed that you'd need a tax-free expat salary to pay for some of those makes of shoe or dress.

There was not much traffic in the side streets, and the only times the driver reduced his frantic speed were to let pedestrians cross the road, even when there were no red lights to stop him. This very un-Parisian habit naturally had Elodie seething with indignation.

'Are you really *obliged* to stop at *every* crossing?' she demanded in clipped French.

'Yes, by law,' the driver replied.

'But it's people like me who *make* the laws!' she complained.

Right, I thought, and it's attitudes like that that are making people say Brussels has got too big for its boots.

I saw the driver eyeing Elodie in his rear-view mirror.

'Vous êtes française, non?' he asked.

'Oui?' she said defiantly, as if it had been an accusation – which it probably was.

We emerged into a wide, congested boulevard, passing a medieval castle that looked like a miniature French chateau. The traffic jam gave the driver the opportunity to turn around and unleash a stream of conversation about the famous French tax exiles he'd had in his taxi. I could hear Elodie groaning with indifference, so I encouraged him with an interested 'vraiment?' or two.

'And there's another one, really famous, just arrived as an exile this week,' he said, grinning. 'Have a guess. A female singer.'

'Edith Piaf,' Elodie hissed, and never before had the legendary *chanteuse*'s name been uttered with such vehemence, except perhaps by someone discussing her dubious activities under the Occupation.

The driver took the hint and went into a sulk. I gave Elodie a reproachful look.

'It's his fault,' she said to me in English. 'He needs to concentrate on driving. I'm late.'

'Late for what? We have a meeting, and here I am.'

'You think I would dash to Brussels just for you, Paul?' She laughed. 'You're so cute. No, I have to sign the MEPs' register before seven or I won't receive my daily allowance. It's more than three hundred euros. A poor MEP needs every cent she can get.'

'So you've been working all day for the EU in Paris, have you?' My question came out even more sarcastically than I'd intended, but Elodie just shrugged.

'I'm an MEP. Every breath I take is working for the EU.' She giggled and repeated the line to the tune of the famous Police song. It's still very popular in France, and the French really know how to murder it.

I gazed longingly out of the car window at the neon-green cross of a *pharmacie*, which, being in Brussels, was also an *apotheek*. I guessed this was one reason why the EU administration was set up here – the Belgians were already good at bilingual signs before they had to add the twenty-odd new languages.

'Oh, Paul, it's so refreshing to see you again,' Elodie said, in a sudden outbreak of friendliness. 'No one answers me back like you do.' She looked across at me, almost affectionately. 'But what have you done to yourself? You look terrible. Have you been drinking?'

'Oh no. Given it up,' I said. 'Haven't drunk a drop since, ooh . . .' I waved my hand about, as if trying to conjure up an abstinence of anywhere between six hours and six months.

She laughed.

'Honest,' I said. 'I was up all night revising my irregular Breton verbs.'

'That's not what I've heard, Paul. What's this about you and a prostitute?' She gave me an accusing grin.

'What are you talking about?'

'The manager called me at dawn this morning complaining about you. Honestly, Paul, a hooker? Haven't you got a girlfriend at the moment? And why did you take her back to the hotel? I use that place all the time for my guests.'

Her barrage of questions stirred up some memories that my hangover had successfully blanked out. That woman on the street corner. The half a T-shirt. Those miniature shorts. Oh no, I thought, surely not?

'I didn't take her back to the hotel, she took me,' I recalled, dimly. 'And I'm sure I didn't . . . I mean, I wouldn't . . . I've never . . . not with a . . .' I had to admit I didn't sound too convincing, but I was sure that nothing untoward had happened, even with a brainful of Belgian beer. I've never paid for sex in my life. Well, not financially anyway. Emotionally, I've had to fork out a fortune, of course.

'I know you didn't take her up to your room,' Elodie said. 'The night porter stopped her.'

'Oh yes, the night porter.' I got an image of a snarling man in a grey waistcoat. Then one of the same man, suddenly lying down on the job. 'It was his own fault she punched him. She wasn't a happy lady. I'd just explained to her that it was all a big misunderstanding and then he waded in. But I had the situation under control.'

'Under control? From what the manager told me, you were down on your knees while she was trying to pull your wallet out of your jeans. The porter gave her twenty euros and threw her out.'

'Twenty euros from my wallet?'

'Believe me, Paul, you should give him fifty as a reward. If one of those street girls had got into your bedroom, you would now have no credit card, no phone, no passport and probably no willy. They're dangerous. Prostitution is legal in Belgium, but it doesn't exactly attract the best people. I hope you'll stay sober while you're working for me.'

'I told you, I've taken the pledge,' I pledged. 'And by the way, you still haven't told me exactly what I'm meant to be doing with these endangered languages.'

'I'll explain later. We're nearly there.'

The small street we were in looked just as shabby-chic as lots of others we'd driven along, but the parked cars were noticeably bigger, with international number plates. Then we hit a wide avenue and the architecture suddenly got glassy, its modern façades peppered with foreign banks and chic cafés.

We entered a small open square, presided over by a statue of an exhausted-looking politician. On two sides of the square were café terraces hosting a horde of office workers, male and female, all with drinks in hands and smiles on faces. Something about working at the European Parliament clearly made its staff pretty happy.

'Voilà!' the driver announced.

'Merci,' I said, filling in for Elodie, who paid wordlessly, grabbed her receipt and set off at a canter. Her low heels clicking, she jogged into an immense beige-floored forecourt that was ringed by a curved wall of billboard-sized photos publicising successful EU actions. These grateful recipients of euros were smiling even more widely than the civil servants out in the square.

There were more eurocrat-looking people in the forecourt, standing in gaggles or heading towards the cafés. Elodie weaved between them and began bounding up a wide staircase into what had to be the biggest glass construction outside of America or Dubai. Honestly, whoever got the glazing contract for the European Parliament building must have retired straight away to the Caymans. Or started up a window-cleaning business.

'Allez, Paul, move, move, move,' Elodie barked over her shoulder. Now she was my personal trainer.

At the first set of doors she had to dig into her bag for her badge, and begged the security man to let me through, using a mixture of official authority and shameless biting of her bottom lip.

'He will be out again in two minutes,' she promised the man.

He shrugged, apparently blasé about politicians' fake promises.

Elodie bundled me into a revolving door, almost threw me through a metal detector gateway and then we were galloping across a wide, marble-floored foyer towards a reception counter, where she finally skidded to a halt.

The woman behind the desk was chatting amicably to the man she was dealing with, a casually dressed type in jeans – the sort of guy Elodie loves to push around.

'Excuse me, but this is urgent,' she foghorned in French. 'I'm an MEP.'

The casual guy looked around, straight into Elodie's glaring eyes.

'Go ahead,' he said in English, clearly used to being elbowed aside by Parisians.

'Oui, madame?' the receptionist asked.

'I'm going to sign in. It's not seven yet, n'est-ce pas?' Elodie held up her wristwatch arm, so that everyone could witness that she fully deserved her daily allowance because she had arrived for work a whole two minutes before the end of the day.

'Seven? MEPs can sign in after that, madame,' the receptionist said, not quite managing to hide the satisfaction of seeing that Elodie had dashed like crazy for nothing. 'Until eleven, in fact.'

'Eleven?' Elodie's mouth dropped open in shock. 'But I *always* sign in before seven. I missed dinner in Paris for this. Only with my husband, but even so . . . Why does no one inform us about these rules?'

As usual with Elodie – with almost anyone French, in fact – everything was someone else's fault.

'There is a document, madame,' the receptionist replied. She turned around, opened a cupboard behind her and, totally deadpan, dropped a paving slab of paper on the desk. 'MEPs' regulations,' she said.

Elodie reeled back as though she were being asked to take possession of a live badger.

'I can't drag that thing with me everywhere,' she said.

'Maybe Louis Vuitton does an MEPs' regulations holder,' I suggested. 'You could claim it as an expense.'

The receptionist gave me the hint of a smile.

'There is an electronic format I can send you, madame,' she said.

'Thank you, my assistant will read it and pass on any useful information,' Elodie said, waving her arm in my direction. 'Stay here while I go and sign in,' she told me. 'I don't want to badge you through a hundred more security gates. Why don't you get yourself a visitor's pass while you wait?'

She left me standing with the guy she had barged out of her life. An embarrassing moment. He looked me up and down. I was almost as casual as he was – white shirt, jeans and a dark suit jacket – but I had an extra layer of dishevelment thrown in. And he was in possession of permanent plastic ID hanging from a well-worn strap around his neck, while I was just an interloper.

'After you,' I finally said, to break the awkward silence. 'Sorry for pushing in. She's French.'

'Oh yes,' he agreed. 'Very.'

Elodie returned to reception ten minutes later, all smiles, as you would be if you'd just received a few hundred euros in return for one squiggle of a pen. She thanked the receptionist and apologised graciously to the guy she'd pushed out of the way – though I'd since realised he was only there to chat up the receptionist, and would have stepped aside anyway.

Elodie took my arm like an old friend instead of an arresting officer, and guided me, dishing out smiles in all directions like a princess at a charity jumble sale, back through security and into the fresh air.

'I need a drink,' she announced as we descended the steps towards the forecourt and its circle of giant posters. One of them depicted a dusty toddler splashing clear water into his mouth, thanks to the EU.

'Me too,' I said. 'Something pure and fizzy.' I was sure the photo of the toddler had been sponsored by the cafés just outside Parliament. You couldn't walk past it without feeling parched. 'Then maybe you can explain what you want me to do with these languages.'

'Oh, nothing much,' Elodie said. She performed one of those raspberries that French people blow when they don't care a damn about a subject you want to discuss.

'You've brought me all the way to Brussels for *nothing much*?' I asked.

'Nothing much is what brings most of us here, Paul. Didn't you know?' She laughed at her own witticism. 'No, what I mean is that the languages project is what I've got a budget for, but it's just a cover for something much more important.'

'Oh yes?'

'Yes.' She pulled me closer, looking around at the groups of badge-wearing people in the forecourt to see if any of them were snooping. They weren't – they all looked as though they were indulging in relaxed, end-of-the-working-day chat – but she lowered her voice anyway. 'I've got a mission for you, Paul.'

'Really?' This sounded either great fun or, knowing Elodie, potentially catastrophic.

'Yes.' She released my arm and started striding across the beige flagstones towards the cafés out in the square.

'Well, aren't you going to tell me what it is?' I asked, jogging after her.

'Not *here*. I'll tell you tomorrow morning.'

'You dragged me out of bed just to tell me that?' My head started to pound again, clearly blaming me for making it work so hard when it could have been resting on a pillow.

'Out of bed at six in the evening?' Elodie laughed as she waited to cross the road to the nearest café terrace.

'Well, you could at least give me a hint,' I pleaded.

'OK.' She shook her head at me, her bothersome child, and leant in close again. 'You've been following the news about the referendum to decide whether the UK leaves the EU or not?'

'Of course.'

There had been nothing else in the news for months, with everyone trying to predict when it would happen and how it would end. Now that the date had been set, the coverage had risen to blanket level. Even the weather reports were smothered – how many millimetres of rain will it take to affect the turnout?

'How do you think the vote will go?' Elodie asked.

'I don't know, the polls are too tight.'

'Well, anyway, I – or should I say *we*…' She checked again that no one nearby could hear. 'We, the French, don't want Britain to leave.'

'You don't?'

It seemed hard to believe. Back in Paris, people had been saying that getting rid of France's hereditary rival in Europe's power struggle was a highly attractive prospect. It was exactly what Napoleon had been trying to do 200 years ago.

'No, we don't.' Elodie lowered her voice still further until it was little more than a tickle in my ear. 'We need a strong Europe. To oppose the hegemony of the Americans.'

'Ah yes.' The French love using words like 'hegemony' when talking about their biggest bugbear, the Transatlantics.

I have no idea what it means, and I don't think they always do, either, but it sounds good.

'Besides, the British don't realise what advantages they get from being part of a big European team,' she said. 'Britain would never be so powerful in isolation. It would be seen by the world as just another little island, like it really is. A sort of inflated Corsica. You English are closing your eyes to the truth of all this. You are – how do you say? – sticking your head in an ostrich?'

Only when she was really annoyed did Elodie's excellent command of English desert her.

'A dangerous thing to do,' I agreed. 'And where do I fit in? In your plans, I mean, not in the ostrich.'

'You will help us to stop Britain leaving, of course.' She stepped back and gave me a French grimace of incomprehension at my slow-wittedness, including a twist of the eyebrows and a crinkling of the nostrils that it would have taken a litre of Botox to smooth out.

'Oh.' This was a surprise. 'And you think I might want to do that, do you?'

'You don't want Britain to stay in Europe, Paul? You live here. You're a continental.' She gawped at me as if I'd just announced I was going to leave a jacuzzi party before the bubbles had warmed up.

'Well, I'm not entirely sure what I want yet. I'm still weighing up the arguments.'

'That's all very balanced of you, Paul, but weigh this up: I am paying you – very generously – to do a job, so I want you to do it.'

'But how am I meant to stop Britain leaving Europe?'

'We have a plan, Paul. I will explain in full tomorrow. Now, come and get me that drink. You have started work already. We don't want to waste Europe's money.'

With this, she held up an arm and strode out in front of a taxi that screeched to a halt to let her cross the road. It was a move that would have got her killed in Paris. She had obviously acclimatised to Brussels very quickly.

3

'EU to ban singing in pubs.'

Report in the British press, 2002

'WELCOME TO Plucks,' Elodie told me as we walked into the noise of a crowded café.

'Is that Flemish rhyming slang?' I asked.

'No, it's a typically Brussels name. Everything is abbreviated here – except for my expenses, of course. "Plux" is an abbreviation for "place du Luxembourg". That's this square. It's where everyone comes after work.'

By 'everyone' she didn't mean bus drivers, waffle-makers and window-cleaners. She meant everyone who was anyone, the cream of the crop of eurocrats. From the look of them, the city's clothes shops were doing as well as its cafés. Same for the hairdressers and hair-removers. The gyms, too – the café was full of trim waistlines, slim calves, tight butts. Even

26

some of the middle-agers looked in good shape, with that upright stance they get from a mixture of Pilates and exaggerated self-worth.

'Shall I get you a drink?' I offered, though I didn't much fancy the crush at the bar. 'What would you like?'

'No need,' Elodie said, and held up two fingers towards someone I didn't see. 'I have my own private waitress,' she added mysteriously. 'Mineral water OK? I always start with that, before deciding if it's worth staying on for something stronger.'

'Mineral water's great. Make mine a bathtub.'

We went outside on to the immense open terrace, and while we waited for Elodie's mystery waitress, she talked me through what was going on around us.

'The older guys in suits and the older, uptight-looking women are mostly MEPs, lobbyists or diverse civil servants. The young girls with the guys are their "assistants". An MEP can hire whoever he wants here in Brussels, and his wife will never see her, so cute women are in high demand, especially with the ugly guys. The younger guys in the chic suits are mainly MEPs' assistants. Their female equivalents are the same, although some of the very chic girls are *stagiaires* – interns – hoping to get spotted by an important man and given a hand upwards, in all senses of the expression. The not-quite-so-chic people usually want a better job so they can get *really* chic. The bulges in their pockets are business cards. The eccentric-looking older ones are MEPs creating a personality for themselves. There are plenty of them here tonight, because Thursday is our last evening in Brussels, before we leave.'

'You only work a four-day week?' Was there no end to their privileges?

'On Thursday nights I usually go back to my voters, Paul. Well, nearer to them anyway, to Paris. But this week I'm staying here for the whole weekend, especially for you. Which means that I want you to look very different for me tomorrow morning. Get some new clothes. I'll put them on the expense account. You can't go around looking like a drunk English tourist, if you're working for France.'

I only had time to nod before one of the *très chic* women Elodie had been talking about strode up to us, holding two tall glasses of deliciously clear liquid, topped with slices of lime.

'Bonsoir, Manon,' Elodie said.

'Bonsoir, Madame Martin,' Manon replied.

So Elodie wasn't using her married name. Good move, I thought – Martin was classless and easy to remember, whereas her husband was saddled with Bonnepoire, a posh name that meant something like 'gullible idiot'.

'This is Pol Wess,' Elodie said, pronouncing my name as the French always do. 'Pol, meet Manon. She's one of my assistants parliamentaires.'

I shook Manon's hand.

'Bonsoir,' she said, somewhat coolly.

Manon's straight dark hair was caressing her shoulders in that amazing '*ceci n'est pas un style*' way that only Frenchwomen seem to manage, so that it looks as if it grew that way completely by chance and that nature is therefore a brilliant hairdresser.

She was gazing straight into my eyes, as if to make sure I strayed no further south than her tastefully made-up eyelids and full, dark lips. She had one of those lucky faces that don't really need make-up but look even more natural with it, if that makes any sense. Which I wasn't, because I was astonished that Elodie had chosen such a looker as an assistant. Too much competition, surely?

I opened my mouth to begin a bit of 'Oh, you work with Elodie, do you?' banter, but I must have been gawping for too long, because I missed my chance.

'How do you think les Anglais will vote?' Manon asked me, in French.

'No one knows,' I said, trying to make my ignorance sound like wisdom.

'How would you *like* them to vote?' she asked, and from the way she looked at me, I guessed there was only one right answer.

'Well, like you, I'll be working with Elodie, so we'll be on the same side,' I said.

'Yes. Well, I must return to talk to Monsieur Cholpin.' I detected hostility in her tone, as if I'd given the wrong answer. Or perhaps she'd just read my mind. Most men probably had exactly the same thoughts when they first set eyes on her.

'Merci pour le drink,' I managed to say.

The French usually think it's hilarious when you mix languages like that, but she just gave a tepid smile and left.

'She seems very efficient,' I told Elodie.

'Yes,' was all she had to say on that subject, as if efficiency might be out of place in the European Parliament.

We both watched Manon walk stylishly back through the crowd towards a short man with thinning, floppy grey hair whose suit looked frequently worn, but expensive. He was grinning up at a tall thirty-something woman, apparently deciding where to start biting her. Instead, he took a business card out of his pocket and pressed it into her hand like a precious gift. It was a strangely seductive gesture, coming from this nerdy-looking guy who anywhere else would be just a little grey man. He then grabbed the woman in an excessive hug, as though she had just won the World Cup for France's female football team. But there was no look of joy on her face, only sufferance. He released her after a good ten seconds and she backed away, nodding politely, like underlings do in films about Chinese emperors. As soon as she had gone, he turned his hungry eyes on Manon. He was obviously quite an operator.

'Cholpin was Minister of Agriculture,' Elodie said, as if in explanation. 'Now he's an MEP for Normandy.'

'Exiled to Brussels as punishment?' I asked.

'Ha!' Elodie almost choked on her mineral water. 'Pension, you mean. Two terms as an MEP and you are eligible for the full pension. Comfortable for life. French politicians get it as a reward. My team are already working on my re-election.'

'A pension? But you're only in your twenties.'

'Oh, Paul, surely you know it's never too early for a French person to start thinking about a luxurious retirement.'

People kept wandering up and saying polite hellos to Elodie. MEPs were big-shots here, I realised. Another drink materialised in her hand, delivered by an ultra-classy guy in a sharp pinstripe. He was sickeningly slick, with a blond head straight out of a hair-conditioner advert and a suit that seemed ridiculously pleased to be wrapped around his tall frame.

The glass he brought was wine-shaped, and Elodie accepted it with a wide smile, handing me her half-finished mineral water. So that was what MEPs' assistants were – glorified furniture. Manon was a drinks trolley, I was the mantelpiece.

The pinstriped newcomer granted me a brief, indifferent glance and then huddled in close to Elodie, almost literally shouldering me away. It was becoming only too clear how the Brussels class system works – no suit, nobody.

From the snippets I heard of the pinstripe's opening gambit, I could tell he had a faint accent – Scandinavian, probably. He was saying that he'd heard Elodie speak at some meeting or other.

'I was very impressed by your argument that grow and near should work closer together, without excluding regions,' he said, whatever that meant.

Elodie lapped it up.

'Oh, I'm *so* glad you agree,' she gushed. 'Regions are very close to my heart.'

'And I'm sure you have a very big heart,' he said, and even without a hangover I would have felt a wave of nausea. That was a line straight out of a 1980s French film starring a Saint-Tropez lifeguard with permed hair, skin-tight Speedos and a fake-gold name-bracelet. But Elodie didn't seem to mind. She laughed and said she was devoting her heart entirely to Brittany, no matter how attractive other regions might look.

Wondering how long I'd be able to survive in a place where nerdy guys mauled unwilling women in exchange for a business card, and smoothies with suits could spout sub-Casanova come-ons and not be laughed at, I moved away, intending to get myself a refresher. Something stronger than water, maybe.

My route indoors to the bar was suddenly blocked by what initially looked like a glamorous cannon.

It was a tall woman a few years older than me and dressed to impress, with a gunmetal-blue business suit and a blouse that seemed to be having a bad top-button day.

'Bonsoir,' she said.

'Bonsoir,' I replied.

'Sharker,' she said, or something like that. 'Sharker Yar Miller.'

'Pol Wess,' I said, joining her in the fashion for badly pro-nounced names.

'Vous êtes l'assistant de Madame Martin?' she asked, in accented French.

Aha, I thought. I'd only been on the scene a few minutes and already I'd been spotted. I told her that I was indeed 'travailling avec Madame Martin'.

The lady's friendly interrogation went on for a couple more minutes, rather like a TV panel game where a contestant has to work out the identity of the mystery guest. After a few questions, she knew everything I was willing to tell her.

'Et qui êtes-vous?' I asked her. In reply she gave me a short list of initials and abbreviations that I was clearly meant to recognise, ending with the only words I really understood – 'public affairs'.

'I like your style,' she added. 'A parliamentary assistant, but not too chic. Low-key, cool. There should be more like you.'

'Merci,' I said, not that I deserved her compliment in the slightest.

'So what's your job exactly?' I asked. 'Public affairs?'

'No, very private ones,' she said, and raised her eyebrows as if to imply that this really was an outrageous come-on. I couldn't believe it. Did everyone in Brussels attract groupies so easily?

I was trying to work out how to respond when I caught sight of someone over her shoulder. It was a guy with a dark, well-clipped beard who seemed to be eyeing me distastefully. Maybe this Sharker was his girlfriend.

He nudged another guy standing next to him and they both gave me a stare. The second guy nodded, as if in agreement with something unpleasant being said about me. I saw that they were wearing almost identical conservative suits and name badges. It looked as though they were deciding whether to expel this intruder who dared to chat up a classy woman while not wearing visible ID.

'Who are they?' my new female friend asked. So it wasn't her bloke after all.

'I don't know. But I think I've seen the guy with the beard before somewhere.'

'Not surprising. They look like assistants, too. You've probably seen them in the Parliament building.'

'Yes,' I agreed, even though I'd only spent about fifteen minutes in reception.

'Never mind them, let's get a drink,' she said, 'and you can tell me how you're enjoying Brussels.'

'Oh, it's been very interesting so far.'

As we weaved our way towards the bar, she grabbed my hand so that we wouldn't be separated in the crush, and I guessed that things were about to get even more interesting.

I'd split up with my Parisian girlfriend about a month earlier. Amandine was a business student who'd been working for Jean-Marie, Elodie's dad. We got on really well at first, but then Amandine accepted a job in Shanghai, which kind of Peking-ducked our relationship (that's Chinese rhyming slang, of course). She asked me to go with her, but I was too scared of turning into a desperate expat wife, and elected to stay in Paris.

We Skyped for a month – one of us usually waking up, the other going to sleep – but soon it began to feel artificial, and we both agreed that there was no point in prolonging the downward spiral.

So in the Plux café, when this glamorous woman started hitting on me, I was not exactly unreceptive. She was very attractive, and quickly proved that she could be amusingly bitchy. She knew enough about the men in the bar for me to understand that I wasn't her first flirtation by any means, but she was never sordid or boastful about it. She was recently divorced, and getting a bit of revenge on the male gender, I gathered.

Her name, it turned out, was Šárka. She was originally from the Czech Republic, she'd been in Brussels for eight years and been married to a eurocrat from Marseille. Hence her excellent command of French. The only gap in her linguistic knowledge was that she seemed to think I was French, too, and I didn't bother to deny it. If I'd admitted to being *anglais*, she might have started asking me about the referendum, as they all did. And anyway, if she wanted a Parisian playboy for the evening, who was I to disappoint her?

Any French person could tell instantly that I was English (they often say that we Brits have a 'lazy tongue' when it comes to pronouncing their guttural sounds – and doing certain other things, too), but in Brussels no one seemed to speak any language perfectly. Even the English bloke in the bar had spoken laboriously, weighing his words as if choosing from a multilingual dictionary in his head. My French accent probably had the same effect on Šárka, because half of my conversation consisted of pauses while I agonised over the right verb conjugation or strangled vowel sound.

After about three drinks, Šárka nipped to the Ladies, and a flushed-looking Elodie came over and grabbed me by the arm.

'I didn't know you could speak Czech, Paul,' she said.

'You know her?'

'Of course. She is very good at making influential *friends*.' She raised her eyebrows meaningfully at this last word. 'Be in my office at eleven tomorrow, OK? Well dressed and without a – what do you call it? Overhang.'

Elodie looked slightly drunk herself, and I noticed the Nordic god hovering in the background. I wondered if she wasn't intending to indulge in some groupie action, too. Though in her case it wasn't clear who was going to be the groupie.

'Well, you take care of yourself, Elodie,' I said, in a way that was meant to convey a bit of moral disapproval. I mean to say, only a year earlier I'd helped to cook her wedding supper. Had all those sea bass died in vain?

'Oh, I am always careful,' she said, which wasn't exactly what I'd meant.

She swanned off back to her blond admirer.

The gregarious Šárka squeezed towards me, exchanging brief pleasantries with several people along the way, and arrived back smiling. I was still holding her glass, but she crinkled her nose at it.

'Why don't we go and get a drink somewhere more peaceful?' From the look in her eyes, I didn't think she meant a coffee machine in the deserted Parliament building.

'Sure,' I said, downing the last of my white wine and feeling it zing against my gums.

We walked out of the square and into a side street where she stopped to show me an alarming poster. By the door of a building marked '*Studios Intimes*' there was a mosaic of photos, all of them lurid flashlit shots of empty bedrooms. Most were decorated with four-poster beds, mirrors on walls, velvety bordello furniture. The poster announced that the place was open from 9 a.m. to midnight and accepted all known credit cards. Shagpads for hire.

My first thought was 'Nine in the morning?' and my second 'Can I afford to pay for the room?' But to my relief, Šárka told me that this was where the truly unsubtle people came for their *rendez-vous*.

'We are fifty metres from the Parliament. They *want* to be seen. We are going somewhere much more discreet.'

Now I knew for sure this wasn't just a wine-tasting invitation.

Just around the corner there was a newish office building with a main entrance encrusted in company name-plaques. Šárka held an electronic key to the entryphone and the door clicked open. The small reception area was empty, but I saw cameras blinking at us from the ceiling, and wondered whether the security company got a kick out of seeing Šárka come in with a nocturnal visitor.

We went up in the small lift, like two people heading for a civilised business meeting, only Šárka's faint smile giving any hint that something more was in store. I was genuinely surprised that she was interested in me. In the lift's mirror, my reflection looked exactly like someone who'd recovered from a raging hangover but hadn't found the energy to shave, or bothered to check that his shirt collar wasn't sticking up crazily on one side. I straightened myself out, as though it would make any difference.

Another electronic keystroke got us through a featureless wooden door and into Šárka's office. She turned the lights on and I saw a smart but uninspiring room – large metal-framed desk, brand-new leather swivel chair, orderly filing shelves. The only thing that livened it up was the giant poster on the wall. It was a map of Europe, headlined with a bright-green company logo, and showing various European countries partly coloured in with the same green as the logo.

There was, I now noticed, one other thing jollying up the office – a long white couch, where Šárka was already sitting. She reached into a small fridge by the couch and pulled out a bottle of champagne.

'Brussels bubbles?' she said in English, and pointed towards a small battalion of glasses standing on a table by the door. I guessed a lot of drinking went on here.

I fetched two tall-stemmed glasses and sat down beside her on the couch. She handed me the bottle to open.

'Don't worry,' she said, reverting to French and calling me by the intimate '*tu*'. 'You know what they say: what happens in Brussels stays in Brussels.'

'Well, actually, that's not true,' I said, 'which is exactly what the British are worried about. These Brussels laws don't stay in Brussels. They cross over to England and force people to eat straight cucumbers.'

'Why do you care about the English?' she asked, and luckily I was saved from the danger of revealing my true identity by the pop of the champagne cork. 'I hope you're not turning English *now*,' she said. 'I need you to be very, very French.'

With this she clamped her mouth to mine and began exploring my palate with a sprightly tongue. After a few seconds she broke off and held out a glass for some champagne. Definitely a woman in total control, I thought, apprehensively.

We clinked glasses and drank. I hoped the bubbles would liven me up for what promised to be a demanding obstacle course. I've known a few of these career women and they can be as exhausting as army gym instructors (not that I've ever got intimate with one of those).

She began to kiss me again, which I took as an invitation to return the compliment. Her satisfied moan suggested that I'd been right.

'Just a moment,' she said, and leant to one side to hit a switch. The lights dimmed to a dull glow that made her white blouse stand out above the dark material of her jacket. That darkness, I decided, had to go. I slid the jacket off her shoulders, and she let it fall on to the couch behind her.

'In Brittany, do the lights ever dim suddenly like that?' she asked.

'I don't know,' I said, more interested in locating the few attached buttons of her blouse than discussing French power cuts.

'It is good to be in constant control,' she said.

'Yes, in control,' I agreed. After more than a month without a real sniff of female flesh, I definitely needed to stay in control. I felt there was a serious risk of going too far too fast and spoiling everything.

'Of the lighting, I mean.'

'Oh yes, this is perfect,' I said, my eyes half-closed as I leant forward to inhale the perfumed cleft between her breasts.

'Of energy in general,' she said. Which suddenly struck me as weird.

'Excusez-moi?' I lifted my face from the depths of her cleavage.

'I think it's best for a region to stay in constant control of its energy supply,' she said.

I sifted through her remark, looking for some sign that it might be a lascivious metaphor about sexual performance or orgasm intensity, or anything related to what we were currently doing on her sofa. But I couldn't find any.

'I don't believe it,' I finally said. 'I have my nose in your breasts, and you're lobbying me.'

'Engaging in a frank discussion about mutual needs,' she replied, taking a sip of champagne and then licking her lips, as if to remind me what my needs were.

'And what are *your* needs?' I asked.

'Well, to be perfectly frank, I would very much like you to have a serious talk with your boss about aliens,' she said.

'Aliens?'

Šárka laughed, wrongly assuming that I was joking. She pointed towards her big wall map, and I now saw that its green swathes were occupied by an army of white windmills, and that the green annexation hadn't got as far as western France.

'Aliens,' she repeated, and this time I understood. She was saying 'éoliennes', the French word for wind turbines. Presumably she wanted me to help her colour in Brittany with wind farms.

'I don't have influence with Elodie about that,' I said.

'I've heard that you do.'

'No, I'm working on languages. Breton, Basque, Corsican.'

'Only that?'

'Yes.'

With this, Šárka suddenly looked more pensive. She still had her shirt half-open, so she was being erotically pensive, but much less focused on matters physical than before.

'Does that really stop us?' I asked. 'I mean, you're a beautiful woman. I don't mind if you want to lobby me for a few minutes. In fact, I'm all in favour of wind power.'

This jolted Šárka out of her meditations.

'What?' she squawked. 'Make love with you, if there's nothing in it for me? What do you think I am? A whore?' She used the vulgar French word *pute*.

'No, of course not,' I said.

Although I was wondering what else you'd call someone who was willing to have casual sex in return for the promise of income. A footballer's girlfriend?

'No, I am not a whore, and we will not make love tonight.'

'Could you please stop saying "whore"?' I begged. 'Especially with your shirt open.'

She pulled the two cotton walls of her blouse together.

'I think you should leave. I made a mistake.'

What can a boy do, except take a few deep breaths to calm his ardour and grab a consoling slug of champagne?

'Bonne nuit,' I wished her as I made for the door.

'Toi aussi,' she said, annoyingly familiar again. 'I'm sure I'll see you at Plux. Let me know if you obtain more influence over your boss. Then maybe we can . . . *talk* again.'

'Really?'

'Bonne nuit,' she repeated, not wanting to make any promises.

I let myself out into the silent street, wondering what the CCTV guys would make of my all-too-brief visit. Not exactly marathon man.

I was much less drunk than the previous night, but I felt certain that my headache next day was going to be just as painful, albeit for different reasons. Brussels, I had already decided, is the kind of place that can give you a vicious hangover every single day.

4

'According to the EU's animal waste directive, it is illegal to bury dead pets unless you have pressure-cooked them at 130°C for half an hour.'

Report in the British press, 2000

NEXT MORNING at ten to eleven I was all spruced up in a new grey suit and reporting for duty at the European Parliament. Or trying to, anyway.

'This is a visitor's badge dated yesterday,' the security man explained. The headache I'd woken up with grew a notch more intense.

'But I'm the new assistant of Madame Elodie Martin,' I argued.

'This is a visitor's badge dated yesterday,' he said, and I sensed a theme developing.

'Perhaps if I talk to the receptionist, I can arrange things.'

'Sorry, monsieur, but entry is impossible with a visitor's badge dated—'

'Yesterday?' I guessed. He nodded. His eyes stopped focusing on me and looked out into the forecourt. I no longer existed.

Backing off, I phoned Elodie, who gave one of her trademark huffs to imply that the whole universe – planets, stars, black holes and whatever deity was out there – had decided to annoy her.

'Stay where you are,' she barked.

'So you'll come and . . . ?' But she was already gone. 'She's coming to fetch me,' I told the security guy, who didn't seem at all worried by the imminent arrival of a barking French MEP. He probably didn't know Elodie that well.

In the event, it wasn't Elodie who came out to rescue me. It was the beautiful Manon.

'Bonjour,' I said pleasantly.

'We have to go to the other entrance,' she replied. As polite as Elodie, I thought. French diplomacy schools must give classes in tactical rudeness.

Manon turned on her heels. She'd changed out of her stilettos, I noticed, into some leather flatties, and was looking more worklike today, less party-chic. Still highly attractive, though, behind her aggressive façade.

I followed her around the building to an almost identical set of revolving doors, where a flash of her badge and my own passport got us inside.

'So you work exclusively for Elodie?' I asked, just to make conversation. I took a risk and used the friendly '*tu*' form.

'Yes,' Manon said, with a little grunt at the end, as though I'd enquired whether the Pope was still practising his usual religion.

'I thought perhaps you were also working with that Minister.'

'Cholpin?'

'Yes.'

'No.'

'Oh.'

Scintillating stuff. I decided to shut up while Manon went through the procedure of getting me another visitor's badge. Whatever I'd done to annoy her, apart from being born, I clearly wasn't going to change her opinion of me just by showing interest in her everyday life.

But none of us standard-issue males like to be disliked by a beautiful woman, so as soon as we were in forced proximity in the lift, I tried a different tack.

'Please tell me what I've done to annoy you,' I asked.

'Nothing,' she said, looking up at the ceiling.

'Is it because I'm English?'

'What?'

'The French sometimes don't like the English.'

She shrugged.

'Especially when we're causing trouble with the European Union,' I said. 'You know, the referendum.'

'Pff!' she said, as if the referendum was a fly trying to settle on her croissant.

'Maybe you think I'm a spy? You know – why is an Englishman working for the French?'

She laughed at this absurdity.

'You French can be very patriotic,' I said. 'You still blame us for our barbecue with Joan of Arc.'

'I'm only half-French,' she said.

'And what is the rest?'

'A quarter Czech, a quarter Polish, a quarter German.'

'That makes a hundred and twenty-five per cent. So you're a sort of super-femme.'

I winced at the way I sounded like a Parisian chat-up artist, but at least I earned a glimmer of a smile.

'My family got complicated after the war,' she said.

'My family's all English, but they've always been complicated.'

She laughed and looked me in the eye for the first time.

'What have you come here to do, Anglais?' she asked, making my nationality sound like an insult. Which, to many people in Brussels, I guessed it was. But at least she'd called me '*tu*', which had to count as a diplomatic victory.

'The same as you, I suppose. We're both working for the same MEP, right?'

'Yes, but what specifically?'

This was all getting a bit interrogatorial, if that's a word. I wasn't sure how much I was allowed to tell her, even if she was part of Elodie's team, so I recited my usual chorus.

'I'll be working on endangered languages mainly. Breton, Basque, Corsican.'

'Is that all?'

'I don't know. Do you think it's not enough? You think I'm going to get bored in Belgium?'

She laughed again. I got the impression that she was enjoying the interrogation, as if it was a game in which she scored a point for every bit of information she squeezed out of me.

'And what do *you* do specifically?' I asked her.

'Oh, everything.' She smiled as if she also got points for evasive answers.

The lift announced the sixth floor, apparently trying to make it sound as boring as possible in three languages, and we emerged into a corridor that instantly explained the lift's lack of enthusiasm.

We hear so much about European excess and MEPs' over-spending that I was expecting chandeliers, mosaics and medieval tapestries. But this featureless corridor of identical doors and unpatterned carpets could have been the head office of Bland Drab & Stodgy Ltd. If it had been a paint company, this would have been the beige department, recently redecorated after somebody complained that the previous beige was a bit too racy.

The only things dispelling the dullness were the large luggage trunks standing beside a few of the office doors, as though several occupants were about to go on a world cruise.

Even so, to make sure this wasn't too exciting, they were all using the same standardised grey luggage.

Most of the walls were bare and boring, too, except for a couple of posters of Eskimos looking confused amongst melting ice floes. These were signed 'The Greens', and the mention of that particular colour reminded me of the posters I'd seen in Šárka's office the previous evening. As I watched Manon's shapely form striding along in front of me, I felt suddenly depressed about my motley relations with the whole of womanhood.

Elodie didn't raise my mood. She was sitting behind a large desk, prodding at her phone, and only gave me a brief glance before turning to Manon.

'Didn't anyone tell him how to dress?' she demanded.

Manon looked at my suit, crisp white shirt and subtly silky tie and shrugged.

'He looks OK,' she said. 'For an Anglais.' If she was joking, she kept a masterfully straight face.

'No, he doesn't. You don't dress like that on Fridays, Paul,' Elodie told me. 'You dress more casual when the MEPs aren't here. It's – what do you call it in English? – undressing Friday. Take your tie off, or everyone will stare at you.'

I obeyed. Now I understood why Manon was looking less chic. And why the few men I'd seen in the entrance hall had been tie-less, some even in jeans. I was such an obvious outsider.

'OK, sit down, Paul. And give your passport to Manon. She's going to get you a permanent badge.' Elodie switched to French. 'Manon, could you close the door on the way out, please?'

I noticed that even though the two women were more or less the same age, both used the '*vous*' form, with Elodie playing the respectful yet distant boss, and Manon the standard employee. There was some serious hierarchical stuff going on.

As Manon closed the door, she gave me a look as if to say, 'Secret meeting, eh? Told you so.' She definitely knew there was more to my presence than preserving Breton verbs. But what was the problem with that? As far as I'd understood, Elodie's 'mission' was favourable to France, beneficial to Europe, and Manon was presumably on the same page as Elodie, so *pourquoi* the huffiness?

'Have I done something to annoy Manon?' I asked Elodie, who carried on jabbing at her phone.

'You annoy all women eventually, Paul. Maybe she's just good at seeing the future.'

'She was asking me what exactly I was going to be doing here. Doesn't she know?'

Suddenly Elodie's phone was less fascinating.

'What did you tell her?' she demanded.

'Just some stuff about endangered languages.'

'Good.' Elodie turned to stare at the door as if Manon might be eavesdropping, and lowered her voice. 'She's not supposed to know everything about the mission. I think that's why she's been acting a bit strange recently. She knows I've got something going on and she's annoyed at being excluded. She's too ambitious. I wish I'd never taken her on. But I had to – Papa owed her mother a favour. I can guess why *that* was. Huh!'

I could guess, too. Elodie's dad, Jean-Marie, was one of those Frenchmen who'll use any argument to get a woman into bed – or, more often, spreadeagled over his desk. 'Your daughter wants a job in Brussels? I can arrange that, madame. You want planning permission to start fracking underneath the Louvre? No *problème*. Now if you'll just bend over . . .'

'Why don't you want Manon to help with the *mission*?' I asked. It felt weird calling it that, as if I was going to be parachuted behind anti-EU lines and hooking up with pro-single-market resistance fighters.

'I have my reasons,' Elodie said, in a way that suggested further questions weren't welcome.

'And are you going to tell me what I'm not supposed to tell Manon?' I asked.

'Yes. Of course.' She looked at the door as if to check that it was still closed, and then turned to me. 'As I told you last night, the plan is to get Britain to stay in the EU. To do that, we need to influence British public opinion, so your job will be to help us.'

'And how exactly?'

'That, Paul, is something I will explain to you when the time is right.'

'Isn't the time right now?'

'No, it isn't. And I decide when it is. The referendum is in less than two weeks. Every part of the mission has to be perfectly timed.' She spoke very slowly, as though to a chimp that was having trouble learning to grunt once for apple and twice for banana. 'Sorry, Paul,' she added, clicking out of her woman-of-mystery role play for a second. 'It's not up to me. I'm just trying to follow orders from Paris.'

'OK, I understand. So you want me to start with these languages?'

'Yes, right. Exactly.' Now I was being a clever chimp. 'I've set up a meeting for you at the Commission.'

'The Commission? What's that, compared to the Parliament?'

'Oh, we decide things, and they do them. Or they suggest them and we vote. The Commission is full of career civil servants, anyway. All in love with Europe.'

She handed me a business card, and I read the small print.

'A German translator?'

'Yes, take him out to lunch and he'll give you enough bla-bla to write a quick report about these stupid languages.'

'Stupid? So you don't actually care about them at all?'

'Well, Breton, yes, because they're my electorate, but personally, the others? *Bof!*' She gave the French language's verbal shrug its full power. 'If you only knew how much it costs to put up road signs with names in two languages. God, just to change one letter in a place name, France spends millions a year. Who gives a fuck if Perpignan is called Perpinyà in Catalan? It's the same place.'

'Shall I put that in the report?'

She laughed, then abruptly stopped.

'You, Paul, will do exactly what I tell you to do. Please. Perhaps I was being a bit, how do you say, frivolish? Frivolatious?' I nodded my approval of this excellent new word, and she went on. 'Frivolatious about these languages, because they will help us with the bigger mission. If your report can convince the people in Scotland or in – what do you call it? Le pays de Galles?'

'Wales.'

'And Cornouailles?'

'Cornwall.'

'Yes, if these provincials all think they will get money from Brussels for extra teachers for their silly languages, they will vote to stay in Europe, no? We could even get money for that weird patois they talk in the north of England.'

'Geordie, in Newcastle?'

'No, the other one. I read about it. What's it called? Scam? Scum?'

'You mean Scouse?'

'Yes, the thing they talk in Blackpool.'

'Liverpool. Yes, I'd love to see Scouse road signs. Turn left, la. This way to scaggy Manctown.'

'I don't know what you're talking about, Paul, as usual, but it doesn't matter. Ask our German friend about all the minority languages in Europe. Lots of countries must have them, and all of them could be useful for our bigger plan. And meanwhile, just remember that lots of nations don't care if Britain leaves the EU. They think you're troublemakers, arguing about every detail of every law and then asking for exceptions. But we in France do care, and we need you to stay at the heart of a strong Europe.'

Elodie put her hand on her own heart, as if swearing an oath on the exiled soul of Napoleon.

'You think Europe's got a strong heart, do you?' I asked. 'It seems to me it's been pretty close to cardiac arrest recently.'

'Oh, shut up with the negativism, Paul. Anyway, talking of heart problems, how did it go with your new lady friend last night?' Elodie grinned, as if she'd already seen CCTV footage of my failed session on Šárka's couch.

'All she wanted was to lobby me about wind power.'

'Yes, I know that. But did she let you . . .?'

'You *knew*?' I was aghast.

'Of course. I was the one who sent her to talk to you.'

'What?'

'Yes. I told her you were my new assistant, with a special interest in sustainable energy.' While the last remaining dregs of my ego collapsed in a small heap on the floor, Elodie went on proudly, 'Šárka keeps trying to lobby me. But I can't allow wind farms to fill up the countryside in my circumscription. Everyone hates them. But honestly, Paul! I thought you might be intelligent enough to lie to Šárka and get some easy sex. What's wrong with you? I need you relaxed, motivated, focused on your work; not on your hands and knees crawling after girls like Manon.'

This hit me where it hurt.

'And what about your night, Elodie? How was that? Northern lights on the bedroom ceiling? A nice little Viking invasion?'

She gritted her teeth at me. At any other time in our relationship she would have told me to go away and get serviced by a Norseman. But I saw her make a conscious effort to get a grip on her emotions.

'You know, Paul,' she said philosophically, 'it's very hard for a young married couple to be separated by their work. Valéry calls me at eight every evening when I'm here.' (Her husband was one of those unfortunate Frenchmen saddled with a female-sounding name, like all the Emmanuels, Gaëls and – yes – the Jean-Maries.) 'He usually calls from the landline, as if to prove that he's at home. Then he probably goes out and takes some woman to dinner. Honestly, does he think I'm stupid? What man stays home every night when his wife is away?'

I felt almost sorry for her.

'So you think he's cheating on you?' I asked.

'Who knows. None of his uncles are really sure who their father is. Probably one of their own uncles. It's that kind of family. They usually marry cousins, so adultery is a vital way of diluting their DNA. But it's not only his family. It's the whole problem with being married and French. You feel as if divorce is just a wrongly directed text message away.'

It was typical Elodie – if she was shagging a Dane in Brussels, it was all someone else's fault.

'Now where is Manon with that bloody badge?' she growled, rather breaking the philosophical mood.

She leapt to her feet and opened her office door. I couldn't see out, but Manon must have been at her desk, because Elodie started whingeing at her in French.

'I didn't want to interrupt,' I heard Manon reply, matter-of-factly, not taking any of Elodie's bullshit. 'He can get the badge from reception in ten minutes.'

'OK, Paul, go-go-go!' Elodie shooed me out of the room like a skydiving instructor who didn't care whether or not her new recruit was wearing a parachute.

5

'EU to ban Scottish bagpipes.'

Report in the British press, 2005

SOME PEOPLE see Brussels as an exclusive health club for bloated bureaucrats. Or as a Stalinist dictatorship that issues tyrannical laws just for the pleasure of watching its oppressed subjects panicking because the laws are impossible to obey.

Others think it's simply a means that we Europeans have invented of splurging our own money away, a giant equivalent of bathing in champagne every day or using banknotes to light cigars.

Personally, though, as I walked through the streets of Brussels towards the European Commission HQ, enjoying the slap of my new badge on my shirt front, I felt like the member of a religious sect.

It was because of the flag – that halo of stars, a cross between a golden tiara and Jesus's crown of thorns, on a background of an idealised, cloudless sky. It looks like the emblem of a private paradise run by a wacky cult that dictates everything, from the number of bacteria per millilitre of paradise's drinking water to the absorbency speed of its disposable nappies.

You can't escape that flag in Brussels. It was all around me – on nameplates outside countless buildings; decorating office windows; on cryptic posters that seemed designed to tell people how to say 'development' in every European language; and now it was dangling from my neck, both on my badge and on its strap.

Arriving at the Commission HQ, I saw the most massive flag of them all, a blue banner ten storeys high telling everyone in three languages who owns the building – even Google or Manchester United couldn't have been more ostentatious in their branding.

It reminded me of my trip to Los Angeles, when I'd first caught sight of the Scientology building. The idea of all the faithful inside, with their identical suits, badges and bonkers beliefs, sent a shiver down my spine. I hadn't dared to venture in, for fear of being brainwashed or teleported to another planet, but here in Brussels I was wearing the perfect camouflage. If I went in, they'd all assume I was one of them.

Disappointingly, though, at the last minute my German contact told me to meet him at a nearby café. I wasn't allowed to peep inside the believers' inner sanctum just yet.

Even so, the café came as a pleasant surprise. I stood outside and gazed through its plate-glass window. It was a self-service canteen type of place, the sort you get at airports. In Paris or London it would have catered to tourists and the occasional lower-paid office worker, but here it was full of badge people. Admittedly it was dress-down Friday, but they were all dressed-up, by my usual standards – the men in suit jackets, the women in serious skirts and smart shoes.

At the Plux, the Brussels insiders had been in their element, elbow-to-elbow at the bar, chatting loudly amongst themselves, at ease with a drink in their fist; but here they were much more subdued, passively holding their trays of wraps, salads and smoothies, almost embarrassed about being forced to obey city rules and wait in an orderly line to pay.

My phone buzzed, and as soon as I'd pulled it out of my pocket, a boyish guy was standing in front of me, holding out his hand to shake.

'Paul, right? I thought it was you. I just wanted to make sure,' he said. His English was practically accentless. Almost better than mine, I thought.

He was as big a surprise as the café. Like most people, I guess, I have a brain that deals in stereotypes, so I'd been expecting someone Germanic and gymnastic, but he was small, with dark hair and a five-o'clock shadow at lunchtime. Only his pale skin and slightly flushed cheeks hinted that he'd grown up in the north of Europe, while his wide smile suggested that he was genuinely pleased to be in a country where beer was taken as seriously as it was back home.

He introduced himself as Edgar Fürst.

'But please call me Ed.'

'Ed Fürst. OK, great.'

We went inside to choose our airport lunches.

Inevitably we got into the 'How will the Brits vote?' thing, which I deflected by looking serious and saying that the polls were still too tight, as if I'd been up all night studying micro-shifts in public opinion.

With that out of the way, he told me a bit about himself. Two years in Brussels straight after a degree in languages in Berlin, and he was a translator rather than an interpreter. That is, he worked on documents rather than live transla-tions of speeches or negotiations.

'Luckily for me,' he said, examining the sell-by dates on sandwiches. 'Interpreters have to be schizophrenic, always thinking in two languages at once. They get flat ears, because of wearing headphones all the time. And of course they have to listen to all the crap that gets said here, and then repeat it.' He laughed loudly, though I didn't know whether this was to suggest he was joking, or because he really thought the whole system was a joke.

I paid for us both – the cashier gave me two receipts, as though everyone in town needed a copy for their expense account – and we found a free table outside. When I sat down, I was disturbed to notice that I instinctively adopted the gesture of tucking my badge over my shoulder so that it wouldn't dangle in my crayfish, avocado and rocket salad. I was becoming a believer already.

'What languages do you speak?' I asked him.

'English, Russian, French, Polish. And of course a bit of German.' He did his loud laugh again, as if multilingualism were inherently humorous.

'And you sit there all day and translate?'

'Yes, like a cissy fuss,' he answered. I guessed it had to be a German idiom. Not a very well-translated one, though. Maybe he wasn't as gifted a linguist as he claimed. 'You know cissy fuss?' he asked me.

'Like when a drama queen has hysterics?'

At this he just looked confused.

'You haven't read Camus? *The Myth of Sisyphus?*'

'No,' I confessed. The only French book I ever read got confiscated by one of my teachers before I'd finished looking up all the dirty words in chapter one.

'The myth about a man who must spend eternity pushing a rock up a mountain,' Ed said and laughed again, though it didn't sound much fun to me. 'I translate nine or ten pages a day, every day, depending on how technical it is.'

'On every subject?'

'Yes, laws, debates, press releases, policy papers, websites. Everything written or spoken has to be issued in all the official languages of the EU. Altogether, we translate about two million pages per year.'

'Bloody hell.' It sounded as though quite a lot of CO_2 was being emitted in the city's debating chambers and meeting rooms. 'It must cost a fortune,' I said.

'A very British remark.' He guffawed again. With me or at me, I couldn't tell. 'We have to inform all the member countries what's going on, don't we? And you don't expect everyone to speak English, do you?' This got his biggest laugh of all.

'So it's never a waste of money?' I asked.

'Oh, sometimes, yes, of course it is. You know . . .' He put down the meaty sandwich he'd been about to bite into. 'Some MEPs don't do that much work.' I nodded agreement – I'd only been here a day and I understood that already. 'Well, one way they have of pretending that they're efficient is to ask questions. Any question will do: Can the committee confirm that frogs will be protected when Berlin builds a new airport? How many life jackets must be carried on a Danube river cruise? Who is responsible for refrigeration if a container of Chinese fish is held by customs on entry into Hamburg? The MEP doesn't give a damn about the answer, of course. He or she sends in a written question to a committee, it gets published, translated and answered, and it looks as though the MEP is busy. Last year we translated two hundred thousand questions, and each one cost fifteen hundred euros. You do the maths.'

I couldn't, but I still felt dizzy. My crayfish seemed to be wobbling on the end of my plastic fork. Maybe it was quicker at maths than me.

'When it comes to translating the laws and serious deliberations, though, it's never a waste of money.' Ed took an assertive bite of his beef. 'Except, of course, with the Maltesers,' he added, and laughed through a mouthful of sandwich. This was one German who was really keen to show he had a sense of humour.

When he'd regained the use of his windpipe, Ed explained that he worked a few doors down from a team of Maltese translators who, like him, made sure that every EU document was published in their language. But, he told me, Maltese translators have a much tougher job than most. Like everyone else, they have to think up ways of translating innovations like 'app', 'wind farm' and 'quantitative easing'. But they also have other problems: there are, for example, no rivers on Malta, so before becoming an official EU language, Maltese had no word for river. The same went for lots of other northern concepts like trains, frost and curly kale.

So, Ed told me, even today the Maltese translators regularly get together to update their language, mostly using a mixture of English and Italian to create new Maltese terms. They are, in fact, constantly revolutionising their country's dictionary.

'The only thing is,' Ed said, 'that no one ever reads what they write. All the Maltese officials read the documents in English. So these guys are inventing a new language that no one speaks, except them. Translating every single document and knowing that it will never, ever be read. It's like being an invisible mime artist.'

He shook with silent mirth, and I understood his tendency to see the humorous side of everything. He was working in a world as surreal as a Monty Python film about Salvador Dalí.

An horrific thought suddenly struck me.

'You don't think my boss wants to get everything translated into Breton, do you?'

'I don't know. But we only translate into official languages, so it couldn't happen. Unless of course Brittany gained independence.'

'Oh God.' Perhaps Elodie had a secret master plan: independence for Brittany, so that she could become its President. No, Queen.

I asked Ed if he thought that Breton autonomy (which they'd be bound to call *'Bretonomie'*) was a realistic prospect. Again, his first reaction was an amused bark. Then he got serious.

'You know, the sense of identity in these linguistic regions has never been stronger,' he said. 'To Bavarians, for example, their dialect is the verbal expression of their Lederhosen.' I thought he was making a joke about farting into leather shorts, but he didn't laugh. 'I wrote a paper on the German dialects as living symbols of localised independence. That's how I met Elodie. We were at a you-you-too meeting.'

'You-you-too?' It sounded like a polite orgy.

'A meeting of the European Union of European Union Teachers' Unions – EU, EU, TU, also known as UU2. They're organising the EML 2020 project. That's European Minority Languages 2020,' he said, reacting to another of my dazed expressions. 'It's about providing education in all of Europe's languages, even the non-official ones. I'll send you my paper and the minutes of the meeting. In Maltese, if you want.'

He let out a hoot of hilarity that had people at the surrounding tables stopping in mid-chew, and I forced myself to offer up a token giggle, even though I felt as though my feet were being sucked down into a quagmire made up of mulched translations and thrown-away euros.

'However, I doubt if those linguistic regions could ever get independence,' Ed said. 'Big countries like Germany and France will never allow their nation to be splintered like the Balkans. So we don't need to worry too much about Elodie trying to fill Brussels with liberated Bretons. A warning, though.' He was suddenly serious again. 'You have to be careful with these French. At the start of the last EML 2020 committee meeting – just five of us present, and Elodie wasn't there – we had to wait half an hour for a French interpreter. Everyone spoke perfect English, but the French guy – his name was Remou or Remord, something like that – refused to speak or listen until we called in a French interpreter. And then he *didn't even use the earpiece.* Scary guy. You know, deep down, the French patriots have never forgiven Europe for getting rid of Napoleon. Don't forget it.'

I promised not to.

Meanwhile I did my duty and asked about other minority languages in the EU. Ed's answer was a shock. They were all over the bloody place. Germany had a whole list of distinct dialects – not just Bavarian, but Swabian, Saxon, Alsatian and a dozen more. France had its own version of Alsatian, as well as Picard (near the Belgian border), Oc in the south, Creole in the Caribbean colonies, various strands of Polynesian and all the tribal languages in French Guiana. Spain had half a dozen linguistic regions that already enjoyed partial autonomy, the Scandinavians had several Inuit-style minorities, and the Balkans had far more languages than nations. Even the UK had some regional dialects I hadn't thought of, like Manx and Ulster Scots.

So it looked as though Elodie was right – promise EU-funded language teaching and bilingual road signs to all the affected areas in Britain, even in some vague political future, and in those regions the referendum would be a walkover.

Ed and I queued yet again to empty our recyclables into a bin, and then to get a coffee, and I was only half-listening to Ed's hearty chat about all the fun he'd been having in his two years working in Brussels, until he said something that grabbed my full attention.

'And, you know, it's true what they say about Lithuanian girls when they go abroad.'

I didn't know what they said about Lithuanian girls, at home or abroad, but I was keen to find out, so when he suggested meeting up for a drink, I accepted gratefully.

'Never forget: the French will fuck you,' Ed reminded me as he squeezed my hand in a firm goodbye grip. 'They'll do it very diplomatically, but you will definitely get fucked.'

After my recent failures with women, it sounded almost enticing.

I needed another coffee to digest everything Ed had told me. My immediate problem was choosing where to drink it. In the modern avenue leading away from my lunch, the only places I could see where I was likely to get an espresso were a juice counter, a cupcake shop, an Italian deli and some kind of beach bar. All much too euro-chic for me. I eventually spotted a Belgian-beer sign and headed for that.

Sure enough, it was a slightly rundown ordinary café where a couple of people were eating plain-looking steak and chips, and one man was reading a Flemish newspaper. Not a eurocrat in sight. Restful after the EU overdose I'd just ingested. I stashed my ID in my pocket and sat at a table on the terrace.

'Un café, s'il vous plaît,' I told a bored waitress in trousers and a black waistcoat, and after a brief conversation about what sort of coffee I wanted, I opted for what the Belgians seemed to call '*un café*' – an ordinary cup of black coffee with, I was pleased to see, a free Speculoos biscuit perched on the saucer. I was in the mood for some comfort dunking.

While I drank, I surfed around on the internet, checking what Ed had told me. It all seemed to be true.

An official website informed me proudly that an interpreter for each language has to be provided at every formal EU meeting, even if there are only ten people attending. In which case, I reasoned, some of those interpreters would be talking to themselves. At some point they all had a tendency to turn Maltese.

Delving further into the world of minority languages, I came across a disturbing story about Scotland on a Gaelic-culture website. In 2005 a British newspaper announced that the EU wanted to ban bagpipes. And it turned out that, in theory, the story was true – sort of. The paper was interpreting a new European law whereby workers had to be protected against loud noise. It applied to factories, of course, but also to staff at music venues. And so, according to a strict interpretation of the law, if a bagpipe player was planning to keep up an average sound level of eighty-seven decibels (the equivalent of standing two metres from a running motorbike) for a full working day, the music venue's manager would have to offer staff the use of ear protectors. If the manager refused or the staff declined the offer, the marathon bagpipe session would have to be abandoned. QED: bagpipes would have been banned by Brussels.

The disturbing part of the story wasn't only the idea of an eight-hour bagpipe concert. It was the lengths the reporters had gone to, to misinterpret what seemed to be a useful bit of legislation to protect workers' hearing. They'd been twisting the truth for pleasure, distorting facts like kittens unravelling a ball of wool.

The conclusion was obvious: if the EU declared that it was illegal to put cyanide in choc ices, these reporters would say that Brussels intended to scrap the dear old English ice-cream van. If MEPs voted to stop teddy-bear manufacturers stuffing toys with asbestos wool, the story would be that the EU is run by people who don't want kids to have cuddly Christmas presents.

To distract myself from this disturbing thought, I took the opportunity to get to know some minority languages a bit better. They all seemed to have their online dictionaries. Naturally enough, I scrolled around in search of the swear words. In this respect, the compilers had been very thorough. Just typing 'shit' produced some wonderfully fruity translations in every language. And there were so many translations for 'dickhead' that you'd have thought Europe's far-flung regions were full of them.

My phone buzzed at me. It was Ed, who told me he'd had a thought.

'To be fair to the French, the British will fuck you, too,' he said.

'Brilliant. Thanks for letting me know.'

He signed off with one of his ear-splitting gusts of laughter.

In short, I seemed to be sitting in the middle of a Belgian field with British landmines to one side, French to the other. It was just a question of who was going to get the pleasure of blowing me to pieces.

Cac. That was 'shit' in Gaelic.

6

'Brussels will give in to French pressure to force Britain to
rename Waterloo Station and Trafalgar Square.'

Report in the British press, 2003

I'VE ALWAYS had a decent sense of direction. Once, on a school trip to a castle, I got out of the garden maze so quickly that I went back in and pretended to be lost, just to be part of the gang.

These days my homing instinct mostly comes in useful when looking for the toilets in a French café. Somehow I can always sense where they are – a door beside the bar, a curtained-off corridor at the back of the room, a half-concealed staircase down into the basement. Or maybe I've just got a sharp sense of smell.

Anyway, something threw my natural satnav off-kilter when I got back to the European Parliament after my linguistic lunch.

I put it down to a disorienting uncertainty about Elodie's intentions – the most disorienting thing of all being that I suspected she was actually being straight with me. It sounded as if she really did want to talk up the importance of Britain's minority languages to persuade people to vote 'yes' to Europe.

And if I got the feeling she was also playing a private poker hand to get funding for Breton, that was her own business. What did I care about a few extra road signs in western France?

In any case, I was in such a daze that my first attempt at taking a lift to the sixth floor delivered me to a beige corridor that was familiar, but simultaneously strange. Same mind-numbing colour scheme, slightly different positioning of the big trunks outside the offices.

And when I walked along the row of doors looking for Elodie's nameplate, I came across a flag stapled to the wall. It was a gay-rights rainbow banner, printed with the slogan '*No to CO_2*'. It made me wonder: didn't gay people need carbon dioxide? Wouldn't they all suffocate?

The name on the nearest door was German, and when I peeped inside I saw a bearded guy in a faded T-shirt standing by a table with an empty mug in his hand, clearly trying to choose from a veritable tower block of different herbal-tea boxes. Here was an MEP who spent his expenses healthily. A tea for every micro-mood.

It obviously wasn't Elodie's corridor, so I travelled back down and took one of the lifts on the opposite side of the lobby. Sixth floor again, but this time I ended up on a gigantic landing full of art. The walls bore huge abstract paintings in a style probably known as euro-splodge, and the central floorspace was taken up with what looked like a partially constructed hangman's gibbet. A shame it wasn't finished, I thought, because it would have been a good way of getting rid of the artists.

This landing didn't lead to Elodie's office, either, so I went back down and – still applying the standard stubborn male's principle of never admitting we're lost – headed further afield to some other lifts. This trek took me past a wall of MEPs' mailboxes, ranged country by country, none of which seemed to have a lock. Very trusting. In my building in Paris this would have meant no one ever received a single parcel.

After yet another wait for yet another lift, I arrived at a sixth floor that also wasn't Elodie's. It did, however, feature a wall plaque bearing the universal promise that salvation is at hand – a drawing of a steaming teacup.

The cafeteria was an open area dotted with brightly coloured seats – lurid green, lemon-curd yellow, disco orange, psychedelic turquoise – an airport departure lounge from a 1970s film. There were a few people having coffee, most of whom my already trained eye recognised as assistants – dressed-down twenty-somethings with badges. A couple of them stared at me in my suit, wondering perhaps if this overdressed newcomer might be influential or useful in any way.

Merde in Europe

I got myself an energy drink, which quickly provided me with the courage to call Elodie and explain my plight. When I described where I was, she gave a sigh of despair and groaned, 'Mickey Mouse.' A very French insult, I thought, the symbol of decadent English-speaking capitalism.

When Manon turned up a few minutes later, she made it obvious that I hadn't got into her good books by calling her away from her desk to come and rescue me yet again. The charmingly vulnerable male was apparently not her thing. Maybe she'd watched one Hugh Grant film too many.

'Tu fais exprès?' she asked me, meaning was I doing it on purpose? This could have been interpreted as a mild rebuke, except that I knew the full form of the question in French, which often starts with 'Tu es con ou . . .' – Are you a twat or . . .?

'It's the only way we can have a private talk,' I said, but my attempt at French-style smoothness only made her roll her eyes. Very pleasant eyes, but less so when being made to imply you're a knobhead.

'Yes, I know, I'm a Mickey Mouse,' I said. She didn't understand, and when I tried to explain, she shook her head and told me that it was the nickname given to the cafeteria, because of its tacky furniture. This of course only made me feel more of a Mickhead.

'Let me get you a coffee,' I offered. 'I'm sure Elodie doesn't give you many breaks.'

She defrosted a degree or two.

73

'Thanks, an espresso, please.'

'No sugar?' I guessed.

'Yes, please,' she said. Surprise, surprise. So she had a sweet spot after all.

I came back with the coffee and a glass of water, and she nodded her approval at this extra touch. Bloody hell, I thought, two right moves in a row.

'Sorry for losing myself,' I said. 'It's all these lifts. I tried all of them. You know the English word "weightlifting"?' She nodded. 'I've invented a new sport – lift-waiting.'

'Is that what you call English humour?' she asked.

'Apparently not.'

At this Manon actually smiled. A flash of warmth that made me want to make her smile again somehow.

'Working for Elodie can't be one of the easiest jobs in Brussels,' I said.

It worked. I earned a smile.

'Yes, the only job in Brussels that might be tougher would be finding accommodation for all the refugees,' she said. She flashed yet another smile at me. This was turning out to be a bumper harvest.

'God, yes. That would be a real job de merde.'

'Thanks, because that's what I'm doing.'

'Seriously? I'm sorry. I didn't mean ...' Me and my big feet again.

She waved away my apologies and explained that Elodie had given her the task of contacting every mayor in

Brittany – meaning the 1,270 leaders of the local councils of every city, town, village and hamlet in the region – and asking them how many refugees they could house.

'Lots of them are sympathetic,' she told me. 'They offer temporary shelters in empty houses or salles des fêtes. But some of them use it as an excuse to let me know their theories on ethnic cleansing and racial superiority. Especially when I tell them that the idea is to try and create permanent facilities, because people from the Middle East and the southern hemisphere are going to be flooding in for decades. Or, as Elodie puts it, "les salopards ne vont pas nous lâcher".' The bastards aren't going to leave us alone.

'Charming,' I agreed. 'And you're the only person doing this for the whole of Brittany?'

'Yes, I have that honour. The other MEPs say they don't have the personnel.'

'And are you the only assistant working for Elodie?' I asked.

'You haven't met Cédric?'

'No, who's he?'

She stared for a moment as though I might be feigning ignorance.

'Her husband's cousin. He's in the office on the other side of Elodie's. When he turns up.'

'What does he do?'

Manon shrugged, which can be a French way of saying they don't know, they're not going to tell you or it's just not worth talking about. Expressive things, French shrugs.

What a team of assistants Elodie had hired. A cousin by marriage – Cédric; the daughter of one of her dad's squeezes – Manon; and an old friend – me. She was clearly determined to keep the EU's money in the family. I wondered if all MEPs did the same. Perhaps it was the only way to count on people's loyalty.

'Well, if I can help in any way . . .' I offered.

'Thanks.' She laughed. 'If you're learning Breton, maybe you can write some emails to the more racist mayors and give them a few local insults. Though you'll have to be careful who you insult – the worst ones vote for Elodie's and her father's party.'

A thought occurred to me.

'You're not a member of their party, are you?' I asked.

'Why shouldn't I be?'

'Well, frankly you don't look like the kind of person who believes that Napoleon was a saint and that drink-driving should be classified as part of French national heritage.'

Saying all this in French would normally have been way out of my range, but I'd seen a comedy sketch taking the pee out of Jean-Marie's election campaign, and this was how they'd summed up his party's manifesto. It wasn't out-and-out racist, it just harked back to a France where all the men wore berets and all the women stayed at home and cooked *bœuf bourguigon*. It was nationalism as sugary as *crème brûlée*.

Manon granted me yet another smile.

'Thanks, I'll take that as a compliment. But if that's what you think about Elodie's party, how can *you* work with her?'

Touché.

Secrecy prevented me telling Manon that I was dealing with a much wider issue than drunk French farmers being allowed to kill themselves on the roads.

'I believe in defending minority languages,' I said.

'Ah yes, the rights of Bretons and Scots to make pancakes in their own patois. That would fascinate anyone.'

'And I need the money,' I confessed. 'Elodie's an old friend of mine from Paris. In a way she's doing me a favour by taking me on. To be honest, I'm not really qualified for this kind of work.'

'From what I've seen of the way Brussels functions, you're not the only one,' Manon said.

'But from the way you keep calm when talking to Elodie, I think you're probably very well qualified,' I told her. OK, blatant flattery, but in my experience the guy who said flattery will get you nowhere was an idiot. 'Have you worked with politicians before?'

'Occasionally,' she said, getting back to scoring points for evasiveness. 'Now shall I show you where someone has hidden your office?'

As Manon led me briskly back through the maze of lifts and corridors, she took a call from Elodie, who seemed to be asking where the hell we'd got to.

'He said he needed a cup of tea,' Manon replied calmly. 'He's English, after all.'

It was becoming increasingly obvious that Manon was very fond of taking the pee out of guys. Or out of me, anyway. Not that I minded. On the contrary, call me a masochist, but I have to admit it's something I've always liked in a woman. That little flash of intelligent mischief in their eyes as they have a dig at you always makes me want to come back for more. As long as they don't resort to outright insults, of course, which was why Elodie and I didn't stay lovers for long. She was the kind of woman who, when it suited her, used jokes and insults the way Joan of Arc used her sword, to beat men down from the battlements and show them who's boss.

'Sorry to put the blame on you,' Manon said when she rang off. 'It just seemed to be the simplest option.'

'Yes, it usually is.'

'Good, I'll remember that,' she said. I *think* she was joking.

For a moment I thought Elodie had been fired and ejected from the building. I'd only just managed to memorise the route through the Parliament building to her door, and now it seemed that it hadn't been worth the effort.

Her office had been efficiently swept of any proof of her existence. Her desktop was bare, the doors on her shelving cabinets had been shut and her laptop charger lay dead on the floor. There wasn't even a phone in sight.

'She always does this,' Manon said. 'Very secretive.'

There was only one clue that someone had been occupying the office – a large white envelope lying on a small table by the door. Manon handed it to me, and I saw that it had my name scrawled on it, and a brief message: 'No time to wait for you.'

Inside was a sheet of paper and a credit card in Elodie's name. I looked to Manon for enlightenment, but she just did another one of those annoying Gallic shrugs. No help there.

The paper was a printout giving the address of a Brussels '*hôtel de ventes*' – a 'sales hotel'. What the hell was that? My first implausible thought was that it must be a polite Belgian way of saying brothel. Was Elodie taking the pee?

'Ce n'est pas un . . .?' Something made me censor my question to Manon. It was all a bit embarrassing.

'Un quoi?'

'Un . . . bordel?'

Manon gave a joyous laugh.

'You're not serious? Is that English humour, too?'

'I'm serious,' I assured her. 'What's a hôtel de ventes?'

With a single sentence she made it clear that I was a bit of a dork, and maybe a bit of a sexual obsessive, too. *Hôtel de ventes*, it seems, means auction house.

Which I might have deduced for myself if I'd read Elodie's instructions at the bottom of the page, below a map showing how to get there. She had written '10 a.m. tomorrow, use credit card to buy lot 34', underlining the lot number three times. 'Call me for PIN number.'

I showed the note to Manon, who pulled a philosophical face, as if I'd picked up a newborn puppy and it had peed all over my new trousers. Yes, she was implying, this is the sort of thing that Elodies are well known for.

'But where is she now?' I asked.

'Probably in a "meeting",' Manon said, doing the speech-marks thing with her fingers.

I frowned my incomprehension.

'A Friday-afternoon "meeting"?'

Now Manon's fingers clawed the air as if they were carving the speechmarks in stone. This was turning into a French mime festival.

'Oh, you mean . . . ?' I tried to suggest sex without moving my hips.

Manon congratulated me for my brilliance, or perhaps for my subtle hips, with a nod.

'With . . . ?' I did my best to mime a tall, slick Scandinavian with bouncy blond hair. Marcel Marceau would have been proud of me, because Manon nodded again.

So Elodie had gone to dunk the Danish.

But damn her, what was all this crap about going to an auction, when I was meant to be getting some serious work done?

I pulled out my phone.

'I'm not sure that's wise,' Manon said, but I was already speed-dialling.

Elodie picked up immediately.

'What the fuck do you want, Paul?' As diplomatic as ever.

'Sorry to disturb your "meeting", Elodie.' I attempted to do the speechmarks thing with one hand, but probably looked as though I was imitating a limp rabbit. 'It's about your note.'

'Yes, well, it's simple enough, isn't it? Even you can read numbers up to thirty-four.'

'But aren't I supposed to be writing up my stuff about languages?'

'Exactly, so go and buy yourself a computer with the credit card.'

'Oh.' Her sudden generosity stumped me for a moment.

On my way back from lunch I'd walked past a shop belonging to a famous fruit-inspired computer company, so I now asked her if it was OK to buy one of those.

She huffed a hurricane in my ear.

'You're totally missing the point, Paul. As usual. Lot thirty-four *is* a computer. Go and buy it.'

'Buy a computer at auction? How do we know it's not clapped out?'

'Don't worry about that, Paul, just buy it, please.'

'But it's an auction,' I reminded her. 'What if I don't win?'

'What if you don't win? That's such an English question, Paul. Just go and win. And call me as soon as you've succeeded. Which you will do, at all costs, OK?'

'OK.'

'Now please don't disturb me again today. I don't work on Fridays. You know that. Honestly, Paul, you're really starting to put the ass in assistant.' Like I said, when she wanted to, she could be as peace-loving as Joan of Arc.

'Oh yeah?' I groped for a riposte. There had to be a jibe about 'putting the member in an MEP' that I could use. But she was gone.

I looked questioningly at Manon, who renewed our physical theatre theme by holding out both hands as if carrying identical plant pots. *Voilà*, her gesture was saying, I told you that phoning was a bad idea.

The only positive in all this was that my working day seemed to be over already.

I took a chance and mimed going out for a drink. But Manon shook her head, did some air-typing and went back into her office. Her most efficient mime yet.

7

'Smoky-bacon crisps to be banned by Brussels.'

Report in the British press, 2003

AFTER A restful, booze-free early night, I was up early and ambling towards the salesroom in plenty of time for my appointment with the auctioneer. I took the scenic route, keeping to basically the right direction but investigating any side streets that looked intriguing.

And as I strolled, I realised that Brussels seems to have an identity problem. Not only has it been largely annexed by the EU, but its own personality is also marooned in a half-way house. It's not quite sexy Paris, not quite drugged-up Amsterdam. Fortunately, though, it sees the funny side of being only half-cool, and has a twisted sense of humour that it expresses in its quirky choice of statues. The city streets are littered with them.

The most famous is, of course, the Manneken Pis. It's so weird to have a peeing baby as a national symbol. When I visited him that morning, he was performing for a gaggle of tourists who were all photographing or filming him in a way that would have got them arrested if he'd been real.

But walking the city streets, I quickly saw that in fact the Manneken is one of Brussels' more conventional statues. He's just a cheeky lad taking a leak. Much weirder than the male toddler is his female equivalent, a pigtailed prepubescent girl called Jeanneke who squats, peeing permanently into a puddle, exposing her nudity in a way that only her parents really ought to see.

Then there's the dog, Zinneke Pis, a little terrier that dry-pisses against a bollard. I guess the city didn't want to add water here, in case it encouraged real dogs to imitate him.

Brussels does possess a few statues that aren't urinating, but even these are pretty bizarre.

In the middle of a wide boulevard I came across what looked like a naked hippy with one foot stuck to a giant sea-shell – a joke, perhaps, about the hallucinogenic effect of eating too many mussels?

Further on, there was a man in a hospital robe apparently stepping off a roof – probably a satirical reference to their national health service.

And fronting an office building near the Commission, probably the most disturbing of them all, a group of Jeannekes who have had their eyes poked out and therefore don't realise they're wearing dangerously revealing miniskirts. Straight out of a horror porn film.

If all these represent Brussels' self-image as a capital city, I thought, then it's a pretty screwed-up place. Personally, I blame those brewing monks.

My map led me out of the city centre and up a cobbled, pedestrians-only slope that was lined with arty junk shops, the kind of stores that look as though your gran has unloaded all her belongings into a shop window and then got confused when writing the price tags, so that she's added a zero too many at the end of every label. I mean, I wouldn't mind decorating my sitting room with a leather armchair that was still imprinted with the 3D outline of Gran's buttocks, but not if it was going to cost me a month's rent.

At the top of the hill I entered a street that had decided to divide its retail space fifty–fifty between antique shops and hipster cafés furnished with mismatching old tables. Here, next to a gluten-free haven, I found my salesroom – a warehouse with an entrance half-blocked by a Gothic wardrobe and a giant rusted-iron garden vase. Pinned up next to the doorway was a trilingual sign advertising the auction.

I wandered deep inside the building, past a cloud of chandeliers that would have blinded the entire city's population if they'd all been switched on at once, through a room of euro-splodge canvases like the ones I'd seen at the Parliament building, and finally arrived in a section of the warehouse that had been laid out for the sale.

Wisely, the auctioneers had made the most of their supply of old seats, and a dozen or so people were moving around the room, testing them for comfort. I had to try a wooden bench with a truncated leg and an armchair that tried to sodomise me with one of its springs, before settling on a plywood seat that had been polished by several generations of Mannekens and Jeannekes as they sweated through school.

I looked around at my potential opponents in the battle for lot 34. They didn't appear to be an especially tech-savvy crowd, or particularly rich. Mainly middle-aged men in bulky jackets, and one elderly couple who were comparing notes about the catalogue, which was just a collection of stapled A4 sheets. It didn't look as though prices would be going too high.

At a small row of second-hand tables in front of us, an overfed man with a bushy white beard and no hair up top was adjusting a bendy microphone, apparently checking that he would be able to swallow it without lowering his head. He, I assumed, was the auctioneer.

The partition walls of the auction space were made up of office furniture – filing cabinets, desks, a range of chairs, from 'I'm-the-big-boss' down to 'sit-here-new-intern'. All for sale, to judge by the numbered tickets taped on to them, as were the numerous lamps, a jacuzzi-sized photocopier and – yes – on top of a display cabinet containing smaller items, a row of laptops, folded open like loungers on a glass beach.

I went to have a look at lot 34 and found that either I'd got blurred vision or there were several computers with the same number. The lot consisted of *three* identical laptops, none of which inspired much confidence in their ability to download anything bulkier than a passport photo. They were black, as thick as a waffle sandwich and bore the logo of a decidedly non-fruity manufacturer.

I decided to risk it and call Elodie.

'Why not buy one more-recent model, instead of these three dinosaurs?' I suggested after we'd got past her 'God, Paul, will you ever stop hassling me?' greetings.

'Just do what I'm paying you for, and buy lot thirty-four,' she groaned. 'Please,' she added, though I guessed that her one polite word might have been addressed to a man asking if she wanted another helping of pickled herring.

'At any price?' I asked.

'Yes, well, I don't expect it will be as expensive as one of those fancy laptops you wanted,' she said, and then left me to it while she went off to enjoy some more smorgasbord.

I checked again that I'd remembered to bring her credit card, and waited for the sale to begin.

At first I thought that maybe I'd gone partially deaf. Then I realised that the auctioneer was talking in Flemish.

It sounded, to my linguistically challenged ears, as though he was speaking a random series of syllables and was annoyed that he couldn't get them in the right order. Either that, or he was a very drunk German.

I don't say this with any sense of superiority. I have often been told that my middle-class English accent makes me sound like a mildly shocked nun.

But you have to appreciate my anxiety as the sale got under way and I realised that I couldn't understand the most vital part of the proceedings – the numbers. Pretty important when you're trying to bid.

Naively, I'd assumed that the sale would be in French, or multilingual. This was the translation capital of Europe, after all, a city where nothing gets done without the presence of at least twenty interpreters.

My only consolation was that the lot number and a picture of each item for sale were being flashed up on a TV screen in front of the auctioneer.

I got out my phone again and started to hunt for a list of Flemish numbers with phonetic transcriptions, so that I'd actually be able to pronounce them. Even so, I doubted whether my tongue would be able to generate enough spit.

But then, as I listened to the sale getting under way, it dawned on me that maybe I didn't have such a big problem after all. The people bidding on the first couple of lots weren't saying anything. They were just raising a finger or nodding a head in response to the auctioneer. He was the only one saying anything. To buy my lot, I just had to keep waving at him until he banged his hammer in my favour.

I relaxed and watched my fellow buyers acquire a collection of ugly desks and unwieldy shelving. The bidding never lasted more than a minute on each lot, so I didn't anticipate bankrupting Brittany West. I even began to look forward to the pleasure of winning the fight for lot 34. That's the clever thing about auctions, isn't it? – even when you've emptied your bank account for a load of tat you don't need, it feels like a victory. And the great thing was, I could go on bidding for as long as I wanted and it wouldn't cost me a penny personally.

What could possibly go wrong?

The butterflies were fluttering slightly by the time lot 33 – a single computer – came up, but they quickly dispelled when it went for '*fiftig*', which sounded like fifty euros. Ridiculously cheap for a laptop. And if none of my three computers actually worked, what did I care? It would just prove that I'd been right about spending France's money on something more reliable.

My lot started out at the absurdly low price of '*dirty*' (or something like that – thirty, I guessed). I duly raised my arm and the auctioneer pointed his hammer at me. He said another number, which attracted a new bid, so he looked at me while saying something else and I raised my arm again. Simple.

After a couple of rounds, we were at what sounded like seventy. I decided to look around the room, hoping to send out the message that I was here to stay and that whoever was bidding against me might as well give up now.

This was when I noticed something incongruous.

Sitting in one corner, over my right shoulder, was a guy who was much younger than everyone except me. He was dressed very similarly, too – jeans and a crisp white shirt, rather than the saggy outfits being worn by most of the older bidders. And maybe it was my imagination, but I could almost see the imprint on his neck left by the constant rubbing of a Brussels badge. He had that smartly casual international look about him that I'd seen on everyone in the parliamentary building. Unless I was much mistaken, he was from somewhere in northern Europe, to gather by his light hair and fair skin.

He was on the phone, but staring straight at me. As I studied him, he nodded to an order from cyberspace and raised his hand to place a bid.

I was still watching him while the auctioneer called out another number, and I responded with another salute.

Again, the young guy in the corner spoke to his phone, nodded and put in a counterbid. Again, I raised my hand to outbid him.

I wasn't even listening to the numbers now, but I couldn't help noticing that the tubby auctioneer's voice was getting more and more soprano with surprise. One or two laughs broke out amongst the other punters. Who, the Belgians were obviously wondering, were these two foreign idiots, fighting for possession of a trio of clapped-out computers?

I must admit I was wondering the same thing, but I was also beginning to understand Elodie's obsession with lot 34. There was clearly something special about it. I just hoped it wasn't a stash of cocaine under the keyboard or anything that was going to get me arrested or mugged on the way out.

The price climbed into the range of a decent new tablet, and then hit the level where I could have hoped to buy a neat laptop, and still both of us obeyed orders, though I was now shrugging at my opponent with every bid, as if to say: Give up, mate, I'm going all the way.

He carried on reporting events into his phone and looking grimly determined, but then, with one movement, he suddenly put his phone away and walked out. He'd given up.

Amid a chorus of gasps, the breathless auctioneer slammed down his hammer and pronounced the price slowly enough for even an Englishman to understand.

'Negenhonderd negentig,' he said, his voice straining as though Flemish numbers didn't usually stretch that far.

Nine hundred and ninety euros for three bog-standard old PCs. Surely the stupidest computer deal since 1976, when some impatient friend of Steve Jobs apparently sold his 10 per cent stake in Apple for 800 dollars.

Oh well, I thought, I was only obeying orders.

Though I seemed to remember, from my history lessons, that that excuse didn't always go down well.

8

'Brussels rules that oysters must be given rest breaks during transport to market.'

Report in the British press, 2012

ONCE, WHILE I was working for Elodie's dad, Jean-Marie, in Paris, he asked me to take some British clients out to dinner.

'Where should I take them?' I asked, not knowing the city too well at that point.

'Oh, where you want – here's a company credit card,' Jean-Marie said, coming over all rich and generous because there was a woman in the room.

Being a literal kind of bloke, I therefore took my three guests to a world-famous restaurant, the kind of place where portions are as big as a mouse dropping and the bill is the size of a private jet, where the wine couldn't be more expensive if it was liquid gold, and the star chef emerges from his kitchen at the end of the evening to shake or kiss the hand of everyone crazy enough to pay his prices.

I had to go and get a hamburger afterwards, to fill the yawning gap left by the droplets of vaporised duckling tongue and kumquat-flavoured ice suppositories, or whatever it was that we'd been served, but at least my guests were happy.

Jean-Marie was less so. As soon as he found my credit-card slip on his desk next day, he sent me a one-word email consisting of the French for 'what' in capital letters, followed by so many question marks that I thought he'd passed out with his forehead on the keyboard.

'QUOI??????????????????????????????????'

This was more or less exactly the reaction I got from Elodie when I told her about the price of her computers, except that she replied down the phone, so that she sounded like a duck giving birth to an ostrich egg.

Though unlike Jean-Marie, who had threatened to dock me a year's salary, Elodie calmed down with what I ought to have recognised as suspicious speed.

As soon as I told her why I'd been forced to bid so much, she began to 'hmm' to herself and asked me: 'Did you talk to this guy?'

'No. He stormed out when he realised I was going to keep on raising the price.'

'Hmm,' she said again, and sounded strangely satisfied with the outcome.

'Who do you think he was?' I asked.

'Oh, I don't know.'

'Do you know why he was willing to bid so much?'

'For the same reason as me, because he wanted the computers. Now stop asking silly questions, Paul, and bring them to me.'

'At the Parliament.'

'No, I'll text you an address. Take a taxi and get here as soon as you can. Ring bell number two.'

I just hoped that it wasn't the Danish embassy. I really didn't fancy seeing a post-coital Viking.

As it turned out, the taxi took me to one of the most beautiful buildings I'd ever seen. I knew Brussels was famous for its Art Nouveau, but this place was a house-sized Klimt painting, a shimmering palace of gold and cream.

It was tall and slim, with a roof of blood-red tiles, and its façade was decorated with mosaics of sinuous foliage and nymphs combing angels' hair. There was an immense bay window on the first floor, with a balcony of curvaceous iron railings, and the sculpted front door looked like the entrance to a wood-sprite's city residence.

All in all, I had the feeling that the architect had got through a large quantity of opium and flouncy shirts while designing it.

I rang bell number two and was buzzed in.

The entrance hall was as sublime as the façade, all geometric tiles and sheened wood panelling, topped off with an ornate gilt-and-crystal chandelier that would have given my Flemish auctioneer an orgasm.

'Come up, Paul! First floor!' Elodie called out.

She sounded almost happy to see me.

In the middle of a room that was big enough to house a family of full-size billiard tables, Elodie was standing next to a tall, blond man. He wasn't, I was relieved to see, the Great Dunking Dane. It took a brief double-take to realise that it wasn't Elodie's husband Valéry, either, even though he looked almost exactly the same.

This guy was a few years younger, and skinnier. The rest was all Valéry, from the 'I'm-too-tall' slouch and the long blond fringe that needed flipping dramatically backwards every ten seconds, to the expression of someone trying to remember which century they're in.

'This is Cédric,' Elodie told me. 'Valéry's cousin. You met at the wedding.'

'Ah, yes, bonjour,' I said, shaking his limp hand.

In fact I couldn't be sure that we actually had met, because there had been a dozen or more Cédric-Valéry clones there, as well as their female equivalents. Theirs was one of those enormous French tribes that expends most of its energies in breeding, presumably so that they'll always have enough people to pay for the upkeep on their various chateaux.

The family also had an inbuilt distrust of breeding with anyone who was not already a member of the clan, which probably meant that within a few generations they'd all have identical faces, and two heads. Elodie had been a rare outside contribution to the DNA and, judging by her taste for extra-marital Danes, not a wise choice.

'Give the computers to Cédric, Paul,' she said.

'Shouldn't I keep one for myself?'

'No, Cédric's going to check them out. You'll have one on Monday.'

I complied, handing over the laptops and the various cables that had come with them.

'OK, off you go, Cédric,' Elodie said, in French, as if talking to a puppy.

He went, and I hoped for his sake that he'd inherited enough of the thinly spread family brain cells to switch on a computer.

'Great apartment,' I told Elodie when we were alone. 'Whose is it?'

'Yours,' she said, and threw me a set of keys.

When I'd picked them (and myself) up off the parquet floor, which now had a tiny key-print in its perfect varnish, I asked what she meant by this.

'It belongs to France. Diplomats usually live here, but this floor is free at the moment, so I thought you might like to stay here while you're in Brussels. There's no rent to pay. The furniture is a bit old-fashioned, but it's liveable.' She gestured dismissively towards a sumptuous purple velvet settee and its four companion armchairs, a black lacquered dining table and six high-backed chairs, and a Japanese-style screen that partially blocked the view into a leafy garden at the back of the building.

'You can use the garden,' she said. 'No drunken English parties, though, please. And promise me you'll only use one of the bathrooms.'

A rather prohibitive tenant agreement, you might think, but I nodded my consent.

'Do you remember when we shared a bathroom, Paul?' Elodie said, which struck me as a weird thing to say.

'Yes,' I agreed, cautiously.

'Me a student, you just arrived in Paris, you could hardly speak any French except for "café au lait" and "voulez-vous coucher avec moi?"'

Elodie was grinning at me now, taking me back to more innocent days at our shared flat in the Marais, when I was sleeping with her occasionally and she was shagging as many male models as she could get her thighs around. OK, maybe not so innocent after all, but fun.

'The two of us in that tiny HLM,' she said. She meant *habitation à loyer modéré*, low-rent subsidised housing, though it was the poshest block of subsidised housing in Paris, inhabited almost exclusively by the sons and daughters of politicians.

'Don't you think we've come a long way, Paul? Me an MEP, you part-owner of an English tea room in Paris, with this luxury place at our – *your* – disposal?'

I still didn't know what she was getting at, but I guessed that maybe a little gratitude was being called for.

'Well, I'm still accepting your family's hospitality,' I said. 'This place is great, yes. Amazingly beautiful. And thanks for bailing me out with this job. The money is going to come in really useful.'

'Thanks for saying that, Paul. It's good to know I'm helping you out.' She smiled at me, with what looked like total sincerity, which was not something she showed very often. 'Now can you do me a favour?' It was back to business. 'I'd like some photos of the place. Could we use your phone?'

I handed it over and she began taking some snaps, including a few of me in the various rooms. She asked me to sit on a huge iron-framed bed that looked as though it had been forged out of a castle portcullis, then to mime drinking a cup of coffee at the breakfast bar in the kitchen – the only modernised part of the apartment.

'Why do you need to have me in the photos?' I asked as I lay in the bath, an immense white tub standing on gilded lions' feet. I still had my clothes on, I should add.

'It's for the website where we put all our accommodation. Some of these old places look a bit scary for young diplomats. We have to make them look fun.'

I tried to imagine what kind of French diplomat selected his accommodation on the basis of an Englishman being able to lie fully clothed in his bath. But then perhaps I didn't know much about the French foreign service.

'Hey, can you do a few selfies, too? I used to love it when you'd send us photos of all your stupid expressions in Paris.'

This apartment really seemed to be bringing out Elodie's wistful side. I took a couple of selfies depicting an English idiot standing in front of some of the most fabulous furniture made in the late nineteenth century, and then spent a few minutes sending all the photos to Elodie.

'Perfect,' she said when they pinged into her phone. 'Now I'll leave you to move into your new home. Have a great weekend, and if you do use handcuffs on that bed, please try not to scratch the paint.'

I promised to be careful.

'What are you doing tonight?' she asked.

'Going out for a drink with some Lithuanian girls, I hope.'

'Excellent, you know what they say about Lithuanian girls.'

No, but I intended to find out.

First thing I did, when I moved my suitcase and its meagre contents into the stadium-sized apartment, was run myself a bath. Lying there for Elodie's photo shoot had reminded me of the joys of a long, leisurely soak. Having spent so long based in minuscule Parisian attics, I'd got used to having only stand-up washes. In a shower cubicle, I mean, not out on the roof.

This, by the way, is the source of those stupid English newspaper stories about the French not washing. It all started because some bright spark in Fleet Street got hold of a statistic whereby the average French adult spent hardly any time in the bathtub and declared that they didn't wash at all.

Ridiculous. Most of the French people I know well enough to ask about their hygiene habits shower every day, and laugh at us Brits for wallowing in our own dirt.

But there were no Parisians about, so I was free to enjoy the luxuries of watching a perfectly clean volcanic lake being created just for me in the glistening enamel tub, of dabbing my hand into the rising tide to test the temperature and then lowering myself, toes first, inch by inch, beneath the blood-warm comfort blanket of gently perfumed water.

That gentle perfume was my only regret – no bubble bath. I'd only been able to nab a couple of tiny shower gels from my hotel room, so I had to make do with a few drops of aftershave in the bathwater. But even if I say so myself, it was a perfume that gave the nostrils something pleasant to quiver about. And it was a nice fantasy to imagine some lucky woman undressing me and finding out that it wasn't only my chin that smelt good – that evening my whole body was going to be imbued with the French ideal of bottled male sophistication.

I lay back, neck deep, and relaxed.

And started to get bored. That's the trouble with showering. It gets you used to the functional in-and-out wash, the quick lather followed by the rapid rubdown. Five minutes and you're done. Any longer feels like a waste of your life.

Admittedly it was interesting to examine the bathroom tiles for a while – a purple, gold and green vine of what looked like toxic plants, running around all four walls. And the light over the washbasin was a piece of vintage chrome, like something off a pre-war luxury liner. Amazing that it had survived so long.

But soon I started to wish that I had some rubber ducks to play with, or maybe a submarine. Or at least a real bar of soap to drop in the water and fish about for. You can't play bathtub games with liquid soap. Well, you can, but I prefer to play them with a girlfriend.

When my phone started buzzing on the bathroom stool, it came as a welcome distraction. I shook my hand dry and carefully answered.

'Hey, Paul, it goes?'

The unmistakable mix of English words and French syntax, spoken with an American accent and the naive enthusiasm of a five-year-old who's just taken a sip of his dad's champagne and thinks that his sudden *joie de vivre* is natural – it could only belong to one man.

'Hi, Jake.'

This was my American friend who had lived for so long in France that his brain could no longer tell which language it was speaking, and therefore spoke English and French simultaneously. Amazingly he'd found a job as an English teacher, and as well as screwing up his French pupils' chances of passing any English exams, Jake was a part-time poet whose rhymes were so tastelessly pornographic that the USA would definitely decide to repeal its famous free-speech laws if he ever moved back there. 'Is Brussels going well to you, Paul?' he asked.

'Yes, thanks, Jake, it's going pretty well to me. Working with Elodie is a bit like being a poodle, but she's set me up in a great apartment.'

'Cool, man. Big bed?'

This was Jake's only criterion when choosing real estate. Did the place have a double mattress with a woman on top of it?

'Yes, pretty big. How are you getting on?'

I asked this question with a note of sadness. He'd recently split up from his wife, Mitzi. I'd been their best man. And I'd actually thought he might make a go of this relationship. He usually started getting itchy feet after the first night, but he'd seemed really besotted with Mitzi, and she with him. Until, that is, she found him in the marriage bed with a six-foot-tall Somali model.

'Yeah, I am reflecting a lot on my culpability.'

'That's good, Jake, that's healthy.'

'I think I have taken too seriously the marriage calves.'

'The what?'

'The marriage calves? Les veaux du mariage?'

'The *vows*, Jake. I think you mean "les voeux". "Veau" is a baby cow.'

'Right, yes, the marriage voeux.'

'Well, I don't think they included vowing to shag a model in your wife's bedroom.'

'But they said we must honour each other. And what bigger honour than an African goddess? You know, I invited Mitzi to join with us.'

This was the problem with debating the finer points of morality with Jake. It was like discussing stamp-collecting with a rainbow trout. The concept was outside his frame of reference. Even while he was married, he'd been carrying on with his life master plan of sleeping with a woman of every nationality on the planet, and then writing verse about them. He'd got all of the main European nations in his little red book, plus most of Asia and a fair chunk of Africa and South America.

'What have you been up to recently?' I asked him.

'Oh, I have commenced to work on an epic poem. It is for-midable, man. It is inspired by a poor Parisienne who must get a job in a topless bar. It is titled "A Sale of Two Titties".'

Suddenly I needed another shot of scalding water in my bath to take away the sting of his poetry.

'You get it, Paul?'

'Sadly, yes. You're only writing the poem because you thought of the title, aren't you, Jake?'

'Yes, I confess. But now I have another idea.'

'Really?' I prepared myself for the worst, or even worse than that.

'Yes, a poem called "Les Bains Louches".'

I groaned. This was a painful pun – *les bains douches* are French public baths, and *louche* means, well, louche, morally suspect.

'What's that about, Jake? Though I dread to ask.'

'Well, I just got the idea because your baignoire' – mean-ing my bathtub – 'looks enough big for two or three people.'

'What?' I tried to clutch my hands over my privates, and almost gave my phone a fatal dunking. 'You can see me?'

'Yes. I was very admirative of you for playing with your pipi as we discussed. I was thinking: Hey, Paul is become more liberated.'

'Shit!'

'Do not panic, Paul. I have seen it before. You remember, that time with those two girls from—'

'For fuck's sake, Jake, how long have we been on visual?'

'It came on when you put in extra water. You didn't realise?'

'No, I must have hit the wrong button. Shit.'

'Calm, Paul, calm. I know exactly what you need.'

'What's that?'

'Me.'

'Fuck off, Jake, I'm not . . . Although there's no shame in . . . And I totally support the right of men to . . .'

'Stop, Paul. I know you're not gay. What I am saying is that I must come and help you fill your baignoire with European women. I need some more nationalities for my petit livre rouge. I'll take the next train. What is your address?'

One day I'll be able to explain to myself why I told him.

9

'Kilts to be re-defined as women's wear.'

Report in the British press, 2003

I'D ARRANGED to meet Ed Fürst that evening at a French-sounding bar near the place du Châtelain. It was a short walk from where I was now living.

Jake hadn't turned up yet, so I texted him the name of the bar and told him to meet me there.

Châtelain was in an area of low-rise buildings, a sort of dwarf Paris, populated by every kind of bar and pub that the Brussels melting pot could brew up – Spanish, Italian, Brazilian, English, even Belgian.

It was eight thirty by the time I got there, and the place was already teeming with off-duty badge people, all looking casual, *mais pas trop* – one notch down from their rather dressy dress-down Friday. Stiff-collared shirts and pristine jeans for the men, designer trousers or not-too-short skirts for the ladies.

I spotted Ed with a small group of people outside the unimaginatively named Café Noir, a half-empty pint glass in his hand.

'Ah, my English friend!' he called out as soon as he saw me, waving me in. I was greeted warmly by two guys and a woman who immediately asked me the obvious question about whether Britain was going to vote itself in or out of the EU. Oh, help, I thought, I'll have to get a T-shirt printed: 'I DON'T BLOODY KNOW'.

But I did my thing of putting on a studious expression and saying the polls were too close to call, and they nodded sympathetically.

'Anyone want a drink?' I asked, and somehow they all did, although a couple of them had taken little more than a sip from the one they already had.

I used the shoving skills I'd learnt in Paris to get to the bar, and returned with a tray a few minutes later, to an even warmer welcome. They'd all managed to down their drinks in my absence. This was going to be a long, wet night.

I explained who I was, and got the same in return.

'Vadim, Lithuanian, MEP's assistant,' a grinning Slav guy told me. Before I could ask about his female compatriots, the woman chimed in.

'Helga, German, translator with Ed.' She was a classic piece of German architecture, statuesque and blonde, but she quickly diverted any unwanted attention by adding that she was 'the girlfriend of Pierre'. She nodded to the guy beside her, who was a good ten centimetres shorter than her and, presumably to compensate, was wearing sunglasses propped up on his dark, stylishly-coiffed head.

'Pierre, from Paree,' he said with a strong French accent.

'Are you an MEP's assistant, too?' I asked.

He grimaced as though this was a job on a par with cleaning toilets. And I've always had a morbid dislike of people who wear sunglasses after dark, so I was delighted when he replied: 'No, I am a consultant in bonking.'

'Pardon?' I said.

'I'm an industrial bonker.'

He meant, of course, that he was a French banker with an accent.

'Do you charge a lot for your bonking services?' I asked him.

'Yes, a good price.'

'I've heard that people love French bonkers.'

Helga, who must have realised what was going on, swept in and said something about '*englischer Humor*'. Pierre sniffed and turned away.

'Fun place, isn't it?' Ed said.

I agreed. I was enjoying myself already.

'You should come here on a Wednesday, then it is really lively. There is a food market in the square, people bring picnics. It gets crazy.'

'Here on Wednesdays, Plux on Thursdays, right?'

'Exactly,' Ed said. 'Same people, same places, different days.'

'It's like a holiday camp. I'm guessing you have karaoke on Fridays, wet T-shirts on Saturdays, human sacrifice on Sundays?'

'Oh, every day is human-sacrifice day. We come here to offer ourselves to anyone who can advance our careers. Brussels is all about networking.'

Bloody hell, I thought. They have plenty of days off, but they never let up for a minute. I was relieved to be a temporary visitor.

The upside to their constant schmoozing was that people didn't just coagulate in cliques – they seemed to circulate all the time. In the space of two drinks I got talking to three new groups of people, all as international as Ed's friends.

Everyone popped the referendum question, of course, but by now I was up and running, so it never took more than a minute to get the opinion polls out of the way, before we were on to other subjects.

Not that I always understood what they were talking about, even if it was in English. These eurocrats were living in a world of their own.

One guy from Portugal asked me where I'd done my Erasmus. I had to admit that I couldn't be sure if I'd ever done one, not having a clue what it was.

A Frenchwoman kept going on about her DJ. Her boyfriend, I assumed. But then she asked me whether I was with a DJ, too, as if relationships with disc jockeys might be a common occurrence in Brussels. When I told her that I didn't know anyone in the music business, she looked at me as if I was a moron, and said, 'Mais non, Direction générale! Day jay!' I finally understood that she'd meant 'DG', but it was too late. She seemed to classify me under 'not worth knowing', and moved on.

I was feeling tipsy but lucky when I got chatting to an attractive girl with large friendly eyes and a figure to match, who said she was from Estonia. I refrained from asking about her next-door neighbours, the Lithuanians, and managed to remain polite when she quizzed me about the referendum. My self-restraint paid off, because somehow we got on to the subject of sex.

This was looking promising, my third beer told me.

I gave her an edited version of my misadventure with the street-corner hooker on my first night in town, which got her laughing.

'I think it's sick, though, prostitution, don't you?' I said. 'Women forced to have sex against their will, probably getting beaten up by some gangster.'

I thought it best to stress that I wasn't at all disappointed about missing out on what the hooker was offering.

'It's legal here,' she said sadly. I'd obviously gauged her mood just right.

'Yes, and it's so open,' I said. 'There are brothels in almost every street.'

This got her looking confused.

'You see the signs everywhere,' I said.

'Really?'

'Yes, there are two in the street where I live, on completely normal-looking buildings.'

'Signs?' Now she was staring at me as though I was a pervert who toured the city hooker-spotting.

'You must have seen them.'

'No.'

'You really haven't seen any of the signs saying "te huur"?' She laughed. And then she laughed some more.

'You're joking, right?' she said, when she had dried her tears.

'No.'

After she had explained that '*te huur*' was not Flemish for 'the whore', but in fact meant 'for hire', as in 'apartment to rent', I had to laugh, too. And far from feeling an idiot, I started congratulating myself. Sharing a laugh is the first step towards sharing a lot more, right? And I'd made myself sound like an innocent – the kind of bloke that it's safe to sleep with.

Another couple of drinks and a few more laughs, and it might be time, I thought, to mention that I had an apartment in one of the most beautiful houses in the city, just five minutes' stroll away . . .

Which was when a heavy arm slammed down on my shoulder.

'Bon jaw,' said the body attached to it. 'Or should I say bon swa.' It burped.

I turned to see a familiar face. It was the bearded guy I'd seen at Plux. The one who'd given me the evil eye.

His accent was as English as soggy chips, and maybe it was the beer on his pungent breath that finally helped me to place his face. Of course. It was the oyster guy from the pub. The one who'd been so pissed off to learn that I was working for the French.

'You want to watch this bloke, he's a spy,' he burped at my Estonian friend.

'Bonsoir and au revoir,' I told him. He was using the classic drunkard's chat-up technique – barge in and screw things up for someone else.

'He says he's English, but I know for a fact he's spying for the bloody French.' The arm on my shoulder began to get a touch too friendly with my neck. I shrugged it off.

'I didn't tell anyone about your plans for the oyster, if that's what you mean,' I said.

'You didn't?' He looked genuinely surprised.

'Of course not. I'm working for the French, but I'm not French. I don't care about your oysters. I've got much bigger shellfish to fry. Or chew.'

I tried to communicate with a pained expression that top of my list of priorities was a nearby human female rather than any mollusc, but he'd had too much to drink to pick up on subtleties.

'Well, what about the computers, then?' he said.

'The computers?'

'Yeah. Why did you buy our computers?'

This was getting weird.

'*Your* computers? You mean lot thirty-four?'

'I don't know the number, but they were ours, yes. We were selling off some office equipment. Why would a French MEP's assistant want to buy our computers, eh?'

He sloshed a beer glass towards my face as if the answer might be in the dark liquid. But I had no answer, because it sounded like a bloody good question. Why, indeed, would Elodie send me out to buy some computers that had belonged to a British MEP?

'So the guy bidding against me was a colleague of yours?' I asked.

'Yeah, but it got too expensive. We can't spend that much buying back our own office equipment. Our MEPs' accounts are picked over with a toothpick, or a toothcomb, or whatever it is.' He was wilting under the weight of Belgian beer. 'So how come your MEP can dish out the dosh so freely?'

Which, despite his drunkenness, was another very good question.

'I don't know. But how do you know it was me bidding?'

'He took your photo. You know, for someone who's only been in town a few days, you really get about.'

'Des amis, Pol?'

'Merde.' I couldn't think of anything else to say. It was Manon, looking very attractive in a tight dress, with her hair loose, but also looking highly suspicious.

'You are friends with this kind of English political party?' she asked, still in French.

'No.' Not a very detailed rebuttal, but the only one that came to mind.

'Well, if you're not friends, maybe you are working together?' She looked genuinely disappointed in me.

'Of course not,' I said, but having a leering English MEP's assistant propped up on my shoulder didn't help my argument for the defence.

I saw that things were slipping out of my control faster than a bar of soap in a giant bathtub. My Estonian friend had got tired of waiting for me to continue our conversation and was now talking to a couple of women. She was keeping one eye on me, but it was a slightly worried one. Who was this guy, she seemed to be asking, who attracted so many accusers?

'He was asking me why I paid nine hundred and ninety euros for his old computers,' I assured Manon.

'Exactly!' the oyster guy confirmed, waving his beer glass dangerously close to Manon's dress.

'I have heard about this crazy expense,' Manon said, changing to English. 'And I am asking myself the same question.' Her suspicious tone suggested that she didn't like any of the answers she had come up with. 'Why did you do it?'

'I honestly don't know,' I said. 'It didn't make any sense to me, either. But Elodie told me to—'

No sooner had I pronounced her name than it was echoed back at me.

113

'Elodie? She's ici? Formidable!'

A grinning American barged into our group, silencing every-one with his Hawaiian shirt, a suede jacket with what looked like a large bloodstain under one armpit, and a hairstyle that made him look like a sumo wrestler trying to imitate a teapot. His long blond hair had been scooped up into a curved ponytail that was somehow attached at both ends to the top of his head.

'Voilà me,' Jake announced, unnecessarily.

While everyone, including the unflappable Manon, gawped at him in disbelief, Jake sized up his audience, nod-ding hi to the oyster guy, a warmer hello to the Estonian and her two friends, and a beam of approval at Manon.

'Wow, respect, Paul,' he finally said. 'Is this the femme who will bath with you?'

Manon's jaw dropped open.

'Another of your friends?' she asked me, a certain frost entering her voice.

'Cut it out, Jake, please,' I begged. 'This is Manon, Elodie's main assistant.'

'Hey, great name. "Man on", right?' Jake grinned at his leaden wit. Manon didn't. I groaned my disapproval as loudly as I could.

'You choose your friends well,' Manon said, the frost in her voice now chilling to liquid nitrogen. She shot a visual icicle at me and made her exit.

'Et vous, ladies?' Ever the optimist, Jake immediately turned his attention to the Estonian and her companions. 'You want to come to a bath party? Frotty-frotty, yeah?'

The girls moved away, attracting the oyster guy in their wake. He was probably just sober enough to realise that a bit of bitching about me and Jake could get him into their good books.

'Jake, do you have to?' I asked him.

'Do I have to be myself? Yes, always.' Which was the problem. Jake was always overpoweringly Jake. 'Fuck them, Paul, they all have ballets in their butts,' he said, whatever that meant. 'Come, mon ami, offer me a drink and we will find some – how do you say? – des sirènes?'

'Mermaids?'

But one thing I didn't need was a wet woman. I was already feeling as if I'd just been drowned.

10

'Brussels will force lorry drivers to eat muesli.'

Report in the British press, 2001

IT CAME as no real surprise when I woke up next day to find that I had a raging headache and was lying fully clothed in the bathtub.

That I was alone didn't shock me, either.

One thing I couldn't understand, though – the headache turned out to be neckache from sleeping with my head jammed against hard enamel. I didn't have a hangover.

I went to find out why. An unidentifiable smell took me into the kitchen, where I discovered Jake doing a sort of homeless person's version of celebrity chef. Wearing nothing but walking boots, boxer shorts and his bloodstained suede jacket, he was emptying various tin cans into a saucepan.

'Found them in the placards,' he explained, meaning cupboards. 'You want?'

I said I didn't want. Even without a hangover it was going to be hard to stomach a mixture of Bolognese sauce, tinned pears and foie gras.

I'd witnessed Jake's indiscriminate eating habits before. It was a result of his bed-hopping lifestyle. He survived by raiding strange kitchens.

He slopped the mix around a bit, then sat down at the breakfast bar with his saucepan and a spoon. His first taste of the lumpy slop made him gag, but after adding pepper he began feeding himself.

I asked him how I had ended up in the bath.

'Oh, it was triste, man,' he said, meaning sad. 'You said that you refuse to sleep solo in your bed any more. No woman, no bed. Fini!'

He laughed and waved his spoon in the air. Luckily it was already empty.

'But I can't have been that drunk, I don't have a hangover.'

Jake looked at me with a friend's concern.

'No, I think you were just fatigued,' he said. 'And deseseses-per – er, desepress, you know, désespéré.'

'Desperate?'

'Yeah, for half an hour I was chasing women for us, but it was the total merde. Finally I had to save us from that Bulgarian guy, and we came chez toi. You don't remember?'

'Vaguely. Big fella? Long hair and beard?'

'Yeah, crazy because I kissed his girlfriend. I wrote a poem about him – you want to hear it?'

'No thanks.'

But there is no stopping Jake when the poetry begins to bubble inside him.

'We ran from the big Bulgarian, and I don't want to be a vulgarian . . .'

'Brilliant, Jake, you're a genius.'

'But his beard was quite a scary 'un.'

'Thanks, Jake.'

'And I bet his butt was a hairy 'un.'

My only thought was: Open a window, somebody, please.

'You look deprimed, Paul' – he meant depressed – 'but don't worry. Those girls were all snobs.'

'No, Manon is a highly intelligent woman with quite a mischievous sense of humour, actually, which for obvious reasons doesn't include liking crude jokes about her name from someone she's only just met.' I was still pissed off at that whole stupid scene with her the previous night. In the space of a few seconds, she'd been given irrefutable evidence that everyone I knew was either politically suspect or just plain creepy.

'She's very belle, Paul, but you always have problems with intelligent women. You make one bad joke and they larg you.' He meant *larguer*, the French for dump. 'Forget her, Paul. Forget all these Brussels political people. Prostitution is legal here, right? Leave it to me.'

'No, Jake …' Now I was starting to get a hangover. Desperate to change the subject, I asked him about his stained jacket. Had someone stabbed him in the armpit, or what?

His explanation only added to my neckache. Something about buying himself a hot dog at the Gare du Nord, running for the train, having to fish out his ticket to be allowed on the high-speed Thalys and stuffing the hot dog under his arm, where the ketchup … you get the picture.

I was almost relieved when Jake had finished his nauseating breakfast and went out to look for a Sunday-morning hook-up. Sometimes, anything was better than listening to him describe his life or mine, whether it was in rhyme or not.

The one thing I wanted to do on my day of rest, I realised, was sort something out at the office. Well, not at the office exactly, but concerning my new job.

It struck me as vitally important to convince Manon that I was in no way implicated in any funny business to do with those computers. Like her, I was totally in the dark about why I'd been told to spend so much money on them. I wanted to prove my innocence to her as quickly as possible. As things stood, it was a bit like hoping to make friends with a polar bear, but I was determined to give it a go.

Not by phoning from the apartment, though. With my luck, I'd just get to the key moment in the conversation with her when Jake would turn up with some lady of ill repute.

I sent him a message to say I was going out for a civilised breakfast and that 'ON NO ACCOUNT' should he bring home a woman intended for my consumption, and that I wanted 'NOTHING TO DO' with any business involving prostitutes, legal or not.

Outside, Brussels was looking at peace with itself, as if it knew nothing about overpriced second-hand computers, an upcoming referendum or even Jake's presence within its ring road.

My street was almost empty, and I wandered slowly along the narrow pavement, taking in the details. My own house was spectacular, of course, the kind of place where you hope someone is watching as you lock the front door. But the others all had their individual charms – Gothic chapel windows, intricate brickwork, façades painted cream or light blue, a grand balcony spanning the whole façade, a view through a high-ceilinged lounge to a sunlit garden.

And, to cap it all, I noticed for the first time that I was in the chaussée Waterloo – Waterloo Road – the perfect place for a Brit to live in Brussels. Hard to believe that the French government had actually bought a building there. I could only imagine that they were planning to buy up the whole street, house by house, and then knock them all down to eradicate the name from the map.

After turning a few corners I came across a fun-looking café. A trendy place with scrubbed pine tables, industrial chairs, and young waitresses wearing mainly T-shirts and lipstick.

Unsurprisingly, it was in mid-brunch. Off-duty badge people were helping themselves to smoked salmon and scrambled eggs from a buffet, then sitting down in couples and ignoring each other as they read newspapers or their phones. Toddlers were busy wailing in French that they didn't like salmon or cold eggs. Luckily for them, there were a few jars of Nutella doing the rounds.

It all told me exactly were I was – in a Parisian ghetto. So I also knew how to get exactly what I wanted – a simple breakfast of black coffee and a croissant. I sat on a stool at the bar and said a friendly 'Bonjour' to a woman who was fighting with an orange squeezer, before telling her what I wanted to eat and drink. She tried to object that it was '*le service brunch*', but I insisted, in French, that I wasn't that hungry, and smiled to show her that I wasn't going anywhere. My coffee and croissant arrived a minute later. If there's one thing Paris teaches you, it's to get what you want in life. But only from other Parisians.

Once the croissant had been dunked and dismantled, I said a silent prayer and called Manon.

First positive sign – she answered.

'C'est qui?' she said.

'C'est Pol. Pol Wess.'

'Ah.'

Slight negative. It was the resigned groan that she would probably make if informed that her tax declaration was being contested on a Sunday morning.

'I would like to explain something to you, Manon.'

'No need. I understand everything.'

'No, that's why I need to explain.'

It's the only way to corner a French girl – hit her with logic.

'Explain on Monday.'

'Please listen now, Manon,' I begged in French. 'First of all, I'm sorry about my friend Jake. I told him he's a trou du cul,' meaning an arsehole. 'And I promise that I don't know why I had to buy those computers. I don't know why Elodie was OK to pay so much. And I had no idea they were English computers. And this Anglais with a beard is not my friend, in politics or in life.'

Having to explain in French was making me sound a bit slow and dim-witted, but at least it was clear.

'So you don't know which party he belongs to?' she asked, the tone of her question suggesting that she wasn't going to believe a 'no'.

I gave her one, anyway.

'Which party is it?' I asked.

'The Eunuchs, of course.'

'Cacarella!' This was 'shit' in Corsican. Like I said, I'd been doing my research. 'Honestly, Manon, I didn't know he was with the Eunuchs.'

I should perhaps enlighten those who have not been following European affairs by explaining exactly who these political castrati were. Their unofficial moniker was, of

122

course, inspired by the name of their rabidly anti-European party – United Kingdom No Capitulation, or UKNOC for short. Apparently it was meant to be a homage to that Great British anti-foreigner Enoch Powell, but it had backfired and now they were commonly known as the Eunuchs and forced to listen to countless jokes about their campaign to 'dismember' Europe.

'One of them puts his arm around you like an old friend, and you don't know who he is?' Manon's scepticism was withering.

'No,' I promised her. 'A drunk Englishman will put his arm around anybody.' Then a thought struck me. 'But what if Elodie knew that they were Eunuch computers? And she wanted to buy them to see if she could find sensitive information on them?'

'What?'

'Maybe they left something on their hard disk. Maybe Elodie wants to expose them.'

'Why would she want to do that?'

Oh, *cac*, I thought. I shouldn't be telling Manon anything about my true mission to help Elodie influence the referendum. No wonder they call these Frenchwomen *femmes fatales* – they can get you gabbing your deepest secrets just by sulking at you for a couple of days.

'Well, you know,' I began to improvise, wondering what ungrammatical French *merde* I was about to come out with, 'she is an MEP, so naturally she is against the Eunuchs, so naturally she wants to expose any secrets that are on their hard disks.'

'Pff!' She gave her trademark French puff of breath through the lips to imply that she was blowing me – and all my opinions – away like a fleck of dust that has dared to land on the sleeve of her Chanel jacket. 'Political secrets hidden on old computers? You're more credible when you're drunk,' she said. 'I suggest you get a few beers for breakfast.'

A joke at last. Maybe she was softening.

'But surely everyone in Brussels wants to expose the Eunuchs, n'est-ce pas?' I said, trying my best to make it sound like a double entendre. 'So maybe Elodie is just trying to defend Europe. And by doing that, defend la France.'

'La France? So now you are a French patriot, Monsieur l'Anglais?'

'Have you never heard me sing La Marseillaise? Can't you hear – I even pronounce it properly. La Mar-say-aze.'

She gave a grudging laugh.

'I'm not sure that who sings, or doesn't sing, a national anthem is always the best way to judge people,' she said. 'In the past, national anthems have been misused.'

I couldn't think of a joke or a comeback to that.

'I'll see you tomorrow,' she said. 'Bon dimanche,' and she hung up. I was pretty sure she was smiling as she did so, which made me smile, too.

As I stashed my phone, I noticed that the orange-squeezer barmaid was watching me.

'Vous êtes Anglais,' she said.

I nodded and guessed what was coming.

'How do you think your referendum will go?' she asked.

I put on my serious, on-weekdays-I-wear-a-badge expression.

'I think we'll probably vote to invade France and restore your monarchy,' I told her.

I honestly think it might solve a lot of Europe's problems.

11

'According to a new EU law, the Queen will have to fetch her own cup of tea.'

Report in the British press, 1999

STROLLING TO the Parliament next morning, I wondered if I hadn't misjudged Elodie. Despite her family genes and past history of screwing me (and most of humanity) around, there was always the possibility that this time she was being straight with me.

After all, from what I'd heard, she really did want to protect the Breton language, even if there was a bit of self-interest involved. Supporting minority languages was in the EU's interests, and could also help Elodie's own electoral prospects.

And maybe she did really buy those computers so that she could fish out some sensitive info to embarrass the extreme anti-marketeers. Everyone knows that you can't wipe a hard disk 100 per cent clean. Perhaps she honestly did want to keep Britain in the EU – after all, it sounded as if it was in her own country's interests, and therefore hers.

Self-interest is the best reason to help others, right?

My brain was conjuring up sunny thoughts to match the morning brightness of the sky. I was in a positive frame of mind because I'd managed to escape another skirt-chasing bar crawl with Jake the previous evening. Predictably, he hadn't rematerialised for the rest of Sunday. He'd texted me to say that he had met, and I quote, a 'charmant mademoiselle of mixed origins who is a veritable ethnic cock-tail'.

The hyphen in that last word was obviously an attempt at a sexual pun, the kind of thing he did in his so-called poems, and I felt a surge of relief that I hadn't been present to listen to the whole monstrous masterpiece that the poor woman had probably inspired.

So on that Monday morning I was actually looking forward to sitting down and bashing out my little treatise on the downtrodden dialects of Europe. Maybe I really could help Scousers to get themselves a few road signs; and Geordies, too, so that the roads into Newcastle would just be marked 'Toon'. Millions of Brits driving by every day would know that Brussels cared about them.

I found the office at the first attempt, but entered to hear Elodie ranting at Manon that she was '*débordée*' – the most popular word in the French workplace. Literally it means overwhelmed or overflowing, but people with not much work to do use the word to explain that a tsunami of *travail* is threatening to sweep them and their desk out the window. Could you just sign this piece of paper I printed out for you two weeks ago? *Non!* (Cue waving of arms and tragic expression.) *Je suis dé-bor-dé!* There is so much straw on their camel's back that the poor thing's spine has snapped in five places. And if you keep on hassling them to sign your piece of paper, they're liable to go to the doctor and get three months' psychiatric leave to ease their nerves.

Elodie threw a file on Manon's desk. This was no doubt what had caused the *débordement*. Manon stayed cool, as she always seemed to do, and said she would deal with the file when she had followed up on the morning's batch of emails from Breton mayors.

Elodie was still in diva mode when she pointed to a table in the corner of Manon's office and told me that was where I'd be working. It was a small, metal-legged thing facing a blank wall.

'I'd be delighted to share an office with Manon,' I said, 'but it's a bit gloomy in that corner.'

'Yes, and I'm on the phone a lot. I don't know if he'll be able to concentrate,' Manon said. 'Cédric isn't here today, is he? Paul could work there?'

This only provoked another bout of flouncing.

'If you two want to question everything I do, maybe you ought to get yourselves elected to Parliament,' Elodie squawked, and made her dramatic exit into the room next door.

After sharing a quick 'ooh-er' moment with Manon, I had to go in and confront Elodie again.

'Any chance of a computer?' I asked.

'Ah, oui,' she answered, with surprising calm. I'd been expecting her to prolong the melodramatics, but she got up from her office chair and unlocked a cupboard. Inside I saw the three laptops.

'Here you are, all cleaned up and loaded with new software. French, of course, not Belgian.' She even grinned chummily as she said it. I didn't dare retort, 'Not British, you mean?' I wasn't supposed to know where the computers came from.

I thanked her and handed back her credit card.

'This has lost some weight,' she quipped, chuckling. The transformation from hell's fury to mild-mannered comedian was positively disturbing. 'How was your weekend?' she asked, giving me something approaching a leer.

'Oh, very good, thanks.'

'Success at last, then?' Now she was sounding like a school nurse enquiring after my bowel habits.

'Yes,' I lied.

'Anyone I know?'

'No, just a girl in a bar.'

'The best sort. Anyway, you're looking much more relaxed, which is excellent news for all of us. Oh, Paul, while you're here, could you sign this?'

She unlocked a drawer in her desk – everything was permanently under lock and key – and fished out a slim grey file, much like the one she had thrown at Manon minutes before. Laying it on her desk, she opened it and pointed to the single sheet of paper inside. There was a dotted line at the bottom, and in case I hadn't understood what this was for, she placed a pen next to it.

'What is it?' I asked, naturally enough.

'Oh, just a rental agreement for the apartment. You don't have to pay anything, obviously, but I need to say who's living there. Insurance and all that. You don't need to read it all.'

She handed me the pen. It felt suspiciously like one of those movie scenes where someone is getting tricked into signing away their life savings. I tried to read the document, which did, as she'd told me, quote the address of my new home, but a lot of extra stuff, too, in French legalese.

'You think I'm getting you to sign for its demolition, with your precious suitcase inside?'

Snooty bitch, I thought.

I signed. Satisfied, Elodie shut the file and locked it away in her drawer. She then walked to her door and closed it, an open gesture to shut Manon out.

'I want you to spend today writing up what you learnt about minority languages from our German friend,' she told me. 'And I've sent you an email giving you the contact information for a meeting tomorrow with DJ Communication.'

Yesterday this would have sounded like a musical act promoting cultural understanding, but now of course I knew that she meant 'DG'. My only question was: What the hell was the *Direction générale* of communication? I phrased it more politely.

'It's the press service at the Commission,' Elodie answered. 'This guy will tell you all the unkind things that your compatriots have been saying about Europe.'

'Great,' I said. It sounded fun. And at last I'd get to go inside the head office of the EU sect. 'But why should I want to hear them?'

'This is part two of your mission. OK?' Elodie widened her eyes at me in case I hadn't understood.

'OK,' I agreed. 'But sorry to be dense – am I missing something here? You want me to go and see this guy and listen to a bunch of nasty things that Brits have said about the EU? That's it?'

'Yes, that's it.'

'And what do I do with them exactly?'

'Ffff.' This was Elodie doing one of her trademark puffs. It struck me that she wasn't at all used to explaining her actions, or briefing people on why they should do things. To her, we were all her cleaning ladies – we should just start hoovering where she told us to hoover, and shut up.

'You listen to them, Paul,' she finally said. 'And then you write them down so that I can read about them. It's quite simple, really.'

'OK.' I thought about this for a second. 'How many do you want? What if there are hundreds of them?'

I was pretty sure I could hear Elodie's teeth grinding with frustration. I hoped for her sake that an MEP's salary package included dental treatment, because enamel had to be avalanching off her molars. She took a deep breath before replying.

'Use your judgement, OK, Paul? Choose the best, the really bitchy ones. Your tabloid newspapers have always loved, how do you say, snipping at Europe?'

She made it sound like a vasectomy, but I knew what she meant.

'OK, that seems clearer now,' I told her. 'You want a best-of compilation. I get it.'

She smiled with relief.

'Enfin,' she said. At last. 'Oh, yes, and you can tell this guy anything you need to about our mission. No need to keep secrets from your compatriots. We can always trust les Anglais, n'est-ce pas?'

'Yes,' I agreed, warily.

'I have to go out now, so I'll see you later,' she said – so much for being *débordée* with work. Overwhelmed with invitations to have coffee, lunch and extramarital sex, more like. 'Oh, Paul, by the way, I hear Jake is in town. Is he staying with you? If so, maybe we should add his name to the rental agreement.'

While I was still recovering from the shock, she grinned and made for the door.

'You can't keep any secrets in Brussels, Paul.'

That, I guessed, was why she never left her office with a single piece of paper or even a Post-it lying around.

It didn't go down too well with Manon when I asked if she was the one who had told Elodie about Jake staying with me. It wasn't an accusation at all, but that was the way she took it. I just thought Manon might have mentioned the arrival of my louche American friend in conversation, but she reacted as if I'd accused her of calling in the Gestapo.

The French hate it when you suggest they might have told anyone in authority anything. It's their communal hang-up from the Second World War, when half the country was writing letters to the Nazi occupiers to rat on their neighbours for being Jewish, anti-Nazi or just guilty of living in a larger apartment.

I was forced to apologise, and to acknowledge that Manon couldn't have snitched on me because she had no idea where Jake was staying. And I conceded wholeheartedly that, after the way he'd greeted her, his address was not something she would have wanted to find out. But she wasn't appeased by all this, or when I said sorry yet again for Jake's joke about her name and his unwanted offer of a communal bath.

'Forget it. Though I really don't know why you would think I'd tell Elodie any of your secrets,' she snapped in angry French. 'You and she seem to share a lot of secrets anyway.' Constantly having the office door closed in her face seemed to be rankling.

I apologised again, as profusely as my French would let me, and sat down to face my wall as punishment.

For the next hour or so, her computer clicked away behind me as I tried out my 'new' laptop. It was clunky but it worked. And a quick dig-around in the deleted files seemed to prove that Cédric had indeed cleaned out the hard drive.

I got in a session of cutting and pasting from EU reports about the viability of Swabian, Valencian, Manx and all their underprivileged cousins, and managed to look up a useful selection of their dirty words, before I turned around and tried another peace offering.

'I'm going to get a coffee, Manon. Would you like one?'

'Non, merci,' she said.

'Or tea?'

'Non, merci.'

'Juice? Water?'

'Merci, non.'

'Coke? Wine? A mojito with fresh lime and a little umbrella in the glass, with an EU flag on it?'

Finally, I got a smile.

'OK, a latte, please, with one sugar.'

'Avec plaisir,' I said, and got the hell out of there before I ruined the moment.

I also left the file up on my screen so that, before it went into power-saving mode, she could see that friendly, innocent Paul had nothing to hide.

Even if in fact, he did.

I found my way to the Mickey Mouse cafeteria and decided to have a sit-down in one of the colourful chairs before getting back to the office.

I was flicking through some private emails on my phone when a familiar voice rang out.

'Bon jaw!'

It was oyster man again, the shellfish superhero. He sat down with me and plonked a large frothy coffee cup on the table. He was looking pretty frothy too, much too jolly for a Monday morning.

'Great fun, that mate of yours,' he said. 'Wish I had his way with the ladies. I mean, asking *every single one* of them for a shag. It must work occasionally.'

'Yes, it does, weirdly.'

'So, busy day, then?' He really was getting chummy.

'Yes, I've got a report to write. What about you?'

'Yeah, my MEP's here all the bloody time at the moment. Didn't even leave for the last Green week.'

This, it turned out, was neither a week devoted to ecology nor seven days of non-stop broccoli at the cafeteria. It was the name for a week that MEPs generally spent back home in their constituencies.

'Frankly, I'm surprised your MEP is *ever* here,' I said.

Surprisingly, he laughed.

'What, you mean because of his slightly eurosceptic stance?' he said.

'Eurosceptic? Your party practically wants to bomb Brussels. Electing one of them to the Parliament is a bit like voting for Goering as Mayor of London.'

This shut him up for a second, but not for the reason I expected.

'*My* party?' he said. 'Listen, I'm all in favour of the EU. Without it, we'd have tomatoes that look like baboon's backsides, two-legged mutant carrots and cucumbers suffering from erectile dysfunction. Who else cares so passionately about the sexual well-being of our vegetables?'

'So that's all the EU is, is it?' I said. 'An international salad inspectorate?'

'Course not. I'm like you,' he said. 'I'm not a party man. I'm doing my job. I've been here for ten years and in that time I've worked with a Tory, a Green, a Scot and now this guy. He took me on because I know how the place works, not because I want to bomb it. Of course I didn't say no to the chance of pissing off the French by banning the oyster. Great fun. And I'll keep on working here whatever happens in the referendum, so quite frankly I'm not too bothered about a British exit. "Brexit". Sounds like an early-morning laxative, doesn't it? "One spoonful of Brexit on your cornflakes – your passport to a healthy morning dump." And you know the funny thing about these Eunuch MEPs?'

I could imagine a few, but shook my head.

'Secretly, they all fucking *adore* the EU.' He guffawed and got the coffee-drinkers around us staring. Lowering his voice,

136

he leant in close. 'When my guy got elected, he made a speech: "If Britain is the mother of all parliaments, then Brussels and Strasbourg are the ugly sisters – overweight, bulimic and out of breath from gobbling too much oily foreign food paid for by *our* taxes!" But now he fucking loves it. They all do. Where else are they going to earn so much bloody dosh? With free booze practically every night at some lobbyist's cocktail party? Hordes of groupies? And the chance to go back home and dish the dirt on the place, as if they've escaped from a concentration camp? You know, when they leave Brussels, we say they take the "Zaventem shower". It's named after the airport. It decontaminates them of impure pro-European thoughts before going back home. Believe me, these so-called eurosceptic MEPs are having the time of their fucking lives. If they win the referendum, they'll be blubbing all the way to the dole office.'

All of which put a new perspective on things for me.

'I'm Danny, by the way,' he said, tapping his badge.

'Paul,' I said, doing the same.

We shook hands.

Which was probably the worst possible time for Manon to catch sight of me as she arrived at the cafeteria, no doubt impatient for her latte. Or just maybe she'd decided to come and drink it with me and make peace after our little scene. A guy can always hope.

She shot a brief 'Oh, so that's how it is?' look in my direction and turned to queue at the counter. My peace offering had been declined before it had even been delivered.

I told Danny the oyster that I'd see him around, and went to put Manon straight.

'C'est un mec bien' – he's an OK guy – I told her. The back of her head, anyway. She didn't turn to look at me.

'To you, maybe,' she said. 'I know what his sort thinks of France.'

'It's not what you think.' Well, not exactly.

She finally turned round.

'You seem to spend most of your life apologising or explaining, Paul. Maybe you should think about that.'

'Let me explain why.'

It was meant to be a joke, but she didn't get it.

'I thought you said he attached himself to you because he was drunk. Well, he doesn't look drunk now.'

'No, he's not. But—'

'Look, Paul,' she interrupted me. 'If you and Elodie want to plot secret policies behind closed doors, and link up with the Eunuchs, you're free to do so.'

'We're not. Well, I'm not.'

'You know what is in that file she gave me?' I had to confess my ignorance. 'I'm supposed to write a communiqué for her explaining why her region should only have to take a minimum number of refugees. While I'm contacting mayors to ask them to take refugees. Quelle merde!'

'Well, you've got to believe I'm not working on anything to do with that. And you've got to listen to what that English guy just told me.'

'Oh, putain,' Manon moaned. Literally it's like *pute*, another vulgar name for a prostitute (French has a suspicious amount of those), but they also use it as an expletive of despair or frustration.

She walked away.

At first I was going to stay on and buy her coffee, but then I thought: *Putain*, the reason why I seemed to spend all my time with Manon explaining things was because she was constantly judging me. And if she wanted to play the judge, she was going to damn well listen to my defence.

Admittedly, part of me was thinking that it was best to steer well clear of French women with strong political opinions – I'd had a girlfriend like that before, and I never knew when I was going to offend her accidentally by liking the wrong book or wanting to live in the wrong part of Paris. But an even stronger part of me wanted Manon to know that I wasn't some double-dealing jingoistic idiot.

I followed her along the corridor, speaking loud French at her back.

'Danny works for the Eunuchs,' I informed her, 'but he's not one of them. He is in favour of Europe.'

'Pff!' she said, which at least proved she was listening.

'You should hear what he just told me about his MEP,' I said, still trailing her. She arrived at a lift, but apparently decided she didn't want to be my captive audience in such a confined space and veered away into a ladies' loo.

No problem. I began talking through the door, translating as best I could the funny stuff that Danny had just told me. I had a few problems with the bit about Brussels gobbling oily foreign food, but I think I summarised the gist. I also promised her that I was as horrified by the Eunuchs as she clearly was. We were on the same Eunuch page.

Still no reaction from inside the loo.

The absurdity of the situation reminded me of something I'd stumbled across on the internet that same morning while compiling my blurb for Elodie. It was about a campaign to harmonise male and female toilets. Some woman MEP for Bavaria was campaigning to abolish urinals, which, she said, expose female cleaning staff to the danger of being confronted by male exhibitionists. This MEP wanted cubicles for everyone, and was gleaning major support from German men, lots of whom apparently prefer to pee sitting down. German even has a special word for this, I learnt – the *Sitzpinkel.*

I delivered my one-word punchline through Manon's toilet door and waited. I heard footsteps. It sounded as though she was coming out. The door opened.

'Très intéressant,' I was told by a middle-aged lady I'd never seen before in my life.

Smiling to herself, she walked away and left me feeling a total *Sitzpinkeler.*

As the door swung closed, I saw that it was a two-cubicle toilet with a washbasin in the little lobby area.

'Is that true?' Manon said when she emerged a moment later, smiling ever so slightly at her victory.

'Yes, der Sitzpinkel. Or maybe *das* Sitzpinkel. I don't know.'

'No, I mean all that about your friend's Eunuchs? The stupid speech, secretly loving Brussels and everything?'

'Yes,' I confirmed.

'Then maybe you can buy me that latte after all.'

We went back to the colourful chairs and actually had a friendly chat. Manon apologised for blowing up at me, I sympathised for the shitty way Elodie was treating her, and after a couple of minutes we even got to the life-story stage.

I told her some tales about my time in France, leaving out a few of the romantic entanglements, but letting her know that I'd recently broken up with a girl who'd buggered off to work in China. Obviously I didn't use the word 'buggered', because I was speaking French, which has no literal translation for this bizarre English concept. I just said Amandine had departed, which made her sound like a train.

In return, Manon told me that Elodie was her third MEP – her second as a full assistant. Before that, she'd been one of the ambitious interns trawling Brussels for business cards. And no, she stressed before I could be tactless enough to ask, she hadn't had to earn jobs on anyone's casting couch.

She, too, had recently emerged from a relationship.

'He was a Greek journalist,' she said, 'and ironically he did keep borrowing money from me, and then getting annoyed when I asked him to repay it.'

'So this was one Grexit that was welcome,' I said.

'Yes, and I'm enjoying my independence,' she said. I guessed this was a hint that she wasn't in favour of a Brentrance into her life.

She asked me how I really felt about the potential Brexit, and for once I decided to answer seriously.

'Honestly, I can't decide,' I said. 'I know Britain is being invaded by war refugees, but that doesn't seem to be caused by being in the EU. I know that the southern European countries' economics are as stable as their plumbing, and we often have to deal with their shit. But maybe we'd have to do that anyway, even if we weren't in the EU. All I really know is that I'm based in France, so if Britain leaves, I will probably have to start queuing up for a residence permit again. That would be hell.'

Manon examined me with her large, lively eyes, obviously wondering whether I was being serious. But I was. Call it petty, but don't most of us think of politics in these personal terms? Will this or that policy guarantee me a job? Will this referendum force me to endure the horrors of a French government waiting room?

'Well, I'm glad you're not one of the Brexiteurs,' she said. 'They're so absurd. You know what they've been trying to do, just to annoy us?'

Well, yes, I did – ban oysters – but I shook my head.

'For example, they have been trying to make it obligatory for all queues in Europe to follow the British system,' she said. 'You know: "Cashier number three, please".' She did a good imitation of the food shops at St Pancras station. 'They say Britain is the only country that knows how to queue.'

'They haven't tried getting served in a London pub recently,' I said. The last time I'd had a go, the queuing system was to wave your money at the barman and shout, 'Oy, over here!'

'And they have been trying to force every hotel in Europe to provide "tea-making facilities", as you English call them, in every room. Honestly – and they complain about wasted European money!'

I tutted disapprovingly at my errant countrymen, though I had to agree with that last policy. Why should any hotel guest be deprived of a wake-up cuppa, even if it is French tea that needs to brew till lunchtime before it gets strong enough to drink?

'I don't understand people who stay in Europe just to cause trouble, or who campaign for years to join the EU and then campaign to get out. It's not just a waste of money, it's a waste of life.'

Clearly Manon was more of an existentialist than I'd imagined.

'You know, if the Brexiteurs win the referendum and Britain leaves the EU, you might not get that residence permit so easily. France might just throw out all the English immigrants,' she said. 'We're pretty mad at you for refusing to take your fair share of the Middle Eastern refugees.

So we might deport you all. You'd be condemned to stay in Brussels,' Manon added in a lighter tone, and her smile made me think this might not be an unpleasant exile. 'The question is: Would Elodie prolong your contract? I mean, that language study isn't going to take you very long. Does she have other things that you can do for her?'

I considered this for a moment, and then suspicion hit me like a Belgian beer glass bouncing off my skull. Disappointment churned my entrails even more efficiently than the beer itself.

I thought: Please somebody tell me that Manon isn't Šárka the lobbyist all over again. Surely this cosy chat wasn't just a way of getting me to reveal why Elodie always wanted to talk to me behind closed doors? Did no one ever stop lobbying, job-hunting or plotting in this bloody place?

'Talking of work, maybe we should get back to the office,' I said.

'Yes.' Perhaps Manon picked up on my sudden unease, because she looked me right in the eyes and said, 'You know, Paul, I'm really glad you're not working with those Eunuchs. Their hypocrisy makes me sick. I'm so relieved you're not one of them.'

At any other time I might have said, 'Eunuch, moi?' in a falsetto voice. Or anything jokey that made it sound as though we were on the same team. Now, though, Manon had steered us straight back into Brussels' game of badges.

Back at my desk, I was spared any awkwardness because Manon had to go and attend the presentation of some award or other, with its associated drinks and nibbles. She seemed to realise that something was up, when all I did was half-turn in my seat to say goodbye and give her one of those workmate smiles you put on for a split second when you know you have to.

I was still feeling peed off that what had felt like a genuine rapprochement had fallen flat, like a Belgian waffle that blackens in the waffle-maker instead of rising up, all golden and fluffy.

While we'd been exchanging life stories, it had been great. She was fun to listen to as well as a total hottie, and I'd really felt that getting closer to her could have been one of life's more golden, fluffy experiences. But then she'd come over all conspiratorial and our shared waffle moment was over.

Merde, as they say in Brussels, in twenty-odd languages, plus dozens of dialects.

I got back to my Art Nouveau palace after work to find that Jake had been there. He'd done some food shopping, but sadly this consisted of a giant sack of coffee beans. Very useful – the apartment didn't even own a coffee grinder.

I messaged him to find out what he was up to, but he didn't reply. So I nipped out for a hot dog (which tasted as though it might actually have been made with canine by-products), and then settled down to watch a Bond movie.

As usual, 007 didn't know if the babe he found in his bed was on his side or the opposing team. The thing about Bond, though, is that he always beds them first and asks their allegiances later. You never see James Bond staying home alone, curled up in front of a Bond movie.

12

'Brussels wants to ban British barmaids' cleavage.'

Report in the British press, 2005

THE CAPITAL of the European Union is a vast bureaucracy with so many moving parts that the organisers have clearly had problems choosing different names for them all. There is, for example, a Council of Europe as well as a Council of the European Union and a European Council – all different bodies with different functions.

There's also the European Court, the European Commission and dozens of European Committees. All those 'EC' initials – no wonder they changed the EEC to the EU.

Added to the problem of names, there is the question of roles. We hear a lot about the European Parliament, the European Commission and the Council of Europe taking decisions. But who has the last word on what becomes European law?

Personally, I don't have a bloody clue.

And, quite frankly, as I walked through the early-morning streets towards my meeting at the Commission, I didn't really care. All I had to do was go in there and get a juicy list of twisted news stories about Europe from the man at DG Communication, and then report back to Elodie. She wasn't asking for a flow chart of the whole organisation.

Call it a lack of conscientiousness, if you want, but in my view life is too short to try and understand the exact work-ings of the European Union. Unless, of course, you want to make it your permanent profession, which, to judge from what I'd seen so far, was a fate I preferred to avoid.

On the large roundabout outside the Commission building I saw my first political action of the day. A group of about two dozen men and women were waving flags and banners and chanting slogans I couldn't understand. Most of the guys had dark facial hair, and the women wore headscarves, so I guessed they were of Middle Eastern or North African origin. Libya, maybe, Syria, Tunisia or Egypt. Or one of the old southeast Russian republics. I didn't recognise the flags, and the banners were calling obscurely for 'ACTION NOW'. I just hoped for their sakes that the badge people, who were wandering into work carrying their coffees, cases and phones, knew what the pro-test was about, otherwise it all seemed to be a waste of time.

There was a small flood of grey-suited men and women flowing into the Commission building, which was an intriguing three-winged tower, a cross between a giant glass propeller and one of those spiked traps that resistance fighters used to throw on roads to puncture tyres.

It was impossible to see what went on inside because all the windows were covered by sunshades, making it look like a fortress defended by rows of arrow slits.

To get into the Commission I had to walk past a long line of flagpoles, all flying the blue EU standard. It felt as if I was arriving at a stupendously clean beach.

My badge got me as far as a reception desk, where I gave the name of the guy I was due to meet – an Englishman called Peter Marsh. Strange, I thought, a Brit working in the press department of the place that the British press loved to denigrate. But then again, who better to unravel the devious workings of the British journalistic mind?

While I waited for him to come down and fetch me, I had a quick nose around. There was a stand for a freebie newspaper, clearly a Brussels-only publication, to judge by its headline: 'Wave of outrage over dismissal of European Digital Single Market director'. Here was one wave that seemed to have passed the rest of the world by.

I also saw evidence that there were some older badge people. At the Parliament, most of the non-MEPs were youngish, but here I saw career bureaucrats who'd obviously been around the block a few times. Some were dressed ambitiously in sharp suits and zingy ties, or bright heels for the women, but there were plenty of creased-looking office workers, strolling comfortably through a job for life towards a cosy pension.

My man arrived, jacketless, his badge bouncing on a shirt with just a touch of purple in its whiteness. A maverick touch to show he was in the press section, no doubt. He had the almost-shaven haircut that only Eastern European ex-soldiers and Brits seem to adopt in office life, and a firm handshake.

'Hello,' he said. 'Peter.'

'Hi, Peter. Paul,' I replied.

'All we need is a Mary,' he said. I didn't know why. Probably a generation thing.

'So you're working for the enemy, then?' he went on.

'The French, you mean? Oui, temporarily.'

'What are they saying about the referendum?'

'That the opinion polls are too close to call.'

He seemed satisfied with this.

We chatted as we walked to the lift, and I tried to detect his accent as he ran me through his CV. There were a few grains of Liverpool in there – the way he pronounced 'work' as 'where-k' – but most of it had been filtered out by twenty years of where-king in Brussels, straight after uni. And even more than Danny the oyster man, he often paused before words, as if sifting around for the right language.

Peter's office came as a pleasant surprise. The corridors here were much wider and plusher than at the Parliament, as if Europe wanted to be more attentive towards its permanent staff than towards short-term MEPs. His desk was in a large, bright open space shared by four people facing each other companionably. Again, nothing like Elodie's cramped, divide-and-rule enclave.

He introduced me to his colleagues, who were all very friendly, unstressed-looking and of varying nationalities. Then, to my relief, he took me off to a meeting room, before everyone could ask me to predict the result of the Brexit poll.

'Best to have a private chat,' he said as we settled into a room with a long wooden meeting table that was bigger than Elodie's office. I sat close to an enormous window, and understood the arrow-slit effect that I'd seen from outside. The windows had all been protected by angled sunshades. Peter saw me studying them.

'No one realised that glass walls would create an oven,' he said. 'Typical out-of-touch architects. So they added these things. We can't see out any more, but at least we don't fry. Or bake, I should say.' The communicator's desire to choose the right word. 'How can I help you?' he asked, and leant back in his chair, lifting his arms as if he wanted to reveal a total lack of sweat patch. His really did seem to be a cushy job.

'Well, first, what is your role exactly?'

'I'm a head of unit in DG Communication, which, as I'm sure you've noticed, is one of the more sensibly named DGs. I mean, "Mare" for the fisheries? "Fisma" for financial stability? And how come they called the DG for enlargement of the EU "Near"? It should be "Next" or "Not Yet", the plonkers.'

He was telling me all this in his slow, I'm-not-really-Scouse voice, smiling good-naturedly as he spoke.

'I deal mainly with press releases about EU decisions. We produce them for every new law or ruling, and after summit meetings – that sort of thing. We have spokespeople who give press conferences downstairs to all the Brussels correspondents.'

'Including the journalists who work for the anti-EU press?'

He laughed.

'Well, they don't generally turn up. Real news doesn't interest them.'

A pained expression flitted across his face for the first time.

'I've seen what they do,' I sympathised. 'Taking news stories and turning them on their heads.'

'Exactly. On most issues we don't even bother publishing a press release for the UK. No point.'

'Isn't that discrimination?'

'No, it just saves paper. It's better for us if we shut up. You know the old principle: if a drunkard starts mouthing off at you in the pub, walk away. We've walked away.'

Bloody hell. Things were worse than I'd imagined.

'So the EU has given up defending itself against attacks from the British press?'

'Yup.' He folded his arms. This was final, he seemed to be saying. Decree nisi.

'So you're not campaigning in the referendum, then? Putting out stories to let people know all the good stuff you do, like . . .' I couldn't think of any.

'Like putting together all the rules on safe online payments, forcing global corporations to pay tax, or giving more money to the British Council for cultural events than the British government does? Nope, no point. They'd ignore us.'

'Isn't that a bit defeatist?'

'No, just realistic. And, between you and me' – he looked over his shoulder at the closed door as if it might be listening – 'I wouldn't want to go anywhere near the referendum campaign. If my press releases flopped or created a backlash, my career could go on permanent hold. That's the reason why most Brit civil servants here in Brussels want the UK to stay in. If it leaves, we'll be stuck halfway up the career ladder. No one will trust us any more, whereas now they like us. We're never extreme left or right, never too green or pink, we just get on with the job. Brussels loves that. So a Brexit would be a bloody disaster for us. I think I'd cash in the old passport and turn Belgian. God help me!'

Depression seemed to be getting a grip on poor Pete, so I gave him the good news that I was here to help, backed up by the whole of France. Well, Brittany West at least.

'Yes, that Madame Martin, classy lady,' he said. He'd obviously been subjected to an Elodie charm offensive. 'Worked for her long?'

'No, but I've known her for years.' No point going into a detailed history of our sex and fruit-throwing. 'Now she's hired me to do what you've given up trying to do – counterbalance all the negative campaigning and tell the Brits what

Europe is really about. The French want the UK to stay in, you know. They don't want to weaken the team.'

'Hard to believe,' Peter said. 'I must admit I was a bit suspicious when she first contacted me. Most French bureaucrats I've spoken to reckon Europe would be better off without Britain. They say all we do is whinge. And whingeing is meant to be a French monopoly, of course. At a pinch, the only reason they want the Brits to stay in is so we'll take a few refugees off their hands. And maybe take back responsibility for Calais, like we did in the sixteenth century, so they don't have to police the tunnel.'

'Yes, well, for whatever reason, Elodie is heading a campaign to keep us in. And it's all top secret, by the way. I don't think she even wants other French people to know what we're up to.'

'French resistance turned upside down, eh? Building bridges instead of blowing them up. That's a new one. The French don't usually ask the Brits to build their bridges. They usually like to do it for themselves.'

'Elodie's not like most French people,' I said, though, even as I spoke, it struck me that in many ways that was totally untrue. 'What we need from you is a list of the craziest stories that have appeared in the UK press. And the truth behind the rumours, so that I can contradict them.'

'No sweat. Hang on a minute, I'll get my laptop.'

Thirty seconds later he was back, opening up a file as he walked.

'How about this? "EU to rename Waterloo Station and Trafalgar Square." That was rubbish, it was just an off-the-cuff remark by some eurocrat who said he thought the names were a bit provocative towards the French.'

He scrolled down.

'Here's a classic: "Brussels bans smoky-bacon crisps." Total balls, it was just a ruling about possible carcinogenics in smoked foods. And this one was bloody unbelievable: "Euro banknotes make men impotent." What happened was that the EU released the results of tests on the inks used, and said that a man might be affected if he ate two thousand five hundred euros a day, for six months.'

'In five-euro notes or hundreds?' I asked. He gaped at me. 'Joke,' I added quickly.

'Yes, but you see the lengths they'll go to?'

I did, and I was wondering how I was going to counter such creative journalism.

He was scrolling again.

'Then, of course, there are all the out-and-out scare stories,' he said, 'mainly about evil things the French want to do to the Brits, like redefining Christmas crackers as firearms or making sex toys in metric lengths. All total bollocks.'

'Can you send me a list?' I asked.

'I can send you a bloody book. An encyclopaedia of them. And most Brits still seem to believe them all. You really can't blame the DG for giving up the fight.'

Below his calm Brussels-bureaucrat surface, as smooth as
the laminate on his badge, this was a deeply troubled man. A
beaten man.

He escorted me to the lift, and I noticed as he walked that a
sweat patch had appeared below his nearest armpit. I'd obviously rekindled some old traumas. Halfway along the corridor, we passed a set of pigeonholes, each containing a stack
of printouts.

'Look at this,' he said, handing me one. 'It's a list of countries that have infringed EU laws, and what each one did
wrong.'

I perused it. Austria, it seemed, had not implemented some
clause in the laws on working conditions. Croatia had forgotten something to do with wheelchair access. Even Germany
had disobeyed some minor EU ruling on food labelling.

'Notice anything?' Peter asked me, and answered before I
could reply. 'No mention of Britain. This is the official communiqué about legal requirements not respected by all EU
members throughout last year, and we don't bother even
mentioning it when the UK fails to comply. It would only
spark off a retaliation campaign in the British press. We let
them get away scot-free. Well, mainly English-free.'

Bloody hell, I thought, if the combined might of the EU
had thrown in the towel against these raging-bull reporters,
what chance did Brittany West and I stand?

But then again, the British tabloids had yet to face Elodie.

13

'EU to force British fish-and-chip shops to use Latin names for fish.'

Report in the British press, 2001

I WENT into Parliament via the back entrance, where Manon had first escorted me through the security checks. For the first time I noticed a sculpture there, another example of Brussels' bizarre taste in public statues.

It was a bronze woman triumphantly holding aloft a euro symbol that she seems to have stolen from the defeated man slumped at her feet. A subliminal message to the Brits, I wondered? Europe's currency is going to stomp all over the pound? It wasn't working too well so far.

I went to give Elodie a quick breakdown of what I'd learnt from Pete, the depressed press man. As usual, she shut all doors and windows and more or less swept the place for bugs before she let me speak.

She seemed delighted by what I told her, and chortled merrily at the 'euros make you impotent' story.

'Perfect, list all the best ones for me. Maybe twenty will be enough. I'll have Cédric translate them into French.'

'Why would he need to translate them, if I'm going to be doing a press release aimed at the Brits?' I asked.

This threw her for a second.

'For my French colleagues. I'm not working alone, Paul.' She raised her eyebrows towards heaven to suggest that much higher authorities were involved.

'Where should I work? I can't really do it with Manon looking over my shoulder. And I must admit I'm getting a bit pissed off with all this secrecy. Can't we tell her what I'm doing? It's all for a good Franco-British cause, isn't it?'

'No.' I hoped she was answering the first question, not the second.

'Manon suggested I work in Cédric's office. How about that?'

'No,' Elodie snapped immediately. 'No one goes in there. He doesn't like it.' She frowned painfully, as if to blame the family inbreeding. 'You can use my desk this afternoon, I won't be here. If you want, I can find an excuse to send Manon out.'

This really was cloak-and-dagger stuff.

'No, she's got a ton of work to do. I don't want you sending her out on my account. Are you off out for lunch?'

'Yes, I have a . . . uh, appointment,' she said, suddenly feeling the need to fiddle with her phone.

'Going to sample some of the local cuisine?' I asked.

'Oh God, no,' she spluttered. 'Greasy, watery merde, a mix of English and Dutch, the two worst cuisines in the world. I never eat it unless we get force-fed at some public dinner. Give them good ingredients and les Belges will fry them, and then boil them. It's like their language – it can turn pleasant things into a horror story. I'm sure they call a parfumerie a stinkeshop in Flemish. The other day I was in a street called Go Fart. I mean, how can you have an international parliament here?'

'Where do you think it should be, then?'

'Paris, of course.'

Which was a surprise.

'I thought we were campaigning to get everyone working happily together in Brussels?' I reminded her. Again, she was thrown for a second.

'Of course, Paul,' she finally said. 'I don't want to change world history. I just want it to work better.'

I didn't know what that meant, and I didn't get the chance to find out, because she jammed her phone into her bag, made sure all her office furniture was locked down and left. A bit early for lunch, but maybe she couldn't wait to get nibbling at her Norseman.

With the wicked witch out of the way, Manon popped in to say 'Bonjour'.

I replied the same.

'Tout va bien?' she asked.

'Yes, great,' I said. 'Elodie has said I can work at a real desk. Promotion.'

'Congratulations.'

It was beginning to feel like awkward office banter, and Manon was the first to mention the elephant in the room. Not that there was space for that size of animal in Elodie's cramped quarters. A piglet, perhaps.

'Is there a problem between us again?' she asked. 'I told you I was sorry I got you wrong. I don't think you're one of the extremists any more. But do you have a problem with me?'

So the boot was on the other foot. The high-heeled shoe, anyway. And a very shapely foot it was. But that, I reminded myself, was not the point.

'Sorry,' I said. 'It's just embarrassing for me that I can't discuss what I'm doing for Elodie. I asked her, but she said no. I don't understand why not, because it's nothing suspicious, but voilà. Sorry.'

I genuinely was sorry, too. I was sure Manon would be a great help. She was bound to be as horrified as I was at all the bollocks being broadcast by the tabloids. And she had more experience of Brussels than I did. She would be able to advise me on how to proceed.

And, of course, it would be fun going out for a drink to discuss our joint project, maybe dinner, too . . .

But that was not possible.

'OK,' she said. 'I believe you now, it's nothing suspect.'

'Exactly, and it was just a bit' – I looked for the right French word, and came up with a weak one – 'sad that you thought I was suspect.'

'I'm sorry. But now we know we're both on the same side, don't we?'

'I hope so,' I said, and saw a flash of irritation cross her face. 'I mean, yes. I think so. Yes, of course. Yes.'

'Well, you certainly sound very sure.'

She laughed and retreated back into her office, shutting the door behind her.

Bloody hell, I thought. It's so difficult talking to a beautiful woman. That's why they all get great service in shops and restaurants. No one wants to make them frown, and risk giving them premature wrinkles.

As soon as Manon had gone, I opened up Peter's file and picked out some peaches for Elodie.

There were outright false rumours about darts being banned from pubs, village fêtes having to get home-made jams tested for E. coli before they could be sold, and fish shops being forced to use Latin names for the species they fried. Then some brilliantly perverse misinterpretations of EU laws, like the story that pub barmaids would have to stop flashing their cleavage – this was an over-interpretation of a rule about protecting employees from developing skin cancer. And a familiar-sounding one about giving oysters rest breaks – an absurd application of the laws governing livestock transport. All beautifully crafted, but ultimately harmful, bullshit.

The difficulty was going to be choosing the top twenty.

Anyway after a fun, albeit frightening, few hours of this, I packed up and left the office. Manon was on the phone, apparently with some mayor who was insisting that every square millimetre of his constituency was occupied, and I gave her my best sympathetic smile. She replied with a friendly-looking wave.

Back at the apartment, there was still no sign of Jake, though there was a new tenant, and an unwelcome one.

A cat was in the kitchen – a ginger monster that rubbed itself against my leg when I went in there, presumably to apologise for having crapped in the corner.

I wondered how the hell it had got in. Through a half-open window, I guessed. Or maybe there was a concierge who'd come nosing in and let the cat slip through.

I bunged up my nose with toilet paper and scooped the poop into a plastic bag with a wooden spoon, which I binned along with the bag. Then I went out to hunt for the owner.

The door on the next floor up was answered by a teenage boy who looked half-asleep, as all teenage boys do. Especially if they've been smoking weed, which this one had, to judge by the acrid pong seeping out on to the landing.

'Vous avez un chat?' I asked.

He looked at me dumbly.

'Vos parents sont ici?' I asked, though I guessed they couldn't be. Unless it was a family of potheads, which I doubted, because of the swanky logo on his polo shirt and the brand of his glasses. He was classic posh French. *Papa* or *Maman*, or both, would be cogs in the Brussels machine. That was presumably how they'd got an apartment in this building.

'Il y a un chat chez moi.' I pointed through the floor. 'Il est à vous?'

'Non,' he said. This seemed to be the full extent of his vocabulary, so I left him to smoke the rest of his brain away.

The door on the top floor was smaller and not Art Nouveau. An attic conversion, I supposed. I rang the bell, and was surprised to see a familiar face.

'Cédric,' I said. 'Paul,' I added, because he seemed even more stoned than the kid downstairs. Maybe the smoke was seeping through the ceiling. Or it could just have been that Cédric's genes were slow to get into gear.

'Oui, Paul, salut,' he said.

'You live here?' I asked, stupidly. Though it was weird that Elodie hadn't told me.

'Oui.'

I explained my problem, and he sympathised (if an 'Oh, merde!' can be called sympathy), but told me he didn't have a cat, and had never seen one in the building. He asked me how I was settling in – I said *très bien*, apart from the *chat*. I asked him how he was enjoying working with Elodie – he said *très bien*, and didn't seem keen to elaborate when I broached the subject of the computers I'd bought. After that our conversation ground to a halt.

I told him to pop down for a drink sometime – when I'd bought some drinks, anyway – and went back to try and evict my new furry room-mate. It was probably not much less hygienic than Jake, and was not likely to write excruciating poetry, but I wanted it out.

What the hell do you do with a feline gatecrasher, though? You can't call the police. And the EU doesn't have a 'DG Up' (Unwanted Pets) – I checked.

In the end, I took a photo of the moggy, captioned it with my phone number and '*Found, Trouvé, Gevonden*' – surely everyone in the neighbourhood would understand those three languages – and went out to a little Middle Eastern phone-home shop to print up a couple of dozen posters.

Half an hour later I was proudly taping portraits of the cat to the front of my building, as well as every tree and lamp post in the immediate neighbourhood. It made a change from all those starry blue flags that usually decorate the streets of Brussels.

Being a natural pessimist, or fatalist anyway, I also stocked up on cat food, cat litter and the recipients to contain them. And, as extra insurance, I invested in a tin of spray guaranteed to stink so much that cats wouldn't pee on it. I thought I owed it to the antique sofa and armchairs to protect them from this new, unwanted house guest.

I gave myself twenty-four hours, and then I'd look for a pet refuge. Or maybe I'd go and have a quiet word with the bloke who'd sold me my hot dog the previous night. My digestion was still trying to work out which animals were in that. He might be in the market for a few kilos of ginger mog.

14

'God Save the Queen must be sung in all immigrant languages.'

Report in the British press, 2015

SOMEONE ONCE told me that gazpacho is named after the sound people make when they suddenly find out that their soup is cold.

I'm sure that must be true, because it's exactly what I said when I took a gulp of my spicy mango-and-breadfruit concoction. This wasn't something I'd cooked up from the tins remaining in my apartment's food cupboards. It was served to me by a charming Asian girl in a Laotian restaurant.

I was surprised, not least because when I first saw the 'Laotian' sign I instinctively assumed that, being in the capital of Europe, it said 'Latvian', and I couldn't understand why I'd walked into a bamboo-walled jungle of plants, jangly muzak and photos of water buffalo. Global warming hadn't got that bad, surely?

It didn't occur to me that a small, non-European country like Laos might have inspired restaurants in Brussels. Croatian, Estonian, Basque, Catalan, Swabian – those I could understand. These were all communities represented here in the capital of the EU. Chinese, Indian, Japanese, Vietnamese, Lebanese, Turkish, too – the usuals. Nepalese, Brazilian and African as well, but Laos seemed too obscure.

Oh no, Danny the oyster guy explained to me – he was the one who'd issued the dinner invitation – there's so much disposable income in the city that it has to keep titillating people with new, exciting food. Bog-standard French or Italian is much too boring. These sophisticates want gastronomic adventure. They might spend all day sitting at a desk, but they want to send their taste buds trekking across the Andes, through the swamps of Borneo or even up into deepest Scotland.

Danny was also the guy who recommended the spicy mango-and-breadfruit soup, or whatever the Laotian word for gazpacho is.

We were part of a rowdy group that was hogging half the restaurant. The owners had set up a long table to accommodate ten of us, all off-duty badge people. Danny was there with his girlfriend, though 'girlfriend' seemed to be a loose term, judging by his admiration for Jake's seduction skills. She was a Spanish-looking woman called Maria, or maybe Isabella or Sofia – honestly, these days I couldn't remember anyone's name if they weren't wearing a badge.

There were a couple of other Brits, as well as an Italian guy with stereotypically curly black hair, an impeccably trimmed beard and a loud voice; some Germanic types, both male and female, and Eastern Europeans who were arguing in a mixture of their own languages and Russian. They were all so effortlessly multilingual that it made me wonder why my brain doesn't get bored with all the free time I give it.

An older couple came into the restaurant and looked startled to see us speaking in tongues and waving our arms about, like people do when they see a giant flock of starlings massing above their home town – as if to say: These creatures live *here*? The wrinklies wisely went elsewhere for their peaceful dinner à deux. From what I'd seen so far, once Brussels badge people got drinking and talking, they rarely shut up until they passed out.

The trouble with a dinner table, rather than a bar crowd, is that you're stuck with your neighbours, and I'd sat down between Danny and Cédric. Yes, I'd invited my upstairs neighbour along, too. It seemed the diplomatic thing to do. At first, though, he was so tight-lipped that I wished he'd stayed at home. He just sat there eating and drinking – mostly drinking – and apparently making a huge effort to follow the conversation. It didn't look as though international-speak was his forte.

This left Danny and the Italian guy opposite me to batter my eardrums with their opinions.

The Italian was saying that his country didn't need to take any more African or Middle Eastern refugees, because Italy was already dedicating half its navy's resources to saving boat people from drowning in the Mediterranean. Britain, Scandinavia and the Baltic nations should take the lion's share, he said, because they were furthest from the Mediterranean and Aegean coasts. And Brits would vote 'no' to Europe in the referendum, he predicted and, even if they didn't, 'We must expel them from the EU because they do nothing but ask for special membership conditions.'

I thought: Special conditions? Isn't that what the Italians got, when they were bailed out so that they wouldn't go bankrupt and have to leave the euro? But I didn't want to start a European war at the dinner table.

Danny, however, had no such scruples, and said, 'At least we don't come crawling with the begging bowl every five years, like you southern Europeans. We're paying for your bloody navy, anyway.'

The Italian shrugged this off and moved on to his thesis that the only reason the Belgians wanted Britain to stay in the EU was so that house prices in Brussels wouldn't fall when all the British MEPs left town.

He explained that this was a joke, aimed at Danny and me, about the way all Brits are obsessed with the value of their house. I told him I wasn't, because I didn't own one, and he looked at me as if I'd just admitted not possessing my own socks.

'His family owns villages. They own wines,' Danny said, waving his soup spoon at Luigi or Giovanni, or whatever his name was. The Italian recoiled, protecting his shirt, which was as white as a Californian's teeth. For the moment, at least.

'Why come to Brussels?' I asked him. 'Your place in Italy sounds great.'

'Lobbyist,' Danny answered for him. 'You fuck with Italian wine, he'll fuck with you.'

'Yes, you try to make English Prosecco, we break your legs,' the Italian said, smiling dangerously.

'You try to serve me *any* kind of Prosecco when I ask for champagne and I'll break *your* legs,' I told him.

The Italian guy looked for a second as if he was going to cross himself to ward off bad English magic, then he laughed.

'I will send you a dozen bottles that will change your mind, you Franco-Englishman.'

It sounded like a great offer, but before I could give him the address, he turned away and got into conversation with a Germanic girl on his left.

This gave Danny the opportunity to broadcast to the whole of central Brussels that his MEP had had a long meeting with some French people that day.

'A bit of funny business going on between France and the UK,' he trumpeted. 'You think it's got something to do with the referendum?'

'Who were the French people?' I asked, in a soft voice that I hoped would be contagious.

'My guy didn't say. He mentioned your minority-language project, though, and asked me to find out how it was being financed. Do you know?'

'French government, I think,' I said.

'Nah. Highly unlikely. France hasn't even signed the charter on minority languages. They're dead against giving any kind of autonomy to their regions. Scared the Corsicans will campaign for independence and reclaim Napoleon's body. Can't be that.'

'Money straight from Europe, then?' I suggested.

'Maybe. Perhaps there's a regional project. Has your thing got a project name? Like Linguapick or Babelbird, or something? These European projects usually get given daft names like that.'

'Not that I know of,' I told him.

'Mystery, then.' He shrugged. 'Which reminds me – did you find out why your boss bought those laptops of ours?'

'No. She's given one to me to use. Works OK.'

'But why didn't she just buy new ones?'

'No idea,' I confessed.

'You're not exactly well informed, are you, Paul?' He clapped me on the back, sending a spoonful of cold orange soup flying out of my spoon and across the table towards the Italian's white shirt. Fortunately, he didn't notice his faint new orange polka-dot pattern.

'What about your French mate here? You know anything, mon ami? About anything at all?'

171

Danny bellowed at Cédric, and leant across to nudge him when he got no response. Cédric had been hitting the wine in silence and wasn't at his most attentive. Finally, though, he removed his nose from his wine glass.

'Bonswa, Seddrick,' Danny yelled in his worst French accent. 'Vous savez ce que la France fait avec les Anglais?' This caught the attention of half the table, and several people gazed at Cédric to see what he would say.

'Bien sûr,' he grinned, and emptied his glass. Into his mouth, but only just.

'Well, are you going to tell us, or what?' Danny hollered, in English.

'Bien sûr que non,' Cédric replied and reached for a refill.

People laughed and returned to their conversations.

'See what I mean,' Danny murmured in my ear. 'Secretive bastards. Once you start working with the French, you enter a world of murk. Your conscience gets to be like a goat's cheese. You feel mould growing on it, and the core grows harder by the day. You know, Paul, you're starting to smell a bit goaty already.'

He sniffed my cheek and somehow I managed to stay diplomatic and not punch him on his twitching nose.

We'd just received our main courses – mine was duck, decorated with sprigs of a lemony herb that smelled a bit like the cat deodorant I'd bought for the flat – when a couple of new dining companions arrived.

'Hey, man, I received your texto!'

It was Jake, looking very pleased with himself, his arm around the shoulders of a squat woman with pale skin and short black hair. Older than him, too. Not his usual sort at all. He introduced her as Rini, and said she was part Russian, part Finnish and part Inuit.

'We won't tardy long, because we're going to have sex,' Jake announced, instantly stopping every other conversation at our table. At this Rini smiled broadly. 'Her husband returns tomorrow from voyage, so we must profit of the night. But, Paul, I just wanted to come and say: Excuse me for the intrusion, you know.'

'You're not intruding at all, Jake. You're never there. No need to apologise.'

'No, no. I'll explicate later. We must go now. Rini wants sex.'

And they were off, waving farewell to their audience.

'Genius,' Danny said, a bit too loudly. I saw his girlfriend glare at him from the end of the table.

The rest of the evening went off smoothly, with gossip about MEPs' bad habits, some unfair cracks about our hosts the Belgians, a short enquiry as to who had stained someone's expensive Italian shirt, and a few jibes at the French, to which Cédric finally responded by standing up and giving a tuneless rendition of the Marseillaise, made even worse than it normally is by his attempts to translate the words into English.

'Let us go, children of ze nation! The day of glory is arrived! Between us is ze tyranny! Ze, uh, ze thing which I don't know what it is called is high,' he wailed, until I pulled him back into his seat and apologised to the waitress for the noise.

The gathering broke up pretty early – no one wanted a headache at work tomorrow. Though the number of empty bottles on the table suggested that some people would be needing high doses of caffeine in the morning.

When the bill came, the Italian made a feeble crack about persuading the Germans to pay for us all, but Danny killed the joke by telling him to 'Get your wallet out, you rich fucker.' Not for the first time, the Italian winced at our British vulgarity.

It was only when I left the restaurant that I realised the full extent of my lunacy in inviting Cédric along. He was so pissed that he could hardly stand up, and I had to march him along the street, trying to swing his long legs forward one after the other, to keep up a rhythm.

'Do you 'ear, in our country, ze ferocious soldiers who are mooing?' he sang. This was more of the Marseillaise, presumably. 'To your arms, citizens! Form your – how do you call zem?'

Luckily it was early enough, and there was enough traffic about, to save us from getting yelled at or arrested. I kept him bouncing along, helped by the fact that he was light and not yet totally legless.

As we got closer to the house, Cédric seemed to forget patriotism and become more maudlin.

'Tu es un chic type,' he kept saying, meaning that I was a good guy. Though it was scary at first because I thought he was saying something about 'sick' and was about to vomit on me.

When we got into the entrance hall and I began hauling him upstairs, he repeated this a few times and then started gibbering something about '*tomates*' – tomatoes.

Oh no, I thought, here comes his dinner.

But as he repeated it, I worked out what he was saying. It wasn't *tomates* at all.

'Dommage. C'est dommage. C'est vraiment dommage.'

'What's a shame?' I asked him.

'Tu es un chic type. C'est dommage,' was all he answered, before hiccuping and lapsing into silence.

I heaved and shoved him as far as the top floor, fished his keys out of his pocket and managed to drag him as far as his sofa, where I carefully laid him out in the even-if-I-puke-my-guts-up-in-my-sleep-I-will-live-to-clean-up-the-mess position.

'C'est dommage,' he mumbled as I left him.

I wondered what he meant.

Until, that is, I opened the door of my own apartment and was assaulted by the pong of cat.

That's what's a shame, I thought. Home alone yet again, to be greeted by no one but a bloody cat. I'm turning into a cat lady. I'm a spinster.

15

'No alcohol sales during the week, says Brussels.'

Report in the British press, 2005

NEXT MORNING I decided to go into work on the underground. Apart from anything else, I felt incapable of the twenty-minute walk to work.

A certain queasiness was on the menu, both as a starter and a main course. Why do continental Europeans always think that Asian food goes with wine? Asian food goes with beer, everyone knows that. Wine and spices are a lethal combination – your stomach thinks it's Christmas, a time of mulled wine and general excess, and goes into self-protective mode.

And if the first thing you see when you go into the kitchen next morning is a cat-litter tray full of what looks like shit-flavoured muesli, who wouldn't be queasy?

That wasn't the only reason I was feeling a little delicate, though. During the night Danny's remarks about Anglo-French goings-on had fermented in my mind. I needed to ask Elodie some questions, and was a bit worried about the answers – or lack of answers – I might get.

To make things worse, there hadn't been any calls from cat owners yet. I promised myself that if nothing happened during the day, I'd get on to a pet refuge that evening. Sorry, mog, I told it, as it munched happily on the vile-stinking meat that came out of the can with a cute furry name printed on it, but I'm much too young to turn into a cat lady.

You have to laugh at the Brussels Métro. Fondly, of course. The city is trying so hard to be an international capital that it claims to have six underground lines. But in the city centre, they all seem to follow the same tracks. Some lines don't have any stations to themselves at all, they just duplicate what other lines are doing. Most of the network consists of a circle around the centre, with a little criss-cross in the middle. The rest is just a few short excursions out to the suburbs.

But I got on a little train that had its face painted orange, and that was fast, clean and airy, so I had no complaints at all, except that the colour reminded me of the damn cat.

I was just wondering how you transported an unwilling feline with claws and teeth to a pet refuge – drugs, perhaps? alcohol? for me, not the cat – when I recognised one of the passengers. It was Cédric. Funny, I hadn't seen him walking to the station.

He was standing up, slumped against a metal pole, looking like a partially deflated balloon. Not that he was ever that puffed-up to start with. I was tempted to go and hang on to him, so that he wouldn't get dislodged by the speed of the train and start floating down the carriage.

'Bonjour,' I said, but he seemed to be asleep. Maybe he was on his second trip around the Métro's inner circle.

'Cédric,' I said, louder, and he groaned in reply.

'Too much wine,' he said, needlessly. His eyes struggled to focus on my face. 'Yesterday evening, I didn't say any stupidities, did I?' he asked. He used the word '*bêtises*', which I've usually heard used applied to trivial things.

'Beaucoup,' I said, and he shot me a look of panic. 'But you didn't *say* them, you sang them. It was very interesting to hear what the French national anthem actually means. I enjoyed the part about watering the fields with impure blood.'

I realised as soon as I'd said it that this wasn't the right morning to talk about gigantic outdoor pools of blood, and both of us took a moment to let the repulsive image fade away.

'You said something was *dommage*,' I told him. 'What was that?'

He looked embarrassed for a second.

'Nothing, nothing. I can't remember. I was drunk.'

Despite his dopey look, this was, I reminded myself, a guy who worked in a locked office that no one else was meant to venture into. I decided to push him while he was looking vulnerable.

'Did you find anything on those English computers?' I asked.

'You know they're English?' Again, that look of panic.

'Oh yes, we Anglais tell each other everything.'

This falsehood had Cédric wilting on his metal pole like a climbing plant with altitude sickness.

'Everything?' he said.

'Yes. And what are you going to do with the other two computers?'

'Oh, Elodie is keeping them in her office,' he said, looking brighter. Somehow I'd let him off the hook. I wondered how. 'If you want to take one, I'm sure it's OK. Is yours working well?'

'Oui, très bien.'

'Très bien,' he echoed. Now he was almost frisky, like the current occupant of my kitchen.

Feeling slightly queasy again, I decided to get off and walk. We were just arriving at a station called Arts-Loi or, as the Flemish call it, Kunst-Wet. What a charming language.

I walked along Loi (aka Wet), possibly the world's most boring avenue. It was lined with lots of slightly different but equally boring new office buildings that were just too short to be exciting. The avenue looked artificial, like a computer-generated street in an urban driving game, and I half-expected cartoon people with blank expressions to emerge and start loping along the pavement, firing guns or getting knocked over by a careering urban racer.

As it was, I was part of a caravan of office workers trooping along the avenue. Walkers were peeling off at regular intervals to disappear inside one of the glass boxes. Only a few of us carried on to the end, towards the Parliament building.

The trance-like monotony of the march had given me time to decide how I was going to address my worries with Elodie – who was the cause of most of them.

'You're going to think I'm a bit slow,' I told Elodie when I walked into her office.

'Going to?' She laughed without looking up. As usual, she was busy massaging her phone.

'Thanks, Elodie. Is that your French motivation technique?'

This had been her dad's strategy. Jean-Marie's theory of management was to show his underlings who's boss. His message was: Shut up, obey and maybe I'll allow you training days so that you can learn to act like a superior bastard, too. The attitude of his employees was therefore: Fuck you, monsieur.

Not exactly motivational, and yet Elodie had obviously decided to follow in the family tradition.

'Sorry, Paul,' she said. She looked up. 'You know I only say things like that because we're old friends.'

I knew that wasn't the only reason – she was also a power-mad control freak – but I smiled as if I forgave her.

'I need you to explain some things to me again,' I said.

'Yes?' she said, suspiciously.

'Yes. First up, I have a question about how the language project is useful in this plan to keep the UK in the EU.'

I could only speak that freely because I'd seen that Manon's office was empty, and Cédric's door was closed. Either he was already shut away, or he'd passed out again in the Métro and was now on his third or fourth underground circuit of the city centre.

'OK.' Elodie placed her hands on her desk in the praying position. I think it's a pose they teach politicians. It's meant to suggest sincerity. Except now, of course, it just suggests training in politicians' bullshit. 'I thought it was clear,' she said. 'If we can suggest to the uncivilised regions of the UK that there is a possibility of EU funding for their local languages, then they will vote to stay in. Right?'

'I know all that. But from what I hear, France doesn't want to support local languages in France itself. It's scared that the regions will lobby for independence. So isn't it a bit of a contradiction for Paris to be commissioning a report into the importance of local languages elsewhere in Europe?'

'Oh, bloody fuck, Paul.' Her hands weren't praying any more, and her English expletives were all over the place, proving that I'd struck a nerve. 'France is not the country that is having a referendum, so what does that matter? And when have the French ever been worried about contradictions?'

181

Which was a good point.

'And don't forget,' she added, 'supporting Breton at a purely local level might win me votes. So who cares about the rest of France?'

Another good point. I decided to let that one rest.

'OK, second question,' I said. 'Can you explain again how it's going to help if I give you a report on all the absurd rumours that the British press have started about the EU? Even DG Communication says it's never been able to stifle them. What are you going to be able to achieve in so short a time?'

'Ah.' Elodie was praying again. Perhaps, I thought, for a credible answer. 'In this, Paul, you have to trust me. To trust France.' She held her hands pleadingly towards me, which was going a bit far, even for a drama queen. 'I know it is difficult for an Englishman to trust France, but after all, in history, we French have been the victims more than you English. Who burnt Jeanne d'Arc? Who called their train station Waterloo? Who sent Napoleon to St Helens?'

I agreed that exiling him in the north of England would have been extreme victimisation, but didn't say anything as Elodie put on an expression of wounded pride.

'Is it not wonderful, Paul? Even after everything you have done against us, we want to help you. It is, as you call it, pay-back time.'

Well, I thought, payback time was something slightly different. That would mean revenge – France burning Helen Mirren or exiling Prince Charles to Tahiti.

'Anyway, Paul, you have to admit that I don't really need you, do I? If I wanted to find out all this information for myself, I could. N'est-ce pas?'

This, I had to admit, was true. Nothing I was doing required much expertise at all. Even Cédric could have done most of it. Which was a slightly disturbing thought.

'I just hoped you would be interested in playing your role in our Anglo-French friendship, Paul. In the Entente Cordiale.'

It had always struck me as strange that this '*entente*' was only cordial – a word meaning coldly polite – rather than friendly. An '*entente sympathique*' would have been much more neighbourly.

'Of course,' I said.

'And, as you yourself have said, you will be richly paid for all this. I am actually helping you out, so what's the problem?'

'Ah yes, I was wondering about that, too – where is the money coming from? Paris? Brittany? Brussels?'

She looked as though it would only take one more question to make her pop like an over-inflated balloon.

'Paul, why do you insist on biting the hand in the horse's bush, or whatever you call it in English? The funding is origine Union européenne garantie.' She made it sound like the ingredients of a sausage. 'And I have chosen to spend it on you, OK?'

I had to admit I was OK with that.

All in all, I felt as though Elodie had rather skilfully avoided giving me any answers, but that it would have been impolite – and frankly dangerous – to keep on questioning her. Time, perhaps, to let things drop. For a while, at least.

'I should be able to finish a first draft of the list of twenty rumours today,' I told her.

'Perfect,' Elodie said, smiling warmly now. 'Because tomorrow you're coming to Strasbourg with me.'

'Oh, for the languages project?'

'No.'

'For the rumours thing?'

'No.'

'What for then?'

'Shitty damn, Paul! Because I'm paying you and I need an assistant with me.' We were back in who's-boss-around-here mode. 'Normally I would take Manon, but I've asked her to work on something else. There is some rumour that the British want to declare oysters an endangered species. They're trying to sabotage Brittany's entire economy. Have you heard anything about this?'

'No.' Ban their sale, yes. Make them all perfectly round, yes. Declare them endangered, no.

I could just picture Manon's face when Elodie gave her this new task. She must have been bloody furious.

'In fact you can be useful in Strasbourg, Paul. Your Anglais friends always get drunk together in the hotel bar. It takes a hell of a lot of Alsace beer for them to blow all their expenses, and they always try to blow the lot. You can mix with them and try to find out something about these oysters. All it means for you is getting less drunk than the others. I hope I can count on you to do that?'

'No problem,' I promised her. 'Ever since I moved to France I've lost the ability to keep up with English drinkers. Even Englishwomen can outdrink me now. My liver has turned French. It rots slowly day by day, instead of losing big chunks every weekend. So no danger of me getting hopelessly drunk. None at all.'

'It's OK, Paul, you can stop now. You've convinced me.' She stood up. 'You can work in Manon's office. She will be out all morning. I have to go. If I don't see you again today, rendez-vous here tomorrow at nine with your toothbrush and a spare pair of underwear. I assume you have one, Paul?'

'Maybe you could bring two pairs of yours? One for me?'

She shot me a look: this is an MEP you're talking to. I riposted with a smile: this is your old mate Paul, whom you taught to make vinaigrette in a Paris kitchen while you were totally naked.

Finally, she cracked a smile.

'Like I said, Paul, we've come a long way.'

There was nothing on her desk, so she checked all her locks, grabbed her handbag and left.

All I could do was finish up the jobs I'd been given and see how the game played out. If the worst came to the worst and Elodie and her French masters were up to some funny business, I would hand over all my info about computer-buying and contradictory French attitudes to minority languages to Peter at DG Communication and persuade him to use it somehow. And I'd put the corrected rumours out there myself. That's what social media are for, aren't they? Letting the small guy talk to the whole planet. And right now I was feeling particularly miniature.

So, alone in the office, I had a quick look through what I'd written about minority languages and decided it hung together well. It was, as Elodie's dad used to say about marketing presentations, 'like a skirt should be: long enough to cover the essentials, but short enough to hold the attention'.

No doubt about it, I thought: the Scots, the Welsh, the Cornish, Corsicans, Basques and Bretons alike would love what I was saying. If they got their *kaoc'h* together, the EU money could come raining down.

Then I got stuck into the surreal world of British rumour-mongering. There were some classics still on the loose.

The story, for example, that the EU wanted to close British off-licences on weekdays. Several papers had reported this as fact. The truth, though, was that the Commission had merely asked member countries for suggestions to reduce binge-drinking in the week, which was affecting Europewide productivity because of working days lost. No matter: 'Brussels says no booze before Friday night' was the kind of headline that Brits were being fed.

Another cracker was that there were '600,000 migrants on benefits in the UK'. The guys over at DG Communication had studied this one in detail, but never dared release their results. In fact, they said, there were less than 200,000 asylum seekers in the UK. It was true that there were 60,000-odd EU citizens on jobseeker's allowance, but most of them had earned the right to benefits by paying British taxes first. The most startling thing for me was that, of the three million or so EU nationals resident in the UK, about 300,000 of them were French, lots of them earning shitloads of money and paying equally large shovelfuls of tax. Perhaps that was why the DG hadn't published the truth – one-third of a million Frenchies established in Blighty? That's more than Napoleon ever dreamt of. Best to leave that scare story out of my report, too, I decided.

One I did keep, though, was the brilliant misinterpretation of France's favourite bit of world politics, the Common Agricultural Policy. According to certain sections of the British press, the CAP was being used to subsidise bullfighting. Yes, British taxpayers' money was being gifted to Spaniards who wanted to stab cattle.

This story was pure art for art's sake. The journalists had taken the notion that all Spanish farmers are eligible for EU subsidies, and combined it with the fact that some of them produce bulls for bullfighting. Ergo, the EU finances the torturing of animals.

For once, the term 'bullshit' was wholly appropriate. The reporters might just as well have said that the EU subsidises other rural pursuits, like getting pissed and falling off your tractor into a pile of dung. Which I suppose, strictly speaking, it does. On second thoughts, I decided it might be best to leave that one off the list, too.

In any case, there were plenty more headlines to choose from: British chocolate to be called 'vegelate'; EU to ban church bells; Brussels to impose 50 per cent Mother Christmases in department stores. All pure fantasy.

I took a quick coffee break to decide whether I should be laughing or crying. Choosing a soothing blue seat in the Mickey Mouse bar, I got out my phone and opened up a message that Jake had sent me an hour or so earlier. I usually need to be seated and full of caffeine to read anything he's written.

'This evening chez toi I will explicate. Towards 19 p.m.? At later,' he'd written, freely translating his thoughts from French into gobbledygook.

I still didn't understand what there was to explicate, or even explain. He had always shagged anything that had more legs than an oyster and less than a hippo – and no feathers, of course. So what if he'd gone and shacked up with a married woman while her husband was away? Nothing very new there. Until he'd got married himself, it was more or less his whole lifestyle. And I really didn't mind if he wasn't at my place every morning to mix up one of his fetid breakfasts. So why this sudden need to explain?

Refreshed, but none the wiser, I went back to my office, to be confronted by a skirt.

It was made of what I took to be cotton, with perhaps a touch of linen in the weave. Grey-blue, almost turquoise, like the Mediterranean on a day with muted sunlight. A very pleasant vista.

The buttocks inside the skirt were fidgeting slightly, as if they were in a hurry to do something.

'Manon?' I said, and the buttocks flinched.

She turned around.

'I was just . . .' she said, but we both knew what she'd just been doing. Nosing into my computer. The screen was lit up. She'd been consulting something.

That was impossible, I thought.

'You know my password?'

'I watched you over your shoulder,' she admitted.

'Cacarella,' I said.

There was a heavy silence in the room.

Then suddenly, everything changed. I could hardly breathe, because someone else's mouth was stuck to my own. A firm mouth, yet enticingly soft. Meanwhile my breathing was also being restricted by the female chest that had been slammed against my ribcage. There, too, everything was firm, yet enticingly soft. I closed my eyes and relished the sensations.

But then reason kicked in. Which is one of the reasons I hate reason.

No, I told myself. Kissing Manon was what I'd been want-ing to do pretty well since the first time I saw her. But now it was wrong. Wasn't it? Yes. I'd just caught her doing something highly suspicious. Hadn't I? The memory was fading as her lips did their work, but I still seemed to recall something about a computer, a password, snooping on me.

I grabbed her arms and pushed her away. Softly but firmly. She was staring at me, wide-eyed.

'Sorry, I panicked,' she said.

'Do you do that every time you panic?' I asked. 'We must go and do some dangerous sports together. But why . . . ?' I pointed to my computer.

'I know, it was wrong. Sorry to spy on you, Paul, but let me show you something.' She leant over the computer and clicked into a window. 'Look at that,' she told me.

I felt she was trying to distract me from the central issue here, which was: why the hell was she prying into my computer? But I did as she asked, for the next minute or so.

'Mokordo!' I finally said. 'Shit' in Basque.

As she clicked around, I realised that I was looking at some kind of software that generated a copy of everything on the computer. Not just a history, but a sort of film of my screen, showing emails sent and then deleted, songs listened to, photos viewed (a bit embarrassing that one, thanks to Jake). Everything. And all of it was being permanently streamed to some outside source.

'Do you know who installed that software?' Manon asked.

'You?' I hazarded.

She almost hit me.

'Look at the date it started working,' she said.

I did. It had recorded the first-ever things I'd done on the screen, including a cringeworthy Skype with my mum along the lines of 'I was wondering when you'd do me the honour of calling. I hope you're not eating microwaved rubbish, you look as though you've got a hangover.'

This meant that the spyware had been installed as soon as Elodie had got the computers, presumably by her cousin-in-law Cédric. Which had to explain why he kept saying 'Tu es un chic type' and 'C'est dommage'. I was a nice bloke and he felt guilty spying on me.

'So Cédric is a kind of Q?' I said, meaning the guy in James Bond who provides all the gadgets.

Manon looked confused, and I quickly realised why. In French, 'Q' is pronounced the same way as '*cul*', meaning arse.

'A scientist spy,' I explained.

'No, Paul, he installed it, but any fool can download this software from the internet. The real question is: why is Elodie doing this to you?'

'Yes.' The betrayal hit home. 'She was right when she said we'd come a long way since Paris. She doesn't trust me at all any more. She's become totally paranoid. But then, if you were looking into my computer, you don't trust me, either. None of you Français trust me. Merde!'

Having to explain my feelings in French seemed to over-simplify things. Maybe that's why the French are so good at romance, I thought. Everything becomes so straightforward when they say it. Or maybe it was just because I was crap at talking about feelings.

'I'm sorry, Paul,' Manon said, interrupting my thoughts. She seemed to be slumping slightly beneath her share of the national guilt. 'I was obliged to investigate. It's become very urgent. There are rumours all over Brussels about Elodie doing something suspicious with the British.'

'And you still think *I* was doing something suspicious? After all our conversations?'

'Sorry, but you're British and you're working with Elodie, so I had to check.'

'Why is it your job to check?'

'I'm here representing the French government. Look.' She went to fetch her bag and pulled out a small ID card. It sported a tricolour band across one corner, a not-very-flattering photo of Manon and a job title that ended in 'Ministère des Affaires étrangères'. She was a Foreign Ministry bod. So *she* was the spy, not Cédric. She was a sort of double-O-*sept*. Sexy, I thought. Unless of course she had a licence to kill *les Anglais*.

'But Elodie told me that you were imposed here. By her father,' I said.

'Yes, but not for the reasons she believes. He was told that if he didn't get me this job, he would be investigated for tax fraud.'

'Ah.' That would hit him right where it hurt.

'We're afraid that Elodie's party is engaging in extra-governmental activities concerning the referendum,' Manon said.

'She told me that she is engaging in *governmental* activities,' I replied, borrowing Manon's convenient phrase. 'She wants to keep Britain in the EU.'

'Well, that's certainly what the French government wants. We don't want anyone to leave, not even Greece. We want to share all our problems. But we're not sure that's what Elodie is working for.'

'But I know what Elodie is doing,' I said. 'It's me that's doing it.'

'Are you sure?'

'You mean: am I sure I'm doing what I'm doing?'

'I mean: are you sure you're doing what you think you're doing?'

Now I was lost.

The only solution was to tell her everything I'd been doing. *Merde* to Elodie's pleas for secrecy.

'Everything I've done sounded logical to me,' I concluded. 'Well, as logical as Elodie can ever be. Supporting British minority languages, contradicting false rumours in British newspapers – all that could help keep Britain in the EU. The only really bizarre thing is why she spent so much money on those computers. I still don't understand that. I can't believe the Anglais would leave sensitive information on a computer.

And Elodie could spy on me using a new one. She didn't need three old ones.'

Manon gave it some thought.

'I don't know what it all means,' she finally said. 'But time is short – we have to find out the whole truth.'

'Why don't you just bug Elodie's phone?'

'I can't do that to an MEP. It would be illegal. The most important thing is that I don't want Elodie to know that we suspect. Maybe you can get a look at her phone or her laptop while you're in Strasbourg?'

'You know I'm going to Strasbourg?' I don't know why I was surprised.

'Yes. She told me. Meanwhile she wants to me look into this merde about oysters. Can you imagine it? Thousands of refugees to house, and she wants me to save a few oysters.'

I had to laugh, which annoyed her until I told her what Danny was really up to. Then she laughed, too.

'Ah, sacrés Anglais,' she said, smiling. And yet again I'm ashamed to say that my stereotypical male brain veered back to the subject of kissing.

Why do we do that, as soon as a woman smiles at us? Jake told me that it's all down to the Neanderthal bit of our DNA. Our distant ancestors got a smile and a shag every time they came back to the cave with a hunk of mammoth, he said. Arg, grin, bang. So when a woman smiles, prehistoric urges kick in. Which is why, if I were a woman, I'd think twice before smiling at Jake.

'Schiss!' I said, which is 'shit' in Alsatian. 'Cédric will know that we found his thing.' I couldn't remember the French for software. 'He sees everything I do on my computer. So he saw what you just showed me.'

'Merde!' Manon agreed in French.

But then I had a brainwave that, for once, had nothing to do with kissing.

I wrote Cédric an email saying that he *had* in fact said a few *bêtises* while he was drunk – he had told me what he'd done to my computer. I added that I was rather insulted that he and Elodie didn't trust their English colleague, but that I hoped that he had seen enough to know that I was just doing my job. I signed off in French: 'Bonne journée.'

Manon laughed as she read it.

'Yes, that will make sure he says nothing to Elodie,' she said, almost admiringly. 'He knows she would kill him for revealing their secret. And it reads as though you suspect nothing more than a bit of paranoia on Elodie's part.'

I hit Send.

'Brilliant,' Manon said.

Then, given that I'd been brilliant in the eyes of the French government, I decided that maybe it was time for us to resume our earlier Franco-British *entente très sympathique*. We were both leaning over my computer, our heads close together as we looked at the screen. So it didn't take much effort on the part of my neck muscles to turn towards her and tilt my mouth in the direction of her own slightly parted lips.

'Non, Pol,' she said, backing away.

'But you . . .'

'Yes, I'm sorry. I told you, I panicked.'

'Can't you panic again un petit peu?'

'No. It wouldn't be reasonable.'

Bloody reason again.

'In reality you've got a boyfriend, is that it?' I asked.

'No.'

'Was it true about the Greek? Have you really ruptured?' This is how the French describe a break-up. I know because I've had to deal with the word many times before.

'Yes, that was true. But I promised myself I wouldn't get involved with anyone else for at least three months.'

'When was that?' I had to stop myself consulting my diary.

'Five weeks ago.'

'Merda.' 'Shit' in Catalan.

'And, anyway, we have serious work to do here. Let's not confuse things.'

I didn't see what could be confusing about kissing Manon. Pretty straightforward, as far as I could tell. No grey areas at all.

But I recognised one of those times when a guy is being called upon to man-up, be mature, respect a woman's wishes, and all that reasonable stuff.

'You're right,' I said. 'We absolutely have to stay focused on the big issue.' Luckily I knew the French for this. It was a phrase Elodie's father used to use all the time. Normally before going off to shag someone from the marketing department.

'Merci, Pol,' Manon said, stroking my forearm in a strictly non-erotic way. 'I have to go and see my bosses about all this. I'll be in touch.'

It wasn't until a few minutes after she'd left that I thought: 'Bosses?'

So there was a whole gang of French Foreign Ministry spies in Brussels in the lead-up to the British referendum? That was one of the scariest things I'd heard since I got here.

That evening I was still in something of a daze when I got back to my Art Nouveau palace.

For the second time that day I was faced with a backside. But this one was hairy and ginger. The damn cat.

I got out my phone and began hunting for the Belgian RSPCA. They have a royal family, too, I thought, so they must have an RSPCA. All royals love animals.

I heard the front door opening.

'Bonsoir, man!' It was Jake.

'Close the door quickly,' I told him as I left the kitchen. 'There's a—'

Somehow I didn't manage to get the last word out. It was meant to be 'cat', of course, but on seeing Jake it had suddenly become redundant. Not that Jake himself looked like one, even if he had been known to adopt predatory feline behaviour towards a group of women. And to show a certain allergy towards bath water.

No, the reason I didn't need to say 'cat' was that there was already one in the equation, as it were. Jake was carrying a large tabby under his arm. It wasn't altogether pleased to be in the equation with us, and its hissing finally persuaded Jake to let it jump to the floor and race towards my antique sofa.

'Shit,' was all I could say, and regretted it immediately, in case the cat was bilingual and mistook it for a command. 'Did you find that in the hall?' I asked him. 'The bloody things seem to be attracted to the place. It's Lourdes for cats.'

But then reason kicked in, as it so often had already that day. I'd been an idiot. It was obvious that the cats had to belong to the previous tenants. The displaced animals must be returning to what they still thought of as their home. All I had to do was find out who'd been living here before me, and where they'd moved to, and my problem would be solved.

'No, I haven't found the cat. I've imprinted it,' Jake said.

'Printed it?' Surely even the newest 3D machines weren't capable of reproducing mammals?

'No. How do you say – emprunter?'

'Borrowed?'

'Yes, borrowed. This one from Rini's friend, the first one from Rini. You still have it?'

I must have been looking confused, because he tried to explain.

'Rini, you know? The girl in the restaurant?'

I told him that it was the word 'borrowed' that had got me stumped, not the name of his adulterous friend.

'Yes, sorry, I must explicate,' he said. 'You and moi, we are going to be millionaires. No, not millionaires, silly-onaires. Come.'

I grabbed the unwilling tabby, earning myself a neat bloody scratch on the thumb, and followed him into the kitchen, even more dazed than when I'd arrived at the flat.

Jake pointed to the sack of coffee beans he'd bought, which was still lying slumped in a corner, much as I felt like doing myself.

'The other day Rini has took me to this incroyable café,' he said. 'She loves a special coffee, the most dear in the world. Like, ten thousand euros per kilo, man. It is from Indonésie, coffee from grains that are shit by an animal. A civet. *Like a cat.*'

He said the last three words as though he was Einstein pronouncing his famous $E = mc^2$ for the first time.

It took a few seconds for the full craziness of Jake's idea to seep through, like coffee through a thick filter paper. When it finally seeped, it was pungent enough to make me utter a stifled growl, the kind a civet probably makes when it excretes an extra-large coffee bean.

'You mean you were going to feed this coffee to the cats, then sift through their shit and sell the result?'

'That's a ten-kilo bag, man. A hundred thousand euros.' Again Jake was back in Einstein mode. Economy equals the *merde* of a cat squared. Or rather, multiplied by ten thousand.

'Well, for a start, Jake, I've read about that stuff, and I'm pretty sure the civets eat the fresh, undried coffee berries, not the roasted beans. And secondly, I don't want my kitchen turned into a cat-shit factory.'

'I could get some fresh coffee berries,' Jake offered.

'You can buy a containerload of fresh civets and sift through a ton of fresh shit a day, if you want. But not in my kitchen. Now can you please take both of these animals back to their owners? Along with the tins of smelly food I bought. And take the cat litter, too. I won't be needing it. I'm planning to carry on using the toilet.'

I gave the bag of cat litter a frustrated kick, scattering gravel to the far corners of the kitchen floor.

For the next half a minute Jake stared mutely at his bag of coffee beans, and watched the two cats squabbling about whose kitchen this was. He seemed to be picturing his new-found fortune slipping away.

'Wow, Paul, man,' he finally said. 'It looks like you had a really stressed day. Let's leave these cats in the cuisine for now. I am taking you out for a fucking drink.'

Which is exactly why he's my best friend.

16

'EU will force cows to wear nappies.'

Report in the British press, 2014

I WAS on time at the Parliament building next morning, feeling considerably less stressed about life than I had the previous day. Say what you like about Jake (and lots of people do, often to his face), but he's great at taking your mind off a crisis.

He'd dragged me out to a bar the previous evening – a completely ordinary Belgian café, the kind of place the badge people don't even notice – and cheered me up. Not with an excess of alcohol, fortunately, but by being his usual self.

'Merde to Elodie, man,' he lectured me. 'She was always une ambitieuse, and politique has made her a total freak du power. What she does is not against you, it's not personnel, it's just what les politiciens do to everyone.'

201

It was great to hear him cut through all my problems in so few words. And for once he'd even restrained himself from writing a poem.

We also got on to the subject of Manon, of course. Here, Jake was encouraging but maddening at the same time.

'She was kissing you? Spontanément . . . uh, spontan-uitously . . . Like, without you asking? Oh, you were so close, man!'

'Close to what?'

'Close to sex. You just had to use the French technique, Paul. All you had to say was this: Oh, ma chérie, you tell me that you must not fuck a man for three months, but . . .'

I tried to explain that using words like 'fuck' to Manon might not have got me close to anything except a cold shoulder, but I quickly gave up and let him go on.

'You say you will not have sex for three months, OK, bla-bla-bla,' he said, getting back into character. 'Well, ma chérie, three days ago I promised myself that I will drink no more alcohol. But for you I would break that promise. If I had a bottle of champagne now, I would drink a glass with you and it would be my best drink ever . . . She would say, Oh, Paul, tu es si romantique – and, boom, you fuck her on the office table.'

'Thanks, very romantic, Jake.'

But in a twisted way he was right – I'd probably given up too quickly. Maybe Manon secretly wanted me to crush her in an irresistible embrace, instead of saying in my hopeless English way, 'Oh, OK then, sorry to have bothered you.'

I just didn't have the French guys' technique. I'm sure they learn it in the cradle. It's like skiing – I seem to fall flat on my face every time, while others glide effortlessly down the pistes. Jake was right. If I'd come on with the French charm, Manon might well have been bouncing on my iron-framed bed before she'd even realised what was happening.

'Zut,' I said. That's 'shit' in Norman French, which is of course where the expression 'Zut alors' comes from. I was learning some fascinating stuff from all this minority-language work.

'I don't know how you get away with it, Jake,' I told him.

'I know what I want, man, that's all, and I tell them. And I don't chase after difficult women, like you do.'

This was true. His demands were simple – he just wanted his women human.

'Of course I have ideals,' he went on. ' My ideal woman is a nymphomaniac with an apartment in the Marais. Though I wouldn't say no to Bastille or the Quartier Latin.'

'What about your shagging-a-woman-of-every-nationality thing? I thought your ideal woman was any citizen of a country that's not in your red book.'

'That's just sport. A man must keep himself amused until the ideal woman arrives. You know what the song says: if you can't be with the one you love, fuck the one you're with.'

'I'm not sure that's exactly what the song says, Jake.'

'It's what it *means*, man. I bet you think "White Christmas" *isn't* about drugs?'

Somehow, listening to Jake's bullshit always makes me feel slightly better about myself.

I ended the night by texting to Manon – completely sober – that I was glad we were on the same side. And she replied immediately: 'Moi aussi.'

Things weren't so bad after all.

I thought about this as I waited for Elodie the next morning, loitering outside her office door. Everything was locked up, including the connecting door to her office from Manon's cubbyhole. The mouse wouldn't be playing while the cat was out of town, it seemed.

Elodie turned up almost on time.

'Good, Paul, you look presentable,' she said as she granted me the honour of brushing her cheeks with mine and saying 'Mwa'. She seemed her usual self – brusque and mildly insulting, but not looking at all suspicious. Cédric obviously hadn't told her anything.

She double-checked that the doors were locked and said, 'Allons-y, we're late.'

'Don't you need anything else?' I asked. She was carrying nothing more than a slightly oversized handbag.

'No, I keep a change of clothes at my office in Strasbourg.'

'And is there no trunk to carry? I thought MEPs always went to Strasbourg with those huge boxes full of documents and stuff.'

'Oh no, Paul, no need. This is a special session. You're lucky. Nothing to carry for me.'

With this, she shooed me towards the lifts, explaining that there was a railway station beneath the building exclusively for the use of MEPs and a very few select staff.

'We get a direct private train to Strasbourg,' she said, as we emerged into a corridor crowded with suits and brief-cases. 'But usually the assistants and translators go on the regular service, which takes five hours and goes through Luxembourg. Can you imagine?' She grimaced.

I've never been to Luxembourg myself, but I gathered from her expression that it probably didn't possess many designer shops or manicurists.

There was, as Elodie had promised, a real railway sta-tion below ground level, complete with a gently purring French high-speed train. It was, of course, much cleaner than a real station, and had no homeless people sleeping on its scrubbed floor. It felt almost eerie to see the elite population of eurocrats hurrying towards the lone train as if this were a nuclear bunker with an emergency exit on rails.

Elodie elbowed us politely through the crowd towards her carriage, apologising as she nudged her colleagues aside, and very soon we were sitting opposite one another in plush red-velvet seats, watching as several hundred MEPs of all shapes and sizes ambled on to the train, which wasn't going to leave without them. Only a Parisian like Elodie felt the need to shove her way on board first.

'At least this is going to be a twenty-four-hour trip,' she said. 'Usually we have to go to Strasbourg for three whole days. God!'

'So it's an extra journey?' I asked.

'Yes, specially for you. You Anglais, I mean. We are going to debate the referendum.'

'Couldn't you do that in Brussels? This must be costing a fortune.'

'Exactly. You know what your English press calls this – the gravy train. A stupid name – gravy is that tasteless, greasy sauce, isn't it? Well, I guess that does describe some of your English MEPs. But anyway, each trip to Strasbourg costs about twenty million euros. And this one is all your fault.'

'I'm sure the British MEPs didn't demand to go to Strasbourg. They're all against excessive spending.'

'No, but your government has been demanding special membership conditions, and we are going to debate them.'

'In Strasbourg.'

'Take it as a compliment, Paul, a sign of your country's importance. It is probably France who wanted to hold the debate there. We need to make some more money out of the MEPs, before Britain leaves and the EU goes bankrupt.'

I couldn't tell whether she was joking or not. In any case, our conversation was interrupted by the arrival of two Frenchmen, who said a perfunctory 'Bonjour' and then proceeded to argue about who was going to sit beside Elodie, facing the engine.

'Do you mind if I sit here?' one of them asked.

'Well, no, but I also prefer to face forward,' the other replied.

'If you prefer to sit here, go ahead.'

'No, no, you sit here.'

'No, you go ahead.'

Elodie watched them politely annoying each other, but never offered to let either of them take her seat facing the engine. One of them finally said, 'Oh, si vous insistez' and, with a big show of reluctance, sank gratefully into the seat he'd wanted all along.

I recognised him as Cholpin, the ex-Minister, the guy who'd been hugging non-consenting women in the Plux pub. He was looking as grey, well worn and pleased with himself as ever.

The other guy was a similar model, a few years younger, with a classier suit and stiff hair that looked like a wig, but was obviously real because I could see from his roots that it was dyed. He could have been quite a handsome bloke, I thought, if it weren't for his disgruntled expression, which seemed to be permanently wrinkled into place.

Elodie gave them a brilliant smile – the youngster acknowledging her elders.

'Vous êtes . . . ah?' Cholpin stared at her face, then down towards her shirt, which as usual had one button too many undone. Perhaps that was how he remembered women.

'Elodie Martin,' she said.

'Martin, oui,' he said. 'The daughter of the MP, n'est-ce pas? We have met before.'

'Oui, bien sûr, Monsieur le Ministre,' Elodie confirmed, not at all shaken by the overt ogling of her cleavage. 'This is Dominique Cholpin,' she informed me, 'ex-Minister of Agriculture.'

'And of Commerce, Education and, briefly, Defence,' he added, waving his hands as if modesty almost – but not quite – prevented him from mentioning them.

'And this is Yves Remord, MEP for Picardie, in the north of France.'

'Bonjour,' I said to them both. 'Pol Wess. Assistant de Madame Martin.'

Remord twisted his neck to look at me, the underling sitting beside him.

'You've brought an assistant?' He scowled even more than usual, as if everyone except him had been given a biscuit. 'I thought we didn't need assistants for this trip?'

'Yes, but I am in the fortunate, yet ambiguous and ultimately fascinating, position of having an assistant of British origin,' Elodie said, adopting the inflated wordiness that the French use when they're trying to impress people.

'Un Anglais?' Both of the men chorused the word and stared at me, Cholpin with amusement, Remord with a display of angry-looking wrinkles.

I remembered where I'd heard his name before. Yes, Yves Remord – Ed Fürst had mentioned him. This was the man who refused to let meetings go ahead if there was no French translator present.

'You know why les Anglais don't respect the EU?' Remord demanded and, as the French so often do when they want to rant at you, quickly answered his own question. 'Because you don't understand it. How could you? You weren't there at its creation. You begged us to join in the 1960s because you thought you could get something out of it, and when you realised that it came with responsibilities as well as advantages, you started to complain. Well, in my opinion you can go away and play the poodle of your American masters – see how well they treat you. Go on, foot the camp!'

He used the classic French insult '*foutre le camp*', and I really felt as though he would prefer me to get off the train and out of his life, along with all my compatriots.

'Of course, that isn't official French policy,' Elodie said, with an uncharacteristically meek giggle.

Cholpin had been sitting there smiling, not giving a damn, but took the opportunity to stroke Elodie's hand encouragingly.

'Très juste,' he said, moving his hand up her arm.

'Well, it should be our policy,' Remord retorted. 'Let the Anglais go, kick them out – they don't give a damn about Europe. They never have.'

Now I am of the generation whose grandparents spent the early 1940s either tramping across Europe getting shot at by men in jackboots or having bombs dropped on their rooftops. And I'm afraid that, after a couple of years of living in Paris, I had reached my threshold of listening to middle-aged French people telling me that France had been liberated in 1944 by General de Gaulle and a few men in French berets. Not everyone in Paris was so forgetful of Britain's role in the Liberation, of course, but when I met one of the forgetters, I found it hard not to rise to the bait.

'I think my great-uncle cared about Europe,' I said. 'He was on the beach on D-Day. And my grandfather was in the RAF. He cared about Europe so much that he used to fly here every night.'

There was a silence, filled only by Elodie giving a little squeak of alarm at my misbehaviour.

Then Remord groaned loudly as if I'd made a bad pun.

'And you won't let us forget it, will you?' he said. 'Petit con, go and fetch us some coffees.'

Petit con is one of the French language's worst insults. Not only are you a twat, you're an undersized one.

'Boubourse,' I replied.

'What?'

'Oh, is that the wrong word?' I asked. 'Sorry, I am studying the different French patois. You come from the north, and I was trying to translate what you said into your local language. Boubourse. Con.'

Remord growled. Elodie squeaked again. Cholpin laughed and stroked her shoulder.

'I think Yves is right,' Cholpin said. 'Our English friend should leave our little European Union. He can sit in the bar for the journey.'

The growling Remord got out of his seat to let me pass and I made my exit, wishing them, 'Bonne continuation.' It's one of those polite-impolite expressions that the French are so good at. It means: 'I hope you enjoy whatever you're going to get up to in the future, not that I really give a toss.' No wonder French used to be the international language of diplomacy.

It wasn't unpleasant sitting in the buffet carriage, dunking a Speculoos in a surprisingly decent coffee while watching MEPs of all nationalities progress quickly from hot drinks to beers to little snifters on the side. Their main subject of conversation seemed to be the fact that these trains left Brussels at an inconvenient time, so that the VIP passengers had the choice of eating railway sandwiches or starving until a very late lunch in Strasbourg – and a rushed one at that, because meetings usually started in the early afternoon. It was, they agreed, a scandal. Only the subsidised booze seemed to console them.

I was expecting Elodie to come and bawl me out, or at the very least force me to play the waiter and bring coffees, so when I saw her striding into the bar, I braced myself.

'God, Paul!' she puffed. 'I envy you.'

'You're not mad?'

'Of course I'm furious with you for annoying my colleagues, but I envy you for getting away from those two. I'm stuck between a python and a scorpion. One trying to squeeze me to death, the other spitting poison. I need an antidote. Get me three coffees and a schnapps, will you?' She thrust some euros at me. 'And don't forget the receipt.'

Once she had ingested her caffeine-and-alcohol boost, she told me how she'd had to sit for an hour listening to Remord ranting on about British ingratitude towards Europe, and moaning at her for employing one of the 'perfidious Albions'. At last, though, he'd fallen asleep and she'd managed to escape.

'If he sees you again, Paul, he will explode. You've got to stay out of sight. So when we get to Strasbourg, go straight to the press office at the Parliament and stay there. You'll be able to listen to the debates without bumping into Remord or any of his friends. And I want you to – how do you say in English? – keep your ears peeled? I want to know if any of your compatriots start talking about France. Not just about oysters. As we all know, most English politicians think they're still fighting the battle of Waterloo.' She pronounced it 'Wah-t-air-lo'.

'OK.'

Tipping up her tiny schnapps bottle to suck out the last few drops, Elodie announced that she was going back to her seat.

Before she picked up the two coffees for her travelling companions, she fastened the top button of her blouse, presumably to reduce the target area.

'The things I do for France,' she said.

'Ah, but *are* you doing them for France?' I asked, once she was safely out of earshot.

To my eyes, the EU Parliament building in Strasbourg looked very much like a cross between a shopping mall and a nuclear-power station.

It was a huge, curved glass construction embracing a taller, circular tower, the whole thing set beside a river basin that probably provided the water necessary for cooling the hot air pumped out by the debating chamber.

Inside I found the same chic but corporate decor as in Brussels, with modernistic furniture that probably cost a fortune, but could have been bought from Ikea. The press centre was an impressive lounge equipped with comfortable chairs and TV screens, as well as desks where journalists from all over Europe could plug in and listen to the debates in whatever language they wanted.

It was easy to blend in with the crowd of laptop-toting journos and grab myself a console. I put on the headphones and switched to English, but heard nothing. The debate hadn't started yet. I kind of expected a pre-match commentary giving the opposing team line-ups, but the silent TV screen showed the MEPs still shuffling into the immense circular amphitheatre, chatting in the aisles, shaking hands or hugging, dividing up into national and political groupings.

They got going about half an hour later, and I felt an almost instant need to fall asleep. It wasn't so much a cut-and-thrust debate as a face-off between zombies. The opening speech went on for at least twenty minutes, with some grey-suited, grey-haired, grey-voiced guy churning out soporific clichés about the need for political unity. They were made even more sleep-inducing by the drone of the interpreter.

After that, various MEPs were given the chance to contribute to the slumberousness, most of them repeating their countries' view that the UK would do better to stay in the EU, but that the EU would survive perfectly well without it. I pitied the poor interpreter, who was trying to find different ways of expressing exactly the same ideas.

The only person to liven things up was the leader of the Eunuchs, a guy called Nick Rummage, who was simultaneously one of the most popular and most despised men in England. When his turn came, he waited for the cameras to get him in focus, gave one of his famously lopsided grins and said simply: 'Au revoir, les amis.' In a surprisingly good French accent, I thought.

The English interpreter in my headphones hesitated for a moment and then translated: 'Not tonight, Josephine.'

This got a loud laugh from the press room and, looking round, I could see that the journalists had already decided which speech would be making their headline.

It was an astute move from Rummage, you had to give him that. A great soundbite, a fuck-off message that would go down well with his supporters back home, but was polite and French enough to earn the grudging respect of his MEP colleagues. A classic case of a politician managing to have his cake and eat it (and then charge it to expenses).

When the following speaker, a southern European, began his drone, I wasn't the only one who decided he'd heard enough for the time being. Several of us took off our head-phones. I stretched my legs and made for the water cooler.

'Classic Rummage, eh?'

A friendly-looking guy was grinning at me as he waited for me to fill my plastic cup. He was dressed pretty smartly. No tie, but everything ironed. One of the serious media outlets, I guessed. Southern English, to judge by his accent.

'Du roomage classique,' I agreed.

'He's the only one who makes these Strasbourg safaris worthwhile, don't you think? I come down here every bloody month for the plenary sessions, feeling guilty about my share of the millions it costs a year, and he's the only thing that makes me think it's money well spent. Even when he's not pissed.'

'Fond of a drink, is he?' I asked.

'Oh, yeah. Haven't you seen him in action?'

'No,' I confessed.

'Really? Who are you with? Don't recall seeing you here before. Or in Brussels, for that matter.' He glanced down at my badge. 'A parliamentary assistant,' he read. 'For a French MEP. But you're a Brit?'

Now he was examining me with frank curiosity.

'Just a temporary job,' I said.

'Pretty key time for a Brit to be working with the enemy,' he replied, obviously mulling over the significance of all this as he spoke. 'What are the French saying about the referendum?'

'Oh, just that it's too close to call.'

But for once my brush-off didn't brush anyone off.

'I don't mean the result, I mean the fact that we're having the referendum at all. Do you think they want us in or out?'

Oh, *kaoc'h*, was what I was thinking. *Merda, schiss* and *mokordo*. I didn't want to be quoted by a British journalist.

'From what I'm hearing, they want us out,' he said. 'It'll give them a chance to rule the roost with Germany, get rid of the whingeing Brits. Is that what you're hearing?'

What I was hearing was Elodie's screech when she read next day that Paul West, British assistant to the French MEP for Brittany West, had given this guy an interview.

'Not at all,' I finally said. 'They want a strong, united Europe. The French are team players, you know. That's why they're so annoyingly good at football.'

'Bullshit! All they ever care about is France. French agriculture, French nuclear power, French companies. That's the only reason we have to trek to Strasbourg every month. It's so that they can siphon off a few zillion euros into their hotels. Even the bloody train that brings us here is French. The only team they play for is Team Frog.'

Maybe he wasn't with one of the more serious newspapers after all, I decided.

'Well, that's not what I'm hearing at all,' I told him. 'I think you've been listening to too many of Rummage's clichés.'

'Some clichés are clichés because they're so bloody true,' he said. 'You want to do an interview about all this? I don't have to quote your name.'

Even if he kept his promise, I thought, Elodie was bound to identify this French MEP's British assistant giving an 'anonymous' interview, so I declined the invitation and decided it was time to go for a tactical toilet break.

I had just located the sign showing a white silhouette with splayed legs, when somebody grabbed my elbow and shoved me into the Gents.

Some journalists just won't take no for an answer, I thought, but turned to see a surprising face. A woman's face.

'Pol,' it whispered, and propelled me into the nearest cubicle.

'C'est les hommes,' I replied, though I guessed that Manon must have known which toilet she was in. I just didn't know why she was in it, with me as a partner, spectator or whatever I was going to be. For a second or two, every possible fantasy flitted through my brain, and I fought hard to swat each of them away.

'Listen,' she said in whispered French, 'we haven't got much time.' A couple of the fantasies came back to life. 'Your phone is being bugged,' she added, which killed them off again.

'Are you sure?'

'Yes.' She was looking grave. She did it very well, in my opinion. 'I enquired about getting Elodie bugged – totally impossible – and discovered that your number is being listened to.'

'Merde!'

'Exactly.'

'Why?'

'I don't know. I'm trying to find out what's going on. I still don't understand what Elodie is trying to do.'

'Who's listening to me?'

'I'm not exactly sure who requested the bug, but I know Elodie has access to all the information. So I have brought you this.' She fished into a small handbag and pulled out a phone. 'Use it for any sensitive conversations from now on. My number is in it.' She blushed ever so slightly. 'We don't want Elodie to suspect anything. She must think everything is normal. So use your old phone to call her, and for any call that you don't mind being recorded.'

'OK.'

There was a brief, breathy silence.

'It's all very exciting, isn't it?' Manon said. 'I didn't expect to be playing the real spy like this.'

'Me neither. It's much more fun than learning Breton grammar.'

She laughed, and we looked at each other for a few moments, suddenly aware that we were crammed almost chest-to-chest in a toilet cubicle.

'Did you come here just to give me this?' I asked.

'Yes. I tried to catch you before you left this morning, but I was too late. So I sat for five hours in the regular train. Via Luxembourg. I suppose I could have waited until you got back to Brussels, but . . .' She blushed again.

'Wow, I'm honoured. Are you staying in Strasbourg for the evening?'

'No, I must get out of here before anyone sees me. There's a train back to Brussels in half an hour.'

'Oh, quel dommage,' I said. What a shame. Maybe, I thought, I could persuade her to stay. How would a Frenchman do it? Ah yes, Jake had explained it to me.

'You know, Manon,' I began, 'three days ago, I decided that I didn't want to drink any more alcohol. But now, if you gave me some champagne . . .'

'Champagne, in a toilet?' Manon laughed.

'Well, not necessarily here and now, but . . .'

'Anyway, it's a bit premature to celebrate,' she said. 'And I must go.'

Oh, bollocks, I thought, I'm just not cut out to be a Frenchman.

'Don't let anyone see your new phone, will you?' she said.

'No. I'll call you when you're on the train, to test it.'

'Yes. I have five more hours to kill. It will be nice to have someone to talk to.'

She listened to make sure no one else was in the toilets, then slipped out of the cubicle. But before doing so, she gave me a French *bise* on each cheek and a smile so warm it seemed to make my insides simmer.

17

'English Channel to be renamed "Anglo-French Pond".'

Report in the British press, 2010

ELODIE HADN'T booked me into the same hotel as all the MEPs. They were in the city's grandest 'palace', five stars-worth of luxury paid for by the taxpayers, whereas I was relegated to a mere four-star business establishment.

But I didn't mind at all – in hotels, the bland corporate chic actually makes sense. All I really want from a hotel is a decent bed, a big TV, drinkable coffee, wi-fi and a power shower. If I'm on my own, that is. At other times, a jacuzzi can come in handy.

When Manon and I left the toilet cubicle, I went back to the hotel, cracked open an Alsace beer from the minibar and lay back on my bed for a muse.

Elodie was beyond paranoid, I decided. First my computer, now the phone. I'd have to check my apartment, to make sure Cédric hadn't installed cameras there. Lucky I hadn't got up to anything embarrassing in the bath. Or in bed, for that matter.

But the question remained: What could Elodie possibly gain from watching and hearing me do everything that she had ordered me to do in the first place? Was she scared I'd reveal her plans to someone? If so, to whom? And why?

It was just a shame I couldn't confront her. It would be nice to see her try to bullshit her way out of it.

There was one thing I could do, though. A bit of fun that might cause her a satisfying smidgen of pain.

I got out my bugged phone.

'Hi, Jake?'

'Bonjour, Paul, how are you going?'

'Fine. I'm in Strasbourg, at my hotel. But I need a bit of advice.'

'Yeah?'

'Yes, I'm feeling lonely and I thought you could give me some chat-up lines.'

Let's hope Elodie gets to listen to this, I thought.

'Hey, man, formidable news. So you're forgetting that Man-killer girl? Good idea, she'll break your boules. You want chat-up lines. Yeah, yeah. D'accord.'

I could hear Jake's instincts clicking into gear.

'Voilà a great one,' he said, almost instantly. His instincts didn't hang around. 'You meet a femme, and straight away you ask her, "Do you know the origin of the word sex?" OK? You with me so far?'

'Yes, Jake.' And somehow wishing I wasn't.

'OK. She is surprised by your question, right?'

'Slightly, I'd say.'

'Yeah. So you tell her, "It comes from the German 'sechs', meaning six. It is the number of seconds before I kiss you." Works every time. Well, almost. Are you writing this down?'

Jake had misinterpreted my stunned silence.

'Yes, got it, thanks. Any more?' I prayed that Cédric would also hear this and be idiotic enough to try it out.

'Oh, yeah, full of them, man. Next one: you go to a femme in a bar. It must be a bar where it is interdit to smoke. You say to her: "You can't smoke in here." She is surprised, she says, "I'm not smoking." You say, "Yes, you are, you're *smoking*."'

Again, he didn't understand why I was silent.

'You see, Paul, it means she's hot, n'est-ce pas? Smoking-hot. They adore it. But be careful, it doesn't function in French. If you tell them, "Tu fumes", I think it kind of means they stink. Not a good technique.'

'I can imagine.'

'Yeah, you need encore?'

'No, no. Thanks, that should be enough. I'll try them out tonight. What have you been up to?'

'Oh, I had a bit of merde with the flicks.' He meant *flics*, police.

'Nothing serious, I hope?'

'No, I was walking in the park, I needed to go pipi, so I went behind this tree, and this flick came and started on-girling me.' This, I knew, was a verb he'd invented, based on the French *engueuler*, to yell at someone. 'I was like: come on, monsieur de la police, can't you just imagine I'm a statue? Like, your little Manneken? But he got furious and I had to pay like eighty euros. Frankly, these Belge flicks, man, it says "politie" on their jackets, but they're not polite. They tell me I'm a "klootzak" and my "moeder" is a "hoer".'

I had to laugh at the amoral and yet somehow innocent anarchy that was Jake's life.

'See you tomorrow, Jake, and thanks for the advice.'

'You're welcome, klootzak.'

Next, to put my new, unbugged phone to use. I texted Danny the oyster man, telling him I was in Strasbourg, that I'd lost my phone and he'd need to use this number from now on. I didn't want Elodie overhearing any more of my conversations with him.

Danny called me back immediately on the new number.

'Hi, Paul. Phone nicked, eh? By a femme fatale? That's the kind of thing that goes on during these Strasbourg jaunts.'

'No, I . . . uh, dropped it in the loo, if you really want to know.'

'Ah, browsing while browning, not a good idea. Anyway, what have you got planned for tonight?'

'A drink, maybe. Preferably with the Brits. I don't really want to bump into the French guys.'

I told him about my little disagreement with Yves Remord.

'Oh, don't worry, he'll probably be out in some fancy restaurant with a tart. That's what all the French MEPs do. The
guys, anyway. The women go straight to the bedroom with
their regular lovers. But if you want to see some good Brit
action, go and have a look at Rummage. He'll be in his hotel
bar, and pissed as an anal trombone. Great entertainment.'

I thanked Danny and promised to go along.

I'd saved the best till last. Time to call Manon. I lay back on
my firm corporate mattress, settled comfortably on a glacier
of pumped-up pillows and ran my finger over her name on
the screen of my new phone.

She picked up straight away and sounded pleased to get my
call. I guessed that it wasn't all down to my natural charm. In
the background I could hear the telltale signs of an intermin-
able rail journey – a wailing kid, a loud teenagers' conversation and the slow clickety-clack of a non-express train. But it
gave me a kick to think that she'd put up with all that just to
bring me the phone that was now enabling us to talk together.

We had what seemed to me like a long chat – more than
twenty minutes, which is a summit meeting by my standards – both of us reliving the thrill of knowing we were
outwitting phone-tappers, computer snoopers and general
international plotters. It was like in the films, when a man
and a woman are thrown together by the need to save the
world. Only us two knew what was going on, and it created a
real sense of closeness.

Well, only two of us if you excluded her government bosses, of course, who were probably remote-controlling her, but that's not the kind of thing you talk about when she's on a train and you're on a bed, and you can tell from her voice that she'd probably prefer to be where you are. I don't mean she wanted to be in the bedroom while I was on the train, of course. And I'm not sure she was saying she wanted us both to be in a bedroom, either. It simply felt as though both of us agreed it would have been nicer speaking face-to-face. A warm sensation that you don't get with every phone call.

Before we said goodbye and wished each other 'Bonne soirée', I took a risk and said it was a *dommage* that she hadn't been able to stay in Strasbourg.

She replied, 'In other circumstances', which was a put-down, but a gentle one. At least it wasn't 'In your dreams'.

Elodie called to ask me where I'd got to. The referendum debate was over, she said, and really hadn't been worth the millions it had cost us all.

'Parliament voted to issue a statement saying that we hope Britain will stay in the European Union, but we don't care if you leave,' she told me. 'So basically we've decided to announce that we don't have an opinion. A useful day's work, n'est-ce pas?'

I laughed with her, wondering how she could play this double-game with me – sharing jokes like an old friend, while spying on me as if I was her worst enemy.

'Now why don't you go out and interview a few drunk Englishmen,' she suggested. 'I'll expect a full report in the morning, OK?'

'And I can expect a full refund on my expenses?'

'Of course. As long as they're below the limit of a drunk English MEP.'

Which was fine by me. I wasn't even in that league.

And so, later that evening, after a quick *choucroûte* in one of central Strasbourg's narrow medieval streets, I strolled into the lobby of Elodie's fancy hotel, scanning the horizon for hostile French MEPs.

The lobby was impressive, to say the least. If all the money, perks and self-esteem weren't enough, that hotel would have convinced anyone to become an MEP. The French really know how to do luxury. Not British-style luxury, which usually involves paying some trendy designer to install uncomfortable chairs, lighting that makes everything look alternately blue and purple, and piped music recorded at an Ibizan beach party. This Strasbourg place was old-school chic, with a chandelier that had been updated to electricity but probably used to light up the same room with candles, and staff so discreet and well-dressed that they must have been trained while that candlelight was still the latest technology.

There were a few MEPs about, none of whom looked particularly French, and I crossed the lobby towards a wooden archway. The faint roar of after-dinner drinkers led me to the end of a carpeted passageway, where the hubbub got suddenly louder. It sounded very well oiled, an impression that was confirmed when I entered a panelled room full of men and women with drinks in their hands.

It was an older version of Plux, with more of a sit-down feel. Most of the MEPs were chatting loudly and merrily in padded armchairs, apparently unconcerned about the grave implications of the referendum they had just been discussing.

Practically the only people standing were in a small gang propping up the bar. They were creating as much noise as all the other drinkers put together. And the gang leader making the loudest racket was Nick Rummage.

An almost-empty glass of lager in his fist (not his first drink of the night, I suspected), he was playing the persona he depicted for the journalists, except that he was singing a song that would have had the British tabloids dashing into a headline meeting.

'Ne me quitte pas,' he was bawling, in a fair approximation of Jacques Brel's tune and accent. He crooned the chorus, then began singing one of the verses, something mawkish about how he'd be his lover's dog if only she agreed not to leave him. I could only assume that the hotel had promised to keep journalists out of the bar.

Sticking to the shadows, I got out my new phone and started to film. Or tried to. It was a bit of a cheapie, and kept taking photos of my feet as I fought to get the bloody thing started. Keep singing, Nick, I begged him silently. If he stopped now, I'd have to shout, 'Encore!' and beg for another verse.

Eventually I managed to begin filming my shoes, so I pointed the phone towards him and recorded a full chorus, in which he was joined by several of his colleagues, most of whom had very deep voices for Eunuchs. At the end of it all, they cheered, and the freely sweating Rummage, his shirt half-untucked, drained his glass.

'Remettez-moi ça!' he called to the barman, demanding a refill in very acceptable French. 'Pour tous mes amis.' A generous party leader, it seemed. With whose money, I wondered?

'You'll have to watch it, Nick,' one of his disciples said. 'You know drinks can only make up ten per cent of meal expenses.'

'I can't eat that much,' Nick replied. 'God, I love this job,' he slurred. 'If we vote to leave, I'm going to become a Froggie, get myself elected as a French MEP. Buy a house in the Dordogne, then campaign to kick out all the English immigrants. Go home, you fuckers, back to England! Make the Dordogne truly French again!'

This had all his followers howling with laughter, and attracted disapproving glares from the seated areas. The small group of rowdy Eunuchs was performing the minor miracle of uniting the whole European Parliament on one issue: the sooner these uncouth English slobs leave the EU, the better, the looks seemed to say.

It all made for a wonderful short film, and I made sure it was safely stocked in the memory of my new phone.

Now to get in even closer. Heading for the bar, I switched the phone over to record sound only.

I took a chance and went straight towards Rummage.

'Do I count as one of your amis?' I asked him.

'Depends,' he said, squinting at me as if trying to recall my face. 'Which way do you swing?'

I guessed this was a question about my attitude to the Brexit, rather than an invitation to his hotel room.

'Well, maybe I ought to vote to stay in, otherwise you'll lose the job you love so much.'

'Very sporting of you,' he slurred. 'Donnez une bière à ce monsieur,' he told the barman, and I ordered a half-litre, which the metric-loving French sportingly call *une pinte*. 'And will you lose your job too, if we leave?' Rummage asked me.

'No, I'm strictly temporary.'

'Temporary what?'

'Researcher.' I thought it best to be discreet.

'Oh yes, more research, that's what Europe needs right now,' he said, piling on the sarcasm. 'Research into what? How many migrants it takes to fill the Channel Tunnel? How many MEPs it takes to change a light bulb? Thanks to the EU, you can't change just one – you have to change the whole bloody lot, over to energy-saving bloody darkness.' It sounded as though he had clicked into campaign mode.

'No,' I said. 'Oysters.'

He burst out laughing.

'Donnez une autre bière à ce monsieur avec un grand whisky,' he ordered the barman, even though I hadn't got my first drink yet. 'Et la même chose pour moi.' He finished his own beer in one efficient draught. 'So you're the chap doing that?' he asked me, burping in my face. He'd obviously got me mixed up with one of his own team. 'Have you worked out how to get them banned yet? Best way I heard was that guff about transport. Drivers have to stop and give them rest breaks and fresh water. Excellent scheme!'

He clapped me on the shoulder.

'Yes,' I agreed. 'One question, though: Do you want all this to be public knowledge before the referendum?'

'Ooh, ah.' He seemed to be in pain. 'Finer points of strategy. I don't do much of that myself. Especially not when I'm pissed.'

All our drinks arrived at the same time – three beers and two whiskies. Following Rummage's lead, I took a long swig of lager, then downed the whisky.

'I bloody love oysters, don't you?' he said. He grabbed my shoulder and pressed his face close to mine so that the air I was breathing was about 50 per cent alcohol. 'My sex life wouldn't be the same without them. Not because of all that aphrodisiac' – it took him three attempts to pronounce the word – 'nonsense. No, it's because a woman looks so bloody sexy when she's slurping them down. Ohmygod.' He groaned beerily. 'Hey, Tim!' Rummage turned to one of the other men propping up, or being propped up by, the bar. 'Let's oyster some orders.'

Tim, a flushed forty-year-old with a five-day blond beard, was predictably confused.

'Oyder some orsters,' Rummage tried again. The booze had finally taken control of his tongue.

'You what?' Tim joined us, and closed one eye to examine me. 'You're not a journalist, are you?' He looked down at my phone-holding hand. He seemed a bit too sober for my liking.

'No, researcher.' I slurred the word as best I could.

'Researcher for whom?' Tim asked, confirming with his use of grammar that he wasn't too drunk to ask some embarrassing questions.

I lifted my glass inaccurately to my mouth. One half-inhaled mouthful later, I was bent double, coughing up beer. I put my glass on the bar and croaked, 'Excuse me, back in a sec' and staggered away, spluttering.

As soon as I had stumbled through the door into the lobby, I bolted for the exit – only to bump into Elodie. She was deep in conversation with her Danish dish. Probably deciding whose room had the best jacuzzi and how much champagne they'd need to fill it.

'Paul.' She excused herself to her chum and marched me a few paces away. As we walked, she bombarded me with questions: 'You're leaving already? The English are all in the bar, right? Did you talk to them? Did you hear anything useful?'

Instinctively I decided I didn't want to share any information with the woman who was listening in to practically every conversation I had, whether written or spoken. How, though, could I avoid the issue?

Luckily, my silent indecision helped me out.

'You're not drunk?' Elodie demanded.

'No way!' I burped.

She punched my arm.

'Didn't I tell you to stay sober?'

'Accident. No tea-making facilities in my room. Only a minibar. And then they were forcing me to drink beer . . .' I held up my hands in surrender to the onslaught of alcohol I had suffered.

'God, Paul, you're so English.'

'Yes. Come and celebrate with me. Bring your friend the scandalous Scandinavian.'

Predictably this got her so mad that she frogmarched me – and for once it was an accurate use of the word – to the door and launched me into the street.

'If you're not on the train tomorrow morning, you can walk back to Brussels,' she told me, as I waved goodnight and staggered towards the nearest street corner.

Result, I thought, as I breathed several sighs of relief.

I had a great excuse to call Manon again. She was going to love my film of Rummage's concert, and his opinions about oysters.

What's more, my minibar would have to be empty by morning, to back up my story to Elodie.

The party was about to get started.

18

'Great British banger to be outlawed by Brussels.'

Report in the British press, 2001 (and most years since)

I SPENT the whole Strasbourg-to-Brussels train journey
in the buffet car, feigning a hangover and hoping that my
large collection of minibar bottles and cans wouldn't leak
into my bag. The previous night I'd decided that sobriety was
the best bet, but my hotel bill was going to tell the opposite
story.

When we arrived back in Brussels, I told Elodie I needed
to go and lie down, and she seemed relieved to see me disap-
pearing back to my apartment.

Almost as soon as I was out of the Parliament building, I
put my new phone to use, setting up a late lunch with Manon.

She joined me in an anonymous Belgian café near Bruxelles-
Midi, where she recommended the cheap *moules-frites*.

I was on my best behaviour. When she said that it was rare to meet an Englishman who liked mussels, I didn't even smile. I could have done a lot worse than that, because, having been around Jake for so long, I knew that '*moule*' in French is a slang word for vagina. But Manon's comment provoked not even a whimper. Like I said, best behaviour.

Picking through our heaps of shellfish and (in my case, anyway) dunking our fries in the salty *marinière* sauce, we went over what we knew about Elodie's trickery – if, that is, there was trickery involved, beyond bugging my phone and computer. The referendum was now only three days away, and both Manon and I were sure that the Brexit was at the heart of the matter.

I argued that the subterfuge might just have been a sign of over-caution on Elodie's part, a fear that I was going to cock up her attempts to help the pro-Europe vote, either deliberately or through sheer incompetence. Not very flattering, but plausible.

Manon was convinced there was something more malevolent going on. Elodie, she said, was a born double-dealer, just like her father, and I had to concede that she was probably right. We needed to put Elodie to the test.

So we hatched a plan, or conceived it, anyway. 'Hatch' sounds as though it just pops out ready-formed. Ours was a plan that would involve careful timing, improvised play-acting and convincing bullshit. If we didn't get all these components right, then Elodie would be free to finish off whatever scheme she had been cooking up.

The first part of this plan involved Manon leaving the café at about 5 p.m. so that she could keep an appointment with Elodie. Everyday life had to continue exactly as normal, so Elodie wouldn't suspect that she too was being observed. She and Manon were due to go to some function chaired by the French ambassador and attended by all the French MEPs.

'Probably an early celebration of the Brexit,' Manon said. 'I'm joking,' she added, but she didn't look amused.

Next morning I called Manon from the doorway of one of the planet's most boring buildings, on the street the Flemish speakers call Wet. Appropriately, it was raining.

Manon took a few rings to pick up.

'Allo?' she finally answered.

'Bonjour, Manon, ça va? Do you want to join me for a cup of coffee before work?'

'Is that Paul?' Her voice was as chilly as a Frappuccino.

'Yes, of course.'

'Ah. Non merci. I am débordée today. Thanks to you, as it happens.'

'What do you mean?'

'I suppose you don't want to tell me anything more about this English plot to ban oysters?'

'I can't tell you any more.'

'I really don't care myself – I can live without oysters – but I've got to find out who's behind the idea and then suggest ways to stop it. Fast. The French ambassador has heard about it, and he is furious. He was yelling at Elodie yesterday evening, and she's been yelling at me.'

'Well, maybe I can help you un petit peu.'

'Un petit peu? No, don't bother. I have to go, I'm too busy to talk.'

'I'll ask my British contacts.'

'Just forget it. I have to go.'

The phone went dead.

I waited a couple of seconds, then turned to Manon. We gave each other a thumbs-up. She was standing in the next doorway. This call, made from my bugged phone, was part of the plan we'd conceived together the previous afternoon. We needed Elodie to think we were still on bad terms. I had to admit that Manon was frighteningly convincing.

'I'll get back on the Métro,' she said.

'I'll follow in ten minutes or so. Bonne chance.'

I moved in for a hug. We were partners in crime, after all. I'm sure partners in crime hug all the time. I placed my chin gently on Manon's shoulder, made sure my backside was sticking out, to avoid any inappropriate pressing, and held the position for five seconds, then let go. All good, clean stuff.

She trotted through the light rain to the Métro steps and looked back as soon as she got under cover. We exchanged a wave and a smile. Partners in crime, that's all, I told myself.

Elodie was at her desk, clicking away on a laptop. I wondered if she was waiting for me to start work, so that she could monitor everything I did onscreen while I was actually doing it.

'Bonjour, Paul. Comment vas-tu?' She was in a good mood.

'Bonjour, Elodie. Ça va.'

'How was your soirée?' she asked, somewhat maternally. 'Less drunk than in Strasbourg, I hope?'

'Yes, very quiet.' This she probably knew, thanks to a conversation I'd had the previous evening with Jake on my bugged phone. He had told me that he'd found himself what he called a 'Slovak-Polonaise', and offered to 'arrange' me with one of her friends. I'd said thanks for the offer, but my head was still sore after my encounter with the minibar in Strasbourg. I told him I was going to take it easy, with one of my discomfort-food hot dogs for company. And that was what I'd done, while Manon and Elodie were glugging champagne with the ambassador.

'I suppose I have to work in Manon's office?' I said. I looked towards Manon's closed door and grimaced, as if the forces of opposition were being beamed through the woodwork. 'She's pretty pissed off, because I haven't been able to tell her anything about the oysters,' I whispered. Scene one of today's play-acting.

Elodie nodded sympathetically.

'OK, but she must not be able to . . .' Elodie mimed being watched over her shoulder.

'I'll sit on the other side of the table, facing her. I've already told her I'm not allowed to discuss what I'm doing for you. She won't be insulted. I don't think she likes the Brits, anyway.'

'I can fully understand that, Paul.' Elodie gave a self-satisfied grin. 'I don't know why I'm trying so hard to keep you in the EU, I really don't.'

That makes two of us, I thought.

I went into the other office and made a big show of apologising to Manon for moving the furniture around. She told me to go ahead – 'Pas de problème.' She was a better actress than I was, very minimal. Taking her lead, I stopped talking and made room for my chair between the table and the wall, then opened up my laptop and got down to work. I took the risk of shooting Manon a complicit glance, but she was concentrating on her screen. A perfect performance.

I settled down to reading my list of British tabloid stories, setting them out as bullet points, checking details online, giving Cédric or whoever was watching my computer a show of passive diligence, waiting for scene two to begin.

With his innate sense of barging in when he wasn't wanted, Jake called me on my bugged phone. I'd given him the new number, but appeals for discretion never worked with Jake.

Manon raised her eyebrows. She must have recognised the ringtone of the old phone.

'Hey, man, got some weird, like, nouvelles for you.' Jake meant news. 'My Slovak-Polonaise knows this Italian-Hungary guy. He has told her, and she tells me, and I am telling you.'

A typical Jake speech, but whatever it meant, I didn't really want it to continue on this phone.

'Can I call you back, Jake? I'm kind of busy.'

'OK, but do it très vite. It's à propos of the French. Crazy stuff, man.'

'I really haven't got time for any conspiracy-theory shit,' I said quickly. 'I've got two reports to finish up. I'll talk to you later.'

I rang off, walked a few paces along the corridor and called him from the new phone.

'What's this you've heard?' I asked.

'Wow, it all, like – how do you say? – sticks together. It glues. Like, gels, man.' God knows what he'd been smoking or drinking, but he was at half-speed this morning.

'What does, Jake?'

'My friend tells me that the French are dispensing Europe money for purely French stuff. Like, giving it to patriots for doing some patriot shit. All about the referendum. And my amie mentioned Elodie. She named her. *Elodie*, man.'

Something about this sounded very bad. 'Patriots doing patriot shit' never sounds good, except perhaps if they're organising a raffle to save an indigenous butterfly. I'd met some of these French patriots – Yves Remord, for example. His kind didn't usually go around trying to improve

Anglo-French relations in any way. And he'd stomp on any butterfly, home-grown or not, to further his political ambitions.

'What kind of patriot shit?' I asked Jake.

'I mean, this is only rumour, you know. He-tells-her-and-she-tells-me stuff. But when I have told my fuck-buddy about you working with Elodie, she has said, like: Wow, tell him that the French patriots could be exploiting him. Attention! You know?'

'Exploiting me how? More than by bugging my phone and computer?'

'Don't know, man. Exploiting is what she said. Something très sérieux.'

'Thanks, Jake. And tell your Slovak-Polish friend thanks for the warning. What's her name, by the way?'

'Her name? Oh, man, you really expect me to remember *everything* she said?'

Typical Jake.

Back in the office, I had to sit down opposite Manon as though nothing had happened and keep on feigning work, waiting for the real spy action to kick in.

At around eleven I went into Elodie's office to ask her if she wanted a coffee. She was bashing with uncharacteristic speed on her laptop.

'Ah, oui, merci,' she said, giving me a genuine smile of gratitude. She was in real need of caffeine.

'You going out for lunch later?' I asked.

'Mm, no – no time today, I think. Maybe you can get me a sandwich later?'

'Sure,' I agreed and went back into Manon's office to grimace at her. This wasn't in our plans at all. We needed Elodie out of the office for a nice long Danish lunch.

While I was queuing up for coffee chez Mickey Mouse I got a text from Manon on my unbugged phone: 'Tu dois la sortir du bureau. 20 minutes.'

She meant that somehow I had to get Elodie away from her desk.

'OK,' I replied, wondering how I was going to do it. It would have been a perverse pleasure to pour coffee all over Elodie and escort her to a dry cleaner's, but, knowing me, my attempt to stage the 'accident' would look too much like a man deliberately assaulting his boss with a hot drink.

Something less crude and physical was called for. I ordered myself a double espresso to kick my brain into creative mode.

Arriving back at the office, I set a paper cup down on Manon's desk.

'Are you ready now?' I whispered.

'Merci,' she said, loudly. 'Yes, if you want,' she added at minimum volume. She opened her bag and pulled out a set of keys. They were, I knew, pass keys to the office furniture. Amazing, really, but one of the advantages of EU centralisation. Someone with Manon's connections could get hold of the keys to unlock any desk and cupboard supplied by Parliament.

Time to bullshit some conversation and make sure Elodie was out of her office long enough to let Manon do her stuff.

I went to give Elodie her espresso, with a Speculoos biscuit to sweeten her up. She broke off from her typing.

'Ah merci, Paul.'

I closed the door to Manon's office behind me.

'Can we drink our coffees in private? I need to have a quick chat with you.' I nodded towards the corridor.

'Is it urgent?'

'A bit. Sorry.' I did my best to look embarrassed.

'Shut the door, then, let's talk.'

'I'd prefer . . .' I tilted my head pleadingly towards the corridor again, wishing that I'd learned hypnosis techniques.

'What's it about?'

This time I nodded towards Manon's door.

'Oh God.' Elodie grumbled, bowing down beneath the responsibility to perform human-resources counselling for her underlings. But, even as she complained, she was getting out of her seat. It occurred to me that the bitching between me and Manon might actually amuse her.

She locked her computer and bag away in her cupboard and followed me into the corridor. As soon as we got to the nearest corner, I dived straight in.

'I've been hearing some worrying things,' I said.

'Yes?' Elodie looked disappointed. This wasn't bitching, it was work.

'I know who is trying to ban the oyster.'

'Yes?'

'It's the Brits. The Eunuchs.'

'Quelle surprise. Have you got any proof?'

'Not really, no. But I just remembered: the other night in Strasbourg, they were laughing about it.'

'OK, but why don't you just tell Manon what you heard?'

'That's the problem. I don't trust her,' I said. 'There's something not straight about her.'

'Ha!' Here, at last, was a topic that really interested Elodie. 'What do you mean?'

'Well, she's suddenly gone cold on me. I offered to find out about the oysters, and she didn't want to know.'

Elodie thought about this. I wondered if she'd already heard my staged phone conversation with Manon.

'Has she said anything negative about me?' I asked.

'Well, when you first arrived she wanted to know why I am employing an Anglais. I told her: at least I *chose* you. You weren't forced on me by Papa. She didn't like that.'

Elodie was warming to her subject. She even leant back on a huge photocopier that was taking up half the width of the corridor, not just with its own bulk, but with the mountain range of paper boxes next to it. There was more photocopy paper by this one machine than I'd ever seen in my whole life. More proof of the EU's capacity to churn out wordage.

I knew that I had to keep churning it out, too, for twenty minutes, so I spent a few precious seconds looking silently embarrassed, working down the clock like a footballer hoping to protect his team's slender lead.

'Manon didn't mention that I followed her to the ladies' toilets, did she?'

'What?' Elodie barked a laugh.

'Good. Because I stayed outside.'

She laughed again.

'No, she didn't mention this, Paul. Please tell me more.' Now Elodie was hooked. She finished her coffee and lobbed the empty cup into the waste-paper bin.

I began to spin out the story of how I'd tried to plead innocent to the charge of being a British Eunuch, through a toilet door. I gave Elodie all the dialogue, almost word-for-word, and had her chuckling with delight. As long as the minutes were passing, I didn't care that I came out of it looking like a *boubourse*.

'Oh, Paul,' she groaned after the lady had emerged unexpectedly from the ladies' loo. 'You and women – it's such an unequal match. We win every time. I feel so guilty.'

'Why would you feel guilty?' I asked, innocently. Both of us knew she wasn't doing anything blameworthy to me, *n'est-ce pas?*

'Oh, well . . .' She looked flustered for a moment. She'd said too much. 'I was just remembering when I got you into trouble with Papa by inviting you to live with me. And then your old girlfriend, what was her name? Alicia?'

'Alexa.'

'Ah yes, she bounced you around like a rubber ball, didn't she? Poor Paul. Please take my advice. After Brussels, you must stand up for yourself. Stop acting like an idiot around every woman you see.'

'After Brussels? Why not *in* Brussels?' I asked.

'Well, yes, OK – you can start now by not caring what Manon thinks about you. You've got no chance with her, so give up. Why don't you stick with that girl you met in a bar the other day?'

'It's complicated,' I said, although in fact it was perfectly simple, of course. She didn't exist.

'Somehow you always manage to make it complicated, Paul. Now let's get back to the office, I have to—'

'There's something else,' I blurted out, only just stopping myself from grabbing her physically. 'Something very urgent.'

'Yes?' This definitely interested her.

'Yes. Even more urgent.'

The question was: what?

'The thing is,' I began, having no idea what the thing was.

'Yes?'

'It's difficult.' Which was just about the first true thing I'd said to Elodie all day.

'Well, maybe you'd better think about it and tell me later, Paul.'

'No!' I hoped I didn't sound too scary. 'I need your help.'

'My help?'

'Yes.'

'With what, exactly?'

This was what I was wondering, too.

'Well, Elodie, it's like this. As you yourself just said, I've been having some problems with women,' I went on.

'Yes?'

'Well, it's worse than you think.'

'Really?' Her expression suggested this was hard to imagine.

'Yes. It's, well . . . When I told you I'd met a girl in a bar the other day, I was lying.'

This had Elodie shaking so much with laughter that I thought she'd jolt the photocopier into action. I took the opportunity to sneak a peek at my watch. It was getting painful, but I was using up the time pretty effectively.

'Honestly, Paul, this is what I mean. Who cares? You shouldn't tell me this. There have been plenty of weekends when I haven't got laid, either.'

She shook her head and seemed to think this ended our conversation.

'Well, the thing is . . .' I had to find some way to stop her going back to the office. 'The thing is . . .'

'I wish you'd stop saying that, Paul.'

'Yes, sorry, but the thing . . .' She raised her hands to strangle me if I uttered the wrong word. '. . . I was wondering, Elodie, is . . .'

'Are you going to tell me before I get arrested for murdering an employee?'

'How about we go out to dinner, you and I?'

'What?'

Elodie's knees almost buckled, as did mine. What the hell was I saying?

'You know,' I went on, feeling my internal organs knotting themselves with horror, 'we used to . . . you know . . . And I thought, if we went out for dinner and . . . you know – candles, champagne, the good old days, who knows . . . ?'

Elodie's mouth opened wider with each word, if that were possible. It looked as though she couldn't make up her mind whether to scream for help or screech with laughter.

'I've always admired you, Elodie,' I trudged on, deeper into the quicksand of my immediate future. 'And seeing you again, working with you, watching you handle real political power, it's . . . well, it's very . . .'

I thought she might make a run for it, so there was nothing else I could do – I leant forward and kissed her. A good old-fashioned bout of lip suction.

For a moment I thought she was going to punch me, or lift one of her slim but solid knees where it would do the most damage. But then, as I'd seen before, she made a deliberate effort to control her feelings. She pushed me gently away. I could only assume that, for some reason, I was too necessary to her to cripple.

'Sorry,' I said. 'I couldn't stop myself.'

She looked at me in disbelief, combined with amusement, and a touch of something else that I couldn't quite identify.

'Well, Paul,' she finally said. 'I suppose I should be flattered that you want to take me to dinner. You could have tried to chase me to the toilets, like you do with other women.'

'No, I . . .'

'I'm a married woman now, you know,' she went on.

'I know,' I said, ignoring the dealings she'd had with a certain Dane.

'It is not unpleasant to be fantasised about by a man, even if he is English and a bit of an idiot with women.'

Bloody hell, I thought. Being given an unwanted snog at the photocopier was 'not unpleasant'? Maybe the 'Sorry, chérie, but I can't resist you' speech was the key to Frenchmen's success.

'But you have to admit that it all feels very uncomfortable, Paul.' She was right there. I was in agony. But yet another minute had passed, and we were still in the corridor.

'I know, and I'm sorry, Elodie. Desire can be an uncomfortable thing.' I cringed at this almost unbearable bullshit, but she didn't. I could only imagine that she'd had this type of conversation before.

'Let's forget it and get back to the office,' Elodie said.

'Can't I buy you another coffee, to say sorry for molesting you? Or a stronger drink?'

'No, a drink is the first step to dinner, and we all know where that leads.' She smiled almost fondly and began to walk back towards her office, shaking her head. 'Honestly, Paul, you are a disaster on legs. But thanks. I feel less guilty now.'

'I'm glad I could help.' I looked at my watch and prayed that my attempt at self-martyrdom hadn't been in vain.

Manon was at her desk, working on her computer. I glanced over to her as I sat down, but couldn't see her face properly. She didn't look up to acknowledge me.

Elodie's door was open a crack. I watched her unlock her cupboard, get out her bag and computer, sit down. She consulted a phone message, opened up her laptop, got back to typing. Nothing amiss, it seemed.

For a count of ten, neither Manon nor I reacted, or even breathed as far as I could hear. Then she raised her head, looked me between the eyes and gave a barely visible thumbs-up.

I began my ritual of clicking about in my browsing history, filling screen time, for Elodie's sake. I sent her my report on false tabloid rumours, then answered a few innocent emails, waiting until the pre-arranged time for me to leave the office. When it came, I told Elodie I was off to lunch and offered to bring back a sandwich for her.

'Don't bother, I'll order one,' she said distractedly, still typing, so I went, giving Manon nothing but a polite 'Bon appétit'. She replied without looking up.

I got a table in one of the Belgian cafés that Manon and I had been using for our *rendez-vous*. It was a bright, airy place, decorated with beer adverts and framed slogans in Flemish that could have meant anything from 'Merry Christmas' to 'No smoking in the toilets'.

It was so practical to know that the badge people steered clear of any eating or drinking establishment that was local. If it wasn't international, they weren't interested.

Fifteen minutes later, Manon turned up, as agreed. What hadn't been agreed, though, was that she wasn't alone. Standing beside her as she reached my table was the tall, uncomfortable figure of Cédric, who looked as though he hadn't had much sleep the previous night, or had been drinking, or both.

I raised my eyebrows enquiringly.

'He walked in when I was opening Elodie's cupboard,' Manon explained.

Cédric was rocking from one foot to the other, which seemed to indicate some sort of brain activity. Even with his goldfish-sized share of his family's grey matter, he must have realised instantly that something was fishy.

'I told him it wasn't a good idea to tell Elodie what I was doing,' Manon went on, 'because we knew about the phone.'

'I didn't bug the phone,' Cédric said, finally emerging from his stupor.

'No, but I bet you've been passing on recordings of conversations to Elodie,' Manon said, 'or transcribing them.'

'Oui, et ça, c'est un crime, Cédric,' I told him in my clearest French. 'Think of your family's reputation' – though as private bankers, I doubted they could sink much lower. 'Think of your grandmother.'

Both of us shivered involuntarily at this. I'd met his *grand-mère*, and she was terrifying. Back at the time of the French revolution she wouldn't have been down in the front row knitting and cackling as the guillotine did its work, she'd have been up on the scaffold, playing football with the aristocratic heads – and stealing the deeds to their chateaux out of their pockets. 'Sharp' didn't do her justice. She was a human razor.

'He agreed to keep quiet and join us for lunch,' Manon said. 'And I think maybe he can help us understand what Elodie has been doing, and tell me where to look in all the stuff I copied off her computer and phone.'

The three of us ordered some plates of Belgian food and discussed what Cédric had been up to since my arrival.

As we spoke, I enjoyed an unhealthily tasty plate of *stoemp*, a dish that sounded as though it might be a horrifically truncated limb of some sort, but was in fact creamy mashed potato with little pieces of leek mixed in, topped off with a sausage that was delicious enough to be English, the whole construction sitting like an iceberg on a sea of gravy. It was exactly what a man needed to calm his nerves after a blood-tingling morning.

Manon went for an only slightly lighter *chicons au gratin* – endives under a cheesy crust, which also had a name in Flemish that no one southwest of Brussels would be able to spell or pronounce.

As if in sympathy with me, Cédric opted for *stoemp*. Making the most of this atmosphere of a communal feast, we tried to pick his brains, or what brains there were.

'Where did she get the money to employ me?' I asked him.

'I know she got an award from a charity called Europe Avenir,' he said.

'Avenir', I knew, meant 'future'.

'Interesting,' Manon said. 'MEPs are obliged to declare gifts worth more than a hundred and fifty euros. A watch, say, or a handbag.' As usual I had to fight down the urge to ask why any handbag could cost that much. 'But they don't have to declare cash. So if you want to give an MEP a perfectly legal bribe or, for example, enough money to carry out a project without supervision, you give the MEP a prize.'

'Was it a French charity?' I asked Cédric.

He shrugged.

'She just said that the award was for "services to the economy".' He shrugged again, and chewed on *stoemp*.

'What does that mean?' I asked Manon.

She had obviously caught Cédric's shrugging bug.

'I don't know who Europe Avenir are,' she said, 'but with a name like that, one thing is for sure – they don't want to leave anything about Europe's future to chance. No room for democracy or any merde like that.'

We tried to get Cédric to explain why Elodie had been spying on me, and what her real motives were. But the overall picture in his mind was predictably blurred. He'd simply been told to make sure the bugs on my phone and computer were working OK, and to keep an eye on me, informing Elodie if I seemed to be revealing sensitive information to anyone except her.

Cédric didn't speak great English, so he'd been forwarding to Elodie any emails or conversation that he had doubts about. She'd moaned at him for 'débording' her with trivia, he said, but she had had a good laugh at Jake's chat-up lines.

'Maybe we can go out with Jake for a drink sometime?' Cédric asked me. He wasn't so stupid after all.

After lunch, all of us left separately, though I stuck close behind Cédric to make sure he returned to work. He had to keep up the appearance of normality, as we all did. I watched him disappear into his cubbyhole, then went to sit at my own desk to kill time while Manon trawled through the files and messages that she'd copied.

This she was doing at her apartment. She'd called in to tell Elodie that she was feeling sick after her lunch. I heard Elodie's side of the conversation.

'What did you eat . . . ? Really? I've told you before – avoid that Belgian merde . . . OK, hope you feel better soon.' She hung up. 'That will teach her,' she grunted to herself. Such compassion.

For three whole hours I tinkered with my sentences, turning commas into full stops, trying out different-coloured bullet points. Not just killing time, but boring it to death.

And then, at last, Manon sent me a text on my new phone, giving me a brief summary of what she'd found out, at which point I was the one suffering from stomach cramps. It was a low blow, even by Elodie's subterranean standards.

It was much more than a stab in the back. It was as if she'd tricked me into sitting on a load of multicoloured drawing pins, then posted a photo of my bouquet-like backside on Facebook so that everyone on the planet could 'LOL' at it. And as Manon explained each different drawing pin that Elodie had used, the humiliation stung more and more.

19

'British toilets to be replaced by "euro-loos".'

Report in the British press, 2013

MANON SUMMONED me to one of our Belgian cafés, and by the time I arrived she was trembling under the pressure of everything she wanted to share with me. And almost as soon as she began her whispered revelations, I was trembling, too.

In a nutshell, I had been shafted once again.

· I should never have trusted Elodie. It's like old Breton ladies probably tell young farmboys – if you have been stung once by a bee, why on earth would you cover your head in honey and stuff it into a bees' nest?

What it boiled down to was that everything I had done for Elodie in Brussels was going to be turned against me – her plan wasn't to swing the British referendum result towards a

'Yes, please', it was to convince the Brits to vote a resounding 'Fuck off, Europe.'

According to emails that Elodie had been exchanging with a group of French people, including my good friend Yves Remord, she was about to reveal to the British press that an Englishman (guess *qui*) had been working for France while living in a massive luxury apartment – with a signed rental agreement and selfies of said Brit in a bathtub as proof. All rent-free, despite the fact that I was getting paid a fortune (well, at least that bit looked good) for betraying my country's interests.

Apparently I had been advising the French government how to screw even more money out of Europe to subsidise its many semi-independent regions. Working with one of France's most patriotic, anti-British political parties (*touché*, I really ought to have thought twice about Elodie's affiliations), I'd advised them how to obtain millions of euros with which to pay for the teaching of obscure, defunct French dialects. My strategically-edited report proved this beyond any doubt.

Not only this, but I had been spying on British eurosceptic politicians by buying up their computers for an absurd amount of (taxpayers') money and retrieving secrets from their hard disks. Judging by emails that Manon had read, I was to be made the villain in a news story she wanted to create about France spying on the anti-EU radicals, which was guaranteed to whip up fury in certain sections of the British press.

My worst crime, though, was my co-authorship of a report that Elodie was planning to release, itemising the crazy new laws that the EU would be free to inflict on Britain if the referendum vote was a 'yes' to Europe.

It looked as though Elodie hadn't waited for me to send her my report on the false tabloid stories about EU laws. She'd grabbed it, half-finished, from my computer, using the spyware. She'd then cut out all my partly written explanations and kept only the bullshit rumours, leaving the reader with a top-twenty chart of the best reasons for Brits to vote 'au revoir' to Europe and thereby save the British sausage, the kilt, Waterloo Station and even the good old English water closet from being flushed away by Brussels.

Also faithfully preserved were my occasional comments about how brilliantly creative the rumours were, so that it looked as if the report was praising the journalists. 'Creative' is usually taken to mean brilliant, but of course if you're creating havoc, then it's not quite so positive.

All in all, Elodie was dropping me right in the *mokordo*.

I felt certain that the British tabloids were going to be having orgasms about all this, as were some of the main TV and radio news programmes. On the morning of the referendum, everyone in Britain would wake up to an irresistible call to get the hell out of Europe. Crowds were going to flock to the White Cliffs of Dover to start paddling the island further away from the continent.

And all thanks to me.

It was much worse than those old stories of sailors having to weave the cat-o'-nine-tails they were to be whipped with. I'd cleaned and loaded the rifles of my own firing squad, and then painted a massive bullseye on my forehead.

My first conclusion was that I was a dickhead, and a blind one at that.

Why hadn't I listened to my own doubts about my two 'missions'? I'd been all too aware that they both involved transcribing what anyone else could have found out. Even Cédric could have copied out the names of minority languages and downloaded British rumours about Europe. What Elodie really wanted was for *me* to do the jobs. Not only were British journalists more likely to believe reports written by one of their own (in English, too, so they were easy to read), the anti-Europeans would also have a brand-new hate figure to use in their Brexit campaign. Those evil French europhiles had recruited a treacherous Brit – *moi.*

My second conclusion was an even more obvious one. When Manon had finished laying out the painful truth before me, I could only think of one word.

'Bitch!' I also translated it, into French, Corsican and Breton. 'Salope, puttana, gast. Who does this to an old friend? Has Elodie forgotten what I did for her at her wedding?'

Manon laughed bitterly. 'It looks as though she's even forgotten what *she* did at her wedding.'

'But why is she doing this? Isn't it true that France wants to preserve a strong Europe? Even the anti-Anglais? Aren't you all terrified that Britain and the USA will be in an anti-French gang?'

My basic French made it sound like playground rivalry, but maybe that wasn't a bad analogy for some of the infantile hysteria that the referendum was throwing up.

'That's what I think,' Manon said, 'but from what I've read, it looks as though Elodie and her friends believe that if Britain leaves the EU, then all the big international banks will come to Paris. And so will all the brains, especially the French ones that have emigrated to London. France will loosen its tax laws and become the financial capital of Europe. The right wing also thinks that, with Britain out, the migrant crisis in Calais will be solved, because the refugees won't be able to get into England with EU papers. So they'll all go straight to Germany, or at least to the south of France. Your friend Remord blames the English for turning the north coast of France into one big refugee camp.'

'But a vote to leave Europe won't change that,' I said. 'The migrants don't go to England because it's part of the EU. They go because they think it's easy to get a job, easy to get unemployment money, and because of the language.'

'I know,' Manon agreed. 'If Britain leaves the EU, it might make the migrants *more* determined to get to Calais. They'll want to escape the EU quota system. If they can't stay in Germany, they don't want Romania or Greece as a second choice. They'll try to get to Britain. But that's not what Elodie and her friends think.'

'I should have known it was all an *arnaque*.' This was a word meaning 'scam' that seems to crop up suspiciously often in French conversations. 'The Martin family hasn't said a true word for ten generations.'

'Oh, I don't think you can blame Elodie's father for this,' Manon said. 'He doesn't seem to be involved at all. I haven't seen any emails between Elodie and him.'

This was hard to believe, but she was adamant.

Revenge was all I could think of.

'I'll give Elodie that dinner,' I said. 'And then afterwards, when she takes off her *culotte*, I'll say: Ha! You think I want to have sex with *you*?'

It sounded like a scene from a clichéd French film, but this wasn't what shocked Manon.

'What dinner?' she asked. 'And why would she take off her *culotte*?'

Oh, *cacarella*, I thought. I hadn't told Manon how desperate I'd been to keep Elodie talking in the corridor.

I described the scene for her – leaving out the kiss, of course, and being careful to imply that Elodie had been horrified by the whole sordid idea of dinner, with a sex dessert.

'Why would you even *think* of telling her you wanted to sleep with her?' Manon demanded.

'I had to do something to stop her returning to her office. I'm not a professional spy like you.'

This argument seemed to calm Manon down, and I managed to steer the conversation back towards ways of disarming the time-bomb that Elodie was about to unleash on the British press.

Meanwhile, I couldn't help wondering why Manon should be so mad about me pretending that I wanted to sleep with Elodie. A bit of pre-emptive possessiveness?

It wasn't an unpleasant idea. Jealousy is always so flattering.

'You have an historic opportunity,' Manon told me.

My first thought was that this sounded like an advert for apartments in a new dockside development in Hull. But we were back on the subject of what to do about Elodie, apart from sleep with her.

'If you want revenge, you can ensure that Britain stays in the EU,' Manon went on.

'Well, I'm not sure I have that much power.'

'You do, Paul. We can sabotage Elodie's campaign so badly that it has the opposite effect and pushes marginal voters towards staying in Europe. As you keep saying, the vote is going to be very tight. Just a few per cent will make the difference.'

This last bit seemed to be true. According to the polls, it looked as though plenty of voters were going to make their decision at the last minute.

But it suddenly struck me that there were other possibilities.

First up, leaving aside the fact that Elodie was planning to drop me personally in the *zut*, was her plan really so bad? All things considered, would it be so terrible if Britain voted to leave?

I mean, I'd only been in Brussels for a short time, but I'd witnessed its absurdities for myself.

At the most basic level, I wasn't sure that we really needed to fill half of Belgium with commissions, councils, courts and committees.

And was it sensible for Britain to be paying its share of the fortune spent translating every Brussels hiccup into more than twenty languages?

The same went for the 200 million euros a year it cost to keep the French happy by shipping all the MEPs down to Strasbourg every month. Who (apart from Manon, of course) cared if the French were unhappy?

And, perhaps the biggest question of all: Did we Brits really need to have all these shaggers and boozers making extra laws for us, when we already had our own shaggers and boozers in Westminster?

I tried to explain some of this to Manon, leaving out the bit about not wanting to make France happy. If you work for the Ministry of Foreign Affairs, that must be your top priority.

'I mean, I'm angry with Elodie for tricking me,' I said, my French forcing me into wild understatement, 'but maybe it's enough if I just stop her using my name.'

'No, Paul, that's not enough,' Manon said. 'You've got to face up to the fact that you're certain to influence the outcome of the referendum. Whatever we decide to do, or not do, it's going to have an effect.'

This was also true. I was obliged to make a clear choice.

Option one was the closest I could get to neutrality. I could help Manon stifle Elodie's campaign so that she had no influence at all, either for or against Europe. This would be the equivalent of letting nature take its course. But it would also mean missing out on the opportunity to expose Elodie's double-dealings and thereby help the 'Remain' campaign.

That was option two: I had the chance to take sweet revenge by totally screwing Elodie (metaphorically, of course). We could turn Elodie's campaign against her so badly that it nudged the undecided over to the 'yes' side of the euro-fence.

Manon repeated that she favoured this last idea, 'as did the whole of France'. It struck me that all the French people in Brussels – Elodie included – were very keen to stress that they spoke for the whole of France.

As we talked on into the evening in that little Belgian café, I started to see things more and more starkly. I had to make a very quick decision. And it had better be the right one, because it was going to be irreversible.

Manon and I went our separate ways with a brief, workmatey *bise* and an all-too-brief hug.

We agreed to sleep on it before taking any decisions. Or, in my case, *not* sleep on it at all.

To get the lesser reasons for my insomnia out of the way first:

At about one in the morning, some idiot, no doubt under the influence of a Belgian brew, phoned to ask if I still needed to get rid of a cat. He asked this in French. I told him what to do with himself, in Corsican, which proved to be a very effective way of getting rid of nuisance callers. No wonder the French police are so terrified of Corsicans.

Then of course there were my mental and hormonal rumblings about Manon. Not a priority in this time of crisis, you might think, but anyone who has ever had to confront a rutting elephant or a disgruntled human teenager knows how hard it is to argue against hormones.

And it struck me during the night, with a mixture of pleasure and pain, that Manon could have used her physical wiles to get me to agree to her plan. If she'd wanted to force me over to the 'stop the Brexit' camp, there was a very easy way to buy my support. And she'd chosen not to use it. Which was comforting and maddeningly frustrating at the same time.

Anyway, those were the two lesser issues preventing me from getting much shut-eye. The main things preoccupying me were three questions relating to our discussion in the Belgian café. These were, in no particular order:

What?

How?

And who?

As in, what exact measures should we take? How could we ensure that they worked? And which of our Brussels contacts could we enrol in our scheme?

Notice that I'd already got 'why?' out of the way. The answer to that was obvious – I couldn't let Elodie and her family get away with it.

Bugger Europe, this was personal.

20

'EU wants to measure how badly workers smell.'

Report in the British press, 1996

NEXT MORNING before leaving for work, I called Manon to share my nocturnal conclusions with her. Despite the fact that it was 8 a.m. and I hadn't had any coffee, I remembered to use the unbugged phone. Maybe I did have a few strands of James Bond DNA, after all.

As before, Manon saw things in terms of acting. I think she must have taken classes.

'Elodie is going to be out of the office from mid-morning onwards,' she said. 'So scene one will be between you and her, and then we will be free to work on our finale.'

We discussed the details of our matinée show. My only worry was that Manon seemed a bit too keen on dashing straight from scene one to the ending. Amateur actors like myself need time to get into our roles.

Elodie was at her desk, fingers prodding and swiping at her phone. She was looking even smarter than usual today, her blonde hair gleaming and pulled tightly back, her cream blouse silky, just a shade darker than the pearls caressing her collar bone.

'Bonjour, Paul!'

She shot me a predatory smile, the look of a *charcutier* welcoming a pig to his workshop.

'Bonjour, Elodie.' I played it casual, as if nothing were the matter. I wished I could nonchalantly light a cigarette to prove how steady my hands were. And to stop them twitching with impatience to strangle her. 'Did you read my report about the false rumours?' I asked.

'Yes, of course. Thanks, Paul, very useful. I liked your little English jokes. Très drôle.' She sounded friendly, but looked as devious as a cat with a goldfish bowl and a fishing rod.

'Great. I was wondering whether I should prepare the press release? It ought to go out today, surely?'

'Thanks, but it's being dealt with.'

'Who by?'

'Oh là là, Paul, don't you mean "by whom?" Really, it's your language.'

As if she had answered the question, she went back to her screen.

'By whom, then? If it's being done by French people for the British press, maybe I ought to have a look. You know, a pair of English eyes.'

'Honestly, Paul. Do you know how many qualified translators there are in Brussels? Do you think I can't find one?'

'No, of course not. But I've spent years reading the tabloids.'

'Looking at the photos of girls with naked breasts and no brains? Your ideal woman, Paul.'

Ignoring the slur, I ploughed on.

'I'm not sure your average Brussels translator knows how a British tabloid works, Elodie. They spend most of their time reading reports about sewage disposal in the Adriatic, and stuff like that.'

'Which is a good metaphor for your British press,' Elodie snapped. 'The shit they say about France! Now please, Paul, trust me to know how to find someone to write a press release, and leave me to my work!'

'OK, just trying to be thorough,' I said. 'I know that DG Communication won't help you write it, so I thought I could help.'

'Mais lâche-moi les couilles!' she suddenly screeched. It's a very common French phrase, but not one usually used by women. Loosely translated, she was telling me to let go of her testicles. Well, I thought, if any woman has them, it's her.

Elodie's outburst seemed to prove that she was feeling the pressure as much as I was. And for the tenth time in a few days, I saw her almost physically getting a grip – not on her testicles, but on her outward calm.

'Paul, I can only think that your positively anal obsession with work this morning must be explained by your lack of female company. Or friendly female company, anyway,' Elodie added, nodding towards the wall of Manon's office. Manon was in there rounding up our anti-Elodie troops via mail and message.

'Why don't we have that dinner tonight?' Elodie said, suddenly all smiles. 'I'm not promising anything more, of course. But some decent food in a quiet restaurant will do you good. Perhaps I can give you some advice. Or pay a waitress to sleep with you.'

Was I imagining things, or did I hear a phone being dropped in Manon's office?

'Oh. Sure – great,' I managed to say.

All things considered, it would be a good idea to keep Elodie occupied that evening. Though it occurred to me that she might be thinking exactly the same about me.

I wondered if we both drew the line at keeping each other occupied all night.

When Elodie went out, I devoted a full fifteen minutes to convincing Manon that I had no intention of distracting Elodie from her propaganda campaign by handcuffing her to my bed. She had been giving me silent looks ever since she'd overheard that dinner invitation.

Once we'd got all that out of the way, Manon and I adjourned to a corner of the Mickey Mouse cafeteria, where we set up a little HQ consisting of a small posy of coloured chairs around a coffee table.

I sat on turquoise, Manon on yellow, and for the next hour or so we held short briefing meetings with friends and contacts we'd invited along. I was grateful that I'd played the Brussels game and kept everyone's business card. All of my new acquaintances had stepped up to the plate when we told them what was at stake – Danny, Ed Fürst, Peter Marsh, even Šárka the lobbyist.

Our conversations were urgent and businesslike. The orange seat opposite us got red-hot.

Each of our co-conspirators listened to our horror story about Elodie, and agreed to bring their own expertise to the table. They would, they promised, take immediate action to help counter the damage Elodie was hoping to inflict. I couldn't help scanning the horizon as we talked. If Elodie had walked in on any one of our conversations, I was sure she would have picked up a chair and added the red of my blood to the already lurid colour scheme.

We'd taken the risk of holding the meetings in the cafeteria because we had no time to lose. Only forty-eight hours or so until the voting in Britain began. And in any case, we knew that Elodie was out for the rest of the day. If she got to hear about our Mickey Mouse sessions, it would be too late for her to do anything about them.

Of course these brief impromptu meetings attracted attention despite the size of the cafeteria. I saw that we were provoking envious conversations. A succession of badge people appearing for a few minutes, nodding a lot, talking quickly and then leaving with a hearty handshake? How come we're not in the loop, they seemed to be wondering? Haven't we been handing out enough business cards? Have we been under-schmoozing?

At last one of them plucked up the courage to sidle over to our corner and ask. I recognised him. It was the Italian guy I'd met at a restaurant one night. I hadn't taken his card because he seemed too much of a *toni*. That's dickhead in Lombardian.

'Hi – John, isn't it?' he said.

'Yes,' I confirmed, guessing that my badge must be hidden from view.

'And hi, er?' He held out his hand to Manon.

'This is Elodie,' I lied.

'Ah, la bella Elodia.' Like I said, a *toni*.

'What is all this?' He pointed to the orange chair that had recently welcomed a trio of Brussels backsides.

'Speed-networking,' I said.

'Ah.' This seemed to be an intriguing concept.

'Yes, we're part of the MEPs' assistants' speed-networking network.'

'Ah.'

'You must have heard about the European network of speed-networking networks?'

'No.' A look of mild panic.

'We've got funding from the EU's new networking DG. Haven't you heard about it?'

'No.' Spicier panic.

'DG Nessie.'

'Wow!'

'Give me your card, I'll hook you up.'

'Thanks.'

The Italian whipped out an impressively embossed card. Antonio Spumante. So he was a genuine *Toni*, and from a truly famous wine family.

'Sorry, we have to keep on networking or it stops being speedy,' I told him. I could see our next arrival on his way in, trying to spot us. 'I'll be in touch.'

The Italian stepped aside to let Peter, the British guy from DG Communication, sit down. Then he went back to his small group of friends or associates, looking sceptical but slightly impressed.

Peter was grinning as if I'd got him tickets to see England in the World Cup Final – and not against Germany or Brazil, but someone like Moldova, half of whose team had gone down with flu, while the other half had been bribed to let in goals. In any case, his delight suggested that enjoyment was guaranteed.

I'd called him previously to convince him that this, at last, was the right time to step in and defy the British press. I'd also hinted that we might be playing dirty enough to get a result. He'd immediately agreed to come and talk.

'I've been rooting around,' he said as soon as he sat down. 'And I've heard an incredible rumour. Someone's put it out there that there's going to be a ferryload of French people turning up in England on the night before the referendum. Bretons claiming UK residency. They're going to be demanding Breton-language teaching in local schools, Breton-speaking nurses in hospitals, et cetera, saying it's their right, according to European law. All bullshit, obviously, but brilliant propaganda.'

'Kaoc'h.' Never had the word been used more appropriately. This was something new. It added another operation to my long list.

'You think Elodie Martin, our MEP, might be behind this?' Manon asked Peter in French.

'Pourquoi pas?' he replied, with a *très* French accent, and went on to tell us that he'd traced the story back to a communiqué by some people called 'L'Avenir de l'Europe, ou quelque chose comme ça'.

'Europe Avenir,' Manon and I chorused. So it was Elodie.

'Are you going to put out a press release to counter this?' I asked.

'No. I told you, the DG doesn't bother on individual issues. But I can help you write one, and advise you on how to get it out there to the right people.'

'That would be excellent,' Manon said.

'Right.' Peter seemed to be thinking something over. 'OK, before we get down to business, I couldn't have a coffee, could I? Skinny latte? I'm parched.'

'Sure, I'll get you one,' I said.

'No, I'll go,' Manon offered.

'Glad she went,' Peter said quietly, when Manon had left. 'So you're helping the French against the French? Are you sure you know what's going on here?'

'I think so.'

'I'm never sure we can trust them at the best of times, never mind when they're at each other's throats. Don't want to get hit in the crossfire. Or crossblades, or whatever.'

'I think I can trust Manon. She's French Ministry of Foreign Affairs.' I looked over to where she was ordering at the bar. She turned and smiled back brightly, the kind of woman you wanted to trust.

'Wow. Ministry, eh? Big guns,' Peter said. 'And are you sure you want to help them influence the vote? You might be adding a lot of weight to the "Remain" campaign. Is that something you want to do?'

Like I said, this had been giving me twinges of conscience.

'I'm all in favour of staying in,' Peter went on. 'If all the Poles got kicked out of the UK and went to Germany, nothing would ever get built in Britain again. Not on time, anyway. And without EU workers, all the restaurants in London would be self-service, and all the hotels would insist on DIY bed-making. Plus the NHS would lose half its nurses. But don't forget that there are equally valid reasons for getting out. Freedom to pass our own laws. Immigrant quotas. All that. So are you really sure about what you want to do?'

I considered this.

'We'll just be giving people an even playing field,' I said. 'I don't think we can stop Elodie coming out with her bullshit. So let's give people some alternative bullshit. Then they can decide whose smells better.'

'OK, fair enough. Then I'm your man. As long as you're sure we can trust the French.'

'Yes,' I said.

I just prayed it was true.

21

'New Brussels law: worn-out sex toys must be given back to retailers.'

Report in the British press, 2004

I DON'T know who in the design world decided that chic modern bars and restaurants should have entirely square furniture. The occasional spherical lightshade is OK, it seems, but everything else – tables, chairs, the bar, even plates – has to have right-angles. You're lucky if you get your drinks served in glasses without corners.

Elodie had arranged to meet me in one of these places, a hotel restaurant that also went in for absurdly dimmed lighting and music that was probably meant to sound cool, but just made me want to go and smash the computer that had generated it.

There was, of course, a sultry woman in painfully high heels, whose only job was to check your DNA against the list of reservations and make sure you weren't uninvited.

The restaurant was divided into three sections – a long mirrored bar, which seemed to be where the anorexics sat for their liquid dinner; a large open section with a chequerboard of tables; and a corner with a dozen or so discreet booths where you needed night-vision glasses to check that you were meeting the right person.

Predictably, and scarily, Elodie had booked a table here. I arrived on time, and followed the woman in high heels to a booth, guiding myself for the last few metres by the sound of her shoes on the floor. I slotted myself in between a square table and a rectangular leather bench seat. Despite the gloom, I could see that there was no one else at the table.

A waiter, or it might have been a waitress with a deep voice, asked me in French whether I would like a drink while I waited for Madame. To match the linguistic mood, I ordered a '*coupe de Champagne*'. Connoisseurs will know that this is not a teacup full of fizzy wine. '*Coupe*' is the name of an open, rounded champagne glass. And it always puzzles me why French restaurants invariably serve a '*coupe*' in a tall, slim '*flûte*'. But maybe that's just because I'm turning Parisian.

Being French, Elodie was twenty minutes late. And being Parisian, she didn't apologise.

I stood up to welcome her (once I'd recognised her through the darkness), and we kissed on both cheeks as we wished each other 'Bonsoir'. It was all feeling very ceremonial. But then both of us were acting out a ceremony of sorts – the prelude to dropping each other in the proverbial *merde.*

'Is that champagne, Paul? Are we celebrating something?'

'I don't know yet.'

It was meant to be an ironic reference to my undercover revenge campaign, but it probably came out more like a plea for sex.

'Well, maybe I need a glass, too, then. Will you order it for me, Paul?'

The man ordering the drink? We were getting even more ceremonial, I thought. I ought to have kissed her hand when she arrived. Or rather, as the truly posh Frenchmen do, held her hand close to my lips and pretended to kiss it.

Hypocritically, I complimented her on her choice of restaurant.

'Oh, I'm staying in this hotel at the moment. It's convenient.'

'That must be expensive. Don't you have a longer-term apartment?'

'Yes, Paul, but you're staying there.'

'Oh.'

She'd told me that diplomats usually lived in the Art Nouveau apartment. Had she forgotten about this earlier lie?

'It was either you or me in the hotel,' she went on, 'and I decided that I deserved a couple of weeks of luxury.'

'I just hope Valéry won't turn up at the flat on a surprise visit and get the wrong idea about me being in your bed.'

'He wouldn't dare!' Elodie laughed. I gathered that Monsieur was trained to obey orders, like everyone else in her life. Everyone except – for the past few hours, at least – me.

'How's Valéry doing?'

'As well as the last time you asked, Paul, about a day ago. I didn't know you were so worried about him. Which reminds me – have you seen Cédric recently?'

'Not since yesterday. He said he wasn't feeling too good.'

'Honestly, that family! They have an immune system as strong as the fences around the Channel Tunnel.'

Elodie clearly wasn't the nursemaid type. But I knew that Cédric wasn't suffering from anything life-threatening. To prevent gaffes on his part, I'd suggested that he go off sick. A true French worker, he'd taken me at my word and gone to a doctor to get himself a month's 'stress leave'. He was probably sitting in his flat browsing a website of cousins he might be able to marry.

We ordered food from a menu that seemed to contain nothing but flame-grilled, *a la plancha* and gluten-free, with a bottle of white wine. French, *bien sûr*. A Pouilly-Fumé, which – despite its name – has not been smoked. But then, of course, neither is there any mutton in a Mouton Rothschild.

'So everything's going ahead as you planned?' I asked Elodie.

It was too dark to see whether she looked embarrassed as she replied that it was. I'd have to ask the waiter for a torch if I wanted to analyse her facial expressions. There was a candle in a (square) bowl on the table, but apparently it was only lit on request.

'Press release done?' I pressed her.

'Yes, all done, Paul. Don't worry, I know how to organise things. And how do you think your compatriots will vote?'

Even in the near-blackness I was sure I detected a look of self-satisfaction on her face. Her smugness was so strong it was generating light.

'Oh, the polls are too close to call,' I replied, as usual. 'For the moment, anyway.'

'Anything could happen, n'est-ce pas?'

Elodie held up her wine glass and we clinked, each of us no doubt smiling at our own interpretation of the toast. It was, if I got it right, an 'I-know-what-you-think-you-know-and-I-don't-but-I-think-I-know-something-you-don't' moment. From my point of view, anyway.

'I invited you to dinner to thank you, Paul,' she said. 'Even though it's been a short job, you've helped me more than you can imagine.'

'Really?'

'Yes.'

'How?'

'Oh . . .'

I understood more than ever the importance of the darkness. Surely even Elodie must be betraying some signs of guilt about shafting one of her old friends?

'In many ways,' she finally said. 'But whatever happens, you'll be getting a nice fat payment to thank you for your help.'

'What do you mean, "whatever happens"?' I asked, as innocently as possible.

'You know, a delay with the funding, that sort of thing. Brussels is a complex place, lots of broken promises.'

That was the biggest understatement I'd ever heard from her.

'It must make your job difficult,' I said. 'Do you enjoy it? Do you get a sense of doing something worthwhile?'

She laughed.

'Oh, are you becoming anti-European, Paul? Don't you think that MEPs are useful?'

Perhaps it was a serious question, and if I'd answered, 'No, I think you're all a bunch of wasters getting a free ride on a gravy train paid for by my taxes, and some of you forget who's paying your wages and spend your whole time undermining Europe,' maybe she would have come clean. But I had a serious question of my own.

'I mean, does what you're doing fit in with your beliefs about Europe? What are your beliefs exactly?'

Elodie made a puffing noise, as though 'belief' was a joke in her very own minority language.

'It's really tough being an MEP, Paul. Everyone wants to influence you – lobbyists, other MEPs, the party back home in France. Consultants and journalists want to know what you think about every subject they can think of. And you must never forget the electors. What will they want you to think and say before the next election? So sometimes I don't know what I believe.'

'That must be slightly inconvenient whenever you have to vote on a new law?'

She laughed. 'All I know, Paul, and you must believe me – whatever happens during your referendum – is that I want what is best for France and for Europe. In that order, admittedly.'

Merde alors, I thought. She's actually being sincere. I ought to note the date and time in my diary.

We ate and drank. The food was good, and in surprisingly generous portions. This was probably the Belgian element to the restaurant's design.

'Now to your personal problem,' Elodie said, after delicately wiping her lips with her napkin. 'Women. Are there any in this restaurant that you like?'

'No.' I didn't even bother turning around to look. Mainly because I wouldn't have been able to see any, except for the illuminated silhouettes at the bar.

'Oh no – you're not going to say that I'm the only one you want to look at, are you, Paul?'

'No, I'm not that French.'

'Thank God for that. But why can't you find yourself a woman? You're not a bad-looking guy. Sweet, sort of naive.'

(Yes, I thought, naivety had been my greatest quality, where she was concerned.) 'Women adore that. Except if they're Manon, of course.' Elodie laughed. 'Maybe she's in love with my papa, and he's been telling her nasty things about you. He's probably sleeping with her *and* her mother.'

I might have defended Manon against this slur if we hadn't been interrupted.

'Elodie?'

There was a shadow standing by our table. All I could see of it was an elegantly trousered groin.

'Let me help you,' a male voice said.

A hand dipped into view, followed by a second of similar size and colour. They flicked a match against a small matchbox, and after a brief spit and fizzle, our candle was emitting light. I blinked a few times and looked up into a face I knew.

I could see that Elodie recognised it too, and that she was shocked.

'Gustav?'

It was the dunking Dane. Although, having done some research, I now knew that he was Swedish.

'I didn't know you were dining here tonight, Elodie,' he said. He didn't look bothered by this. It was just an observation.

'Yes, well, I . . .' Elodie's reply petered out as she caught sight of a female figure who now came into view, and whose hand Gustav clasped possessively.

'Manon?' she said.

22

'EU wants all condoms to be of uniform size – small.'

Report in the British press, 2000

I HAD been play-acting for most of that dinner with Elodie, hamming it up as her innocent victim.

But seeing Manon's hand clutched by the Swedish seducer in the dim light of the restaurant elicited my first non-acted reaction of the evening, a twisting of the upper intestine that made me grit my teeth.

It was no consolation to remind myself that I had set up the whole scene.

I had contacted Danny the oyster man and reminded him of that first night at Plux when he'd given me the evil eye. I described the Dane (as I thought he was) who'd been in the bar, and asked if Danny knew him. He didn't, he said, but he could ask around. Less than half an hour later he came back with a name, a phone number and a new nationality. Gustav the Swede.

Vive the Brussels high-speed networking network.

I'd phoned Gustav and asked if I could come and see him, explaining that it was a 'delicate matter concerning Elodie'. This had caught his attention. I went over to his office, which was on the centre-left side of the Parliament building, where most of the Scandinavians seemed to be, except the Viking supremacy extremists.

He turned out to be a virulent pro-European, full of pity for his Norwegian neighbours who opted out of the EU and now found themselves obliged to apply EU trading laws anyway, if they wanted to do business with Europe.

He was also very much in favour of keeping Britain in the EU, so that it could, as he put it, 'accept its full share of our common responsibilities at this difficult time'. I was secretly pleased to see that someone so smooth and handsome could come out with dull politician's clichés.

Once Gustav heard about Elodie's plans to sabotage the vote in favour of a Brexit, she seemed to drop down several places on his sex-friend chart. He immediately agreed to my plan: he would turn up at the restaurant that night and 'surprise' Elodie dining with me.

Admittedly, my main reason for doing this to Elodie was spite. It had nothing to do with the referendum, except that I thought it might be good to destabilise her and get her thinking about non-political matters on the day before the vote. I wanted to knock her off her self-satisfied perch.

But it was also a promise to Cédric. Valéry was his cousin after all, and he'd confided in me that he was sick of seeing Elodie 'se foutre de la gueule du monde', as he put it, which more or less translates as 'fucking everyone's face', but means something less violent – taking the piss.

Cédric had begged me to try and mess up Elodie's Scandinavian fling. In return, he was willing to guarantee his silence about my messing up her propaganda campaign. He seemed to be forgetting the blackmail hold we had on him, but I agreed anyway.

'The only question is: Why would I be in the restaurant alone?' Gustav had asked me, and when I suggested that he invite a woman along, he replied that he wouldn't be able to find a date at such short notice.

This was almost certainly a lie, but it was also a challenge. He wanted me to set him up with some new tottie.

'Why not Elodie's other assistant, for example?' he said. I guessed he didn't mean Cédric.

To my annoyance, Manon agreed all too easily. And I couldn't really object.

But when I saw them standing together at the restaurant, I found myself asking: Did she really have to hold Gustav's hand?

It took all my self-discipline not to call Manon when I got back to the apartment after dinner with Elodie. It would have looked as though I was checking up on her. Which of course I would have been.

And the fact that Manon didn't phone to check up on me only made things worse. Did she no longer care whether I slept with Elodie? Or was she too busy doing Stockholm somersaults?

I would have liked to consult Jake on the matter. Where sex was concerned, he had been through every complication known to humankind. But he wasn't at the apartment and when I called him, he replied breathlessly that he couldn't talk: 'I'm in full invasion of the empire Austro-Hungarian.' It didn't take much imagination to guess what that meant.

Of course I didn't go up to Elodie's hotel room after dinner, even though she put on a great show of seductive play-acting, all for Gustav's benefit. Once he and Manon had gone to their table, she leant towards me as we spoke and kept her face in the candlelight, probably knowing that the flickering flame picked out the gold in her hair and the pearls at her throat. And when we left the table, she gripped my arm and swayed against me as though our hips were beginning the foreplay on our way upstairs.

But once we were in the lobby she brusquely wished me a 'Bonne fin de soirée' and suggested that I go and solve my problems at a '*bordel*'. Then she was striding towards the lift, no doubt on her way to the minibar. I almost felt sorry for her. Almost.

It was of course me who gave in and called next morning. The day before the referendum.

'Bonjour, Manon.'

'Bonjour, Paul.'

'Ça va?'

'Oui très bien, et toi?'

'Bien, merci.'

We spend so long asking what we don't really want to know.

'How did it go with Gustav?' I finally asked.

'Oh, very well. He's très sympathique.'

'Yes, très.'

'How did it go with Elodie?'

'Oh, very badly. She is a crazy hypocrite.'

'She seemed to be very affectionate towards you.'

'You saw that? Did Gustav see? That's what she wanted. As soon as we left the restaurant, she disappeared.'

'Ah. Were you disappointed that she rejected you, Paul?'

'No, of course not. And she didn't reject me. I'm not interested in her.'

There was silence. Sometimes I really hate silence.

'What about you and Gustav?' I asked.

'He's very seductive. It's flattering for a woman when a man is so direct. He wants to make love with you and he shows it so . . . honestly.'

Yes, the smooth, efficient bastard, I thought.

'But I told him that I have just suffered a separation, and I have promised myself not to get involved with a man for three months. Naturally, he asked me when the three months would be finished,' she added.

'Did you tell him?'

'Yes. He put a reminder in his phone. Very flattering.'

'Seriously?'

'Seriously. Oh, come on, Paul, he's nothing but a gros dragueur' – a serial womaniser – 'I hated him.'

'Really?'

'Of course. Frankly, who gets out their phone to write down the date they hope to sleep with a girl?'

'Huh, yes – disgusting. So cold and cynical.'

I hoped I wasn't laying on the disapproval too thick.

'Shall we meet in our Belgian café for breakfast?' Manon suggested.

'Yes, I could go for a gaufre.'

'You must tell me what Elodie said. Was she mad at me?' Manon laughed and for the first time in eight hours or so, my intestines unknotted themselves and I was hungry for everything the day would throw at me.

Breakfast was short but sweet. Very sweet, in my case, with a sugar-coated waffle dunked into coffee that gradually became a black soup encrusted with pastry crumbs and sugar floes.

This amused and disgusted Manon in equal measure.

'Why do men always have to dunk everything?'

Now it doesn't take much of a dirty mind to raise an eyebrow at that. I'd heard the French expression 'tremper le poireau', to dunk your leek, meaning – well, the meaning is obvious.

So my right eyebrow performed the aforementioned vertical movement, and Manon frowned at me in mock disapproval.

We shared a chuckle about our respective nightmare dates. Manon's had ended with Gustav practically clinging on to the back bumper of her taxi as she escaped.

'You know, I'm glad you didn't sleep with Gustav,' I told her.

'Did you think I would?'

'You seem to be a woman who decides for herself what she wants to do. If it would be fun or interesting, you would do it.'

'Well, that wouldn't have been fun or interesting. And I'm glad you didn't sleep with Elodie.'

'That wouldn't have been possible. Not all men dunk everything everywhere.'

She laughed. My attempt at a French joke had worked. The day was beginning well.

Elodie wasn't in the office when Manon and I arrived – separately, of course. We had already divided up our tasks for this vital last day before the referendum. I was going to keep a close eye on the polls and the news reports. I wanted to check whether Elodie's press releases or ours were having any effect. Even if my computer was being monitored, it would be a logical thing for me to do. I was meant to be helping Elodie influence the referendum result, wasn't I?

Meanwhile Manon was to liaise with the people we had met at the Mickey Mouse café the day before. The only exception was Peter, the DG Communication guy, who was in contact with me by phone. He still didn't completely trust anyone French.

Elodie rolled up at about eleven, in a foul mood. It was almost fun to watch. She'd probably had a bust-up with Gustav over the phone. Or, even more likely, been ignored by him.

I couldn't resist suggesting that my next task for her could be to lobby for a Breton entry in the Eurovision song contest. That, I said, would win her votes back home.

'Only joking,' I added, when Elodie didn't reply.

She murmured something about me going to get myself sodomised by Astérix the Gaul, and slumped behind her desk.

After half an hour of her customary phone-poking, she announced that she was going out. We were left in peace.

As far as I could tell, the British news reports were as yet untouched by Elodie's hand, or mine. It was the usual stuff, divided between dire warnings about Europe's plans to end the British way of life, calm reassurances that the status quo was the way to go, and long, boring lists of economic pros and cons. Nothing new yet.

Meanwhile there seemed to have been an explosion in the number of polling organisations. All the news outlets had a mosaic of pollsters' logos, each with different percentages for 'in', 'out' and 'you decide, I can't be bothered'. Funnily enough, overall the opinion polls genuinely were too close to call. It looked as though Britain's future might be decided by a few yeses or nos getting lost on their way to the polling station.

Manon told me that everyone we'd asked for help had kept their word. When Peter sent me a copy of his (anonymous) press release, I forwarded the news to Manon, and she said that was the final link in our chain. We were up and running. It was just a matter of hoping that our propaganda would get picked up and outweigh Elodie's.

We grabbed a quick sandwich at the cafeteria, where everyone was abuzz with expectation. There were anxious pro-Europeans shaking their heads, anti-Brits (mainly with French-sounding accents) wishing us a hearty *au revoir,* and nervous-looking neutrals debating what-ifs. I bumped into Danny the oyster man, who winked at me and said, 'Plux tonight – it's going to be massive.' I gave him a thumbs-up.

My sandwich was a tasty combination of salad and shrimps, and when we got back to the office, I wondered whether one of the shrimps hadn't been past its sell-by date. Either that or the mayo had contained LSD.

Because, during our brief lunch break, Elodie seemed to have gone bald and put on men's clothing.

Then I saw my mistake. This wasn't Elodie; it was her dad, Jean-Marie.

23

'EU bureaucrats decree that Britain is not an island.'

Report in the British press, 2003

'AH, POOL!'

He got up from Elodie's desk to shake my hand.

'Jean-Mary.'

His smile of welcome flickered for a second, before resuming normal service. It was a childish thing we did. He often called me 'Pool', a mispronunciation of my name as '*poulé*', the French for chicken. In reply, I stressed the feminine sound of his name. Infantile, but I wasn't going to let him get away with it, especially now.

'Et Manon!' He came out from behind the desk and grabbed her hand for a stylishly delivered kiss.

While I was wondering what the *mokordo* he was doing here, he began questioning Manon about her work. She

294

looked annoyed about his prying, and at first I thought this was because he was stepping out of his role as blackmail victim. The French government had obliged him to organise Manon's job with Elodie in return for not prosecuting him for tax evasion, right? So surely he ought to be keeping his head below the parapet?

But then his questions started to get even more detailed, and I wondered why she didn't just tell him to mind his own business and get back to his tax returns?

'And the passwords worked?' he asked Manon in French, before turning to me and adding in English, 'I gave Manon the codes to Elodie's computer. She always uses the same numbers, since she was at school. She is so charming.'

So he'd helped Manon snoop into Elodie's computer? Again I got the impression I was under attack from an out-of-date shrimp.

'Quoi?' I asked – meaning 'what?' I didn't think it needed a more detailed question.

Manon squirmed.

Jean-Marie, meanwhile, did what he does best, which was to look even smugger than his daughter. His artificially suntanned cheeks widened in a huge grin, his salmon-pink shirt seemed to flush red and his royal-blue tie knot appeared to bulge.

'Oh, you didn't know, Pool? Manon works for me.'

The look on Manon's face seemed to confirm this.

The shrimp felt as if it was crawling back up my oesophagus.

If I'd had anywhere better to go, I would have stormed out. As it was, I stood there feeling the events of the past few days ricochet about in my head.

So Manon had been play-acting, even while play-acting?

'You're not with the French government?' I asked her, somewhat feebly.

She stood there mutely.

'Elle est avec moi,' Jean-Marie said, attaining even great heights of smugdom.

'Cacarella,' was all I could say.

'Corsican, n'est-ce pas?' Jean-Marie said. 'I have a house there, you know.' His smugness left the Earth's orbit and began its journey towards the planet Pompous.

'Sorry, Paul,' Manon said, 'but I knew you wouldn't trust me if I said I was working for *him*.'

Something in the way she pronounced 'him' dented Jean-Marie's spaceship just a little.

'I am a patriot,' he said, in English. 'And a true European. I couldn't allow my daughter to – how do you say? – rip Europe to shreddies. This great edifice that we have erected since the terrible war of 1945! France, England and even Germany friends again! With the Belges and the Hollandish and all the others, of course.'

Manon curtailed Jean-Marie's attack of idealism with an outburst in quick-fire French.

'He is afraid that if Britain leaves Europe, it will destroy his meat-export business,' she told me. 'He sells tons of French meat to England now. And imports from there, too.'

'I buy cows from the royal family,' Jean-Marie said, in English again. 'I received a medal from your Queen. What a sexy lady.'

God, I thought, only a Frenchman would fantasise about Her Maj.

'He also thinks that if Britain stays in the EU, it will work with France to reduce the pressure on Calais from all the migrants,' Manon said. 'His lorries keep getting held up at the Tunnel.'

'Intolerable, n'est-ce pas?' Jean-Marie agreed. 'A few months ago, when I have heard that my daughter is working with the "no to Europe" campaign, I was afraid. Elodie is an excellent organiser, you know. She has learnt it from me. I knew she could make their plan a reality. So I was forced to – how do you say in English? – stab her in the backside?'

'You see, everything you and I have done is valid, Paul,' Manon said. 'The only difference is that he was paying me.'

'That's a very big difference.'

'It's like your footballers, Paul,' she said. 'When they play a match, are they trying to make the owner happy? No, they want to win. And for their team. They don't care a damn about the owner.'

'Eh-yo.' Jean-Marie made the French noise that means 'watch what you're saying'. He shook a finger at Manon.

But she wasn't going to be stopped by a waving male digit.

'And don't forget, Paul, that just by birth I'm playing for the Czechs, the Poles, the Germans, as well as the French. And our team is immense – all the countries in Europe. Much bigger than the business plans of one Frenchman.'

'Ey!' Jean-Marie objected. 'Do not – how do you say in English? – sub-estimate my sincerity. You know, Pool, to hire Manon, I had to recruit her from a Socialist. Me, on my knees to a Socialist!'

I understood his pain. Jean-Marie was so right-wing that he thought OAP bus passes were borderline communist.

'But it was necessary, because I saw how the European situation was developing. You know, Pool, I am a visionary,' he said, like any politician who gets any decision vaguely right. 'You think I am just a businessman, but I am a true – how do you say? – strategicist? Strategian?'

'Excusez-nous.' Manon grabbed my arm and pulled me out into the corridor. We walked in silence until we got to the corner with the massive photocopier and its Alps of paper. She stood me against it and began speaking in quiet but urgent French.

'Paul, you have to believe me, please. I was sent to work for Elodie by that idiot, it's true, but what he doesn't know is that I really am working for the Ministry of Foreign Affairs.

When he first explained why he wanted to hire me – because his daughter was organising a secret pro-Brexit campaign – I told my MEP, and we got in touch with the Ministry. They instructed me to accept his offer and act as a sort of double-agent for them. How else do you think I found out about your phone being bugged? That kind of thing is an official secret. So you see, this whole time my aim has always been to stop Elodie. Her father's not important. He just has to carry on thinking that he is controlling me, that's all. What I told you about him being investigated for tax fraud was false, but everything else I have told you has been true and sincere.'

She had given me her most impassioned speech yet, and she certainly looked convincing. But then, as I've said before, we guys always want to believe a beautiful face.

'So you really were in Brussels before?' I asked.

'Yes, I was working for a French MEP who deals with international trading laws. That's how Jean-Marie heard about me.'

'And you're being paid by Jean-Marie, but working for the French government?'

'Yes. He's giving the government a sort of accidental subsidy.'

'And all the rest is true?'

'Yes, I promise you.'

'So your Greek ex-boyfriend – he's real?'

'Sadly, yes,' she said.

'And your promise to yourself – no relationships for three months?'

'True.' She smiled. 'But I read in the news that the orbit of the Moon is changing.'

'What?'

'Yes, it's like science fiction come true. Apparently the months are getting shorter. Last month was only three days long. And yesterday was a whole month.'

'What?' There was a short pause while I did some translation from French to English to make sure I'd got this right.

'Mon Dieu, Paul, that means: kiss me, now!'

Even in Brussels there are times when translation can wait.

It was a rather different Paul who walked back into the office a few enjoyable minutes later.

Jean-Marie was sitting at Elodie's desk, on his phone, looking understandably deflated. His audience had walked out on their star performer.

And now Manon was at my side, her lips probably looking slightly less shiny than before, my own gleaming with transferred gloss. Honey-flavoured.

'Alors?' he asked.

'Manon has explained everything. I didn't realise you had been so important, Jean-Marie,' I flattered him. Characteristically, he took it at face value. He smiled philosophically, as if his brilliance was a gift from heaven.

Manon gave him a strategically edited account of what had been happening over the past twenty-four hours or so. She didn't have time to go into details, she told Jean-Marie, but she had definitely set wheels in motion, some of which ought to derail a few of Elodie's stratagems.

'Très bien, all I ask for is results. Now can you come for a quick drink, Manon?' he asked, using the familiar '*tu*' form.

'Merci, but not really. We have work to do here. I'll let you know how things progress,' she replied with the distant '*vous*'.

'Let's all meet up for a drink later,' I told Jean-Marie. I was feeling magnanimous. 'It should be fun. The cafés outside Parliament will be heaving.'

'Heaving? Isn't that a word for vomiting?' he asked. 'I don't find that English habit fun.'

I explained what I meant, and hinted that Plux would be full of female badge people and lobbyists, most of whom liked nothing better than a man with a sharp suit and influence.

He left with a new spring in his step.

A few hours later Plux was, as I'd promised, heaving. So far, not at all in the way that Jean-Marie feared, though plenty of alcohol was on its way down throats. The roar of conversation was even louder than usual, the drinking more frenetic.

This was the night before the referendum, the eve of something massive. It really did feel as though we were surfing on a wave that could smash us head-first on to the rocks or make us world champions. Same wave, different fates, but everyone was looking thrilled by the ride.

The first time I'd come here, such a short time ago, I'd felt a total outsider. Now I had a badge in my pocket and a eurobabe on my arm. I could raise a glass and say 'Bonsoir' to a whole host of people whose business card I carried in my wallet.

The only person who wasn't there, so far at least, was the woman who'd introduced me to it all – Elodie. She was still AWOL. Hardly surprising, really, given the unpleasant shocks she'd planned for me and Manon that evening.

Slowly our small team of undercover agents gathered near one of the TV screens that was broadcasting British news. Apart from the occasional weather update and calls to buy cars, burgers and insurance policies, the imminent referendum was top of the agenda. Poll percentages were permanent fixtures at the bottom of the screen. Politicians, journalists and 'experts' swapped places alongside the anchor-people.

We all drank and waited for news that we had created.

Danny the oyster man was at the heart of our huddle, alternately cheering and booing politicians, though without much consistency in his allegiances. Beer might have had something to do with that.

Peter was sipping nervously at mineral water. He was with one of the women I'd seen in his office, who was fiddling with his shirt front a lot as they spoke. I didn't think it was to cover up the space left by his absent badge.

Gustav the Swedish Dane was there, and seemed to be making some generous promises about wind power to Šárka, if her body language was anything to go by.

Ed Fürst and his girlfriend were being monologued by Antonio the Italian, but at least he was plying them with fizz. Ed broke away to come and whisper in my ear.

'So you're no longer in the market for a Lithuanian girl, Paul? It's a pity, because they can be extraordinary.'

'Don't worry about me,' I told him, 'Manon is anything but ordinary.'

I flinched as he laughed at full volume against my eardrum.

It was ten o'clock before we saw something relevant onscreen. Going into an ad-break, a headline flashed up: 'THE END OF BRITISH LIFE AS WE KNOW IT?'

Sure enough, the news resumed with the fallout from Elodie's press release. A journalist, who had clearly been invited because he owned a Union Jack tie and could talk total bollocks, ran us through the shock article that his paper was planning to publish the next morning. Everything truly British was about to be crushed beneath the Brussels jack-boot, he said, from sausages to buses, chocolate to bingo halls. Even the Great British penis was going to get the squeeze, because of EU plans to reduce condom sizes.

The last rumour, I knew, was a completely twisted interpretation of an EU idea that contraception and disease control might be more efficient if people used the right size of condom, so that it would neither split nor slip off. But the anchor-lady was too busy giggling to contradict her guest, and British male viewers were probably left with the impression that staying in Europe would be a vote for castration.

All this had to be true, the man with the patriotic tie said, because the report had been written by a Brit working inside Brussels who had access to secret French papers. It was straight from the horse's *bouche*.

The anchor lady grimaced silently into the camera, as if she'd just seen footage of a gruesome accident. This was distasteful news, she was implying, but it was her duty to break it to us.

One up to Elodie.

Peter came over and told me that he'd told me so: it was pointless trying to oppose the rumour-mongers, he said, they were too shameless. His pessimistic rap was only truncated by Danny blundering up and promising us all that he could get 'giant johnnies' from a sex shop. In fact he had some in his pocket, if anyone was interested.

When nobody was, he went to get himself yet another drink.

Next up, about half an hour later, was a story about minority languages. Manon grabbed my hand and squeezed.

A woman who was being interviewed at home via Skype, giving us a blurred close-up of her nose and teeth, explained how it was possible for France to get EU funding for its minority languages, because, as in Spain, they were officially recognised as part of regional identity. She read out a list of millions of euros to be spent per French region. France, she concluded with toothy indignation, was going to be raiding Europe's coffers just to teach people how to swear in its various dialects.

The news-anchors looked appropriately shocked. Elodie seemed to have won again.

But then another speaker came on, a young woman apparently straight out of university, all smiles and enthusiasm, to say that this was a great opportunity for Britain. She quoted some meaty-sounding amounts that might be granted to Wales, Scotland, Northern Ireland and Cornwall, to fund their own language programmes.

One of the anchors asked: What about Liverpool and Newcastle?

Manon kissed me on the cheek. That question must have come from my press release.

The young woman laughed and said that any mention of Geordie and Scouse dialects was probably a joke. But she added that these EU regional grants might take the burden off existing cultural funding in the less-privileged parts of England, freeing up extra money for, say, music and theatre. Or even sport for kids. I could almost hear the whole of

Liverpool and Newcastle reaching for their voting pens. EU money for football? Yes!

We had drawn some blood. Ed broke away from his Italian friend's grasp to come and pat me on the shoulder. I bought him a drink to say thanks for his help.

When I got back from the bar, I saw that Manon had company. Jake had turned up with a tall, dark woman in tow. She stood a good six inches taller than him and seemed to be looking down on everyone from her olive-skinned, dark pony-tailed perch. As I moved closer, I saw that she was dressed in something approaching national costume – a round-necked white blouse, green cardigan and wide red skirt. It was urban wear, but with a bit of the Alps woven in.

Jake was chatting to Manon, while the new girl was already deep in conversation with the rich Italian.

'Hey, Paul! Man on, man!' Jake greeted me. 'So you kissed her? Formidable!'

Manon glowered and blushed simultaneously.

'Is this giant dirndl a new friend of yours?' I asked him, to prevent any blunt enquiries about developments beyond kissing.

'Yeah, she's my Austro-Hungarian. Works for one of the extremist parties. Très nostalgique about her old emperor. It's bizarre, like dating an Aztec or a Roman.'

'You call it dating, after one night?' I asked.

'And one afternoon. Long enough to discover that her sort of extremism has its disadvantage. She's très, très traditionnelle. But she has inspired me. Want to hear my poème?'

'Yes,' Manon said. She didn't know him well enough to say 'no' or just dash for the emergency exit.

'OK.' Jake took a deep breath.

So did I, but for different reasons.

> 'A nostalgic Austro-Hungarian,
> Is no sexual revolutionarian.
> Sole position: the missionarian.'

Mercifully, that seemed to be that.

'Great one, Jake. Up to your usual standard.'

Manon was simply looking confused, which was probably for the best. It wasn't healthy to think too much about Jake's poems.

Fortunately we were distracted when Danny meandered back through the crowd to bellow in my face, 'Paul, you're famous!'

I looked up to see myself on TV, waving stupidly at the camera while lying fully clothed in a bath, and then selfying – if that's a verb – from a sexy-looking iron-framed bed.

The male news-anchor was frowning in that concerned manner they adopt when they want viewers to realise that things are more serious than they seem. He was looking deeply disturbed by my ridiculous photos, and began talking us through the revelations that a (fortunately unnamed) '*British* civil servant working for a *French* MEP' (this paradox provoked an extra-deep frown from the newsman) had been living it up in Brussels while working for the 'yes' camp. Vested interests were obviously at play, he surmised – corruption even. The screen showed a photo of my tenancy agreement, with the rent-free clause highlighted, for all to see that I was a freeloader.

The co-anchor then led straight into an allegation that this same '*Englishman* in the pay of the *French*' had bought a *British* MEP's computers and helped the *French* to hack into them – a segment that was illustrated with stock shots of a shadowy figure typing at full speed on a laptop. You'd have thought I was sending out naked photos of Princess Kate to the French press, or issuing death threats to all of England's kittens.

A pollster-type in a stiff collar and tie came on and said this was a nail in the 'Remain' vote's French-built coffin.

Another blow landed by Elodie, and a painful one.

'Merde,' Manon commented, and she wasn't only talking about what we'd seen on TV.

Into the crowded bar, its conversation even louder after the recent revelations, had walked an anxious-looking Jean-Marie and a furious Elodie.

She barged past Gustav, hardly giving him a second glance, and stopped in front of Šárka. Waving a phone under Šárka's nose, Elodie unleashed the full force of a Parisian rant, which Šárka could only counter by holding out a hand in my direction.

I knew what this was about.

Elodie seemed to breaststroke through the few metres of crowd towards me, and within seconds she was brandishing her phone in my face.

'What is this?' she demanded.

'An iPhone?' I guessed, but the joke only made her madder.

She held the screen motionless long enough for Manon and me to read what was on it. Neither of us were good enough at acting to stop ourselves giving a little smile of satisfaction. A story we'd planted had got into the French news.

When Šárka had come to see us at the Mickey Mouse café the previous day, I'd fed her the white lie that Elodie was all in favour of installing a wind farm in her constituency – a dozen or so giant windmills in mid-countryside. I'd been careful to spell out the name of the site. It was right next to a famous historic monument, a group of ancient stones that might well have been laid out by Astérix and Obélix themselves, and which were rumoured to be the home of Celtic fairies, ghostly Gauls and magical lobsters, or similar Breton creatures.

All Elodie wanted in return, I'd told Šárka, was an immediate press release announcing the plan, so that she could be hailed in her region as an energy-efficient MEP. True to her word, Šárka had given exactly this to the Breton local newspaper, which had instantly sent it viral. 'Famous fairies to be blown away by windmills' was the gist of the story.

'What is this merde?' Elodie demanded.

'This kaoc'h, you mean,' I corrected her. 'Or koniriou, if you mean bullshit.' Before she could bludgeon me with her phone, I added that the wind-farm story was only as *merdique* as the stuff we'd just seen on TV about me hacking into English computers.

This stumped her for a second.

'The same goes for the edited version of my report about false EU rumours that you gave to the press,' I added. 'And which you stole off my computer using spy software.'

I could see that Elodie was not only stumped; she also felt that she was being caught and bowled at the same time. So I hit her with my final googly.

'Do you think the TV will be showing anything about a certain ferry?' I asked her. 'A load of Bretons arriving in England to demand linguistic refuge with their EU neighbours?'

Elodie was obviously wondering how the hell I knew all this. Her suspicions fell on Manon.

'Have you been spying on me?' she hissed.

Manon simply laughed off the accusation.

'Until yesterday Manon didn't know what I was working on, or what you were doing,' I said. 'Maybe someone else betrayed you.'

'Cédric? I'll cut him up and feed him to his cousins.'

'No, do you think he even understood what he was doing?'

Elodie seemed to accept this argument. She swept an accusing glare over the crowd. Ironically she ignored her father, who was hovering in the background, eyeing up Jake's Austro-Hungarian friend. Her gaze landed on Gustav.

'What did he reveal while he was fucking you?' Elodie sneered at Manon, using not only the '*tu*' form, but one of the crudest French words for sexual intercourse, '*niquer*'.

'I didn't fuck him.' Manon used the same word, but somehow kept it matter-of-fact. 'And all he revealed during our dinner was that he likes to nibble little pieces of pickled herring off women's bodies. I was wondering: Did he use the sauces, too? They must have been very sticky.'

Elodie could only squeak with fury. Despite the volume of the chatter and the TV, people had noticed that something confrontational was going on, and Elodie knew it wasn't cool to lose your cool in front of the influential Plux crowd.

'I think both of you will need to find new jobs in the morning,' she told us.

'Our jobs are done anyway,' Manon replied.

'You think so?' Elodie said, icily. 'You really believe you can keep your country in the EU, Paul? I don't know why you bother. Nobody wants you. I am doing everyone a favour.'

'You haven't been doing me any favours, Elodie. Honestly, all those selfies you got me to take, the bullshit computer auction, even your little speeches about the good old days. You must think I'm a real dickhead.'

'No, Paul. Honestly. You were just the Anglais de service. How do you say? The convenient Englishman. You were an old friend, but I couldn't let that stop me. This was a battle, I was the general, and I took the decision that you were the one who had to face the music of the cannons.'

'You sound like Napoleon.'

'Merci, Paul.'

'We Brits don't mean that as a compliment. How the hell did you think I was going to react this evening, when I saw myself on TV?'

'I thought you might see the humour in the situation. That's what you English are famous for, isn't it? And I supposed you would be consoled by a pile of euros – of which you have already received half. Isn't that a consolation?'

'You really think everything can be bought, don't you? It must be in your DNA.'

'Eh-yo!' Jean-Marie had been listening to our last exchange and stepped in to defend the Martin honour (not that there was much left to defend). He put an arm around Elodie's shoulder, which would have been cutely paternal if he hadn't been directly implicated in spoiling his daughter's evening.

'Don't listen to him, ma chérie,' he told her in French. 'He's English. He doesn't understand Europe. Let's go, before he says any more bêtises.'

What he probably meant was: Come away before anyone reveals that your own papa hired Manon to screw up your scheme.

'Yes, let's go.' Elodie laughed triumphantly. 'You stay here, and keep watching the TV, Paul. The battle isn't finished yet.

Look out for that ferry. It will sink the "stay in Europe" vote to the bottom of your precious so-called English Channel. We will see who has the last laugh, and whether you English really do have a sense of humour.'

With this, she turned and sailed out of the bar, accompanied by her father, who, with masterful hypocrisy, was saying, 'Great words, ma chérie . . . but what's all this about a ferry?'

The cross-Channel ferry from Cherbourg wasn't due to arrive in Poole until late. Before it docked, the news programme had time for another couple of referendum items.

First, a story about the EU paying France a fortune to build wind farms. The French, it was reported, were accepting so much cash from a Brussels-based energy lobby that they had even agreed to erect windmills near national monuments. The journalist with the Union Jack tie declared that the money was almost certainly going to go straight into French farmers' pockets, and predicted that only half the wind farms would actually 'see the light of day – or rather the breeze of day'. Cue a studio chuckle, and an acknowledgement that the 'Leave' camp would be loving this.

I had to admit that Elodie and her people had been very quick to retort with that twist on Šárka's story. As Elodie said, the battle was far from over.

Again Peter came across and commiserated with me. Ever the euro-pessimist, he seemed sure Elodie was going to win the war of words.

Almost immediately, though, there was good news.

First, an intriguing teaser in which an obviously drunk man was giving a bleeped-out speech in a pub. A few minutes later, after the adverts, we got the full story.

I gave Peter a friendly punch on the shoulder for doubting me. It was my film of Nick Rummage in Strasbourg.

Despite my shaky camera work, the coverage it got was gleeful. Everyone in the news studio – anchors, politicians and experts alike – thought it was hilarious to see the head of the anti-Europeans singing in perfect French, boasting about his cushy job within the EU's cosy walls and even issuing veiled threats of violence to innocent Brits in the Dordogne. The clip ran again and again, with each word relished, sub-titles added at key points, and freeze-frames on Rummage's flushed and drooling face.

'The Eunuchs have lost it – no pun intended,' said a grinning pro-Europe politician, before the anchor gravely announced that they'd invited a UKNOC party member to comment, but had received no reply. They cut to another ad-break.

Manon and I exchanged a kiss.

'Now it all depends on the ferry,' she said.

I nodded. Dealing with that had been our toughest call. We were far from sure that we'd get a result.

Our co-conspirators all came over to shake hands and pat backs, or in Danny's case, sing in French, about the Rummage film. No one in Brussels liked Rummage. Even his allies were said to hate him really.

The TV anchor-man announced that they were just getting 'astonishing footage' of a ferry that had arrived in the south of England. It was, he said 'a whole new migrant problem on our doorsteps'.

We all stopped talking and watched.

Sensing the tension emitting from our small group, other people near the TV screen shut up, too. The silence seemed to spread as the white ship docked at a floodlit quay, so that when the car port began to open, there was little more than a low hubbub of conversation in our section of the bar.

The camera pulled back for a wide shot. This late in the evening, the port area was deserted except for people waiting for the ferry. The journalists amongst them were easy to spot. They were the ones carrying cameras, lights and sound equipment.

A group of about a dozen foot passengers began to walk down the ferry's car ramp, preventing the vehicles from disembarking. It was clearly some kind of demonstration. The camera zoomed in. Some of them were carrying placards. The voice-over said that these were rumoured to be Bretons, coming to demand refuge in Britain.

Manon's hand squeezed mine even tighter.

We could hear the Bretons chanting. One of them broke away from the group and started walking towards the cameras. It was a middle-aged guy in a striped fisherman's jumper, and he was looking very pleased with himself.

But before he could start issuing his demands, there were shouts from the ferry, and the camera panned over to investigate. When it focused, everyone watching our TV gave an involuntary laugh.

Rolling down the ferry ramp, rather like tanks emerging from the landing craft on D-Day, was a small squadron of mobility scooters. A tight V-formation of electric-powered four-wheelers, all painted glossy red, accelerated at the Bretons, forcing them to scatter, and headed for the barrage of cameras at top speed – just over walking pace.

The old people hunched over the handlebars were all wearing baseball caps and sweatshirts emblazoned with the Union Jack. The commentator said that it was probably a reunion of the 1948 London Olympics cycling team.

The first scooter overtook the lead Breton, who had stopped to see what the fuss was about, before screeching – or purring anyway – to a halt in front of a TV camera. A white-haired lady with rosy cheeks and a backwards baseball cap blinked into the lights. A microphone was held out towards her for comment.

'Excuse me, dear, where's the nearest loo?' she asked.

Before anyone could answer, a second scooter pulled up. Another elderly lady beckoned for the microphone and waited for the cameras to focus on her.

'We're all British citizens who've been living in France,' she said, in a slightly wavering voice, 'but now we're coming home. If Britain votes to leave the EU, all of us British pensioners living abroad will lose our automatic right to free medical care on the continent. So here we are, back home again. Can anyone tell me where to sign up for a GP?'

The lady who needed the loo butted in: 'Oh yes, and my husband George needs his pacemaker resetting. He says it's because of the one-hour time difference. Where's the nearest A&E?'

More scooters were arriving.

An old guy wearing a fleece over his sweatshirt called out, 'It's bloody freezing here in England. How do I claim heating allowance?'

A frail-looking lady with her sweatshirt on backwards hobbled off her scooter and grabbed a reporter's sleeve. The camera focused on her eagerly smiling face.

'Are you my husband?' she asked him. 'What's my name?'

I joined in the round of spontaneous applause from the bar crowd that greeted this performance.

Unlike almost everyone in the room except Manon, I knew that it really was a performance. It was English Peter's idea. He'd told me that his mother was a retired actress who lived most of the year in Normandy. There, he said, she had started up an expat pensioners' theatre group. And they would probably be more than happy to put on a travelling show for me.

It had taken a few Skypes, an express delivery of printed hats and sweatshirts, and a costly but effective bit of haggling between Manon and a French medical-supply company, but we'd got everyone and their scooters to Cherbourg in time for the ferry.

Now our OAP actors were really getting into the swing of things. One of the guys was mooning a large white backside at the camera, demanding his daily insulin shot. A woman was complaining that she'd just been molested by a Breton farmer and wanted round-the-clock police protection.

'Tell Mrs Thatcher I voted for her!' she yelled, and then lunged at the nearest Frenchman.

The lady who'd asked for the loo came back into shot.

'If you vote "Leave", we're all coming home. And there are millions more Brits on the continent, just like us,' she warned, and then winked to camera.

Suddenly Manon and I were enveloped as a grinning Peter, sagely nodding Ed, drunk Danny, cool Gustav with his arm around Šárka, and hands-on Jake – who's always up for a group hug – closed in to congratulate us. The only ones to stay aloof were the Italian guy and the Austro-Hungarian woman, who were standing almost nose-to-nose, no doubt plotting the Austrian annexation of Tuscany, or vice versa.

In the crush, it was only natural that Manon and I got closer than ever.

'So do you think that's a definitive *oui* to Europe?' Jake asked, when we'd all moved apart a little. Apart from Manon and myself, that is.

'Impossible to tell,' I said. 'The polls are too ...' I looked up at the screen, and the percentages had disappeared. It had to be midnight. No more opinion polls. At bloody last.

'At least the British voters know everything now,' Manon said.

'Yes, people will decide for themselves in the morning,' I said. 'Time to sleep on it.'

I raised an eyebrow at Manon. She smiled.

'Hey, man, you're not really going to *sleep*?' This was Jake, of course. 'Allez, Paul, look at Manon – even you can see that she is totally desesper . . . uh, deseprest, uh . . .'

I dragged Manon away before Jake could finish dispensing his own brand of relationship therapy.

By common consent, Manon and I stopped on the threshold of the café, hand-in-hand, to look back at the scene we were leaving, the scene we had helped to create.

The TV screen was rerunning the mobility-scooter display, and a whole bar full of semi-drunk Brussels badge people were cheering the OAPs' invasion.

I wondered why the eurocrats cared so much. Whichever way the vote went in the morning, the Plux crowd's jobs were all pretty secure. Maybe the British civil servants' careers would be slowed down by a vote to leave Europe, but the other nationalities of Brussels eurocrat were more or less assured of a stable, well-paid future.

Even so, they didn't look the least bit complacent about Europe, or their place in it. They really did care. They were cheering for their team. They believed in Brussels. It was strangely touching.

'Allez, Paul!' Manon was tugging at my hand. 'You should listen to your friend Jake. Three months is a very long time for a girl to wait.'

She was right. For tonight at least, the EU could solve its own *merde, zut, cacarella, kao'ch, kaka, mokordo,* and all the other ways it has of describing its troubles.

I had a purely personal European union to forge.

And a French-subsidised bed in which to forge it.

24

'EU is backing out of its promise to prohibit excessive data roaming charges in Europe.'

Report in the British press, 2016

WHEN YOU wake up on that first morning with someone new, it's a very special feeling – all night there have been smells, tastes, sounds, sensations, and now, with the dawn light, there's going to be vision, too.

That was exactly how it felt on the morning after my showdown with Elodie. I drifted awake to find a warm presence in the bed beside me, and reached out to let my fingers run along its unfamiliar curves. Manon turned to face me and we enjoyed a long morning 'Bonjour'.

We were at my apartment – I guessed Elodie's eviction notice would be arriving very soon, but for the time being I was happy to squat there, if only to make the most of that iron-framed bed. There was something about gripping the thin, cool bars of a metal bedstead, or watching someone else do so, that made you want to try it again and again.

Eventually I got up to make coffee, and we took a look at the referendum news. As usual, it was all about contradiction – '*We're* going to win' . . . 'No, *we* are' – but the majority opinion seemed to be that the whopping lies told by the 'Leave' campaign would swing the vote against them.

While the Brits were out marking their ballot papers – or staying home and hoping for the best – Manon went off to talk to her mysterious bosses, and I packed my bags in case Elodie sent round some bouncers to throw me out. I then called Jake to bore him about the pleasure of hooking up with a woman you actually respected and wanted to spend more than one night with.

'Does she have an apartment where you can live?' was his answer to that. Same old Jake.

Manon and I spent the evening of referendum day in the bars at Plux with Danny and his euro-mates, and the general mood was summed up by the Italian Toni when he said that 'Next week, everyone will have forgotten the word Brexit.' Most people in Brussels would have agreed with him.

Waking up after a second night with Manon, still undisturbed by Elodie, my first impressions were the same as before: softness, contentment and calm, coupled with a desire to snuggle up and ward off the slight Belgian chill in the air. No T-shirts or pyjamas with a new lover, right? Nudity is, as the French

say, *de rigueur*. And talking of rigour, or vigour, I knew before
I even opened my eyes that I had a vigorous appetite for all
the physical and emotional perks that the new day was going
to offer. Life felt pretty good.

What I didn't expect was an acute pain in the earlobe,
accompanied by the sort of hissing you'd probably hear if
you accidentally sat on a cobra's eggs.

I dragged my eyelids aloft to find Manon, naked from the
waist up, as far as I could see (and from the waist down, as
far as I could remember), pinching my right ear while stage-
whispering me to 'get up!' in several languages.

Instead of the dreamy, contented gaze I had been expecting from her on our second morning-after, there was a furious snarl aimed right between my eyes.

'Are all your compatriots idiots?' she demanded in English.

I blinked at the small screen she was holding in front of my
face, and answered. 'No, apparently only fifty-two per cent
of them.'

It didn't seem possible. The Brexiteers had won.

We went into the lounge to watch the fallout on TV, and sat
side-by-side on the velvet sofa, wrapped in the white duvet,
like some two-headed maggot.

On a Belgian channel, a French-speaking reporter was
standing beneath the row of EU flags outside the Commission
building, giving a sort of elegy for the twenty-eighth flag,
which would soon be taken down and locked away in the

EU's archives or, knowing the Belgians, transformed into a wacky sculpture – underwear, maybe, to protect the decency of Jeanneke, the Manneken Pis's naked female cousin.

Then – surprise, surprise – Elodie popped up beside the reporter for an interview. On her face there was that infuriating mixture of false compassion and genuine glee which shows that a French person has just won a victory. The French can be bad losers, but they're even worse winners.

Asked what she thought of the vote for Brexit, Elodie all but ignored the interviewer and made a direct appeal to camera in husky, seductive French.

'We are ready to welcome foreign banks to Paris,' she promised. 'The British economy will now be too unstable for them to stay in London. And their employees will find Paris a much more accommodating city than London – cheaper housing, a far better lifestyle. And no need to import champagne at absurd English prices, of course.' She gave a well-rehearsed laugh, before getting suddenly serious. 'Now is also the perfect time for all those French citizens working in London to come home – they and their children will receive much better healthcare, and enjoy much better food. And who knows if, as EU citizens, they won't be deported by the British one day soon? Yes, time for everyone to come home to Paris,' she concluded, looking spookily like a young Margaret Thatcher, her womanly smile failing to conceal steely eyes.

'Quelle salope!' Manon said. What a bitch.

'She'll be going on every French-language channel there is, trying to hypnotise the expats into running home,' I said. 'Switch her off, for sanity's sake.'

I reached for the remote, but Manon was more awake than me and grabbed it.

'No, look, Paul, it's your best friend.'

Elodie's professionally smug mask wilted just a little as a man came into shot on the other side of the reporter. It was the French politician, Yves Remord, his usual grimace of distaste at everything in the world around him looking more pronounced than ever.

'This result proves what we've always known,' he lectured. 'The British disdain for Europe, their total lack of solidarity for anyone except themselves, their ancestral need to withdraw to their islands and busy themselves with their petty parochial concerns. It's as De Gaulle said in 1946, "The British are our true enemies in Europe, not the Germans."'

'Did he say that?' the reporter asked, but a sharpened scowl from Remord killed any debate about the matter.

'What we are demanding now,' Remord went on, 'is the right to a similar referendum in France. Let us vote; let us decide to stop immigration, to empty the refugee camps that have been imposed upon us. We will allow all the Calais refugees to walk into the Tunnel. If they want to go to England, let them . . .' For the first time I'd ever seen, a look of joy came over his face.

'That's not at all what the French people want,' Elodie butted in. 'The French people want to stay in Europe, to strengthen the economy from within, to trade with the rest of the world while the British sit alone—'

'What?' Remord's grimace was back again.

The camera had panned out, to include all three figures standing below the row of flags, with the bemused Belgian reporter stuck between the two French politicians, who were now barking directly at each other.

'That is absurd,' Remord said. 'You campaigned for the Brexit, madame, you campaigned to diminish the Union, and now you want to stay in? What hypocrisy! At least I'm honest. I have never—'

But we were destined never to know what he would never do, because Manon gave a grunt of disgust and turned off the TV.

'Quel bordel,' she groaned. What a brothel. Sadly, though, there is nothing sexual about this typically French expression. It just means 'What a mess'. Strange, really, because in all those Impressionist paintings, French brothels look like highly organised places.

Standing in the giant bathtub, I showered and tried to figure out what the hell to do with the rest of my life. Suddenly, being a Brit on the continent was no longer the simple pleasure it had always been – well, when I wasn't going head-to-head with French colleagues, bosses and bureaucrats, anyway.

My main worry was that from now on, the French might look down on me as a quitter – a traitor, even – whereas in the past they'd always had a soft spot for the English, especially if we managed to mangle a few French verbs at them.

After the Brexit vote, France might introduce residence permits, and tell their people at the Préfecture to make damn sure that Brits never had exactly the right number of photocopies or rent receipts. Staying on in France could mean getting slowly choked to death by red tape.

In which case, now that Elodie had fired me, was it a good idea to return to Paris? Or was it better to stay on in Brussels? Or just give up and go home to Blighty?

I was drying off, having reached no conclusions other than that a wise next move would be a cup of superhero-strength coffee, when Manon walked into the bathroom carrying my phone. She was already fully dressed, I noticed with a stab of regret.

'Some weirdo for you,' she said. 'I answered it because I thought it might be important.'

I saw that the call was from a landline, with no caller ID.

'Hello?' I asked.

A deep voice replied, in strongly accented English, 'You Meester Wess Pol? Breeteesh man, yeah?'

'Who is this?' I said, not wanting to commit myself.

'You want buy Europe passport? I get you Romania, Hungria, Polonia, very good price.'

'What?'

'OK, OK, I get Francia, Germania, but expensive very much.'

'Who the hell is this?'

'No names. You Eengleesh, you must get Europe passport, no? Otherwise you stuck on your little island, no travel nowhere. Y viva Espana, por favor? No gracias! But me, I have access to all consulates Brussels.'

'I don't need access to any consulates.'

'No? So you have Irlandia grandmother? You very lucky. You want to sell grandmother to me? Good price, Swiss francs.'

'You leave my grandmother out of this,' I said and cut him off.

'What was that?' Manon asked me. She'd stayed in the bathroom to listen.

'Nothing. Jake, probably – I bet he's inhaled one of his poetry-inducing drugs.'

Manon shrugged and left me to my towel work. No sooner had she gone than my phone buzzed to life again. It was a message from Danny the oyster man.

'Had you going there, Paul? Sorry, mate. But if you do need access to an EU consulate, let me know. Seriously.'

I found Manon in the kitchen preparing a lifesaving brew, and showed her the message.

'Idiot,' she tutted, but then seemed to change her mind. 'Maybe it's not a bad idea, Paul. Why don't you apply for a French passport? You've lived in Paris for a few years. You own a French business, your tea room. I'm sure they'd give you nationality immediately.'

'Really?' The idea had never crossed my mind. Become French, *moi*?

'Yes.' Manon warmed to her topic. 'In fact you *have* to become French, Paul. It's a great idea. As many British expats as possible have to get EU passports. It will show the Brexiteurs what you think of their racist, anti-foreigner vote.'

'I'm not sure *all* of them were racists.'

'Enough of them. You should leave them to their English fantasy island, get a French passport.'

'It's a bit early to start jumping ship, isn't it? Nothing's changed yet.'

'It's exactly the right time, Paul. You must jump ship now, before the lifeboats are all full. Your compatriots have made a hole in the bottom of their own ship. It is already sinking. And the worst thing is: they are the iceberg, and they are *inside* the ship.'

'You can't have an iceberg inside a ship – it would melt.'

'Metaphors can't melt, Paul.'

Oh, *merde*, I thought, it's useless trying to argue with one of these Frenchwomen who studied philosophy till the bac-calaureate. Especially before morning coffee.

We toasted some slices of dry baguette and went back to the TV, me in my bath towel, Manon in yesterday's clothes, as though she was about to sneak out of the apartment and do the walk of shame. Not that there'd been any shame about either of our two nights together.

I tried to give her a breakfast kiss, but it ended up bouncing off her left cheek as she fiddled with the TV remote. She switched to a British news channel. As referendum results slid along the bottom of the screen, town by town, a young woman in a British-looking street of red-brick buildings poked a microphone at a middle-aged guy with a tattoo wandering up his neck.

'How did you vote?' she asked him.

'Leave, a course,' he answered in a fierce Welsh accent.

'Why?'

'Well, what's the EU ever done for us, like?' he asked.

'It funded the renovation of this theatre,' she said, pointing to the blue plaque on the brick wall behind them.

'Never been in there,' the man shrugged.

'Didn't EU money rebuild the bridge, after the floods?'

'Maybe, but what have they done since?'

'The beach down the road has a blue flag. That must attract a few tourists.'

'That's fine for the tourists, but what have they done for the Welsh?'

'I'm pretty sure most Welsh farmers receive EU subsidies.'

'OK, but what has the EU ever done for *me*?'

Manon groaned again, making me think that she'd moaned a lot more about the Brexit result than during our recent lovemaking. Maybe, I thought, she was more emotionally tied up with Europe than with me.

'Do you really want to stay the same nationality as this guy?' she asked me.

'I might not for long, if the UK falls to pieces. Soon, Scotland, Northern Ireland and chunks of Wales might vote to go independent and rejoin the EU. London, too. All that will be left of the UK will be the pro-Brexit bits. The Queen will have to move to Burnley.'

'Stop hallucinating, Paul,' Manon ordered. 'I'm being serious. With people like this guy deciding British politics, it will be an important political gesture to get a new, EU nationality. It will be your protest vote. You have to give Britain a slip in the face.'

'Slip in the face' was a fantastic expression, I thought, because in French '*slip*' means male underpants. It would be great to give someone a slip in the face, a veritable jockstrap on the jaw. But I corrected Manon.

'I don't want to give Britain a *slap* in the face,' I told her. 'I'd love to punch one or two politicians and pee on the printing presses of a few newspapers, but Britain as a whole doesn't need a slap right now – it needs therapy. It needs a sticking plaster on its self-inflicted slash of the wrist. You've seen the vote. The country is split down the middle – young v. old, middle classes against working classes, urban against rural, all of us dumped in the merde by a bunch of gutless, self-serving political careerists. We need to *save* Britain before it splits up into four tiny nations and sinks into the Atlantic, while the Americans sell us overpriced life rafts – probably made in China. It's definitely not time for a slap in the face.'

I must have been looking genuinely sad, because Manon left off her political campaigning and stroked my wrist. She even gave me her first real kiss of the day. Well, since she'd got out of bed, anyway.

'That feels a bit better,' I said, pulling her tighter against me. 'I thought you'd forgotten our non-political activities.'

'Oh no,' she laughed, and gave me a playful slap in the face.

'Good. I remember *everything*.' I began picking at the top button of her blouse.

'There are important things to do,' she said, standing up and walking towards the bedroom.

'Important things?' I asked, hopefully.

'Yes, get dressed, we have people to go and see.'

'Oh, *important* important.' It was my turn to groan. 'But I haven't got a job any more.'

'That doesn't mean your work in Brussels is finished. Allez, Paul!'

A girl beckoning me towards the bedroom saying 'Allez!' had been a fantasy of mine ever since I could remember. Manon had said it to me just the other evening, and made my dream come true. But now, just one referendum result later, she was using the same technique to bully me into getting dressed. Talk about fantasies turning into nightmares.

*

Outdoors, the streets were eerily quiet. It reminded me of the deathly mornings in Paris after France has got knocked out of a football tournament.

There was hardly a soul about, except a couple of dog walkers and a jogging woman pushing her dozing toddler in a sort of offroad buggy. An expat mum, probably.

Manon was trotting along almost as fast as the jogger, as if she couldn't wait to get back indoors somewhere, out of sight.

'Who exactly are we going to see?' I asked.

Manon said she was going to meet some people at the Parliament, to try and make sure that British MPs would lose their privileges as soon as electronically possible.

'You can't do that,' I told her, forcing myself to keep up with her quickstep. 'Britain hasn't actually left yet. All our MEPs are still MEPs.'

'Yes, for now, but after Brexit actually happens, some of them will qualify for the EU pension. Even the MEPs who campaigned for Brexit. I want to make sure that Britain has to pay the pensions, not Brussels. Organising that will take some time. Best to start early.'

'Wow!' I'd seen Manon's tough side before, but this was long-range, premeditated toughness. 'You've been making contingency plans all along, haven't you?'

'Oh yes. The instant that Britain activates Article Fifty and begins the official process to leave, Brussels will have a – how do you say – une batterie?'

'A drum kit?' This was a word I knew, thanks to a musician friend. Though I couldn't picture Brussels putting on a percussion concert to celebrate Article 50.

'No, idiot, a battery – a barrage of diplomatic missiles to shoot at Britain. This pension is just one. The rest will be economic sanctions, import taxes, refusing to do trade deals, things like that. You have to inform the British.'

'Inform them?'

She stopped trotting and took both my hands, looking me hard in the eyes, presumably to make sure I understood once and for all that this had nothing to do with drum kits.

'Yes. Go and see your man at the DG Communication – Peter. While you were in the shower, I told him you'd visit him sometime this morning.'

'You did?' Bloody hell, she was a machine. Her brain waves probably looked like an Excel spreadsheet. Quite a contrast with the girl I'd got to know in the iron bed over the past couple of nights.

'Yes. You don't mind, do you, Paul, if I have organised your morning? This is all very urgent.'

I gave it a moment's consideration.

'No, I don't mind,' I said. 'I thought I could let the EU deal with its own merde, but now I'm not so sure. The DG Communication people need a bloody good talking to. I asked them before the vote why they weren't contradicting all the bollocks that was being broadcast during the campaign. They didn't budge, and now the bollocks has won the referendum. A lot of the blame has to go to the EU itself. They didn't stick up for themselves. They didn't tell people what they were really voting about.'

'Exactly, Paul.'

My little speech earned me a rather pleasant kiss, which I developed into a hug, reminding both of us that our bodies had been a lot closer, and a lot more undressed, in the very recent past.

'Let's meet up later,' I said, still holding Manon in my arms. 'We can't let all this politics distract us from . . . well, us.'

'Yes, of course. But first, work.' She kissed me again, briskly, then broke free. 'To the Commission. Allez!'

There was my French fantasy word again, even less sexily said than before. You couldn't get much further from my fantasy than the European Commission.

Manon hailed a taxi, but I preferred to walk, and as I got nearer the EU buildings, I began to see eurocrats on their way to work. They were dressed for a summer's day – cheerful colours for the women, light shirts and suits for the men – but their way of walking was anything but bright and summery. There was a furtiveness about them, and slouching was the *position du jour*, as if they'd all been up to no good the night before.

The Brit in me couldn't help thinking that, in some eyes, these people had been up to no good for the previous four decades or so. They'd been getting away with their overpaid Kafkaesque lifestyle, and now they'd been publicly taken to task.

I joined a small convoy of pedestrians heading along Kunst-Wet, and it seemed only appropriate to put in a call to the biggest fan of the most boring avenue in Europe.

'Hey, bonjour, Paul, man. How did it go?' Jake asked me.

'Haven't you heard? Elodie did it.'

'Elodie was there aussi?'

'What?'

'You had a ménage à trois?'

'What the hell are you talking about, Jake?' My raised voice began to attract the attention of a blue-shirted eurocrat in dark glasses walking ahead of me, who until then had been lost in his political hangover.

'You, Manon and Elodie? Tell me you filmed it, man.'

The euro-centime finally dropped.

'No, Jake, I'm talking about the referendum. They voted for Brexit.'

'Oh, I know *that*. I was talking about le sexe. You and Manon. For a *second* night. Was it repetitive? Boring?'

'Oh, fuck off, Jake.'

The guy in front turned to stare at me even more explicitly. Though it might have been because of my Brexiter's accent, rather than the words I was saying.

'I know about le Brexit since hours, Paul. I haven't sleep all the night. I was with a girl, half-Scottish, half-Irelandish. Very explosive. Married to an Englishman who is in London. She wanted me to—'

'Yes, thanks for the details, Jake, but I'm on my way to a meeting and I'm trying to prepare mentally. I don't need my head filling with your multinational porn.'

To my surprise, Jake changed the subject and asked me about my meeting, and he actually showed interest when I told him I was going to the DG.

'You're right, Paul,' he concluded. 'Someone has absolutely must got to tell Britain of the consequences of the vote. Go for it. Bon courage, man.'

'Thanks, Jake.' I was about to hang up, feeling freshly motivated, when the old Jake kicked back in.

'This night I have composed a posy that will help you.' He meant a poem.

'No, thanks, Jake, you've been helpful enough already.'

'It is titled "Coalition Interruptus". You want to hear it?'

'No, really, Jake, thanks—'

But it was too late. His poetry voice was already droning in my ear. I gritted my teeth.

'Britain dumped the EU,' he began, 'like a guy who don't want to screw, anyone wearing blue.'

'No, really, Jake . . .'

> 'Brits will throw EU's future into doubt,
> By pulling their seed money out,
> Like a Catholic who won't spray his sperm about.
> But attention, you British, if you turn your backs,
> France will take you up the ass.'

Finally there was silence, or at least nothing more than the sound of footsteps and traffic in the street. Mercifully, the poetry had stopped.

'You get it, Paul? "Butt attention", you know, like "pay attention to your butt"?'

'Yes, Jake. Very poetic.'

'The only problem is with the last line.'

'You really think so?' Most of his lines seemed to me to have fatal flaws.

'Yeah. Will it be only France? I mean, maybe also China? America? India? Everyone will want to take England in the cul, now you're alone and without protection. Scotland also. Hey, er, babe? You want to take the English up the ass, right? No, not your man in London, I mean politiquement, métaphoriquement . . .'

I gathered he was now talking to his new sex friend, whose name he'd already forgotten, if he ever knew it, and I put my phone away. It was the wrong time to stay on the line with Jake. I only had a couple of hundred metres more to clear my brain before meeting Peter, the DG guy.

In front of the Commission the blue flags were hanging appropriately limp. The sun was shining on their yellow stars, but today they were looking jaundiced instead of golden. The curved, metal-clad façade of the building was more fortress-like than ever. I could imagine all the faces inside, peeking out at the hostile world from the slits in their armour plating.

I called Peter to tell him I'd arrived, and loitered in the wide lobby. It hadn't exactly been a buzzing hive of conversation the last time I came here, but now it was a hushed cathedral in mourning, the arriving eurocrats almost tiptoeing in, offering only wan smiles or whispered conversation to their colleagues.

Peter came down, shook my hand and escorted me through the security barriers. His only comment before we reached the lifts was a pair of raised eyebrows and an 'oo-er' twist of the mouth. I wondered if he didn't want to be heard speaking in the language of Brexit.

Once we were behind sliding doors, alone as we travelled upwards, he let rip.

'What a bloody mess. How could they believe all those total fucking lies?' He looked towards the ceiling of the lift, maybe worried that his lips could be read on CCTV.

'Well, partly because you didn't contradict them loudly enough,' I said. He had no answer to that.

On his floor, the atmosphere had changed. When I'd come here last time, they'd seemed a merry, laid-back bunch, chatting amiably and calling out greetings to each other as they ambled along their career path, with little to do except pump out inoffensive blurbs about obscure EU achievements and the occasional report on infringements of Brussels law by various member states (except the UK, of course). Now the wide corridors were empty, and the only people I saw were three middle-aged badge-wearers huddling over a desk as if in a crisis meeting.

Peter ushered me straight into his office and shut the door.

'Well, what are you going to do?' I asked as soon as we had sat down on either side of his desk. No point beating about the bush.

'Apply for Belgian citizenship, of course, like everyone else.'

'No, I mean about the Brexit vote – not how are you going to salvage your career.'

'Oh yes, of course.' To his credit, Peter looked guilty. 'All we can do is express our regret that the EU's wide-ranging ideals haven't been recognised by a majority of Britain's voters, and reaffirm our wish that the UK will ultimately decide to stay in the Union and continue to work—'

'That's going to make a great headline, Peter. Bound to get picked up by all the tabloids. Though they might have to make their front pages a bit bigger to fit it in.'

'It's all we can do.'

'You know it's partly your fault that so many people voted for Brexit.' This time he tried to object, but I talked over him. 'No one in Britain really knew what the EU does. Sure, there are plaques on bridges and the like, but people expect bridges to be built anyway, they don't really feel grateful for that. What you should have been telling the Brexit voters is that when they go on holiday to Spain this summer, the main reason they won't be swimming through shoals of turds is that the EU started its blue-flag beach scheme. And if they turn up in Magaluf to find that their supposed hotel is in fact a car park, they can get their money back, because the EU introduced Europewide consumer protection laws. And from now on, they might have to pay for visas or spend half their holiday at the airport, queuing to get their passports stamped.'

I ran out of breath and ideas. Peter was shaking his head.

'I told you, Paul, the British press wouldn't have listened.'

'Then you should have put up posters in the streets, showing beaches before the blue flag and after.'

'And the British press would have said we were spending their taxpayers' money on propaganda. Face it, Paul, the people who voted to leave didn't want to hear the truth. They were happy to believe the lies. They just don't like foreigners very much, simple as that. And they think that as soon as Britain leaves the EU, we'll get the Empire back and start winning the World Cup again. It wasn't about truth.'

I suddenly felt deflated. He was probably right. You don't believe whoppers like the ones the Brexiteers had been touting, unless you really wanted to.

'Our best chance now is to discreetly lobby British politicians to hold a second referendum,' Peter said.

'You can't do that. That's just being a bad loser. It'd be like wanting to toss a coin until you finally win. What Manon says is that you lot have to warn everyone that once Article

Fifty is triggered, the EU can just walk away and say, "You want a trade deal to import cheaply into the single market? Fuck off, in twenty-odd languages.'"

'We're going to be doing that, of course. But the British press will only call it scaremongering. Project Fear, part two.'

Again, I guessed he was probably right. It all looked pretty hopeless.

'So you're applying to become Belgian?' I asked him.

'Oh yes, and from what I've seen on Facebook this morning, their citizenship website is going to crash. All the Brits I know here are brushing up their French and Flemish, and trying to sort out their King Leopolds from their Queen Mathildes. Either that or they're claiming the same nationality as their spouse. By this time next year there won't be a UK citizen left in the whole of the EU bureaucracy. What about you? Can you become French?'

'I'm not sure. Do you have to do an interview if you apply for a new nationality? When I speak French, it sounds as though I'm taking the piss. And I can't even pronounce the name of their national anthem.'

'La Mar-say-yez,' Peter said, convincingly.

I had a few goes at copying his accent, but like most Brits, I wavered somewhere between 'marshy haze' and 'mayonnaise'. In any case, it never really sounded French.

'Don't worry, Paul. I'm sure it's more about whether you tick the right economic boxes. And I bet the French will be only too pleased to welcome Brits into the fold. They'll send you a French passport as soon as you click "yes" in the box asking if you like Camembert.'

'I can't stand the stuff. Cheese shouldn't be that squidgy. Give me a nice, crumbly Wensleydale any day.'

Peter tutted at me.

'You're forgetting, Paul. We're in a period of history where it's not trendy to tell the truth. You've got to lie, like everyone else. Now, sorry to deport you, but I'd better go and see what kind of press releases my team's been concocting.'

He stood up.

'It's not just about Britain, you know,' he said. 'We've got to rally the European troops. We don't want other countries holding referendums, otherwise before you know it, it'll be just France and Germany meeting in Strasbourg every month to try and decide which bankrupt European nation they can invite to join their dwindling little club.'

'I've got bad news for you, then,' I told him. 'The French patriots are already calling for a referendum.'

'Voilà,' he said, already sounding Belgian. 'If we're not careful, we're heading for total meltdown. The UK will disintegrate and the EU will slowly deflate, member by member. It's la merde généralisée.'

On that note, I left Peter to try and decide what the hell his Communication department was going to communicate. Once he'd got his citizenship application done, of course. First things first.

Heading for the exit, I was accosted by a guy I'd seen somewhere before.

'Hey,' he called as I walked towards him in the lobby, the loudest voice I'd heard all day. He was badged up, but I couldn't read his name. 'You're a Brit, right?' he asked me, shaking my hand. 'Parliamentary assistant? Working for a French MEP?'

I remembered. He was the tabloid journalist who'd tried to interview me in Strasbourg.

'Hi. This is going to be a busy day for you, right?' I pulled at my hand, but he was still hanging on.

'Oh, yeah.' He looked delighted. 'All these politicians backing out and doing U-turns, as if to say, "You didn't really believe me, did you, you fucking idiots?" This is going to run and run. Want to do an interview? You know, the view from inside Brussels?'

'I'm not really inside Brussels any more.'

'You resigned? Brilliant.'

'No, fired.'

'Even better. Brit booted out of Brussels. The backlash begins. Come and grab a coffee, let's talk.'

Something about the way he was still gripping my hand, tugging even harder now, got on my nerves. I pulled my fingers free.

'No thanks, mate. It's because of you lot that we're in this mess. So go fuck yourself! And you can quote me on that.'

The line was as cheesy as a ripe Camembert, I know, but it's something I've always wanted to say, and I walked out of the Commission with a spring in my step, ignoring the loud 'Yeah, well fuck you, too' aimed at my back.

25

'EU wants to ban British beaches.'

Report in the British press, 2014

FEELING PECKISH, I found the Belgian café where I'd taken refuge once before, and ordered *moules-frites*. I thought there would be something therapeutic about picking the little bits of salty yellow rubber out of their shells. The repetitiveness would help me think. And chips are such great comfort food.

Call me cautious, but I tried my best to sound German or Scandinavian when I was ordering. Who knew what Brussels chefs would be doing to Englishmen's food today. It would be all too easy to spit in the sauce or replace the mayonnaise with something unspeakable. I even pulled out my phone and had a brief fake conversation along the lines of 'Yergen splergen nergen, danke!' to convince the waitress I was in no way a Brexiteer.

I saw that there was a voicemail from Manon asking me to call her back, but I didn't dare do it before my meal was safely served. I just sat nursing a Belgian brew and wondering again where I was going to go from here.

That partly depended on what Manon's plans were, and whether she wanted me to be involved in them. Over the last couple of days I'd felt sure we had something going for us. We'd played cat-and-mouse for so long that finally getting it together had felt like a heartfelt decision, rather than a casual fling. This morning, though, she had been worryingly brisk and businesslike. No real romance in the air, as if our bubble had been popped. Well, if it had, I hoped there was a puncture-repair kit.

The big question that I couldn't get out of my head was: if I – or we – did go back to Paris, should I become an apprentice Frenchman?

This was really bugging me. My conversation with Peter had reminded me what the Marseillaise was about. I'd seen the words written down. It was a battle song. There was a line about taking up arms, another about raising a bloody flag, and it ended with a call for 'impure blood to water our fields', which sounded downright racist. Could I really accept the nationality of a country that suggests a massacre on July 14 every year, and before every international football match?

Fittingly, it was while I was imagining hordes of French people spraying their courgettes with blood that Elodie phoned me. I was so surprised that I took the call.

'Bonjour, Paul.'

'Bonjour, Elodie?' I was already regretting this conversation.

'How are you feeling this morning, Paul?'

She sounded sincere and compassionate, which was a sure sign that she was loving every patronising second. But I couldn't accuse her of calling me just to gloat, without alerting everyone around me to my true nationality.

'OK,' I finally answered, internationally.

'I'm so glad. I thought you'd be sad, or angry, or shocked, or all of those.'

She was managing to keep any hint of glee out of her voice, which had to be demanding superhuman self-control.

'No,' I said, with a slight Swedish accent. *Ner*.

'Well, it sounds as if you've been – how do you say? – struck numb. Speechless.'

'Ner,' I repeated.

'Anyway, I want to help you, Paul.'

'Er?'

'Yes, I want to help you get French nationality.'

Bloody hell, I thought, everyone's at it. But all I replied was another vaguely Nordic grunt.

'Are you all right, Paul? You sound as though someone's got their hands wrapped round your testicles. You're not still in bed with Manon, are you?'

I wanted to ask how the hell she knew I'd ever been there, but I guessed it had been pretty obvious the last time Elodie saw us together where Manon and I were going to end up.

'Ner,' I answered.

'Oh, so it's just the shock then. I'm sorry. My fault entirely. I humiliated you. I destroyed you and your political ideals. I crushed your hopes.'

Amazingly, she was managing to make this sound as if she was sorry for committing some social faux pas, like asking me how my grandmother was, the day after she died. But I couldn't let her carry on with the fake sympathy.

'Pah!' I said, which sounded like a suitably non-English putdown.

'I crushed your hopes as if you were an ant.'

'Et tu es un éléphant?' I couldn't keep shtum any longer.

'Ah, awake at last, Paul. But I think you mean "une éléphante", feminine. You must get your grammar right, if you want to become French.'

'Qui dit je veux?' I asked, no doubt using grammar that would have got my application stamped 'undesirable'.

'What is wrong with you, Paul? First you can't speak at all, now you only speak French, or what is probably meant to be French. Are you drunk?'

Making an 'I'll be back in a second' gesture to the waitress, who didn't really seem to give a damn, I went outside so that I could rant in English.

'What's wrong with *you*, Elodie? Why are you calling me up this morning sounding as if you want to give me a consolation shag? Are you hoping that you'll screw things up between me and Manon? Well, it won't work. I'm in a café having a pleasant Belgian beer, so you don't need to worry about me.'

'But I want to *help* you, Paul.'

'I don't need your help.'

'I think you do. And I want to give it.'

'Why? What's in it for you?'

'What's in it for me?'

'Yes, there's always something in it for you, Elodie. If you saved the world from global warming, it would only be so that you could wear your fur coat more often.'

'Honestly, Paul! Do you really think I am so . . . what is the word?'

'Deviously, cynically hypocritical that you would stab an old friend in the back and then sell the photos to the newspapers? Yes, I do. So why don't you just tell me what you want, and what's in it for you?'

'OK, OK. I'll tell you, Paul. I'm worried. Remord and his racist idiots want to campaign to leave the EU. I want France to stay in, at its heart. And the best way to do that is to have lots of French expats coming home, and lots of Brits wanting to join us, becoming French, or Belgian, Spanish – wherever they're living. I want to make becoming a European citizen trendy. I want you to help me make Europe sexy. You remember when you wore that mini-kilt?'

She was referring to a time a few years earlier when I'd earned my fifteen minutes of internet fame by being photographed in America wearing a ladies' kilt, for reasons that had seemed logical at the time.

'Don't try the nostalgia trip on me, Elodie,' I retorted. 'And don't forget you screwed me over pretty badly in America, too. Like you've been planning to do since before you invited me to Brussels. And I'm not even sure I want to get French nationality, so you can forget it.'

'Just apply – just fill in the form. I'll let you stay on in the apartment for another month.'

'I'm already packed and ready to go.'

'I'll pay you, Paul. A hundred euros.'

'Don't insult me.'

'Tell me a price. Five hundred, a thousand.'

I'd had enough of her attempts to mind-fuck me. And in any case, inside the café I could see the waitress carrying a tray of *moules-frites* towards my table.

'Au revoir, Elodie.'

As I hung up, I thought I heard her call out 'Five thousand'. That had to be a joke.

Heeding Danny the oyster man's advice about shellfish, I was careful to chew each mussel to a pulp before swallowing. Even if they had already been boiled to death, there was no point taking chances. And they did their mesmerising trick. I even managed to put Elodie out of my mind, as I devoted myself wholly to the task of pinching mussel from shell.

Once the mussels were gone, the heaped dishful of thin, crisp *frites* was so comforting that I even forgot I was meant to be Scandinavian. After wiping my fingers on the little towelette provided for shellfish-eaters, I called Danny to decline his earlier offer to put me in touch with every EU consulate in Brussels.

Characteristically, he was in optimistic mood.

'I'm going to become a Flem,' he told me. 'The Belgians are fun. Having dual Belgian-Brit nationality isn't really political at all. It's just like having two favourite beers. Hey, which reminds me. Are you up for some action at the pub tonight?'

'What sort of action?' I hadn't forgotten that my first drinking session with him had ended with me on my knees, getting pickpocketed by a prostitute.

'Political action. Sabotage.'

He lowered his voice slightly and outlined his plan, and how I could get involved. Sabotage was right. He was proposing direct action of the directest kind.

'Bloody hell, you're really going to do that?' I asked when he'd finished explaining.

'Oh yes. And it'll all be filmed, of course. It's called getting your just deserts. Or your just hors d'œuvre, anyway.'

'Count me in,' I told him.

Whatever else happened on this mixed-up Brexit hangover day, the evening was going to be pure fun.

Next I phoned Manon, who told me she'd set up shop at the Mickey Mouse canteen in the Parliament building and invited me to join her.

My badge got me through all the security barriers (either Elodie was too busy to have me crossed off the list or the EU's bureaucracy really was as slow as everyone says) and I dashed into the lift, keen to avoid any embarrassing encounters in the lobby – with Elodie herself, Yves Remord or the British anti-European MEP Nick Rummage, who would be in sickeningly triumphant mood.

Most of the brightly coloured seats in the cafeteria were occupied. But the babble of chatter was low, and there seemed to be no networkers flitting from table to table. Shoulders were hunched a few degrees lower than usual, including Manon's. I spotted her in a corner, bent over her laptop, typing fast.

I bought us both cappuccinos and joined her. We kissed soberly on the cheeks, like old colleagues. But then I wasn't expecting a public snog in the workplace.

We discussed my meeting with Peter at the Commission, and her concluding comment was a loud 'Merde'.

Normally, Manon's expletive might have attracted a few curious stares, but suddenly everyone's attention was drawn to a huddle of chairs in the middle of the large room. Voices were raised. Guttural opinions were being exchanged, accompanied by waving hands.

'The Germans and the Dutch are at war already,' Manon said.

As if in reaction to this first outbreak of European discord, another group of coffee-drinkers started having a go at each other. A man and a woman stood up and seemed to be trading accusations.

'She's Italian, he's Greek,' Manon explained. 'Ça commence.'

After a couple of minutes, and a dismissive guffaw from the Greek man, diplomacy won over and a relative calm was renewed, although the general volume of conversation in the room had risen to a tenser pitch.

I told Manon about Elodie's offer of a fortune in cash, just for filling in an online form. She was less shocked than I'd expected.

'You should take it, Paul,' she said. 'You haven't got a job any more, and soon you'll be homeless.'

I noticed that she didn't tell me to bring my bags round to her place.

'I've got enough for a decent hotel,' I said.

'Yes, but if you could get all that money, just for applying…'

'I don't believe she really meant five thousand.'

'Ask her. What have you got to lose?'

'You don't think it's a trap?' I asked. 'With Elodie, nothing is ever that straightforward.'

'Just make sure you get the money first, then you don't care. And you never know, you might decide to go the whole way and become French.'

I had to admit I'd been thinking about it.

'One thing bothers me, though,' I said. 'Do you think I'd have to sing the national anthem?' I didn't attempt to say 'Marseillaise'.

'I don't know. Why?'

I tried to explain my problem with words implying racial differences between blood groups, but as I did so, I saw the expression on her face turn from bemusement to outright disbelief.

'It's a national anthem, Paul – they're all about defending the homeland and things like that, aren't they? What about "God Save the Queen"? How arrogant can you get! You think England is the centre of the divine universe?'

'No, we're just asking nicely. "Please God, if you exist, there's one thing you can do for us as a nation – save the figurehead whose family attracts all the tourists." It's much more polite than a call to massacre people in the middle of a field.'

'What about all that "send her victorious" stuff?'

'That's probably to do with horseracing. They're the only victories the Queen really cares about.'

Manon laughed.

'I hope this is English humour, Paul. You are joking, right?'

But I had to confess I wasn't. Forming battalions and slaughtering people wasn't my thing.

Manon frowned at me.

'Seriously, Paul, I think you should tell Elodie you'll do it. It's not just the money. It's important to me.' She put her hand on mine. 'Like I told you, making this gesture now would show that we're on the same page politically. That we feel the same way about things. If you don't at least make the symbolic move of asking for French nationality, I'll be very disappointed.' She squeezed my fingers and gave me a playful pout. 'And you might be a little disappointed, too, Paul.'

The look in her eyes told me what was at stake here. I couldn't believe it.

'You mean, you want to be able to lie back and think of France?' I asked, at a discreet volume. But she didn't understand. I lowered the volume still further. 'You mean, no French passport, no amour?'

She giggled, but I got the impression she was deadly serious.

'I can't faire l'amour with someone who has the opposite opinions to me,' she said. 'I mean, for example, I couldn't with someone who was crazily religious.'

'What, so no "two nuns in a bath" action, then?'

Manon was lost again. She'd clearly never heard any ancient English jokes about convents and soap.

'This is sexual blackmail, Manon,' I explained.

'Or you can look at it as an offer,' she said. 'Fill in the form, then come to my apartment and tell me all about it.' She squeezed my hand again. So it looked as though I was welcome *chez elle* after all – as long as I had the right passport.

Oh well, I thought, call me a materialist, but if it's a case of 'fill in the form and you'll get a pile of euros, a place to stay *and* a shag', why not?

I phoned Elodie there and then. After a bit of haggling, she confirmed that she really would pay me a whole, insane five thousand, and sounded all too keen to meet up as soon as possible.

'Give me thirty minutes, then come to my office,' she told me. From the sound of it, she was in a car, and before she rang off I heard her tell the driver 'Au Parlement, vite.'

I was suspicious about all this haste, but Manon repeated that I had nothing to lose.

'Just get the cash first,' she reminded me.

Half an hour later I was walking along the bland corridor I knew so well (if you can know one of the EU Parliament's faceless corridors well), lecturing myself that even if I thought I had nothing to lose, Elodie was an expert at digging up things that her adversaries hadn't realised they could in fact lose. I was going to have to tread very carefully.

First I went into Manon's old office, which was exactly as I'd left it two days before. My chair was still facing the way my buttocks had pointed it, so that I could stand up and head over to Plux to watch the pre-Brexit TV debates.

'Paul, c'est toi?' Elodie called from her office next door. She sounded as though an old friend had dropped by for coffee.

I found her sitting at her desk, prodding away at her laptop. As usual, all her other work surfaces were bare. Everything was locked away in the safe.

She stood up and came to give me a *bise* on the cheeks. Again, just like a casual meeting between friends, as if our showdown a couple of nights before had never happened. Eerie.

'I see you're the type of girl who wipes the slate clean every morning,' I said. 'That must make life easy for you.'

She laughed and fiddled with the top button of her crisp white blouse, which was done up for once. She was looking almost prim. Her blouse was uncharacteristically loose and her skirt several inches longer than usual. Her hair was pulled back to reveal discreet pearl earrings. I guessed she'd dressed for the TV shows, wanting to project a mature image.

'Oh no, Paul, our little public argument was one to remember,' she said. 'For all the right reasons, too. It was the contrary of what that Romanian king used to do to his prisoners – you know who I mean? L'empaleur.'

'Vlad the Impaler?'

'The one who used to sit them on a pointed pole, and slowly, slowly their own weight would push it up their – well, you can imagine how painful it got. In French we call it "the punishment that begins so well and ends so badly". Since our little argument, everything has been the opposite of that. The night began horribly, thanks to you, but ended wonderfully.'

Just for an instant, a look of triumphalism flashed across her face.

'I forgive you for trying to impale me, Paul,' she said. 'All your manipulations and your betrayals were in vain, so let's forget them.'

The bare-faced cheek of the woman left me speechless. I opened my mouth to argue, but she held up her hands in a gesture of conciliation.

'Let's forget our conflicts, please, Paul. Today is about helping you – and all the British – move forward. And the best way for you personally to do that is to ask for French nationality. Agreed?'

'Well . . .' I still wasn't sure. 'Have you got the money?'

'Of course!' She looked affronted.

'Hand it over, then. Cash in advance, please.'

Elodie laughed again. She really was in a frisky mood today.

'Oh, Paul. You've been taking lessons from that prostitute you took back to your hotel.'

I ignored the jibe and held out my hand.

Tutting at this show of distrust, she went behind her desk and opened her safe, making sure that I didn't see the code.

She handed me an envelope, and I began to count the stack of crisp green hundred-euro notes it contained. As I did so, I couldn't help remembering that scare-story about the ink on euro banknotes making men impotent. The sight of so much money was having a slightly different effect on me. I'd never touched that much cash before in my life.

'I can't believe you don't trust me,' Elodie said. 'That reminds me: you haven't got a criminal record, have you? It might complicate your application.'

I waited until I'd counted right up to fifty before answering.

'I got a fine for not translating my tea-room menus into French,' I said. I wondered if a sin against the French language might disqualify me from citizenship.

'That's not a crime, that's just a délit,' she said.

I didn't understand the word, but I gathered French crimes were divided up into strict hierarchies, like all aspects of their life.

'OK, are we ready to begin?' Elodie asked.

I stuffed the money into my trouser pocket.

'Now we are,' I said.

'Can you turn off your phone, please?'

'Why?'

'This is a serious moment, Paul. I don't want you to be distracted by one of your friends telling you that he has found a Pokémon.'

She glanced down at my trouser pocket, and I got the message. She was paying, so we were playing by her rules. I switched off the phone.

'Merci, Paul, just one second.' She typed something, then looked up at me and smiled. 'OK, all ready. Now you sit here, we'll do it on my computer.'

She positioned the laptop almost ceremonially in the centre of her desk, and then stood directly behind me as I sat down and began to read the official-looking text on her screen.

'These are the conditions you need,' she said. 'It says five years' residence, but don't bother with that. My father and I can sponsor you. There is a condition that says you can get nationality if you have done something good for France. We will say that you have started a business and given employment to the French nation.'

'But I started it with your dad, and employed your brother,' I objected.

'That doesn't matter. Nepotism is one of France's greatest natural resources.'

She wanted to click elsewhere, but I read on.

'Hey, it says that if you're over sixty, you don't need to speak French. Even my dad could get citizenship, and he hates the French – except for your wine, brandy, cheese, climate, cafés, fast trains, Impressionist paintings and topless beaches, of course.'

Elodie puffed impatiently.

'Get rid of this page, Paul.' She leant forward to open up another tab, and I smelled her perfume and felt the pressure of her breast on my shoulder. Incredible really, when the last time I saw her she had looked as though she wanted to rip my balls off.

'Voilà,' she said. 'Now we can begin. Allez!' That word again, though this time it was said like a film director calling for action. 'So,' she announced, 'an Englishman applies for French nationality. Monsieur Pol Wess, future Frenchman.'

I was going to answer back that we were far from sure that France would have me, but the preamble to the nationality application had caught my attention.

'Do I adhere to the principles and values of the Republic?' I read out loud. 'It's a bit difficult to do that, if you were born in a monarchy and don't see why your monarch should get her head chopped off.'

'All that means, Paul, is that you must agree with the ideas of "Liberté, Égalité et Fraternité". That's not difficult. Everyone believes in those.'

'France hasn't exactly produced Égalité yet, though, has it? When we lived together in that HLM' – meaning subsidised housing – 'right in the heart of the Marais, all the other apartments in the building were rented out cheap to friends of the mayor. Including your dad.'

I chuckled at the memory, but I felt Elodie stiffen.

'That was a long time ago, Paul, when I was a student. And anyway I'm sure that my father paid the full rent, a fair rent.'

It sounded as if she was issuing a public statement.

'What does it mean by the "symbols of the Republic"?' I asked, pointing to the screen. 'The fleur-de-lys?'

'No, Paul, that was the symbol of the old monarchy,' Elodie said, as if explaining the difference between a red and green traffic light to a total moron. 'It means, like, Marianne, for example.'

'The topless woman with the flag? Oh yes, I wouldn't mind adhering to her.'

'Paul, take this seriously, please.' Elodie shifted her grip from the back of my chair to my shoulders, as though she wanted to hold me on-course. 'Look, it gives you a list. The symbols of the Republic are the tricolour flag, the national anthem . . .'

'The national anthem?' I repeated.

'Yes, I'm sure you know how to sing that, don't you, Paul?'

I couldn't help picturing all those red-splattered courgettes.

'You know, "Allons enfants de la Patrie . . ."' Elodie prompted. She obviously wasn't going to be happy until I'd given her a few bars, but I shook my head.

She started again, this time doing the melody as well as the words.

'Allons enfants de la Patrie,' she sang, straight into my right ear. 'Le jour de gloire est arrivé.'

I couldn't help myself – hearing that tune made something English in me go click and I interrupted her with 'Love, love, love.'

'What are you doing, Paul?' She gripped my shoulder again, painfully this time.

'Love, love, love,' I went on. 'Love, love, love.'

'Stop it!'

But the Beatles tune felt right. Instead of a call to take up arms and fertilise the countryside with gore, surely what France really needed was *amour*. It was hippy talk, but it was true. And it was the same thing for Brexit. After all that bitter in-fighting, the haters had won. The people who wanted to divide us, rather than bring all of Europe together. Love, love, love. That was all we needed. I carried on singing.

'Stop this, Paul, you are mocking a serious process. It is intolerable!'

Now, though, I was in full chorus, and didn't feel like stopping.

'On arrête tout!' Elodie shouted, and leant forward to slam her laptop shut. She lifted me bodily out of her seat and shoved me towards the door of her office, ranting all the time in French about me not being 'sérieux', and saying that the 'crétins d'Anglais' deserved everything that Europe was going to throw at them from now on.

'You lied to me,' she growled when we were out in the corridor. Now she was looking a lot less prim. Her blouse was crooked and her face was flushed. 'You said you would apply for French nationality, but you never had any intention.'

'I was going to apply, honest,' I told her. 'But I can't. Not unless you change the words to the Mar-see-ez.'

Elodie flinched only slightly at my mispronunciation.

'Then you can give my money back.' She held out a manicured hand.

'You owed me it anyway. For all the work I did.'

'Give it to me.' Her nails were pointing dangerously at my trousers. I backed away.

'Sue me, Elodie. I'd love to see an MEP explaining where she got five thousand euros in cash, and why she tried to bribe someone to apply for French citizenship.'

In reply, she gave me her most murderous look yet, before suddenly getting a grip on her emotions, as I'd seen her do so often over the past couple of weeks. She smoothed her blouse down, straightened her hair and began to speak, quite calmly now.

'OK, keep it, Paul. Five thousand is nothing to me. Call it compensation for your humiliation in the referendum. Call it unemployment money. Call it a pension. You will need it when your country's economy has a heart attack, like most of your obese compatriots will do, if they carry on eating your disgusting food. And it is in euros, so it will soon be worth a fortune against your pathetic pound. So keep it. One final European subsidy and adieu!'

With this, she exited stage left into her office, slamming the door behind her.

I was tempted to applaud. A true diva's performance. I would have felt well and truly put down, if I hadn't known about the envelope in my pocket.

I was still grinning to myself, rerunning the whole scene through my mind, when I saw Manon jogging along the corridor towards me. She was breathless and holding out her phone.

'You didn't answer,' she puffed when she reached me.

'Elodie told me to switch it off.'

'I was trying to warn you.'

'About what?'

'It was all streaming live.'

'What?'

'Yes, look, it's still online.'

She poked at her screen and brought up a video. Below the title 'Regardez un Anglais qui devient Français', there was a photo of me. I was lying full-length in the bath at the apartment. The scene changed and we saw Elodie, in a smart skirt suit and tricolour sash, grinning as she shook the French President's hand. Then suddenly I came into view, staring at her screen – and her webcam – as I had done a few minutes before.

'What the fuck?' was my initial comment, closely followed by 'How did *you* know, Manon?'

'She or Cédric, or someone, put it out on all the social media just before you started. She wanted to broadcast you live, applying to be French.'

This explained everything. The director-like cue to start filming. The formal statement about paying rent on that apartment.

'Luckily, you screwed it all up for her, by massacring "la Marseillaise".'

I gave myself a self-congratulatory laugh. Meanwhile, on Manon's phone, I heard myself talking about Elodie's dad's subsidised apartment. Yes, I'd really screwed it up for her.

'And I kept the money, too,' I told Manon. 'Five thousand euros.'

'Justice is done,' she said. But she didn't look as pleased as I felt. 'This doesn't stop you applying for French nationality, though, does it?' she asked.

I couldn't believe it. I'd just escaped from Elodie's entrapment and now Manon wanted to shove me into the same cage?

'Well, I don't exactly feel like going online right now and doing all that again,' I told her.

'No, but I mean, eventually. Soon. Like we said, as a political gesture . . .'

She was looking at me as if a hell of a lot was hanging on my reply. Her face was tipped up towards me, enquiringly, expectantly. Under normal circumstances, my natural response would have been to kiss her. But now I was getting the familiar feeling that a Frenchwoman – or a partly Frenchwoman, in Manon's case – was manipulating me. Her phone was now broadcasting my voice singing 'Love, love, love', but the mood between us was more like the French anthem's original words. We were in a battle of wills.

It was best, I thought, to give it to her straight.

'I'm English, Manon. Sorry, but I'm just not French. It'd be like trying to get a bulldog to put on a frilly dress and do the cancan. I haven't got the legs for it. It feels unnatural.'

Suddenly she was looking a lot less as though she wanted to be kissed.

'I thought you understood me, Paul,' she said. 'I thought we were in agreement.'

'You mean you thought I was easier to push around.'

'Is that how you see me, as just another version of Elodie?'

'No,' I assured her. But I was thinking 'not *exactly*', and it must have shown.

'I see,' she said. 'OK, then. I understand now. You don't respect my wishes. You don't share my opinions. You don't care how I feel. I think we have no choice. It must be au revoir.'

She glowered at me accusingly and strode off, the second woman to leave me standing in the space of five minutes. I watched her attractive silhouette until it turned the corner and disappeared. Something told me it wasn't worth trying to stop her.

It looked as if it wasn't going to be my 'jour de gloire' or my 'jour de l'amour'. I'd been given the Brexit.

26

'If Britain leaves the EU, British singers will have a better chance of winning the Eurovision song contest.'

Report in the British press, 2016

A FRENCH surfer once told me about his favourite spot. It wasn't one of the huge Atlantic breaks off Biarritz, he said, it was a miniature wave on a river. Apparently, four or five times a year, when the tide differentials are at their biggest, the Gironde near Bordeaux produces a single wave that can flow towards the sea for up to two kilometres. Its arrival on specific days can be predicted to within ten minutes, so at the appointed hour (or just beforehand), crowds of surfers, paddleboarders and kayakers take up their positions across the width of the river, waiting for the metre-high swell that will embark them on one of the longest, and yet gentlest, rides on the planet. The phenomenon is called a tidal bore.

Before the Brexit vote, the lives and careers of most Brussels bureaucrats had been exactly like that – one long, slow, predictable ride on an unfailing wave. 'Tidal bore' had been a pretty good description of most of them.

And most nights, the mood at the Plux bars had been very similar to the party vibe at the Gironde on wave-days – genuine fun, coloured with an element of self-congratulation about being part of the in-crowd.

Now, however, when I went to the place du Luxembourg to meet up with Danny, the badge-wearers I saw looked as though they'd missed the wave. Far from being long-range surfers, they were floundering about in the river, drowning their sorrows while praying that they would stay afloat.

The result of the referendum seemed to have spoilt everyone's party in Brussels – outside the tiny minority who came to the city just to campaign for its ultimate demise. These included people like Nick Rummage, who, according to Danny, was expected at Plux for a snifter or three, before going into the Parliament to blow his own trumpet at a post-Brexit debate.

It took me a lot less time to get served than on all of my previous visits, and within a minute or so of arriving I was nursing a pint of dark-brown beer and searching for familiar faces.

I recognised one or two MEPs and a few of the regulars from Mickey Mouse, all of them in small, intimate groups, as opposed to the intermingling clusters of networkers on a pre-Brexit night. None of Danny's mates were here yet, and neither was Šárka. But then maybe this wasn't a good time for lobbying, what with the whole European economy thrown off-kilter.

I went out on to the terrace, and soon caught sight of Jake ambling towards me. I'd told him about the entertainment that Danny was planning, and Jake had said he 'would not monk it'. This meant that he didn't want to miss anything – he'd been doing his usual Franglais thing and using the French word '*manquer*'.

Jake looked as if he was in mourning over the Brexit vote – he was sporting a black suit. Uncharacteristically chic for him, even if the jacket was absurdly baggy and the trousers were an inch too short above his white trainers. But at least it was better than his previous ketchup-stained outfit.

'Looking smart,' I congratulated him.

'Yes, it appartenates to the marry of my fuck-friend last night.'

'It belongs to her husband?' I translated. 'You stole his suit?'

'Hey, man, he doesn't know that his femme is fucking Americans, so I guess he doesn't care about his suit.'

As usual with Jake, these things had a perversely convincing logic about them.

'Comment ça va for you, Paul?'

'Oh, OK,' I summarised. I'd already told him about Manon's unilateral vote. And strangely, the pain of getting dumped by her had got mixed in with the shock of the referendum result. Just like the feeling on the pre-Brexit evening that everything would turn out OK, my two nights with Manon now seemed unreal, too good to be true. I felt almost numb.

'You want sex tonight?' Jake asked.

I knew him well enough to realise that he wasn't asking me if I wanted to go to bed with him. He was enquiring whether he should try to set me up.

'I'm really not feeling sexy,' I said.

'Maybe you do need to be Français after all.'

I didn't even bother answering.

'I can help,' he said.

'That's what everybody says.'

'No, vraiment.' Jake began rooting about in the pocket of his jacket – or rather his lover's husband's jacket. 'I have thinked, er …'

'Thought?' I suggested, as he carried on rooting.

'Yeah … on what you have told me about the Marseillaise.' Amazingly, he pronounced it right. 'Voilà!' He held up a folded sheet of paper in triumph. 'I have writed, er, rooted – composed, anyway, some new words.'

'Oh?' I just managed to stop myself adding, 'God, no.' I could imagine what kind of national anthem Jake would invent for France – the topless Marianne was certain to figure in full-frontal close-up, that was for sure.

'Not for all of it yet, but for the end that you detest. You know, "aux armes, citoyens, formez vos bataillons", and the "sang impur". Here …'

He held out the piece of paper. Usually, he took delight in reading his poems out and inflicting maximum pain on his defenceless listener. But now he gave me the single sheet and let me unfold it.

Glancing through his lines of French verse, I had to concede that it seemed to be the least painful poem he'd ever written. I read it out, to the rhythm of the song:

> 'Aux graines, citoyens,
> Semez vos échalotes,
> Plantons, plantons,
> Qu'une eau minérale
> Abreuve nos carottes.'

What it seemed to mean was that instead of forming battalions, the French should sow shallot seeds, and that their fields (of carrots) should be irrigated with mineral water rather than blood.

'Brilliant, Jake,' I told him, sincere for once in my praise of his writing. 'All you need is a first verse about cheese and wine and you've nailed it. I'd sign up for that nationality any day.'

We were high-fiving when Danny stormed in and told us that his show was about to begin.

'Rummage is just downing a pint and a shot at the bar next door. He's shaking his Union Jack tie at everyone as if it was his dick. You ready, Paul?'

'Can't wait,' I said.

'You might get hit in the crossfire,' he warned me.

'No worries.'

'Great. Jake, you want to film this?' Danny asked. 'I've got three people out there already, but we need every angle we can get. We're going to flood social media with this little gem.'

371

'D'accord, man,' Jake agreed.

'Where's the . . . er, weapon?' I asked.

'With one of my mates outside the Parliament building,' Danny said. 'I couldn't very well bring it in here without sending everyone screaming for cover.'

I laughed – the contraption he was planning to aim at Rummage was indeed a chemical weapon that was probably illegal under EU law.

Jake and I went to stand at the foot of the steps leading to the Parliament building's main entrance. The two of us made up one corner of a rectangle of accomplices. The other three were fanned out about twenty metres away from us, each of them with a phone in their hand, ready to close in on the action and start filming.

It was still light, so I could see the giant faces of the thirsty Third World kids on the posters lining the square. It was probably my imagination, but their smiles now seemed to be anticipating much more than a drink of clean water.

I thought back to the first time I'd crossed this square, trying to keep up with the manic Elodie, who was on her way to claim her MEP's daily allowance, even though she'd spent all day in Paris. Then, I'd seen badge-wearers chatting happily in the early evening sun. Now, the few people present who weren't involved in Danny's plot were looking much more subdued, and a man who'd helped to cause their change of mood was about to get his comeuppance.

We only had to wait about ten minutes before Danny sent a message: 'On his way.'

Rummage was preceded, as always, by his loud voice, bellowing out his opinions to everyone within a mile. He was with a couple of cronies, the three of them marching straight towards Jake and me.

I heard Rummage say something about a 'kick in the euro-balls', and waved to him.

'Mister Rummage? Nick? Can we get a Brexit photo?'

As Danny had predicted, the sound of an English voice caught Rummage's attention, as did the prospect of grinning at a lens.

'Mais bien sûr!' he said in his excellent French. There was no doubt about where he was going to spend his EU pension – if Manon didn't manage to take it away from him, of course: at his retirement villa on the continent he professed to despise. 'Haven't we met before?' he asked.

'Yes, big fan. My mate will take it,' I said, as we both turned to look into Jake's phone.

'Oh, good, not a selfie,' Rummage bellowed. 'I do hate selfies. So bloody common.'

This was the last opinion he managed to pronounce before Danny struck.

What a horde of social-media viewers saw, from four different angles, was a textbook ambush. Rummage's self-satisfied grin turned to shock, then twisted fear, as a blue plastic bucket, decorated with a ring of yellow stars, was swiftly but precisely emptied over his head. I flinched, but only because I knew what was in the bucket.

With the foresight that made him such an employable eurocrat, Danny had put together a Brexit contingency plan, and had been storing oysters for the past week or so. In the hermetically sealed confines of a plastic tub, he had left them in full sunlight on his balcony to begin decomposing.

From the few splashes that hit my shirt, I judged that the resulting slurry was a stink bomb worse than a ton of that shark-meat that Icelanders bury for a year and then force-feed to tourists in minuscule cubes as a joke. Danny's grey goo would have put anyone off sushi for life.

A good litre or two of this concoction discoloured Rummage's hair, his face, then his formerly white shirt collar, before spreading down his jacket and patriotic tie.

Worse, his bellow of rage opened his mouth so widely that, watched in slow-motion playback, you could see a large chunk of rotten oyster sliding between his lips, before being ejected by a gagging tongue.

As the victim ducked down in belated self-defence, Danny's grinning face appeared behind him – or rather Rummage's own grinning face, because Danny was wearing a lookalike mask.

'You fuckers!' Rummage yelled, swinging out at everyone around him. 'You just want to stop me speaking tonight. This is undemocratic.'

'You can speak if you want,' Danny said, dancing out of range of Rummage's fists. 'You'll just stink as much as your opinions do. And I'm sure you'll claim the cleaning bill on EU expenses, like you do everything else you spend.'

'Show your face, you cowardly fucker,' Rummage bawled.

'Why? You've never shown your true face, you profiteering twat,' Danny laughed, and gave us the signal to leg it. No point hanging around till the EU security guys came out of the building.

As I ran, a strange thought struck me. Unbelievably, I actually pitied Rummage. Not for the mess we'd made of his hair and clothes, but because all the time he was under attack, neither of his cronies made a single move to defend him. They both just stood and stared. Even his own friends didn't like him.

And that, I decided, was a bit like Brexit itself. We Brits had turned our backs on the people we were meant to be friends with. The risk was that we'd now become a nation of Johnny no-mates.

We all met at a pre-arranged spot just outside Plux, at the place near Šárka's office that rented rooms by the hour for illicit *rendez-vous*. Standing beside the photos of velvet boudoirs, we looked as though we were getting together for a huge gang-bang.

There were a lot more of us than I'd expected, at least seven or eight. As well as Jake, me and the other three camera operators, Danny had clearly let quite a few people in on his plan.

One of them, I now noticed, was Manon. She came over.

'Bonsoir, Paul,' she said, and leaned in for a *bise* on the cheek. I obliged. No hard feelings, I told myself. This was how Brussels worked. We were all consenting adults. *Vive le euro-shagging.*

Even so, seeing Manon flushed and out of breath brought back poignant memories of a very similar sight just a day or so earlier, when we'd first gazed at each other after making love.

'Hi,' I answered, as cheerfully as I could.

'That,' she said, 'was a political gesture.'

'Yes, I guess it was,' I agreed, looking over towards Danny, the planner and executor of the gesture, who was giggling at the film Jake was showing him.

'No, I mean your part in it,' Manon said. 'Trapping Rummage, standing next to him for the film. You know you will be recognised on the security cameras.'

I shrugged. I could always claim to be an innocent victim. And I guessed the Belgian police had better things to do than hunt for someone who might, or might not, have helped one of the least popular men in Brussels get humiliated.

'You said it wasn't the right time, but you helped to give a real slip in the face,' Manon said. 'Or should I say "slap"?' She grinned.

'More like a slop,' I said. 'In any case, it wasn't a slap in the face for Britain, just for one hypocritical dickhead.'

'It was a slap – that's the important thing. And not just for Monsieur Roomage. It was one for me, too. I'm sorry, Paul, it's like I told you before: sometimes I panic. And Brexit has panicked me. So I was an idiot this afternoon. All day, in fact. Will you forgive me?'

I didn't get much of a chance to refuse, because before I knew what was happening, she had clamped herself to me and her body was pressing against mine in all the right places.

'We can't let the Brexiteurs divide us,' she said, kissing my neck as if to prove it. 'We must stick together. And you're the kind of guy I would like to stick with together. Or together with. Together, anyway.'

As I put my arms around her, my previous numbness evaporated and I felt a warm flood of relief. My body seemed to be telling me that it had never really accepted that we were just another case of Brussels' sexual networking. Pretty soon my brain would have hit me with some serious regret about losing this enticing, unpredictable woman.

'You're definitely the kind of principle I could adhere to,' I told her.

'Thank you, Paul, that is the most romantic thing anyone has ever said to me.'

Our kiss was interrupted by Jake.

'Ah, Paul,' he said. 'Après tout, I think you will have some sex tonight.'

'Shut up, Jake,' I said, but something told me he might be right.

Fɪɴ / Eɴᴅ / Eɪɴᴅᴇ

De: Paul West
À: Elodie Martin
Sujet: Silly Euro Rumours

Bonjour Elodie,

Here is my top 20 (or so) of the insane rumours put about by the British press, with the explanation as to why each one is *revr a strouilh*, which of course means 'a pig's anus' in Breton – the only part of a pig not eaten by the Bretons, and therefore apparently used as a term meaning a complete waste of time and space. But I'm sure you knew that.

1 *'Euro banknotes can make men impotent'*

This story emerged in 2002 after a German magazine tested a ten-euro note and found traces in the paper of a stabiliser called Tributyltin. One of its side-effects can be impotence.

However, the same laboratory that carried out the tests for the magazine admitted that, in order to suffer any problems, a man would have to handle thousands of euro notes per day, over a prolonged period of time.

This didn't stop one British paper digging up a German called Wolfgang Fritz (convincing German name, *nicht?*), who said that he hadn't been able to achieve an erection since the euro was introduced.

And we all thought that the euro had triggered inflation.

2 *'Brussels to force farmers to give toys to pigs'*

There is in fact a European law that orders pig farmers to provide their animals with distractions in their pens. This is because pigs naturally snuffle about and would harm themselves, or attack other pigs, if they could not do so. Apparently, frustrated pigs often go in for 'tail-biting' (and that's not a crude joke).

European farmers are therefore obliged to provide all pigs kept in enclosed pens with 'manipulable material'. But this does not usually include toys. It is more likely to be hay, straw, sawdust, sand, peat, earth or compost.

The 'toy' rumour came from suggestions that pigs can also alleviate boredom by chewing on lumps of wood or plastic suspended from the ceiling. Not exactly the same thing as buying them dolls or tricycles.

(Elodie: You might want to explain to your Breton constituents that they don't need to buy actual toys for their farm animals, in case any of them are ordering *pétanque* balls or trying to make their PlayStations hoof-compatible.)

3 *'EU to ban singing in pubs'*

This story emerged in 2002, when the EU announced that it was looking into ways of protecting workers from excessive noise. The maximum safe volume during an 8-hour day was set at 87 decibels, which is roughly equivalent to standing near a motorbike with its engine running.

The EU directive was intended to force employers to offer workers ear-protection if their working environment involved high noise levels. However, this perfectly reasonable measure inspired a whole rash of absurd press stories.

A football crowd, for example, can easily generate more than 100 decibels, and some newspapers suggested that players would have to wear earplugs, and would therefore not be able to hear the referee's whistle.

It was even said that orchestras would not be able to play loud classical pieces, such as Beethoven's 9th Symphony (which, of course, contains Europe's anthem, the 'Ode to Joy').

According to one of these scare stories, English pubs would have to ban singing during World Cup football matches in case the bar staff were subjected to excessive noise levels. The sad fact was that, as usual,

English fans had little to sing about during the 2004 World Cup.

4 *'According to the EU's animal waste directive, it is illegal to bury dead pets unless you have pressure-cooked them at 130°C for half an hour'*

This story, which emerged in 2000, came out of nowhere. It seemed to refer back to the EU's 1992 Animal Waste Directive, which was part of a larger plan to prevent pollution of the environment from the disposal of all types of waste.

During the BSE scare, many infected animals were simply buried or burnt in the open air, which posed a potential health risk. The Animal Waste Directive stipulated that carcasses had to be disposed of using adequately equipped, government-approved incinerators.

This ruling did not include domestic animals – unless, of course, your pet died of mad-cow disease. And no one mentioned pressure-cooking them, which would be just plain impractical.

The story was a straight bit of euro-bashing. The writer might just as well have said that all half-eaten kebabs found dumped in the street would have to be fed into a nuclear reactor. Which might not be a bad idea.

5 'EU to ban Scottish bagpipes'

This was simply a five-year update of the rule mentioned in item 3 – in theory, if for some reason you invited a pipe band to play for 8 hours in a workplace, you would be breaking European health-and-safety laws.

It was also an attempt to turn the Scots, who actually seem to like the EU, against Brussels.

Though, of course, by banning the Scottish howling octopus, there was also the danger of making some English people look favourably upon EU lawmakers.

6 'Brussels will give in to French pressure and force Britain to rename Waterloo Station and Trafalgar Square'

As we all know, Waterloo Station has long been a French *bête noire*, especially since it was chosen as the initial London terminus for Eurostar.

(Elodie: Didn't I hear your patriotic colleague Yves Remord call it '*la gare sans nom*' – the station that shall remain nameless? I'm not sure he was joking.)

The reports published in the British press saying that Europe was going to force a name-change for Waterloo and Trafalgar Square were nonsense, based simply on an offhand comment by the head of the European Investment Fund, an Oxford-educated economist called Francis Carpenter. He seems to have gone native and expressed his opinion that the French probably find these names irritating.

But most rational people accept that you can't just get rid of everything that irritates the French – otherwise Belgium, for example, would disappear.

7 *'Smoky-bacon crisps to be banned by Brussels'*

It is true that in 2003 Europe adopted new rules concerning the types of smoke-flavouring used in food. It tested different smoke-flavourings, most of which are made of 'smoke condensates', to check that none of them contained harmful chemicals.

But no one suggested banning smoky-bacon crisps, smoked salmon or anything similar – unless, of course, they were made with a smoke-flavouring that had been distilled from, say, the emissions from one of the waste incinerators mentioned in item 4 above. In which case, consumers might well have approved of the ban.

(Elodie: I'm sure your dad uses safe sources for his smoked-meat products, right?)

8 *'Brussels rules that oysters must be given rest breaks during transport to market'*

This is another piece of comical over-interpretation. Of course quite often these British reports are deliberately humorous, to show us how absurdly anal Europe's law-makers are.

This story, which also suggested that mussels, whelks and other shellfish might enjoy a quick stop in a lay-by on their way to market, was based on the detailed EU laws governing the transport of live animals. These include rules on the ventilation of trucks, provision of food and water during long journeys, the number of animals carried per cubic metre of trailer space, and even the age of the animals that can be transported (for example, calves less than ten days old cannot be transported more than 100 kilometres, which seems quite a long journey for baby animals without their mums).

There are rules on carrying shellfish, but these mainly involve refrigeration, which most Europeans would probably find advisable.

(Elodie: Rumours that the Brits really want to have oyster sales banned are not true. Yet.)

9 'Kilts to be re-defined as women's wear'

This was clearly another attempt, like item 5 above, to turn the Scots off the EU. But for once it was based on a genuine EU balls-up.

In 2003 the European statistics agency, Eurostat, published a form asking clothes manufacturers about the types of garments they sold. There was no space on the form allotted to the kilt. When a kilt manufacturer questioned this, he was told to record kilt sales in the 'women's apparel' section.

After an outcry in the Scottish press, including of course a quote from Sean Connery, the forms were amended.

The only detail the papers got wrong was that the European forms were actually vetted and sent out by Britain's own Office of National Statistics. And it was an ONS employee who told the kilt manufacturer where to record his sales. Not Brussels' fault at all.

Incidentally, the quote from Sean Connery included the interesting line: 'I have been wearing a woman's skirt for more than 45 years.'

(Elodie: That quote is just a bit of fun for the journalists, designed to cause a stir. The full quote was: '*If this is the case*, I have been wearing a woman's skirt for more than 45 years.')

10 *'Brussels will force lorry drivers to eat muesli'*

The EU laws governing the health, training and safety of professional drivers came into force in 2003. Not surprisingly, they did not specify what British truck drivers should eat for breakfast.

They did warn against the combination of an unhealthy diet and a sedentary job, and suggested that sleepiness at the wheel after a heavy meal might be dangerous for drivers of vehicles weighing several tons.

But then a headline about the EU simply trying to get truck drivers to stay alive might not have been quite so eye-catching.

11 *'According to a new EU law, the Queen will have to fetch her own cup of tea'*

Yet another masterful piece of journalistic embroidery of the facts. It could also have read, 'The Pontiff will have to drive his own Popemobile' or 'The President of France will be forced to nip out for croissants.'

This was all about the Working Time Directive, which gives EU citizens the right to a maximum working week of 48 hours. A reporter managed to find a Buckingham Palace servant who agreed that, if his 48 hours were up, he might not be legally required to fetch a royal cuppa.

In reality, of course, staffing levels in royal palaces rarely reach the critical stage at which a member of the royal family would be forced to phone out for a takeaway.

(Elodie: Didn't the French President actually nip out for croissants recently, and take them to his mistress, who was waiting in their love nest? If so, you might want to cut out the above reference. We don't want to put your *Légion d'honneur* at risk.)

12 *'Brussels wants to ban British barmaids' cleavage'*

Again, employee protection is taken to its absurd limit. The EU does require employers to assess the potential dangers to their staff of working for long periods in the sun, and advises the use of sun cream, hats and sunglasses. But it does not ban low-cut tops for barmaids.

The encouraging aspect to this story was that one article in the British press lamented the possible demise of the low-cut dirndl blouses worn by Bavarian barmaids at the Oktoberfest. A nice bit of cross-European solidarity.

(Elodie: If you're not sure what a dirndl top looks like, Jake has some photos.)

13 *'EU to force British fish-and-chip shops to use Latin names for fish'*

This rumour first emerged in the late 1990s, along with stories about putting the Latin names for nuts and other foodstuffs on labels.

It started out with EU directives requiring food and cosmetics manufacturers to list all potentially allergenic ingredients on their packaging, if they wanted to export. To make these lists understandable across the whole of Europe, some kind of standardisation of the names was suggested, possibly involving Latin. Though of course translation into the different European languages of the names for all nuts and allergenic ingredients was said to be preferable.

This Latin scare migrated over to the fish world when the EU called for more detailed labelling on pre-prepared fish products. The exact species of fish would have to be given – 'fingers' was no longer going to be detailed enough.

Some witty journalist implied that this might involve the Latin genus names and, hey presto, a fishy story was served up in newspaper.

(Elodie: That last line is a joke about the way fish & chips used to be served in Britain. I thought you might like it, given that you think our food usually tastes like old paper and ink.)

14 'God Save the Queen must be sung in all immigrant languages'

This is – to use the technical journalistic term – total balls. Pure scaremongering.

Anthems are, as we know, touchy subjects. There was a kerfuffle about the EU's own anthem, Beethoven's 'Ode to Joy', in 2004 when an Austrian called Peter Roland wrote some new lyrics for the song. These included a line about 'freedom for Europe's people in a bigger motherland', which was lambasted in the British press for its apparently Nazi/Soviet overtones. But in fact these new words were merely Herr Roland's brain-child and have not been adopted as the official lyrics to Europe's anthem.

(Elodie: FYI, Jake has also written some lyrics to Beethoven's tune, but I don't think his will be adopted by the EU, either, because he rhymes 'joy' with 'sex toy' and has replaced '*Götterfunken*' with something unmentionable.

Oh, and is it true that the EU wants France to change that line in the Marseillaise about 'impure blood', because of its racist overtones? *Merde alors!*)

15 *'No alcohol sales during the week, says Brussels'*

In 2005 the British press went into a *delirium tremens* about 'secret EU plans' to ban the sale of alcohol from Monday to Friday, and to hand the alcohol trade over to state-run monopolies.

The origin of these scare stories was a working paper submitted to the European Commission suggesting ways of reducing alcoholism, drink-driving, alcohol consumption during pregnancy and binge-drinking (Elodie: That is what you call 'drinking à l'*anglaise*').

The EU has both a committee and a forum on alcohol, so it is obviously an issue that concerns them, and they probably get together for lots of cocktail parties to discuss it. But they're not planning to ban anything, even though they have identified alcohol as the cause of 25% of the deaths of European males aged between 15 and 29.

So I personally am going to give up binge-drinking until I'm 30, when it apparently gets statistically less dangerous.

16 *'EU will force cows to wear nappies'*

This is all about nitrate pollution. As we all know, animals poo. But if large concentrations of them do so in a small area, and if that poo is not collected up, to be spread out more evenly as fertiliser, it can leak into the soil and rivers, causing algae blooms on beaches and polluting drinking water.

(Elodie: I know you don't really care about this, because you drink bottled water, but lots of people do care. Honestly.)

In 2014 a Bavarian farmer announced that he was fitting his cows with nappies because, he said, the EU bans nitrate pollution in alpine pastures. The British press seized on this as another example of EU lunacy, either not realising or ignoring the fact that it was that rare thing, a Bavarian joke.

The EU does have a Nitrates Directive dating back to 1991, which states that reservoirs used for drinking-water extraction may not contain more than 50mg per litre of nitrates. But the EU doesn't tell member states how to achieve that limit, and the words 'nappy' or 'diaper' – and their various translations – do not appear anywhere in the Directive.

(Elodie: In case you want to reduce algae blooms on Brittany's beaches, the Breton for nappy is *trezh*.)

17 'English Channel to be renamed "Anglo-French Pond"'

This relates to the Waterloo/Trafalgar story in item 6 above. As most French people are coming to realise, almost all British geographical names have been invented to annoy France. Either they refer to some historic humiliation or they're impossible to pronounce (Gloucester, Leicester, Bournemouth, etc).

The 'English Channel' seems to have been named to remind the French whose navy has traditionally been the more efficient of the two. The fact that France is much more neutral and tries to call the stretch of water dividing us '*La Manche*' (the sleeve) hasn't convinced the British at all. We don't name places after bits of clothing. We do it the other way round (eg cardigan, balaclava, jodhpurs, Panama hat, Chelsea football shirt).

Anyway, this news story cropped up after a French economist identified a cross-Channel trading area between southern England and northern France and dubbed it '*la zone Trans-Manche*'.

British journalists seem to have asked what the hell a 'cross-sleeve zone' was, and simply invented something more provocative than the truth.

18 '*Great British banger to be outlawed by Brussels*'

We Brits know that our chocolate isn't really chocolate, that our bread was until recently more like slices of lino, and that our sausages are full of *kaoc'h*. But we don't care. We invented several of the world's most famous chocolate bars and its most complete breakfast, and that's what counts.

So when Brussels decides to regulate the meat content of sausages, to ban manufacturers from counting fat as meat and generally improve the quality of sausages, we are quite naturally outraged.

What actually happened here was that the EU tried to outlaw the use of 'mechanically separated meat' in sausages. This is the leftover scraps of flesh clinging to skin, bones, hooves, etc, after the useful cuts have been extracted from the animal carcass.

Fortunately, though, British manufacturers have since managed to get some of these barely edible scraps redefined as 'de-sinewed meat', so they can continue using them in sausages.

Vive le banger!

19 'British toilets to be replaced by "euro-loos"'

As we all know, the flushing toilet is one of Britain's great contributions to world culture, alongside Shakespeare, the sandwich and driving on the sensible side of the road. The verb 'to crap' even comes from the name of the inventor of the flushing toilet, Thomas Crapper.

So it was easy for the British press to kick up a shitstorm when the EU proposed to interfere with the Great British flush.

In fact, though, this was simply the EU's attempt to reduce the amount of water used by toilets. It involved a purely voluntary eco-labelling scheme for toilet manufacturers, based on the realisation that about 30% of a household's drinking water goes down a toilet, most of it unnecessarily.

An EU study estimated that by reducing the size of cisterns and introducing the double-speed flush system, Europe could save more than a billion cubic metres of water per year.

(Elodie: To put it in a way you might understand, that's about 10 million swimming pools.)

The British press, though, jumped on the opportunity to defend one of our proudest institutions, which has even entered the French language – some older people in France still call toilets '*les WC*'.

(Elodie: You might be interested to know that in English we already had a rhyme encouraging people to save water: 'If it's yellow let it mellow, if it's brown flush it down.' I can get Jake to translate it into French, if you want.)

20 '*EU wants to measure how badly workers smell*'

We Brits seem to have a real hang-up about our armpits. Why else do we continually go on about French women not shaving there (false) and French people not taking frequent baths (true – they take showers instead, much more hygienic)?

So back in 1996, when Britain's male workers had little more to make them fragrant than two deodorants called Brut and Old Spice, the press kicked up a massive stink about the news that the EU was looking into the smells inside buildings. This came about because the Commission commissioned (sorry, can't think of another word) a study into energy efficiency, which looked into double glazing and similar insulation techniques.

A by-product of these techniques was, of course, the creation of a hermetically sealed environment and therefore a higher concentration of smells inside houses, as well as in shops, offices and factories. Deodorant therefore became an environmental issue.

The good news is that this silly rumour has become obsolete. Since 1996, Englishmen have evolved, and young British males now devote approximately half their waking hours to buffing their skin, having bodily hair removed and getting body art, so these days a little story about the need to smell nice wouldn't bother them at all.

21 *'New Brussels law: worn-out sex toys must be given back to retailers'*

This is a very creative bit of over-interpretation, and for once it's based on reality. In fact, only the 'must' in the headline is wrong. It should read 'may'.

According to the EU's Waste Electronic and Electrical Equipment Directive (or WEEE – surely that was an acronym that they could have saved for the toilet-flush directive?), owners of broken or unwanted electrical devices can return them to the retailers for recycling. The idea is, of course, that their motor usually contains toxic materials and should not therefore be put in household dustbins.

WEEE includes a section on 'toys, leisure and sports equipment'. Interesting that British journalists instantly assumed this meant sex toys.

22 'EU wants all condoms to be of uniform size – small'

We all know that any mention of crushing a penis (for non-recreational purposes) instinctively gets men wincing and crossing their legs. It is also a scientific fact that the male readers of British tabloids have the world's largest penises. So this news story about shrinking condoms was a double whammy. It was also totally false.

It was inspired by the EU's recommendations that condoms need quality control, which no one in their right mind would disagree with. The true story is quite fun, because the European Standardisation Committee devised some really wacky experiments to test condom quality.

These included the 'rolled water test', in which a condom is filled with water and then rolled on absorbent paper to check for leaks; the 'European electric test', in which a condom is filled with a salt solution and then tested for high or low electrical resistance (Elodie: Sorry,

I don't get it: why would you electrocute a condom?); and the 'air burst test', which simply involves inflating a condom till it bursts – and if it doesn't inflate, it's obviously got a hole anyway.

Surely the British newspapers could have reported the true story for once, and had great fun describing scientists doing all these goofy things to condoms?

(Elodie: If you use this story, it might also be useful to take the opportunity to tell people that there's no need to do these tests yourself before putting on the condom.)

23 'EU bureaucrats decree that Britain is not an island'

This relates to item 17 above. When that French economist identified a trading area encompassing northern France and southeast England, someone in the EU drew up a map that united the two coastal regions in the aforementioned 'zone Trans-Manche'. This naturally caused primeval jingoistic instincts to kick in. France was claiming that Britain was on the continent; the EU wanted to make Kent part of France, etc, etc.

At the same time, these fears were stoked up by an EU study of the problems facing small island communities. The preamble to the study said that it would not include islands that contained the capital of an EU nation. Obvious really, because you can't define England and Ireland as 'small island communities' and say they have the same economic problems as, say, a village on a lump of rock just off the Breton coast.

But the British press seized on this, alleging that the EU wanted to rob Britain of its island status. The contrary is, of course, the case. Most Brussels bureaucrats are glad that we're on an island, cut off from them by the sea.

(Elodie: FYI, re Kent being part of France. Apparently, due to global warming, climate conditions in southeast England are becoming more like those in northern France, while France is heating up, meaning that soon champagne-style wines made in Kent and Sussex will probably be better than those actually made in France. This is why French champagne companies are buying up land in southern England. If Britain leaves the EU, we might be free to ignore European law and call this British fizz 'English Champagne'. Just thought you might like to pass this news on to your French patriot friends.)

24 *'EU is backing out of its promise to prohibit excessive data-roaming charges in Europe'*

Talk about fake news. This story was so twisted, looking for the truth was like trying to pick out all the little bacon bits from a creamy carbonara sauce.

I'll do my best to re-assemble them into a nicely-formed rasher of reality.

(Elodie: Having lived in France for a while, I know that your bacon bits – *lardons* – are much chunkier than ours and less likely to sink to the bottom of a bowl of pasta. But please bear with me on this.)

In 2015, the EU promised to stop phone companies hitting consumers with huge bills for using internet abroad. As we all know, if you forget to turn off data roaming when you go away on holiday, you're going to have to sell your house.

Which is why the European Commission negotiated a deal with phone companies to let EU citizens phone and roam freely when travelling, paying the same price as when they do it at home. Fantastic news, no?

Well, not if you're anti-EU.

It must have been pure Brexit frenzy that made troublemakers in the UK object to this brilliant plan.

The 'problem' was that the EU had negotiated a 90-day limit on the deal. Ordinary tourists and busi-ness travellers would benefit, but not UK pensioners who spend whole winters in Spain. (Funny – you'd think that these well-off long-term residents would have time to work out the Spanish for 'could I have a SIM card please?') The objectors even said that people who go on long cruises would be discriminated against, the poor dears. Which was rubbish, surely – who goes on a three-month cruise on a ship without wi-fi?

Anyway, rather than celebrate the fact that the vast majority of ordinary people would be freed by a European law from the tyranny of profiteering phone companies, the Brexit brigade complained so vocally that the European Commission actually agreed to re-think its plans.

The British press trumpeted this as a moral victory.

In the report I saw, the newspaper (which shall remain nameless) said that the EU's plans had been 'scrapped' and that the EU had done a 'U-turn' on the roaming deal. Pretty clear, you might think. End of story.

But here come the bacon bits.

The same article went on to quote Jean-Claude Juncker, head of the European Commission, saying that they were looking at this British objection, but that they had 'put an end to' excess roaming charges.

He was also quoted as saying that Brits travel abroad for an average of twelve days a year, so the 90-day cap was perfectly adequate for almost everyone.

These quotations came a few lines below a headline alleging that the EU had been forced to scrap its plans. Did the newspaper think its readers were too lazy to read down as far as Juncker's statement? Or too stupid to understand that the article contradicted its own headline?

Anyway, when I looked at the European Commission's website, I saw that the data roaming plans are going ahead. This British objection has carried no weight at all.

In short, the article seemed to be fake news that got so disgusted with itself that it gave up being fake after about three sentences.

So from now on, I'd recommend ignoring headlines in certain sectors of the British press and just reading the last paragraph of any report. Only there might you find something resembling the truth.

I'm calling it bacon bits journalism. You, Elodie, might prefer 'le journalisme du lardon'.

25 'EU wants to ban British beaches'

In 2014, a British newspaper headline seemed to be announcing that, thanks to those beastly Brussels bureaucrats, Britain was going to lose the right to have sand along its coastline. What else does 'banning beaches' mean?

The article stated that a new EU ruling would make Blackpool 'lose its beach'. Presumably readers were supposed to imagine hordes of European economic migrants carrying off several million tons of sand to a euro-depot somewhere in Belgium, leaving the resort's donkeys to offer rides along the bedrock.

(Elodie: FYI, Blackpool is a seaside town in the north of England, very popular with Brits who want to get roaring drunk, have unprotected sex on cold sand, then spend a day vomiting into their hotel bed. This isn't

Blackpool's fault. It used to be a family resort. But it's not exactly your kind of place. For one thing, I don't think anyone there serves vinaigrette.)

Looking more closely at the article, the reporter was saying that the EU was about to re-jig its water quality standards so that British beaches that had passed previous EU pollution tests would now fail, and no one would even be allowed to walk along them, never mind swim.

The truth, as ever, was very different.

In fact, the EU was going to oblige European (not just British) resorts to publish levels of dangerous E-coli and faecal streptococci in its seawater – not a bad idea, surely, unless you want to spend your holiday swimming in diluted excrement.

The eurocrats also want the award of a blue flag to depend on a three- or four-year survey of water quality rather than just one year, as at present. This would actually help British beaches to keep their blue flag, because it would mean that the occasional bout of heavy rain or tidal surge, during which seawater can be polluted by overloaded sewers, would be less catastrophic. These incidents would be nullified by a good average score over three or four years.

It was actually good news for Britain being presented as bad.

In any case, what the newspaper seemed to be forgetting was that millions of British holidaymakers are safe to swim off beaches all over Europe, including prime Brexiteer territory like Benidorm and Magaluf, thanks to the EU's blue flag scheme. *Gracias, amigos.*

26 *'If Britain leaves the EU, British singers will have a better chance of winning the Eurovision song contest'*

I mean, come off it. This report was really scraping the euro-barrel. Maybe the anti-EU press thought, 'oh, damn, there are some people we haven't targeted yet: the one per cent of the population who think that churning out the universally elected unhippest song in Europe is a national triumph.'

The article was based on a tweet by the 'Leave' campaign saying that 'more countries outside the EU have won than those inside.' This was false: in reality (and I'm ashamed to say I actually looked this up) sixteen EU members have won at least once, compared to only ten non-members, including Yugoslavia which doesn't exist any more. But who bloody cares?

No one really wants to win Eurovision, do they? For a start, the winners host the following year's show, and it costs them a bloody fortune. Honestly, if the UK did start winning Eurovision, I'd seriously think it was a French plan to try and bankrupt us.

You wouldn't stoop that low, would you, Elodie?

ALSO AVAILABLE IN ARROW

The Merde Factor

Stephen Clarke

Englishman Paul West is living the Parisian dream, and doing his best not to annoy the French. But recently things have been going très wrong.

He's stuck in an apartment so small that he has to cut his baguettes in two to fit them in the kitchen.

His research into authentic French cuisine is about to cause a national strike – and it could be all his fault.

His Parisian business partner is determined to close their tea-room. And thinks that sexually harassing his female employees is a basic human right.

And Paul's gorgeous ex-girlfriend seems to be stalking him.

Threatened with eviction, unemployment and bankruptcy, Paul realises that his personal merde factor is about to hit the fan . . .

Praise for *The Merde Factor*

'Has done more for the Entente Cordiale than any of our politicians.'
Daily Mail

'Edgier than Bryson, hits harder than Mayle.'
The Times

arrow books

ALSO AVAILABLE IN ARROW

Dirty Bertie: An English King Made in France

Stephen Clarke

The truly entertaining biography of Edward VII and his playboy lifestyle, by Stephen Clarke, author of *1000 Years of Annoying the French* and *A Year in the Merde*.

Despite fierce opposition from his mother, Queen Victoria, Edward VII was always passionately in love with France.

He had affairs with the most famous Parisian actresses, courtesans and can-can dancers. He spoke French more elegantly than English. He was the first ever guest to climb the Eiffel Tower with Gustave Eiffel, in defiance of an official English ban on his visit. He turned his French seduction skills into the diplomatic prowess that sealed the Entente Cordiale.

A quintessentially English king? *Pas du tout!* Stephen Clarke argues that as 'Dirty Bertie', Edward learned *all* the essentials in life from the French.

Praise for *Dirty Bertie: An English King Made in France*

'A wicked and witty biography.'
Daily Express

'A comic history which manages to combine Clarke's brand of jaunty, bawdy humour . . . with being genuinely informative about French history.'
Spectator

arrow books

ALSO AVAILABLE IN ARROW

How the French Won Waterloo – or Think They Did

Stephen Clarke

Published in the 200th Anniversary year of the Battle of Waterloo a witty look at how the French still think they won.

Two centuries after the Battle of Waterloo, the French are still in denial.

If Napoleon lost on 18th June 1815 (and that's a big 'if'), then whoever rules the universe got it wrong. As soon as the cannons stopped firing, French historians began re-writing history. The Duke of Wellington was beaten, they say, and then the Prussians jumped into the boxing ring, breaking all the rules of battle. In essence, the French cannot bear the idea that Napoleon, their greatest-ever national hero, was in any way a loser. Especially not against the traditional enemy – *les Anglais.*

Stephen Clarke has studied the French version of Waterloo, as told by battle veterans, novelists, historians – right up to today's politicians, and he has uncovered a story of pain, patriotism and sheer perversion . . .

Praise for *How the French Won Waterloo – or Think They Did*

'This is Waterloo as stand-up, funny and caustic by turns.'
BBC History Magazine

arrow books

BC 04/17